Voltaire

The best of all possible worlds

THE BEST OF
ALL POSSIBLE WORLDS

Romances and Tales by
FRANCOIS VOLTAIRE

Short Story Index Reprint Series

With an Introduction by
CLARENCE DARROW

 BOOKS FOR LIBRARIES PRESS
FREEPORT, NEW YORK

First Published 1929
Reprinted 1972

Library of Congress Cataloging in Publication Data

Voltaire, François Marie Arouet de, 1694-1778.
    The best of all possible worlds; romances and tales.

    (Short story index reprint series)
    I. Title.
PZ3.V89Be5 [PQ2081.E5]   843!.5   72-3277
ISBN 0-8369-4165-9

PRINTED IN THE UNITED STATES OF AMERICA

CONTENTS

INTRODUCTION

FRANCOIS MARIE AROUET, known to history as Voltaire, was born in Paris on November 21, 1694. He was a weak, puny and sickly child. His family thought that he could live only a few hours, so he was duly baptized the day after he was born. Had he died, as they expected, his soul would now be saved in glory instead of tortured in a burning hell.

The father of Voltaire was a notary, which in those days meant something less than a lawyer; how much less I would not pretend to say. He had been a linen-draper who was shrewd and thrifty in earthly matters and had accumulated some wealth. He was respected, religious, obstinate and mediocre. His mother was his mother and nothing more. He had a living brother and sister at the time of his birth, and his mother had lost two children in infancy.

In spite of their hopes and fears, the child lived. Although puny and frail in its early youth, and not robust nor strong at any time, it clung to life for eighty-four years. And these eighty-four years perhaps did more for the liberation of man than any other child or any other like period that the world has ever known.

Neither Voltaire's father nor mother, nor the brother and sister that lived to maturity, ever showed any signs of great intelligence, and no one connected with the family, near or remote, seems to have been touched with the divine fire that manifested itself in Voltaire's life and work. The modern eugenists can find no evidence for inherited genius and the potency of the germ plasm in the great Voltaire. But, of course, the eugenists build their theories upon the sparse facts that here and there they seem to find, rather than upon the almost universal experiences that do not prove their theories.

When Voltaire was a mere child, he was placed under the tutelege of an abbé named Chateauneuf. The priest was clever, witty, skeptical and gay. He soon formed a great attachment for Voltaire, who was not only his pupil but his godson—whatever that may mean. It was not long before the child showed an amazing precocity which startled his family and gratified the abbé.

At the time of Voltaire's birth, there was but one church, which of course was ignorant, tyrannical and cruel in the extreme. No one was allowed to write or publish any book or pamphlet that denied the accepted faith. The book was always burned and sometimes the author with it. So far as freedom of thought is concerned, it is well to have more than one church. The more the better. Under these circumstances, they must give some attention to each other. Not only was the church supreme in France in 1694, but poverty, degradation, ignorance and superstition were the common heritages of the time.

At the age of ten, he was sent to a boy's school. It was soon discovered that he had a clever mind. His body was lean and his intellect alert, and in these respects neither one changed to the day of his death. He says that at school he "learned Latin and nonsense and nothing else." And, unlike most boys, he cared little for games and sports. He told his teachers that every one must jump after his own fashion.

One of the church fathers who was a teacher and who closely observed the boy, said to the child:

"Witch, you will one day be the standard bearer of Deism in France."

Voltaire's father sought to make him a lawyer but, luckily for the world, he never was destined for this fate. Later, in speaking of Molière, he said:

"All who have made a name for themselves in the fine arts have done so in spite of their relations. Nature has always been much stronger with them than education."

And again:

"I saw early that one can neither resist one's ruling passion nor fight one's destiny."

When Voltaire returned from school, at sixteen, he startled his father by announcing his intention to devote his life to literature. The practical notary replied in heat:

"Literature is the profession of a man who wishes to be useless to society, a burden to his relatives and to die of hunger."

The advice of his father did not prevent Voltaire from writing verses. Even at an early age they were clever, skeptical and daring. These were followed by the production of his first play, *Oedipe*. This he finished at the age of nineteen. The play immediately attracted the interest of the dilletante of Paris and was accepted and placed in rehearsal for the theater. However much it pleased the people, it was pronounced dangerous and blasphemous by the police and Voltaire was arrested, in 1717, when he was twenty-one years old, and thrown in the Bastile. He arrived at the historical prison May 17th, and on the following Thursday he signed a receipt for a couple of volumes of Homer, two India handkerchiefs, a little cap, two cravats, a night cap and a bottle of essence of cloves. Soon after he was given pen and ink. It was in the Bastile that he dropped the name "Arouet" and adopted the psuedonym which he has made immortal for all time—"Voltaire."

After a short time while he was released from prison on promise of good behavior, which promise he continued to violate to the end of his life.

His first play, *Oedipe*, was completed when he was nineteen years old, and his last play, *Irene*, at the age of eighty-three. No man who ever lived gave as much to the world in sixty-four years as this son of an obscure notary, Voltaire. It is not in my province to go over his works in any great detail. Perhaps he is best known as a writer of plays. His first literary production and his last alike were dramas, but in that fruitful and fateful sixty-four years of the world's history, which should be known as "The Age of Voltaire," the printing presses of France turned out a constant stream of books and pamphlets from the pen of this great genius. In spite of the fact that Voltaire lived in an age of blind faith, deep superstition and dense ignorance, every word that flowed from his illustrious pen was a part of a plea for liberty, humanity, charity and the rights of the submerged.

In sixty-four years, more than one hundred volumes were produced and published by Voltaire. In addition to these one hundred volumes, he wrote and published no fewer than five thousand pamphlets covering every subject of interest to France and the world. These pamphlets were published under various psuedonyms, many of them burned by public executioners who would gladly have burned Voltaire with his heretical utterances. Many of them he denied to save his life. These children of his active brain drove him constantly through Europe, seeking safety and refuge, avoiding pursuers, denying his utterances and committing new offenses before the old ones were forgiven or condoned. Not plays alone, but history, biography, poetry, romances and brilliant pleas for prosecuted men and unpopular causes, filled these tireless years.

Neither was his attention given entirely to books and pamphlets. In the later years of his life he bought a great estate at Ferney, in France, on the shores of Lake Geneva, where he lived for some twenty years, up to the time when he went to Paris at the close of his life. This estate gave him a magnificent view of the beautiful lake and the picturesque Alps and was so close to Switzerland that it furnished him a place of refuge from the French officers, who were always dogging his footsteps on account of his devotion to the freedom of the human mind.

It seems as if there was no form of literature at which Voltaire did not excel. Perhaps his romances have not been as widely read as his other works, but these, like everything he wrote, received the widest notice when they came from the press. The romances are not in the form of the modern novel. Styles in literature change as styles in dress. All of them were written for a purpose, and all of them must be interpreted in view of the age and the cause for which he wrote. Whether the scenes were laid in Persia, Arabia or any other part of the world, all of them meant Europe and described the institutions, customs, follies, crimes and cruelties of the day in which he lived.

The sketches contained in this volume have long passed under the name of romances. They are only romances in the sense that Voltaire used the form sometimes for the sake of self-protection; events lure the reader into the feeling of a story when, in fact, Voltaire was writing about the shams, superstitions and cruelties of man.

Candide was inspired largely by his agonizing over the

Lisbon earthquake. On November 1, 1755, Lisbon was almost completely destroyed by an earthquake. The news reached Voltaire and stirred his whole being. Thirty thousand people were killed in the twinkling of an eye. The earthquake was on All Souls Day, and the greatest loss of life was in the cathedrals and churches of the place. For months thereafter all of Voltaire's letters contained allusions to the catastrophe which moved every fiber of his being.

"The best of all possible worlds! If Pope had been there, would he have said, 'Whatever is, is right?' 'All is well,' seems to be absurd, when evil is on land and sea."

Voltaire used the disaster of Lisbon as the title to a searching poem on the problems of life and death and put the same theme in verse under the title of "natural law." This poem deals with the questions as to the meaning or plan and scheme of things. When the church authorities read or heard of these poems they were promptly burned in Paris, and the Genevans held up their hands in holy horror at Voltaire's theology. However, the world was shocked at the terrible tragedy. Even the King of France had serious thoughts and caused a private entrance to be built to Madam Pompadour's apartments and made her a maid of honor to the queen.

In view of this catastrophe, Voltaire likewise wrote his famous romance, *Candide*. His hero was a young man of prepossessing manners, good understanding and fine disposition and suspected of being of gentle blood. Pangloss was the preceptor and oracle of the family, and the boy listened to his instructions with the simplicity natural to his age and disposition. His teacher had no trouble to prove that this was the best of all possible worlds in which we live and that everything was created for the best end. The natural fitness of all things was easily seen.

"Observe, for instance, the nose is formed to bear spectacles, therefore we wear spectacles. The legs are visibly designed for stockings, accordingly we wear stockings. Stones were made to be hewn, and to construct castles, therefore my Lord has a magnificent castle; for the greatest baron in the province ought to be the best lodged. Swine were created to be eaten, therefore we eat pork all the year round. It is not enough therefore to say that every thing is right, we should say every thing is in the best state it possibly could be."

Of course, it was no trouble to convince the young pupil of the purpose of the universe and that everything was for the best, for what else are teachers provided excepting to convince?

Candide formed an attachment for a girl named Cunegonde who lived in the castle, but the Baron, discovering the situation, promptly used his strength and prestige to break it up. Candide left the castle, laid himself down to sleep in a furrow in the field without his supper, and awoke almost frozen to death. He set off for the next town and arrived almost dead of hunger and fatigue. Then commences a series of adventures—shipwrecks, storms and earthquakes, and imminent perils in a thousand ways, each one more terrible than the others. Not only did Candide and Cunegonde suffer these inflictions but countless others whom they met on their way suffered the same fates—beating, rapine, torture, starvation and disease, until the earth looked to them like a great charnel house, and still Pangloss insisted with all the stupidity of the modern theologian that this was the best possible world, that human beings were endowed with free will and that everything happened for the best.

The story of *Zadig*, while outwardly a romance, was recognized by every one who read it at the time as picturing plainly the people at the French Court, the absurd manners and customs and the stupidity of it all. There was scarcely a custom or habit prevalent at court that was not satirized by the keen wit and facile pen of Voltaire in this romance.

The World as It Goes might well have been written today and anywhere else, although the scenes are laid in upper Asia and Ithuriel was the hero and ruler. Perhaps many of our one hundred per cent patriots had better not read this story. It would be hard to find a piece of literature showing a keener view into life in all of its phases. It is written with the cleverness of a Dean Swift, the insight of a philosopher and the evident feelings of a most sensitive humanitarian.

The little story, *The Study of Nature*, is more an essay than a romance. This reveals some of Voltaire's keenest reasoning. Philosophical questions which seem to be as new today as in the time of Voltaire are dissected by the keenest intellect and the liveliest wit that the world has ever known.

Though the romances of Voltaire have never taken the place with the public that has been given to many of his other books, still all of them are interesting. All of them tell their story and have done their part in his great work. It was not only religion that interested him, but all social questions claimed the same attention. He hated injustice; he hated poverty; he recognized the exploitation of the poor by the rich. Wherever he touches upon this subject, as he frequently does in his romances, his sympathies are with those who need them most.

Voltaire has passed into history mainly as a fighter against the superstitions, the cruelties and the bigotries that are masked under religion, but he was essentially a humanitarian in every aspect of life. When he built his beautiful home and established his fine estate at Ferney, he interested himself in all the activities of the people of the community in which he lived; he established a factory for the manufacture of watches and for several other important industries. These were well managed and were not only prosperous to him but prosperous to his employees. With them he built up something like a coöperative community where every workman had a share of the profits. He was beloved by his neighbors, by the citizens of the place, and by the men who worked with him.

On a monument erected for his honor just outside of his estate in the little hamlet of Ferney, can be read the following inscriptions which show, the affection in which he was held by these people.

(south face)
TO THE POET PHILOSOPHER
Cabas, Sirven, Montbaille, La Barre, Lally.
Emancipation of the serfs of the Jura.
Liberation of the country of Gex.
Essay on the customs and intelligence of the nations.
History of Russia under Peter the Great.
Commentaries on Corneille. Philosophical Dictionary.
History of the Parliament of Paris.
The Chinese Orphan. Tancred. Irene.

(north face)
TO THE BENEFACTOR OF FERNEY
Voltaire builds more than 100 houses.
He donates to the city a church, a hospital,
a school, the reservoir, the fountain.
He lends money without interest.
He reclaims the swamps of the country.

He establishes fairs and markets.
He feeds the people during the famine of 1771.

(front)
TO THE PATRIARCH OF FERNEY
1694-1758-1778

(back)
THIS MONUMENT WAS INAUGURATED
July 27th, 1890
*(This statue was given to the city of Ferney by
its sculptor, Emile Lambert)*

Voltaire's works abound in cynical statements. He seemed to approach the world with a sneer. But, most people have not the subtlety to judge a sneer. Often it is a protective covering against the pain and anguish suffered by the man who feels the sorrows of the world; what seems to be a sneer is the effort to make himself believe that all of it amounts to nothing, and to loose his consciousness of misery and pain in the contemplation of Nirvana. Scattered broadcast through the world are the copies of the bust made by the great sculptor Houdon. These have been reproduced in all lands and in all sorts of books until Houdon's Voltaire has grown to be the image of the man. The work on this bust was done late in life. His face is thin and gaunt; his nose and chin come close together, and a cynical smile marks the countenance as if it was the characteristic attitude of Voltaire.

Of course he joked and laughed and sneered in his deepest miseries. When haunted by the profoundest tragedies which move the sensitive man, he wore his mocking grin and his cynic's smile, but his tireless brain, his constant energy, even his mocking grin, have done more than was ever accomplished by any other man to rid the world of the cruelty and intolerance that has blasted the lives and destroyed the hopes of millions of human beings since man came upon the earth.

CLARENCE DARROW.

MICROMEGAS

MICROMEGAS

A Philosophical Tale

CHAPTER I

JOURNEY OF AN INHABITANT OF THE SYSTEM OF THE STAR SIRIUS TO THE PLANET SATURN

IN one of those planets which revolve round the star named Sirius there lived a young man of great intelligence, whose acquaintance I had the honor of making on the occasion of his last journey to our little ant-hill. He was called Micromegas,[1] a name which is exceedingly appropriate to all great people. He had a stature of eight leagues, and by eight leagues I mean twenty-four thousand geometrical paces of five feet each.

Here some mathematicians, a class of persons who are always useful to the public, will immediately take up the pen, and find out by calculation that since Mr. Micromegas, inhabitant of the country of Sirius, is twenty-four thousand paces in height from head to foot, which make one hundred and twenty thousand statute feet, whereas we denizens of the earth have an average stature of hardly more than five feet, and, since our globe is nine thousand leagues in circumference, they will find, I say, that the world which produced him must have a circumference precisely twenty-one millions six hundred thousand times greater than our little earth. Nothing in nature is simpler, more a matter of course. The dominions of certain potentates in Germany or Italy, round which you can walk in half an hour, as compared with the empire of Turkey, of Russia, or of China, can give but a very faint idea of the prodigious differences which nature has set between various orders of being throughout the universe.

His Excellency's height being what I have said, all our sculptors and painters will readily agree that his waist may be about fifty thousand feet round, which would constitute a symmetrical proportion. His nose being one-third of the length of his handsome face, and his handsome face being the seventh part of the height of his handsome body, it will indisputably follow that the Sirian's nose is six thousand three hundred and thirty-three statute feet in length, and a fraction more; which was the proposition to be proved.

As to his mind, it is worthy to rank with the most cultivated among us; he knows many things, some of which are of his own invention. He had not yet reached his two hundred and fiftieth year, and was studying, as was customary at his age, at the most famous school in the planet, when he solved, by the strength of his own intellect, more than fifty propositions of Euclid, that is, eighteen more than Blaise Pascal, who, after having, according to his sister's account, solved thirty-two for his own amusement, afterwards became a pretty fair geometer, and a very poor metaphysician. When he was about four hundred and fifty years of age, and already passing out of childhood, he dissected a great many little insects less than a hundred feet in diameter, such as are invisible under ordinary microscopes, and composed a very curious book about them, but one which brought him into some trouble. The mufti of that country, much given to hair-splitting and very ignorant, found in his work statements which he deemed suspicious, offensive, rash, heretical or savoring of heresy, and he prosecuted him for it with the bitterest animosity. The question in dispute was whether the substantial form of which the fleas of Sirius consisted was of the same nature as that of the snails. Micromegas defended himself with spirit, and had all the ladies on his side; the trial lasted two hundred and twenty years. At last the mufti had the book condemned by judges who had never read it, and the author was forbidden to appear at court for eight hundred years.

He was only moderately afflicted at being banished from a court which was full of nothing but trickery and meanness. He composed a very funny song in ridicule of the mufti, which in its turn failed to give the latter much annoyance;[2] and he himself set forth on his travels from planet to planet, with a view to improving his mind and soul, as the saying is. Those who travel only in postchaises or family coaches, will doubtless be astonished at the sort of conveyance adopted up there; for we, on our little mound of mud, can imagine nothing that surpasses our own experience. Our traveler had such a marvelous acquaintance with the laws of gravitation, and with all the forces of attraction and repulsion, and made such good use of his knowledge, that, sometimes by means of a sunbeam, and sometimes by the help of a comet, he and his companions went from one world to another as a bird hops from bough to bough. He traversed the Milky Way in a very short time; and I am obliged to confess that he never saw, beyond the stars with which it is thickly sown, that beautiful celestial empyrean which the illustrious parson, Derham[3] boasts of having discovered at the end of his telescope. Not that I would for a moment suggest that Mr. Derham mistook what he saw; heaven forbid! But Micromegas was on the spot, he is an accurate observer, and I have no wish to contradict anybody. Micromegas, after plenty of turns and twists, arrived at the planet Saturn. Accustomed though he was to the sight of novelties, when he saw the insignificant size of the globe and its inhabitants, he could not at first refrain from that smile of superiority which sometimes escapes even the wisest; for in truth Saturn is scarcely nine hundred times greater than the earth, and the citizens of that country are mere dwarfs, only a thousand fathoms high, or thereabout. He laughed a little at first at these people, in much the same way as an Italian musician, when he comes to France, is wont to deride Lulli's performances. But, as the Sirian was a sensible fellow, he was very soon convinced that a thinking being need not be altogether ridiculous because he is no more than six thousand feet high. He was soon on familiar terms with the Saturnians after their astonishment had somewhat subsided. He formed an intimate friendship with the secretary of the Academy of Saturn, a man of great intelligence, who had not indeed invented anything himself, but was a capital hand at describing the inventions of others, and one who could turn a little verse neatly enough or perform an elaborate calculation. I will here introduce, for the gratification of my readers, a singular conversation that Micromegas one day held with Mr. Secretary.

CHAPTER II

CONVERSATION BETWEEN AN INHABITANT OF
SIRIUS AND A NATIVE OF SATURN

AFTER His Excellency had laid himself down, and the secretary had approached his face, Micromegas said:

"I must needs confess that nature is full of variety."

"Yes," said the Saturnian; "nature is like a flower-bed, the blossoms of which——"

"Oh," said the other, "have done with your flower-bed!"

"She is," resumed the secretary, "like an assembly of blondes and brunettes, whose attire——"

"Pooh! What have I to do with your brunettes?" said the other.

"She is like a gallery of pictures, then, the outlines of which——"

"No, no," said the traveler; "once more, nature is like nature. Why do you search for comparisons?"

"To please you," answered the secretary.

"I do not want to be pleased," rejoined the traveler; "I want to be instructed: begin by telling me how many senses the men in your world possess?"

"We have seventy-two," said the academician; "and we are always complaining that they are so few. Our imagination goes beyond our needs; we find that with our seventy-two senses, our ring, and our five moons, our range is too restricted, and, in spite of all our curiosity and the tolerably large number of passions which spring out of our seventy-two senses, we have plenty of time to feel bored."

"I can well believe it," said Micromegas; "for in our globe, although we have nearly a thousand senses, there lingers even in us a certain vague desire, an unaccountable restlessness, which warns us unceasingly that we are of little account in the universe, and that there are beings much more perfect than ourselves. I have traveled a little; I have seen mortals far below us, and others as greatly superior; but I have seen none who have not more desires than real wants, and more wants than they can satisfy. I shall some day, perhaps, reach the country where there is lack of nothing, but hitherto no one has been able to give me any positive information about it." The Saturnian and the Sirian thereupon exhausted themselves in conjectures on the subject, but after a great deal of argumentative discussion, as ingenious as it was futile, they were obliged to return to facts.

"How long do you people live?" asked the Sirian.

"Ah, a very short time," replied the little man of Saturn.

"That is just the way with us," said the Sirian; "we are always complaining of the shortness of life. This must be a universal law of nature."

"Alas," quoth the Saturnian, "none of us lives for more than five hundred annual revolutions of the sun;"—that amounts to about fifteen thousand years, according to our manner of counting—"you see how it is our fate to die almost as soon as we are born: our existence is a point, our duration an instant, our globe an atom. Scarcely have we begun to acquire a little information when death arrives before we can put it to use. For my part, I do not venture to lay any schemes; I feel myself like a drop of water in a boundless ocean. I am ashamed, especially before you, of the absurd figure I make in this universe."

Micromegas answered: "If you were not a philosopher, I should fear to distress you by telling you that our lives are seven hundred times as long as yours, but you know too well that when the time comes to give back one's body to the elements and to reanimate nature under another form, which process is called death,—when that moment of metamorphosis comes, it is precisely the same thing whether we have lived an eternity or only a day. I have been in countries where life is a thousand times longer than with us, and yet have heard murmurs at its brevity even there. But people of good sense are to be found everywhere who know how to make the most of what they have, and to thank the Author of nature. He has spread over this universe abundant variety, together with a kind of admirable uniformity. For example, all thinking beings are different, yet they all resemble each other essentially in the common endowment of thought and will. Matter is infinitely extended, but it has different properties in different worlds. How many of these various properties do you reckon in the matter with which you are acquainted?"

"If you speak," replied the Saturnian, "of those properties without which we believe that this globe could not subsist as it is, we reckon three hundred of them, such as extension, impenetrability, mobility, gravitation, divisibility, and so on."

"Apparently," rejoined the traveler, "this small number is sufficient for the purpose which the Creator had in view in constructing this little habitation. I admire His wisdom throughout; I see differences everywhere, but everywhere also a due proportion. Your globe is small, you who inhabit it are small likewise; you have few senses, the matter of which your world consists has few properties; all this is the work of Providence. Of what color is your sun when carefully examined?"

"White deeply tinged with yellow," said the Saturnian; "and when we split up one of its rays, we find that it consists of seven colors."

"Our sun has a reddish light," said the Sirian, "and we have thirty-nine primitive colors. There is not a single sun, among all those that I have approached, which resembles any other, just as among yourselves there is not a single face which is not different from all the rest."

After several other questions of this kind, he inquired how many essentially different modes of existence were enumerated in Saturn. He was told that not more than thirty were distinguished, as God, space, matter, beings occupying space which feel and think, thinking beings which do not occupy space, those which possess penetrability, others which do not do so, etc. The Sirian, in whose world they count three hundred of them, and who had discovered three thousand more in the course of his travels, astonished the philosopher of Saturn immensely. At length, after having communicated to each other a little of what they knew, and a great deal of that about which they knew nothing, and after having exercised their reasoning powers during a complete revolution of the sun, they resolved to make a little philosophical tour together.

CHAPTER III

THE SIRIAN AND THE SATURNIAN AS FELLOW-
TRAVELERS

OUR two philosophers were ready to embark upon the atmosphere of Saturn, with a fine collection of mathematical instruments, when the Saturnian's mistress, who got wind of what he was going to do, came in tears to remonstrate with him. She was a pretty little brunette, whose stature did not exceed six hundred and sixty fathoms, but her agreeable manners amply atoned for that deficiency.

"Oh, cruel one!" she exclaimed, "after having resisted you for fifteen hundred years, and when I was at last beginning to surrender, and have passed scarcely a hundred years in your arms, to leave me thus and start on a long journey with a giant of another world! Go, you have no taste for anything but novelty, you have never felt what it is to love! If you were a true Saturnian, you would be constant. Whither away so fast? What is it you would have? Our five moons are less fickle than you, our ring is less changeable. So much for what is past! I will never love anyone again."

The philosopher embraced her, and, in spite of all his philosophy, joined his tears with hers. As to the lady, after having fainted away, she proceeded to console herself with a certain beau who lived in the neighborhood.

Meanwhile our two inquirers set forth on their travels; they first of all jumped upon Saturn's ring, which they found pretty flat, as an illustrious inhabitant of our little globe has very cleverly conjectured; [4] thence they easily made their way from moon to moon. A comet passed quite near the last one, so they sprang upon it, together with their servants and their instruments. When they had gone about a hundred and fifty millions of leagues, they came across the satellites of Jupiter. They landed on Jupiter itself, and remained there for a year, during which they learned some very remarkable secrets which would be at the present moment in the press, were it not for the gentlemen who act as censors, and who have discovered therein some statements too hard for them to swallow. But I have read the manuscript which contains them in the library of the illustrious Archbishop of——, who, with a generosity and kindness which cannot be sufficiently commended, has permitted me to peruse his books. Accordingly I promise to give him a long article in the next edition that shall be brought out of Moreri, [5] and I will be specially careful not to forget his sons, who afford such good hope of the perpetuation of their illustrious father's progeny.

But let us return to our travelers. Quitting Jupiter, they traversed a space of about a hundred million leagues, and, coasting along the planet Mars, which, as is well known, is five times smaller than our own little globe, they saw two moons, which attend upon that planet, and which have escaped the observation of our astronomers. [6] I am well aware that Father Castel will write, and pleasantly enough too, against the existence of these two moons, but I refer myself to those who reason from analogy. Those excellent philosophers know how difficult it would be for Mars, which is such a long way off from the sun, to get on with less than two moons. Be that as it may, our friends found the planet so small, that they were afraid of finding no room there to put up for the night, so they proceeded on their way, like a pair of travelers who disdain a humble village inn, and push on to the nearest town. But the Sirian and his companion soon had cause to repent having done so, for they went on for a long time without finding anything at all. At last they perceived a faint glimmer; it came from our earth, and created compassion in the minds of those who had so lately left Jupiter. However, for fear of repenting a second time, they decided to disembark. They passed over the tail of the comet, and meeting with an aurora borealis close at hand, they got inside, and alighted on the earth by the northern shore of the Baltic Sea, July the 5th, 1737, new style.

CHAPTER IV

WHAT HAPPENED TO THE TRAVELERS ON THE
TERRESTRIAL GLOBE

AFTER having rested for some time, they consumed for their breakfast a couple of mountains, which their people prepared for them as daintily as possible. Then, wishing to inspect the country where they were, they first went from north to south. Each of the Sirian's ordinary steps was about thirty thousand statute feet; the Saturnian dwarf, whose height was only a thousand fathoms, followed panting far behind, for he had to take about a dozen steps when the other made a single stride. Picture to yourself (if I may be allowed to make such a comparison) a tiny little toy spaniel pursuing a captain of the King of Prussia's grenadiers.

As the strangers proceeded pretty quickly, they made the circuit of the globe in thirty-six hours; the sun, indeed, or rather the earth, makes the same journey in a day, but it must be borne in mind that it is a much easier way of getting on, to turn on one's axis, than to walk on one's feet. Behold our travelers, then, returned to the same spot from which they had started, after having set eyes upon that sea, to them almost imperceptible, which is called the Mediterranean, and that other little pond which, under the name of the great Ocean, surrounds this mole-hill. Therein the dwarf had never sunk much above the knee, while the other had scarcely wetted his ankle. They did all they could, searching here and there, both when going and returning, to ascertain whether the earth were inhabited or not. They stooped, they lay down, they groped about in all directions; but their eyes and their hands being out of all proportion to the tiny beings who crawl up and down here, they felt not the slightest sensation which could lead them to suspect that we and our fellow-creatures, the other inhabitants of this globe, have the honor to exist.

The dwarf, who sometimes judged a little too hastily, at once decided that there was not a single creature on the earth. His first reason was that he had not seen one. But Micromegas politely gave him to understand that that was not a good argument:

"For," said he, "you, with your little eyes, cannot see certain stars of the fiftieth magnitude which I distinctly discern; do you conclude from that circumstance that those stars have no existence?"

"But," said the dwarf, "I have felt about very carefully."

"But," rejoined the other, "your powers of perception may be at fault."

"But," continued the dwarf, "this globe is so ill-constructed, it is so irregular, and, it seems to me, of so ridiculous a shape! All here appears to be in a state of chaos: look at these little brooks, not one of which goes in a straight line; look at these ponds, which are neither round nor square, nor oval, nor of any regular form; and all these little sharp-pointed grains with which this globe bristles, and which have rubbed the skin off my feet!"—he alluded to the mountains—"Observe too the shape of the globe as a whole, how it is flat at the poles, how it turns round the sun in a clumsily slanting manner, so that the polar climes are necessarily mere wastes. In truth, what chiefly makes me think that there is nobody here, is that I cannot suppose any people of sense would wish to occupy such a dwelling."

"Well," said Micromegas, "perhaps the people who inhabit it are not people of sense. But in point of fact there are some signs of its not having been made for nothing. Everything here seems to you irregular, you say; that is because everything is judged by the measures of Saturn and Jupiter. Ay, perhaps it is for that very reason that there is so much apparent confusion here. Have I not told you that in the course of my travels I have always remarked the presence of variety?"

The Saturnian had answers to meet all these arguments, and the dispute might never have ended, if Micromegas, in the heat of discussion, had not luckily broken the thread which bound together his collar of diamonds, so that they fell to the ground; pretty little stones they were, of rather unequal size, the largest of which weighed four hundred pounds, and the smallest not more than fifty. The dwarf, who picked up some of them, perceived, on bringing them near his eyes, that these diamonds, from the fashion in which they were cut, made capital microscopes. He accordingly took up a little magnifier of one hundred and sixty feet in diameter, which he applied to his eye; and Micromegas selected one of two thousand five hundred feet across. They were of high power, but at first nothing was revealed by their help, so the focus had to be adjusted. At last the inhabitant of Saturn saw something almost imperceptible which moved half under water in the Baltic sea; it was a whale. He caught it very cleverly with his little finger, and, placing it on his thumb nail, showed it to the Sirian, who burst out laughing a second time at the extreme minuteness of the inhabitants of our system. The Saturnian, now convinced that our world was inhabited, immediately rushed to the conclusion that whales were the only creatures to be found there; and, as speculation was his strong point, he pleased himself with conjectures as to the origin of so insignificant an atom and the source of its movement, whether it had ideas and free will. Micromegas was a good deal puzzled about it; he examined the creature very patiently, and the result of his investigation was that he had no grounds for supposing that it had a soul lodged in its body. The two travelers then were inclined to think that there was no being possessed of intelligence in this habitation of ours, when with the aid of the microscope they detected something as big as a whale, floating on the Baltic sea. We know that at that very time a flock of philosophers were returning from the polar circle, whither they had gone to make observations which no one had attempted before. The newspapers say that their vessel ran aground in the gulf of Bothnia, and that they had great difficulty in saving their lives; but we never know in this world the real truth about anything. I am going to relate honestly what took place, without adding anything of my own invention, a task which demands no small effort on the part of an historian.

CHAPTER V

EXPERIENCES AND CONJECTURES OF THE TWO TRAVELERS

MICROMEGAS stretched out his hand very gently towards the place where the object appeared. Thrusting forward two fingers, he quickly drew them back lest his hopes should be defeated; then, cautiously opening and closing them, he seized with great dexterity the ship which carried those gentlemen, and placed it likewise on his nail without squeezing it too much, for fear of crushing it.

"Here is an animal quite different from the first," said the Saturnian dwarf. The Sirian placed the supposed animal in the hollow of his hand. The passengers and crew, who thought that they had been whirled aloft by a tempest and supposed that they had struck upon some kind of rock, began to bestir themselves; the sailors seized casks of wine, threw them overboard on Micromegas's hand, and afterwards jumped down themselves, while the geometers seized their quadrants, their sectors, and a pair of Lapland girls, and descended on the Sirian's fingers. They made such a commotion, that at last he felt something tickling him; it was a pole with an iron point being driven a foot deep into his forefinger. He judged from this prick that it had proceeded somehow from the little animal that he was holding; but at first he perceived nothing more. The magnifier, which scarcely enabled them to discern a whale and a ship, had no effect upon a being so insignificant as man. I have no wish to shock the vanity of anyone, but here I am obliged to beg those who are sensitive about their own importance to consider what I have to say on this subject. Taking the average stature of mankind at five feet, we make no greater figure on the earth than an insect not quite the six hundred thousandth part of an inch in height would do upon a bowl ten feet round. Figure to yourselves a being who could hold the earth in his hand, and who had organs of sense proportionate to our own,—and it may well be conceived that there are a great number of such beings,—consider then, I pray you, what they would think of those battles which give the conqueror possession of some village, to be lost again soon afterwards.

I have no doubt that if some captain of tall grenadiers ever reads this work, he will raise the caps of his company at least a couple of feet; but I warn him that it will be all in vain, that he and his men will never be anything but the merest mites.

What marvelous skill then must our philosopher from Sirius have possessed in order to perceive those atoms of which I have been speaking! When Leuwenhoek and Hartsoeker first saw, or thought they saw, the minute speck out of which we are formed, they did not make nearly so surprising a discovery.[7] What pleasure then did Micromegas feel in watching the movements of those little machines, in examining all their feats, in following all their operations! How he shouted for joy, as he placed one of his microscopes in his companion's hand!

"I see them," they exclaimed both at once; "do you not observe how they are carrying burdens, how they stoop down and rise up?"

As they spoke, their hands trembled with delight at beholding objects so unusual, and with fear lest they might lose them. The Saturnian, passing from the one extreme of skepticism to an equal degree of credulity,

fancied that he saw them engaged in the work of prop-
agation.

"Ah!" said he, "I have surprised nature in the very
act." [8]

But he was deceived by appearances, an accident to
which we are only too liable, whether we make use of
microscopes or not.

CHAPTER VI

WHAT COMMUNICATION THEY HELD WITH MEN

MICROMEGAS, a much better observer than his
dwarf, perceived clearly that the atoms were
speaking to each other, and he called his companion's attention to the circumstance; but he, ashamed as he was
of having made a mistake on the subject of generation,
was indisposed to believe that such creatures as they
could have any means of communicating ideas. He had
the gift of tongues as well as the Sirian; he did not hear
the atoms speak, so he concluded that they did not do
so. Besides, how could those imperceptible beings have
vocal organs, and what could they have to say? To be
able to speak, one must think, or at least make some
approach to thought; but if those creatures could think,
then they must have something equivalent to a soul;
now to attribute the equivalent of a soul to these little
animals appeared to him absurd.

"But," said the Sirian, "you fancied just now that
they were making love; do you imagine that they can
make love without being able to think or utter a word,
or even to make themselves understood? Moreover, do
you suppose that it is more difficult to produce argu-

ments than offspring? Both appear to me equally mysterious operations."

"I no longer venture either to believe or to deny,"
said the dwarf; "I no longer have any opinion about
the matter. We must try to examine these insects, we
will form our conclusions afterwards."

"That is very well said," replied Micromegas; and he
straightway drew forth a pair of scissors with which he
cut his nails, and immediately made out of a paring
from his thumb nail a sort of monster speaking trumpet,
like a huge funnel, the narrow end of which he put into
his ear. As the wide part of the funnel included the ship
and all her crew, the faintest voice was conveyed along
the circular fibers of the nail in such a manner, that,
thanks to his perseverance, the philosopher high above
them clearly heard the buzzing of our insects down below.
In a few hours he succeeded in distinguishing the words,
and at last in understanding the French language. The
dwarf heard the same, but with more difficulty. The astonishment of the travelers increased every instant. They
heard mere mites speaking tolerably good sense; such a
freak of nature seemed to them inexplicable. You may
imagine how impatiently the Sirian and his dwarf longed
to hold conversation with the atoms; but the dwarf was
afraid that his voice of thunder, and still more that of
Micromegas, might deafen the mites without conveying
any meaning. It became necessary to diminish its
strength; they, accordingly, placed in their mouths instruments like little toothpicks, the tapering end of
which was brought near the ship. Then the Sirian, holding the dwarf on his knees, and the vessel with her crew
upon his nail, bent his head down and spoke in a low
voice, thus at last, with the help of all these precautions
and many others besides, beginning to address them:

"Invisible insects, whom the hand of the Creator has been pleased to produce in the abyss of the infinitely little, I thank Him for having deigned to reveal to me secrets which seemed inscrutable. It may be the courtiers of my country would not condescend to look upon you, but I despise no one, and I offer you my protection."

If ever anyone was astonished, it was the people who heard these words, nor could they guess whence they came. The ship's chaplain repeated the prayers used in exorcism, the sailors swore, and the philosophers constructed theories; but whatever theories they constructed, they could not divine who was speaking to them. The dwarf of Saturn, who had a softer voice than Micromegas, then told them in a few words with what kind of beings they had to do. He gave them an account of the journey from Saturn, and made them acquainted with the parts and powers of Mr. Micromegas; and, after having commiserated them for being so small, he asked them if they had always been in that pitiful condition, little better than annihilation, what they found to do on a globe that appeared to belong to whales, if they were happy, if they increased and multiplied, whether they had souls, and a hundred other questions of that nature.

A philosopher of the party, bolder than the rest of them, and shocked that the existence of his soul should be called in question, took observations of the speaker with a quadrant from two different stations, and, at the third, spoke as follows:

"Do you then suppose, sir, because a thousand fathoms extend between your head and your feet, that you are———"

"A thousand fathoms!" cried the dwarf; "good heavens! How is it that he knows my height? A thousand fathoms! He is not an inch out in his reckoning. What! Has that atom actually measured me? He is a geometer, he knows my size; while I, who cannot see him except through a microscope, am still ignorant of his!'"

"Yes, I have taken your measure," said the man of science; "and I will now proceed, if you please, to measure your big companion."

The proposal was accepted; His Excellency lay down at full length, for, if he had kept himself upright, his head would have reached too far above the clouds. Our philosophers then planted a tall tree in a place which Dr. Swift [9] would have named without hesitation, but which I abstain from mentioning out of my great respect for the ladies. Then by means of a series of triangles joined together, they came to the conclusion that the object before them was in reality a young man whose length was one hundred and twenty thousand statute foot.

Thereupon Micromegas uttered these words:

"I see more clearly than ever that we should judge of nothing by its apparent importance. O God, Who hast bestowed intelligence upon things which seemed so despicable, the infinitely little is as much Thy concern as the infinitely great; and, if it is possible that there should be living things smaller than these, they may be endowed with minds superior even to those of the magnificent creatures whom I have seen in the sky, who with one foot could cover this globe upon which I have alighted."

One of the philosophers replied that he might with perfect confidence believe that there actually were intelligent beings much smaller than man. He related, not indeed all the fables that Virgil has told on the subject of bees, but the results of Swammerdam's discoveries, and Réaumur's dissections. Finally, he informed him that

there are animals which bear the same proportion to
bees that bees bear to men, or that the Sirian himself
bore to those huge creatures of which he spoke, or that
those great creatures themselves bore to others before
whom they seemed mere atoms. The conversation grew
more and more interesting, and Micromegas spoke as follows.

CHAPTER VII

THE CONVERSATION CONTINUED

"O INTELLIGENT atoms, in whom the eternal Being has been pleased to make manifest His skill
and power, you must doubtless taste joys of perfect purity on this, your globe; for, being encumbered with so
little matter, and seeming to be all spirit, you must pass
your lives in love and meditation, which is the true life
of spiritual beings. I have nowhere beheld genuine happiness, but here it is to be found without a doubt."

On hearing these words, all the philosophers shook
their heads, and one of them, more frank than the others,
candidly confessed that, with the exception of a small
number held in little esteem among them, all the rest of
mankind were a multitude of fools, knaves, and miserable wretches.

"We have more matter than we need," said he, "the
cause of much evil, if evil proceeds from matter; and
we have too much mind, if evil proceeds from the mind.
Are you aware, for instance, that at this very moment
while I am speaking to you, there are a hundred thousand fools of our species who wear hats, slaying a hundred thousand fellow-creatures who wear turbans, or
who are being massacred by them, and that over al-

most all the earth, such practices have been going on from time immemorial?"

The Sirian shuddered, and asked what could be the cause of such horrible quarrels between those miserable little creatures.

"The dispute is all about a lump of clay," said the philosopher, "no bigger than your heel.[10] Not that a single one of those millions of men who get their throats cut has the slightest interest in this clod of earth. The only point in question is whether it shall belong to a certain man who is called Sultan, or to another who, I know not why, is called Cæsar.[11] Neither the one nor the other has ever seen, or is ever likely to see, the little corner of ground which is the bone of contention; and hardly one of those animals, who are cutting each other's throats, has ever seen the animal for whom they fight so desperately."

"Ah, wretched creatures!" exclaimed the Sirian with indignation; "can anyone imagine such frantic ferocity! I should like to take two or three steps, and stamp upon the whole swarm of these ridiculous assassins."

"Do not give yourself the trouble," answered the philosopher; "they are working hard enough to destroy themselves. I assure you that at the end of ten years, not a hundredth part of those wretches will be left; even if they had never drawn the sword, famine, fatigue, or intemperance will sweep them almost all away. Besides, it is not they who deserve punishment, but rather those armchair barbarians, who from the privacy of their cabinets, and during the process of digestion, command the massacre of a million men, and afterwards ordain a solemn thanksgiving to God."

The traveler, moved with compassion for the tiny human race, among whom he found such astonishing contrasts, said to the gentlemen who were present:

"Since you belong to the small number of wise men, and apparently do not kill anyone for money, tell me, pray, how you occupy yourselves."

"We dissect flies," said the same philosopher, "we measure distances, we calculate numbers, we are agreed upon two or three points which we understand, and we dispute about two or three thousand as to which we know nothing."

The visitors from Sirius and Saturn were immediately seized with a desire to question these intelligent atoms on the subjects whereon their opinions coincided.

"How far do you reckon it," said the latter, "from the Dog-star to the great star in Gemini?"

They all answered together: "Thirty-two degrees and a half."

"How far do you make it from here to the moon?"

"Sixty half diameters of the earth, in round numbers."

"What is the weight of your air?"

He thought to lay a trap for them, but they all told him that the air weighs about nine hundred times less than an equal volume of distilled water, and nineteen thousand times less than pure gold.

The little dwarf from Saturn, astonished at their replies, was now inclined to take for sorcerers the same people to whom he had refused, a quarter of an hour ago, to allow the possession of a soul.

Then Micromegas said:

"Since you know so well what is outside of yourselves, doubtless you know still better what is within you. Tell me what is the nature of your soul, and how you form ideas."

The philosophers spoke all at once as before, but this time they were all of different opinions. The oldest of them quoted Aristotle, another pronounced the name of Descartes, this spoke of Malebranche, that of Leibnitz, and another again of Locke. The old Peripatetic said in a loud and confident tone of voice:

"The soul is an actuality and a rationality, in virtue of which it has the power to be what it is; as Aristotle expressly declares on page six hundred thirty-three of the Louvre edition of his works;" and he quoted the passage.

"I don't understand Greek very well," said the giant.

"No more do I," said the mite of a philosopher.

"Why, then," inquired the Sirian, "do you quote the man you call Aristotle in that language?"

"Because," replied the sage, "it is right and proper to quote what we do not comprehend at all in a language we least understand."

The Cartesian then interposed and said:

"The soul is pure spirit, which has received in its mother's womb all metaphysical ideas, and which, on issuing thence, is obliged to go to school, as it were, and learn afresh all that it knew so well, and which it will never know any more."

"It was hardly worth while, then," answered the eight-leagued giant, "for your soul to have been so learned in your mother's womb, if you were to become so ignorant by the time you have a beard on your chin.—But what do you understand by spirit?"

"Why do you ask me that question?" said the philosopher; "I have no idea of its meaning, except that it is said to be independent of matter."

"You know, at least, what matter is, I presume?"

"Perfectly well," replied the man. "For instance, this

stone is gray, is of such and such a form, has three dimensions, has weight and divisibility."

"Very well," said the Sirian. "Now tell me, please, what this thing actually is which appears to you to be divisible, heavy, and of a gray color. You observe certain qualities, but are you acquainted with the intrinsic nature of the thing itself?"

"No," said the other.

"Then you do not know what matter is."

Thereupon Mr. Micromegas, addressing his question to another sage, whom he held on his thumb, asked him what the soul was, and what it did.

"Nothing at all," said the disciple of Malebranche; "it is God who does everything for me; I see and do everything through Him; He it is who does all without my interference."

"You might just as well, then, have no existence," replied the sage of Sirius.

"And you, my friend," he said to a follower of Leibnitz, who was there, "what is your soul?"

"It is," answered he, "a hand which points to the hour while my body chimes, or, if you like, it is the soul which chimes, while my body points to the hour; or, to put it in another way, my soul is the mirror of the universe, and my body is its frame: that is all clear enough."

A little student of Locke was standing near, and when his opinion at last was asked, he said:

"I know nothing of how I think, but I know that I have never thought except on the suggestion of my senses. That there are immaterial and intelligent substances is not what I doubt; but that it is impossible for God to communicate the faculty of thought to matter is what I doubt very strongly. I adore the eternal Power, nor is it my part to limit its exercise; I assert nothing, I content myself with believing that more is possible than people think."

The creature of Sirius smiled. He did not deem the last speaker the least sagacious of the company, and the dwarf of Saturn would have clasped Locke's disciple in his arms if their extreme disproportion had not made that impossible. But unluckily a little animalcule was there in a square cap,[12] who silenced all the other philosophical mites, saying that he knew the whole secret, that it was all to be found in the *Summa* of St. Thomas Aquinas; he scanned the pair of celestial visitors from top to toe, and maintained that they and all their kind, their suns and stars, were made solely for man's benefit. At this speech our two travelers tumbled over each other, choking with that inextinguishable laughter which, according to Homer, is the special privilege of the gods. Their shoulders shook, and their bodies heaved up and down, till, in those merry convulsions, the ship which the Sirian held on his nail fell into the Saturnian's breeches pocket. These two good people, after a long search, recovered it at last, and duly set to rights all that had been displaced. The Sirian once more took up the little mites, and addressed them again with great kindness, though he was a little disgusted in the bottom of his heart at seeing such infinitely insignificant atoms puffed up with a pride of such infinite magnitude. He promised to supply them with a rare book of philosophy, written in very minute characters for their special use, telling them that in that book they would find all that can be known of the ultimate essence of things, and he actually gave them the volume ere his departure. It was carried to Paris and laid before the Academy of Sciences; but when the old secretary came to open it, he saw nothing but blank leaves.

"Ah!" said he, "this is just what I expected."

ZADIG, OR DESTINY

ZADIG, OR DESTINY

An Eastern Tale

CERTIFICATE OF APPROVAL.—I, the undersigned, who have succeeded in making myself pass for a man of learning and even of wit, have read this manuscript, and found it, in spite of myself, curious and amusing, moral and philosophical, and worthy even of pleasing those who hate romances. So I have disparaged it, and assured the cadi that it is an abominable work.

DEDICATORY EPISTLE OF ZADIG TO THE SULTANA SHERAH, BY SADI.

The 10th day of the month Shawal, in the year 837 of the Hegira.

Delight of the eyes, torment of the heart, and lamp of the soul, I kiss not the dust of thy feet, because thou dost scarcely ever walk, or only on Persian carpets or over rose leaves. I present thee with the translation of a book written by an ancient sage, to whom, being in the happy condition of having nothing to do, there occurred the happy thought of amusing himself by writing the story of Zadig, a work that means more than it seems to do. I beseech thee to read it and form thy judgment on it; for although thou art in the springtime of life, and courted by pleasures of every kind; although thou art fair, and thy talents add to thy beauty; and although thou art loaded with praises from morning to

night, and so hast every right to be devoid of common
sense, yet thou hast a very sound intelligence and a
highly refined taste, and I have heard thee argue better
than any old dervish with a long beard and pointed cap.
Thou art cautious yet not suspicious; thou art gentle
without being weak; thou art beneficent with due dis-
crimination; thou dost love thy friends, and makest to
thyself no enemies. Thy wit never borrows its charm
from the shafts of slander; thou dost neither say nor do
evil, in spite of abundant facilities if thou wert so inclined. Lastly, thy soul has always appeared to me as
spotless as thy beauty. Thou hast even a small stock of
philosophy, which has led me to believe that thou
wouldst take more interest than any other of thy sex in
this work of a wise man.

It was originally written in ancient Chaldean, which
neither thou nor I understand. It was translated into
Arabic for the entertainment of the famous Sultan Oulook, about the time when the Arabs and Persians were
beginning to compose *The Thousand and One Nights,
The Thousand and One Days,* etc. Oulook preferred to
read *Zadig;* but the ladies of his harem liked the others
better.

"How can you prefer," said the wise Oulook, "senseless stories that mean nothing?"

"That is just why we are so fond of them," answered
the ladies.

I feel confident that thou wilt not resemble them, but
that thou wilt be a true Oulook; and I venture to hope
that when thou art weary of general conversation, which
is of much the same character as *The Arabian Nights
Entertainment,* except that it is less amusing, I may
have the honor of talking to thee for a few minutes in a
rational manner. If thou hadst been Thalestris in the time

of Alexander, son of Philip, or if thou hadst been the Queen of Sheba in the days of Solomon, those kings would have traveled to thee, not thou to them.

I pray the heavenly powers that thy pleasures may be unalloyed, thy beauty unfading, and thy happiness everlasting.

CHAPTER I

THE MAN OF ONE EYE

IN the time of King Moabdar there lived at Babylon a young man named Zadig, who was born with a good disposition, which education had strengthened. Though young and rich, he knew how to restrain his passions; he was free from all affectation, made no pretension to infallibility himself, and knew how to respect the foibles of others. People were astonished to see that, with all his wit, he never turned his powers of raillery on the vague, disconnected, and confused talk, the rash censures, the ignorant judgments, the scurvy jests, and all that vain babble of words which went by the name of conversation at Babylon. He had learned in the first book of Zoroaster that self-conceit is a bladder puffed up with wind, out of which issue storms and tempests when it is pricked. Above all, Zadig never prided himself on despising women, nor boasted of his conquests over them. Generous as he was, he had no fear of bestowing kindness on the ungrateful, therein following the noble maxim of Zoroaster: *When thou eatest, give something to the dogs, even though they should bite thee.* He was as wise as man can be, for he sought to live with the wise. Instructed in the sciences of the ancient Chaldeans, he was not ignorant of such principles of natural philosophy as

were then known, and knew as much of metaphysics
as has been known in any age, that is to say, next to
nothing. He was firmly persuaded that the year consists
of three hundred sixty-five days and a quarter, in spite
of the latest philosophy of his time, and that the sun is
the center of our system; and when the leading magi
told him with contemptuous arrogance that he entertained dangerous opinions, and that it was a proof of
hostility to the government to believe that the sun turned on its own axis and that the year had twelve months,
he held his peace without showing either anger or disdain.

Zadig, with great riches, and consequently well provided with friends, having health and good looks, a just
and well-disciplined mind, and a heart noble and sincere,
thought that he might be happy. He was to be married
to Semira, a lady whose beauty, birth, and fortune rendered her the first match in Babylon. He felt for her a
strong and virtuous attachment, and Semira in her turn
loved him passionately. They were close upon the happy
moment which was about to unite them, when, walking
together towards one of the gates of Babylon, under the
palm trees which adorned the banks of the Euphrates,
they saw a party of men armed with swords and bows
advancing in their direction. They were the satellites of
young Orcan, the nephew of a minister of state, whom
his uncle's hangers-on had encouraged in the belief that
he might do what he liked with impunity. He had none
of the graces nor virtues of Zadig; but, fancying he was
worth a great deal more, he was provoked at not being
preferred to him. This jealousy, which proceeded only
from his vanity, made him think that he was desperately
in love with Semira, and he determined to carry her off.
The ravishers seized her, and in their outrageous violence

wounded her, shedding the blood of one so fair that the tigers of Mount Imaus would have melted at the sight of her. She pierced the sky with her lamentations. She cried aloud:

"My dear husband! They are tearing me from him who is the idol of my heart."

Taking no heed of her own danger, it was of her beloved Zadig alone that she thought, who, meanwhile, was defending her with all the force that love and valor could bestow. With the help of only two slaves he put the ravishers to flight, and carried Semira to her home unconscious and covered with blood. On opening her eyes she saw her deliverer, and said:

"O Zadig, I loved you before as my future husband, I love you now as the preserver of my life and honor."

Never was there a heart more deeply moved than that of Semira; never did lips more lovely express sentiments more touching, in words of fire inspired by gratitude for the greatest of benefits and the most tender transports of the most honorable love. Her wound was slight, and was soon cured; but Zadig was hurt more severely, an arrow had struck him near the eye and made a deep wound. Semira's only prayer to Heaven now was that her lover might be healed. Her eyes were bathed in tears night and day; she longed for the moment when those of Zadig might once more be able to gaze on her with delight; but an abscess which attacked the wounded eye gave every cause for alarm. A messenger was sent as far as Memphis for Hermes, the famous physician, who came with a numerous train. He visited the sick man, and declared that he would lose the eye; he even foretold the day and the hour when this unfortunate event would happen.

"If it had been the right eye," said he, "I might have cured it, but injuries to the left eye are incurable."

All Babylon, while bewailing Zadig's fate, admired the profound scientific research of Hermes. Two days afterwards the abscess broke of itself, and Zadig was completely cured. Hermes wrote a book, in which he proved to him that he ought not to have been cured; but Zadig did not read it. As soon as he could venture forth, he prepared to visit her in whom rested his every hope of happiness in life, and for whose sake alone he desired to have eyes. Now Semira had gone into the country three days before, and on his way he learned that this fair lady, after loudly declaring that she had an insurmountable objection to one-eyed people, had just married Orcan the night before. At these tidings he fell senseless, and his anguish brought him to the brink of the grave; he was ill for a long time, but at last reason prevailed over his affliction, and the very atrocity of his treatment furnished him with a source of consolation.

"Since I have experienced," said he, "such cruel caprice from a maiden brought up at the court, I must marry one of the townspeople."

He chose Azora, who came of the best stock and was the best behaved girl in the city. He married her, and lived with her for a month in all the bliss of a most tender union. The only fault he remarked in her was a little giddiness, and a strong tendency to find out that the handsomest young men had always the most intelligence and virtue.

CHAPTER II

THE NOSE

ONE day Azora returned from a walk in a state of vehement indignation and uttering loud exclamations.

"What is the matter with you, my dear wife?" said Zadig; "who can have put you so much out of temper?"

"Alas!" she replied, "you would be as indignant as I, if you had seen the sight which I have just witnessed. I went to console the young widow Cosrou, who two days ago raised a tomb to her young husband beside the stream which forms the boundary of this meadow. She vowed to Heaven, in her grief, that she would dwell beside that tomb as long as the stream flowed by it."

"Well!" said Zadig, "a truly estimable woman, who really loved her husband!"

"Ah!" returned Azora, "if you only knew how she was occupied when I paid her my visit!"

"How then, fair Azora?"

"She was diverting the course of the brook."

Azora gave vent to her feelings in such lengthy invectives, and burst into such violent reproaches against the young widow, that this ostentatious display of virtue was not altogether pleasing to Zadig.

He had a friend named Cador, who was one of those young men in whom his wife found more merit and integrity than in others; Zadig took him into his confidence, and secured his fidelity, as far as possible, by means of a considerable present.

Azora, having passed a couple of days with one of her lady friends in the country, on the third day returned

home. The servants, with tears in their eyes, told her
that her husband had died quite suddenly the night before, that they had not dared to convey to her such sad
news, and that they had just buried Zadig in the tomb of
his ancestors at the end of the garden. She wept, and
tore her hair, and vowed that she would die. In the evening Cador asked if she would allow him to speak to her,
and they wept in company. Next day they wept less,
and dined together. Cador informed her that his friend
had left him the best part of his property, and gave her
to understand that he would deem it the greatest happiness to share his fortune with her. The lady shed tears,
was offended, allowed herself to be soothed; the supper
lasted longer than the dinner, and they conversed together more confidentially. Azora spoke in praise of the
deceased, but admitted that he had faults from which
Cador was free.

In the middle of supper, Cador complained of a violent pain in the spleen. The lady, anxious and attentive,
caused all the essences on her toilet table to be brought,
to try if there might not be some one among them good
for affections of the spleen. She was very sorry that the
famous Hermes was no longer in Babylon. She even condescended to touch the side where Cador felt such sharp
pains.

"Are you subject to this cruel malady?" she asked in
a tone of compassion.

"It sometimes brings me to the brink of the grave,"
answered Cador, "and there is only one remedy which
can relieve me: it is to apply to my side the nose of a
man who has been only a day or two dead."

"What a strange remedy!" said Azora.

"Not more strange," was his reply, "than the scent-
bags of Mr. Arnoult being an antidote to apoplexy." [1]

That reason, joined to the distinguished merit of the young man, at last decided the lady.

"After all," said she, "when my husband shall pass from the world of yesterday into the world of tomorrow over the bridge Chinavar, the angel Azrael will not grant him a passage any the less because his nose will be a little shorter in the second life than in the first."

She then took a razor, and went to her husband's tomb; after she had watered it with her tears, she approached to cut off Zadig's nose, whom she found stretched at full length in the tomb, when he suddenly got up, and, holding his nose with one hand, stopped the razor with the other.

"Madam," said he, "do not cry out so loudly another time against young Cosrou; your intention of cutting off my nose is as bad as that of turning aside a stream."

CHAPTER III

THE DOG AND THE HORSE

ZADIG found by experience that the first month of marriage is, as it is written in the book of the Zendavesta, the moon of honey, and that the second is the moon of wormwood. He was some time afterwards obliged to put away Azora, who became too unmanageable to live with, and he sought for happiness in the study of nature.

"There is no delight," he said, "equal to that of a philosopher, who reads in this great book which God has set before our eyes. The truths which he discovers are his own: he nurtures and educates his soul, he lives in peace, he fears no man, and no tender spouse comes to cut off his nose."

Full of these ideas, he retired to a country house on the banks of the Euphrates. There he did not spend his time in calculating how many inches of water flowed in a second under the arches of a bridge, or whether a cubic line of rain fell in the month of the mouse more than in the month of the sheep. He did not contrive how to make silk out of cobwebs, nor porcelain out of broken bottles, but he studied most of all the properties of animals and plants, and soon acquired a sagacity that showed him a thousand differences where other men see nothing but uniformity.

One day, when he was walking near a little wood, he saw one of the queen's eunuchs running to meet him, followed by several officers, who appeared to be in the greatest uneasiness, and who were running hither and thither like men bewildered and searching for some most precious object which they had lost.

"Young man," said the chief eunuch to Zadig, "have you seen the queen's dog?"

Zadig modestly replied: "It is a bitch, not a dog."

"You are right," said the eunuch.

"It is a very small spaniel," added Zadig; "it is not long since she has had a litter of puppies; she is lame in the left forefoot, and her ears are very long."

"You have seen her, then?" said the chief eunuch, quite out of breath.

"No," answered Zadig, "I have never seen her, and never knew that the queen had a bitch."

Just at this very time, by one of those curious coincidences which are not uncommon, the finest horse in the king's stables had broken away from the hands of a groom in the plains of Babylon. The grand huntsman and all the other officers ran after him with as much anxiety as the chief of the eunuchs had displayed in his search after the queen's bitch. The grand huntsman accosted Zadig, and asked him if he had seen the king's horse pass that way.

"It is the horse," said Zadig, "which gallops best; he is five feet high, and has small hoofs; his tail is three and a half feet long; the bosses on his bit are of gold twenty-three carats fine; his shoes are silver of eleven penny-weights."

"Which road did he take? Where is he?" asked the grand huntsman.

"I have not seen him," answered Zadig, "and I have never even heard anyone speak of him."

The grand huntsman and the chief eunuch had no doubt that Zadig had stolen the king's horse and the queen's bitch, so they caused him to be brought before the Assembly of the Grand Desterham, which condemned him to the knout, and to pass the rest of his life in Siberia. Scarcely had the sentence been pronounced, when the horse and the bitch were found. The judges were now under the disagreeable necessity of amending their judgment; but they condemned Zadig to pay four hundred ounces of gold for having said that he had not seen what he had seen. He was forced to pay this fine first, and afterwards he was allowed to plead his cause before the Council of the Grand Desterham, when he expressed himself in the following terms:

"Stars of justice, fathomless gulfs of wisdom, mirrors of truth, ye who have the gravity of lead, the strength of iron, the brilliance of the diamond, and a close affinity with gold, inasmuch as it is permitted me to speak before this august assembly, I swear to you by Ormuzd that I have never seen the queen's respected bitch, nor the sacred horse of the king of kings. Hear all that happened: I was walking towards the little wood where later on I met the venerable eunuch and the most illustrious grand huntsman. I saw on the sand the footprints of an animal, and easily decided that they were those of a little dog. Long and faintly marked furrows, imprinted where the sand was slightly raised between the footprints, told me that it was a bitch whose dugs were drooping and that consequently she must have given birth to young ones only a few days before. Other marks of a different character, showing that the surface of the sand had been constantly grazed on either side of the front paws, informed me that she had very long ears; and, as I observed that the sand was always less deeply indented by one paw than by the other three, I gathered that the bitch belonging to our august queen was a little lame, if I may venture to say so.

"With respect to the horse of the king of kings, you must know that as I was walking along the roads in that same wood, I perceived the marks of a horse's shoes, all at equal distances. 'There,' I said to myself, 'went a horse with a faultless gallop.' The dust upon the trees, where the width of the road was not more than seven feet, was here and there rubbed off on both sides, three feet and a half away from the middle of the road. 'This horse,' said I, 'has a tail three feet and a half long, which, by its movements to right and left, has whisked away the dust.' I saw, where the trees formed a canopy five feet above the ground, leaves lately fallen from the boughs; and I concluded that the horse had touched them, and was therefore five feet high. As to his bit, it must be of gold twenty-three carats fine, for he had rubbed its bosses against a touchstone, the properties of which I had ascertained. Lastly, I inferred from the marks that his shoes left upon stones of another kind, that he was shod with silver of eleven pennyweights in quality."

All the judges marveled at Zadig's deep and subtle discernment, and a report of it even reached the king and queen. Nothing but Zadig was talked of in the antechambers, the presence chamber, and the private closet; and, though several of the magi were of opinion that he ought to be burned as a wizard, the king ordered that he should be released from the fine of four hundred ounces of gold to which he had been condemned. The registrar, the bailiffs, and the attorneys came to his house with great solemnity to restore him his four hundred ounces; they kept back only three hundred and ninety-eight of them for legal expenses, and their servants too claimed their fees.

Zadig saw how very dangerous it sometimes is to show oneself too knowing, and resolved on the next occasion of the kind to say nothing about what he had seen.

Such an opportunity soon occurred. A state prisoner made his escape, and passed under the windows of Zadig's house, who, on being questioned, answered nothing; but it was proved that he had looked out of the window. For this offense he was condemned to pay five hundred ounces of gold, and he thanked his judges for their leniency, according to the custom of Babylon.

"Good Heavens!" said Zadig to himself, "what a pity it is when one takes a walk in a wood through which the queen's bitch and the king's horse have passed! how dangerous it is to stand at a window! And how difficult it is to be happy in this life!"

CHAPTER IV

THE ENVIOUS MAN

ZADIG sought consolation in philosophy and friendship for the unkindness with which fortune had
treated him. In one of the suburbs of Babylon he had a
house tastefully furnished, where he had gathered all the
arts and pleasures that were worthy of a gentleman. In
the morning his library was open to all men of learning;
in the evening his table was surrounded by good company. But he soon discovered what danger there is in entertaining the learned. A hot dispute arose over a law of
Zoroaster, which prohibited the eating of a griffin.

"How can a griffin be forbidden," said some, "if no
such creature exists?"

"It must exist," said the others, "since Zoroaster for-
bids it to be eaten."

Zadig endeavored to bring them to an agreement by
saying:

"If there are griffins, let us refrain from eating them;
and if there are none, there will be all the less danger of
our doing so. Thus, in either case alike, Zoroaster will be
obeyed."

A learned scholar who had composed thirteen volumes
on the properties of the griffin, and who was moreover a
great magician, lost no time in bringing an accusation
against Zadig before an archimagian named Yebor,[2] the
most foolish of the Chaldeans, and consequently the
most fanatical. This man would fain have impaled Zadig
for the greater glory of the Sun, and would have recited
the breviary of Zoroaster in a more complacent tone of
voice for having done it; but Zadig's friend Cador (one

friend is worth more than a hundred priests) sought out old Yebor, and addressed him thus:

"Long live the Sun and the griffins! Take good heed that you do no harm to Zadig; he is a saint; he keeps griffins in his back yard, and abstains from eating them; and his accuser is a heretic who dares to maintain that rabbits have cloven feet and are not unclean."

"In that case," said Yebor, shaking his bald head, "Zadig must be impaled for having thought wrongly about griffins, and the other for having spoken wrongly about rabbits."

Cador settled the matter by means of a maid of honor, who had borne Yebor a child, and who was held in high esteem in the college of the magi. No one was impaled, though a good many of the doctors murmured thereat, and prophesied the downfall of Babylon in consequence.

Zadig exclaimed: "On what does happiness depend! Everybody in this world persecutes me, even beings that do not exist."

He cursed all men of learning, and determined to live henceforth only in the best society. He invited to his house the most distinguished men and the most charming women in Babylon; he gave elegant suppers, often preceded by concerts, and enlivened by interesting conversation, from which he knew how to banish that straining after a display of wit which is the surest way to have none and to mar the most brilliant company. Neither the choice of his friends, nor that of his dishes, was prompted by vanity; for in everything he preferred being to seeming, and thereby he attracted to himself the real respect to which he made no claim.

Opposite Zadig's house lived Arimaze, a person whose depraved soul was painted on his coarse countenance.[3] He was consumed with malice, and puffed up with pride, and, to crown all, he set up for being a wit and was only a bore. Having never been able to succeed in the world, he took his revenge by railing at it. In spite of his riches, he had some trouble in getting flatterers to flock to his house. The noise of the carriages entering Zadig's gates of an evening annoyed him, and the sound of his praises irritated him yet more. He sometimes went to Zadig's parties and sat down at his table without being invited, where he spoiled all the enjoyment of the company, just as the harpies are said to infect whatever food they touch. One day a lady whom he was anxious to entertain, instead of accepting his invitation, went to sup with Zadig. Another day, when he was talking with Zadig in the palace, they came across a minister who asked Zadig to supper without asking Arimaze. The most inveterate hatreds are often founded on causes quite as trivial. This person, who went by the name of "the Envious man" in Babylon, wished to ruin Zadig because people called him "the Happy man." Opportunities for doing harm are found a hundred times a day, and an opportunity for doing good occurs once a year, as Zoroaster has observed.

On one occasion the Envious man went to Zadig's house and found him walking in his garden with two friends and a lady, to whom he was addressing frequent compliments, without any intention other than that of making himself agreeable. The conversation turned upon a war, which the king had just brought to a prosperous termination, against the prince of Hyrcania, his vassal. Zadig, who had displayed his valor during the short campaign, had much to say in praise of the king, and still more in praise of the lady. He took out his notebook, and wrote down four lines, which he made on the spur of the moment, and which he gave to his fair companion to read. His friends entreated him to be allowed a sight of them; but his modesty, or rather a natural regard for his reputation, made him refuse. He knew that such impromptu verses are never of any value except in the eyes of her in whose honor they have been composed, so he tore in two the leaf on which he had just written them, and threw the pieces into a thicket of roses, where his friends looked for them in vain. A shower came on, and they betook themselves indoors. The Envious man, who remained in the garden, searched so diligently that he found one fragment of the leaf, which had been torn in such a way that the halves of each line that was left made sense, and even a rhymed verse, in shorter meter than the original. But by an accident still more strange, these short lines were found to contain the most opprobrious libel against the king. They read thus:

"By heinous crimes
Set on the throne,
In peaceful times
One foe alone."

The Envious man was happy for the first time in his life, for he had in his hands the means of destroying a virtuous and amiable man. Full of such cruel joy, he caused this lampoon written by Zadig's own hand to be brought to the king's notice, who ordered Zadig to be sent to prison, together with his two friends and the lady. His trial was soon over, nor did his judges deign to hear what he had to say for himself. When he was brought up to receive sentence, the Envious man crossed his path, and told him in a loud voice that his verses were good for nothing. Zadig did not pride himself on being a fine poet, but he was in despair at being condemned as guilty of high treason, and at seeing so fair a lady and his two friends kept in prison for a crime that he had never committed. He was not allowed to speak, because his notebook spoke for him. Such was the law of Babylon. He was then forced to go to his execution through a crowd of inquisitive spectators, not one of whom dared to commiserate him, but who rushed forward in order to scrutinize his countenance, and to see whether he was likely to die with a good grace. His relations alone were distressed; for they were not to be his heirs. Three quarters of his estate were confiscated for the king's benefit, and the Envious man profited by the other quarter.

Just as he was preparing for death, the king's parrot escaped from its perch, and alighted in Zadig's garden, on a thicket of roses. A peach had been carried thither by the wind from a tree hard by, and it had fallen on a piece of writing paper, to which it had stuck. The bird took up both the peach and the paper, and laid them on the monarch's knees. The king, whose curiosity was excited, read some words which made no sense, and which appeared to be the ends of four lines of verse. He loved poetry, and princes who love the muses never find time hangs heavy on their hands. His parrot's adventure set him thinking. The queen, who remembered what had been written on the fragment of the leaf from Zadig's notebook, had it brought to her.

Both pieces were put side by side, and were found to fit together exactly. The verses then read as Zadig had made them:

> "By heinous crimes I saw the earth alarm'd,
> Set on the throne one king all evil curbs;
> In peaceful times now only Love is arm'd,
> One foe alone the timid heart disturbs."

The king immediately commanded that Zadig should be brought before him, and that his two friends and the fair lady should be let out of prison. Zadig prostrated himself with his face to the ground at their majesties' feet, asked their pardon most humbly for having made such poor rhymes, and spoke with so much grace, wit, and good sense, that the king and queen desired to see him again. He came again accordingly, and won still greater favor. All the property of the Envious man who had accused him unjustly was given to Zadig, but he restored it all, and the Envious man was touched, but only with the joy of not losing his wealth after all. The king's esteem for Zadig increased every day. He made him share all his pleasures, and consulted him in all matters of business. The queen regarded him from that time with a tender complacency that might become dangerous to herself, to her royal consort, to Zadig, and to the whole State. Zadig began to think that it is not so difficult after all to be happy.

CHAPTER V

THE PRIZE OF GENEROSITY

THE time had now arrived for celebrating a high festival, which recurred every five years. It was the custom at Babylon, at the end of such a period, to announce in a public and solemn manner the name of that citizen who had done the most generous act during the interval. The grandees and the magi were the arbitrators. The chief satrap, who had the city under his charge, made known the most noble deeds that had been performed under his government. The election was made by vote, and the king pronounced judgment. People came to this festival from the farthest corners of the earth, and the successful candidate received from the monarch's hands a cup of gold decorated with precious stones, the king addressing him in these terms:

"Receive this reward of generosity, and may the gods grant me many subjects who resemble you."

The memorable day then was come, and the king appeared upon his throne, surrounded by grandees, magi, and deputies, sent by all nations to these games, where glory was to be gained, not by the swiftness of horses nor by strength of body, but by virtue. The chief satrap proclaimed with a loud voice the actions that might entitle their authors to this inestimable prize. He said nothing about the magnanimity with which Zadig had restored all his fortune to the Envious man; that was not considered an action worthy of disputing the prize.

First, he presented a judge who, after having given judgment against a citizen in an important lawsuit, under a mistake for which he was in no way responsible, had given him all his own property, which was equal in value to what the other had lost.

He next brought forward a young man, who, being over head and ears in love with a damsel to whom he was engaged to be married, had resigned her to a friend who was nearly dying for love of her, and had moreover resigned the dowry as well as the damsel.

Then he introduced a soldier, who in the Hyrcanian war had given a still nobler example of generosity. Some of the enemy's troops were laying hands on his mistress, and he was defending her from them, when he was told that another party of Hyrcanians, a few paces off, were carrying away his mother. With tears he left his mistress, and ran to rescue his mother; and when he returned to

the object of his love, he found her dying. He was on
the point of slaying himself, but when his mother pointed
out that she had no one but him to whom she could look
for succor, he was courageous enough to endure to live
on.

The arbitrators were inclined to give the prize to this
soldier; but the king interposed, and said:

"This man's conduct and that of the others is praise-
worthy, but it does not astonish me; whereas yesterday
Zadig did a thing that made me marvel. Some days before, my minister and favorite, Coreb, had incurred my
displeasure and been disgraced. I uttered violent complaints against him, and all my courtiers assured me that
I was not half severe enough; each vied with his neighbor in saying as much evil as he could of Coreb. I asked
Zadig what he thought of him, and he dared to say a
word in his favor. I am free to confess that I have heard
of instances in our history of men atoning for a mistake
by the sacrifice of their goods, giving up a mistress, or
preferring a mother to a sweetheart, but I have never
read of a courtier speaking a good word for a minister
in disgrace, against whom his sovereign was bitterly in-
censed. I award twenty thousand pieces of gold to each
of those whose generous acts have been recounted; but
I award the cup to Zadig."

"Sire," said Zadig, "it is Your Majesty alone who deserves the cup for having done a deed of unprecedented
magnanimity, in that, being a king, you were not angry
with your slave when he ran counter to your passion."

The king and Zadig were regarded with equal admiration. The judge who had given away his fortune, the
lover who allowed his friend to marry his mistress, and
the soldier who had preferred his mother's safety to that
of his sweetheart, received at the monarch's hands the

presents he had assigned, and saw their names written in the Book of the Generous, but Zadig had the cup. The king gained the reputation of a good prince, which he did not keep long. The day was celebrated with feasts that lasted longer than the law directed, and its memory is still preserved in Asia. Zadig said:

"At last, then, I am happy." But he was deceived.

CHAPTER VI

THE MINISTER

THE king had lost his prime minister, and chose Zadig to fill his place. All the fair ladies in Babylon applauded the choice; for since the foundation of the empire there had never been known such a young minister. All the courtiers were offended; and the Envious man spat blood on hearing the news, while his nose swelled to an enormous size. Zadig, having thanked the king and queen, proceeded to thank the parrot also.

"Beautiful bird," he said, "it is you who have saved my life, and made me prime minister: the bitch and the horse belonging to Their Majesties did me much harm, but you have done me good. On what slight threads do human destinies depend! But," added he, "a happiness so strangely acquired will, perhaps, soon pass by."

"Ay," replied the parrot.

Zadig was startled at the response; but, being a good naturalist, and not believing that parrots were prophets, he soon recovered himself.

Applying all his energies to the duties of his office, he made everybody feel the sacred power of the laws, but made no one feel the weight of his dignity. He did not interfere with the free expression of opinion in the divan, and each vizier was welcome to hold his own without displeasing him. When he acted as judge in any matter, it was not he who pronounced sentence, it was the law. But when the law was too harsh, he tempered its severity, and when there were no laws to meet the case, his sense of equity supplied him with decisions that might have been taken for those of Zoroaster.

It is from Zadig that the nations of the world have received the grand maxim: "It is better that a guilty man should be acquitted than that an innocent one should be condemned." He held that laws were made as much for the sake of helping as of intimidating the people. His chief skill lay in revealing the truth which all men try to darken. From the very beginning of his administration he put this great talent to good use. A famous merchant of Babylon had died in India and made his two sons heirs to equal portions of his estate, after having given their sister in marriage; and he left a present of thirty thousand gold pieces to that one of his two sons who should be judged to have shown the greater love towards him. The elder built him a tomb, the second increased his sister's dowry with a part of his own inheritance. Everybody said: "It is the elder son who has the greater love for his father, the younger loves his sister better; the thirty thousand pieces belong to the elder."

Zadig sent for the two brothers, one after the other. He said to the elder:

"Your father is not dead; he has been cured of his last illness, and is returning to Babylon."

"God be praised!" answered the young man, "but his tomb has cost me a large sum of money."

Zadig then said the same thing to the younger brother.

"God be praised!" answered he; "I will restore to my

father all that I have, but I hope that he will leave my sister what I have given her."

"You shall restore nothing," said Zadig, "and you shall have the thirty thousand pieces; it is you who love your father best."

A very rich young lady had promised her hand to two magi, and, after having received a course of instruction for some months from each of them, found herself likely to become a mother. Both still wishing to marry her, she said she would take for her husband the one who had put her in a position to present the empire with a citizen.

"It is I who have done that good work," said one of them.

"It is I who have had that privilege," said the other.

"Well," answered she, "I will recognize that one as the father of the child who can give him the best education."

She was brought to bed of a son. Each of the two magi wished to bring it up, and the case was referred to Zadig, who summoned the magi to his presence.

"What will you teach your pupil?" he asked of the first.

"I will instruct him," said the learned professor, "in the eight parts of speech, in logic, astrology, demonology, the difference between substance and accident, abstract and concrete, the doctrine of the monads and the pre-established harmony." [4]

"For my part," said the other, "I will endeavor to render him just and worthy of having friends."

Zadig exclaimed: "Whether you are his father or not, you shall marry his mother."

Day after day complaints reached court of the governor of Media, whose name was Irax. He was a high and mighty personage, not a bad fellow at bottom, but

spoiled by vanity and self-indulgence. He seldom suffered anyone to speak to him, and never to contradict
him. Peacocks are not more conceited than he was, nor
doves more voluptuous, nor turtles more indolent; every
breath he drew was devoted to vainglory and false pleasures. Zadig undertook to reform him.

He sent him, in the king's name, a skilful musician
with a dozen singers and two dozen fiddlers, also a
butler with half a dozen cooks and four chamberlains,
who were never to leave him alone. By the king's orders
the following ceremonies were strictly observed, and this
is how matters were carried on.

The first day, as soon as the pleasure-loving Irax was
awake, the musical conductor entered his chamber followed by the singers and fiddlers: a cantata was sung
which lasted two hours, and every three minutes there
was this refrain:

> "Whose merits e'er attain'd such height?
>   Who with such grace was e'er endow'd?
> Has not his Highness every right
>   To feel self-satisfied and proud?"

After this cantata was performed, one of the chamberlains made him a speech, three quarters of an hour
long, in which he praised him expressly for all those
good qualities in which he was most deficient. The ora-
tion finished, he was escorted to the table to the sound
of musical instruments. The dinner lasted three hours;
whenever he opened his mouth to speak, the first chamberlain said: "Whatever he says will be right." Scarcely
had he spoken four words, when the second chamberlain
would exclaim: "He is right." The two other chamberlains burst into fits of laughter at all the witticisms
which Irax uttered, or which they attributed to him.

After dinner he was favored with a repetition of the cantata.

This first day seemed to him delightful; he thought that the king of kings was honoring him according to his deserts. The second appeared a little less agreeable, the third palled upon him considerably, the fourth was intolerable, and the fifth absolute torture. At last, rather than hear the continual refrain:

> "Has not his Highness every right
> To feel self-satisfied and proud?"

rather than hear the perpetual assurance that whatever he said was right, rather than be harangued every day at the same hour, he wrote to the court entreating the king to be good enough to recall his chamberlains, his musicians, and his butler; and he promised to be less vain and more industrious in future. He was henceforth less tolerant of flattery, gave fewer entertainments, and was all the happier; for, as the Sadder [5] has said:

> "Continual pleasure is no pleasure."

CHAPTER VII

SETTLING DISPUTES AND GIVING AUDIENCE

THUS it was that Zadig daily showed the shrewdness of his intellect and the goodness of his heart. He was admired, yet he was also loved. He passed for the most fortunate of men; all the empire resounded with his name, all the women ogled him, and all the citizens extolled his justice, the men of science regarded him as their oracle, and even the priests confessed that he knew more than the old archimagian Yebor. Far from wishing to prosecute him for his opinions on the subject of griffins, they believed only what seemed credible to him.

Now there was a great controversy in Babylon which had lasted fifteen hundred years and had divided the empire into two bigoted sects: one maintained that the temple of Mithras should never be entered except with the left foot foremost; the other held this practice in abomination, and always entered with the right foot first. The rival sects waited impatiently for the day on which the solemn feast of the holy fire was to be held, to know which side would be favored by Zadig. All had their eyes fixed on his two feet, and the whole city was in agitation and suspense. Zadig leaped into the temple with both his feet together, and afterwards proved in an eloquent discourse that the God of heaven and earth, who is no respecter of persons, cares no more for the left leg than for the right. The Envious man and his wife contended that there were not enough figures of speech in his discourse, that he had not made the mountains and hills skip about freely enough.

"He is dry and wants imagination," they said; "one does not see the ocean fly before him, nor the stars fall, nor the sun melt like wax; he lacks the fine oriental style."

Zadig was content with having the style of a reasonable man. He was a favorite with all classes, not because he was in the right road, nor because he was reasonable, nor even because he was amiable, but because he was grand vizier.

He also happily put an end to the hot dispute between the white and the black magi. The white asserted that it was impious, when praying to God, to turn towards the east in winter; the black were confident that God abhorred the prayers of those who turned towards the west in summer. Zadig directed that men should turn to whatever quarter of the compass they pleased.

He likewise found out the secret of dispatching all his business, both public and private, in the morning, and he employed the rest of the day in providing Babylon with refined entertainments. He caused tragedies to be presented which moved the audience to tears, and comedies that made them laugh; a custom which had long passed out of fashion, and which he had the good taste to revive. He did not pretend to know more about their art than the actors themselves; he rewarded them with gifts and distinctions, and was not secretly jealous of their talents. In the evenings he diverted the king much, and the queen still more.

"A great minister!" said the king.

"A charming minister!" said the queen.

Both of them agreed that it would have been a thousand pities if Zadig had been hanged.

Never was statesman in office obliged to give so many audiences to the ladies. The greater number came to speak to him about no business in particular for the sake of having particular business with him. The wife of the Envious man presented herself among the first; she swore by Mithras and the Zendavesta and the holy fire that she detested the conduct of her husband; then she told him in confidence that this husband of hers was jealous and treated her brutally, and gave him to understand that the gods punished him by refusing him the precious effects of that holy fire whereby alone man is made like the immortals. She ended by dropping her garter. Zadig picked it up with his customary politeness, but did not offer to fasten it again round the lady's knee, and this little fault, if it can be considered such, was the cause of the most dreadful misfortunes. Zadig thought no more about the incident, but the Envious man's wife thought about it a great deal.

Other ladies continued to present themselves every day. The secret annals of Babylon assert that he yielded to temptation on only one occasion, but that he was astonished to find that he enjoyed his mistress without pleasure, and that his mind was distracted even in the midst of the tenderest embraces. The fair one to whom he gave, almost unconsciously, these tokens of his favor was a lady in waiting to Queen Astarte. This amorous daughter of Babylon consoled herself for his coldness by saying to herself:

"That man must have a prodigious amount of business in his head, since his thoughts are absorbed with it even when he is making love."

Zadig happened at a moment when many people say nothing and others only utter terms of endearment, to suddenly exclaim: "The queen!" The fair Babylonian fancied that he had at last recovered his wits at a happy moment, and that he was addressing her as his queen. But Zadig, still absent-minded, proceeded to utter the name of Astarte. The lady, who in this agreeable situation interpreted everything in a flattering sense, imagined that he meant to say: "You are more beautiful than Queen Astarte." She left the seraglio of Zadig with magnificent presents, and went to relate her adventure to the Envious woman, who was her intimate friend. The latter was cruelly piqued at the preference shown to the other.

"He did not even condescend," said she, "to replace this garter which I have here, and which I will never use again."

"Oh!" said her more fortunate friend, "you wear the

same garters as the queen! Do you get them from the same maker?"

The Envious woman fell into a brown study, and made no reply, but went and consulted her husband, the Envious man.

Meanwhile Zadig became aware of his constant absence of mind whenever he gave an audience or administered justice; he did not know to what to attribute it; it was his only subject of annoyance.

He had a dream, in which he seemed to be lying at first on a heap of dry herbs, among which were some prickly ones which made him uncomfortable, and that afterwards he reposed luxuriously upon a bed of roses, out of which glided a snake that wounded him in the heart with its pointed and poisoned tongue.[6]

"Alas!" said he, "I lay a long time on those dry and prickly herbs; I am now on the bed of roses; but who will be the serpent?"

CHAPTER VIII

JEALOUSY

ZADIG'S ill luck arose out of his very happiness, and was mainly due to his merits. He had daily interviews with the king and with Astarte, his august consort. The charm of his conversation was doubled by that desire to please which is to the mind what ornaments are to personal beauty; his youth and graceful manners insensibly made an impression upon Astarte, of the strength of which she was not at first aware. Her passion grew up in the bosom of innocence. Astarte gave herself up without scruple and without fear to the pleasure of seeing

and hearing a man who was so dear to her husband and
to the State; she never ceased singing his praises to the
king; she was perpetually speaking about him to her
women, who even went beyond her in their commenda-
tions; everything served to fix more deeply in her heart
the arrow of which she was unconscious. She bestowed
presents upon Zadig, into which more love making entered than she supposed; she meant to speak to him as a
queen satisfied with his services, but the expressions she
used were sometimes those of a women of tender sensibility.

Astarte was much more beautiful than that Semira
who had such a detestation of one-eyed men, or that other woman who had intended to cut off her husband's nose.
Astarte's familiar manner, her soft speeches at which she
began to blush, her eyes which, despite her efforts to
turn them away, were ever fixed upon his own, kindled
in Zadig's heart a fire which filled him with astonishment. He fought against his feelings; he called to his
aid the philosophy which had never before failed him; he
drew from it nothing but a clearer perception of his
folly, and received no relief. Duty, gratitude, and out-
raged majesty presented themselves to his view as so
many avenging deities; he struggled, and he triumphed;
but this victory, which had to be repeated every moment, cost him groans and tears. He no longer dared to
address the queen with that delightful freedom which
had had such charms for both of them; a cloud over-
shadowed his eyes; his conversation was constrained and
abrupt; his eyes were downcast, and when, in spite of
himself, they turned towards Astarte, they encountered
those of the queen moistened with tears from which
there shot forth arrows of flame. They seemed to say to
each other:

"Our adoration is mutual, yet we are afraid to love; we are both consumed with a fire which we condemn."

When Zadig left her side it was with bewilderment and despair, his heart oppressed with a burden which he was no longer able to support: in the violence of his agitation he let his friend Cador penetrate his secret, like a man who, after having endured the most excruciating pains, at last makes his malady known by a cry which a keener spasm than any before wrings from him, and by the cold sweat which pours over his forehead.

Cador addressed him as follows:

"I have already divined the feelings that you would fain hide from yourself; the passions have symptoms which cannot be misinterpreted. Judge, my dear Zadig, since I have been able to read your heart, whether the king is not likely to discover there a sentiment that may give him serious offense. He has no other fault but that of being the most jealous of men. You resist your passion with more vigor than the queen can contend against hers, because you are a philosopher, and because you are Zadig. Astarte is a woman; she lets her looks speak for her with all the more imprudence that she does not yet believe herself blameworthy. Assured of her innocence, she unfortunately neglects appearances which it is necessary to observe. I shall tremble for her so long as she has nothing wherewith to reproach herself. If you came to a common understanding, you would be able to throw dust into all eyes; a growing passion, forcibly checked, gives evident tokens of its existence; but love when gratified can easily conceal itself."

Zadig shuddered at the suggestion of betraying the king, his benefactor; and he was never more faithful to his prince than when guilty of an involuntary crime against him. Meanwhile the queen pronounced the name of Zadig so often, she blushed so deeply as she uttered it, she was sometimes so animated, and at other times so confused when she addressed him in the king's presence, and she was seized with so profound a fit of abstraction whenever he went away, that the king began to be alarmed. He believed all that he saw, and imagined all that he did not see. He particularly remarked that his wife's slippers were blue, and that Zadig's slippers were blue; that his wife's ribbons were yellow, and that Zadig's cap was yellow. Terrible indications, these, to a prince of such delicate sensibility! Suspicion soon became certainty in his envenomed mind.

All the slaves of kings and queens are so many spies over their hearts. It was soon discovered that Astarte was tender and that Moabdar was jealous. The Envious man got his wife to send the king her garter, which was like the queen's; and, to make the matter worse, this garter was blue. The monarch thought of nothing now but how to take his revenge. One night he determined to poison the queen, and to have Zadig strangled as soon as it was light. The order was given to a merciless eunuch, the usual executioner of his vengeance. Now there happened to be in the king's chamber at this time a little dwarf, who was dumb but not deaf. He was allowed to wander about when and where he pleased, and, like a domestic animal, was oftentimes a witness of what passed in the strictest privacy. This little mute was much attached to the queen and Zadig, and he heard with no less surprise than horror the order given for their death. But what could he do to prevent this frightful order, which was to be carried out within a few hours? He did not know how to write, but he had learned how to paint, and was particularly skilful in making likenesses. He spent part of the night in portraying what he wished the queen to understand. His sketch represented in one corner of the picture the king in a furious rage, giving orders to ..is eunuch; a blue bowstring and a cup on a table, with garters and yellow ribbons; the queen in the middle of the picture, expiring in the arms of her women, and Zadig lying strangled at her feet. A rising sun was represented on the horizon to indicate that this horrible execution was to take place at the earliest glimpse of dawn. As soon as this task was finished he ran to one of Astarte's women, awoke her, and made her understand that she must take the picture that very instant to the queen.

In the middle of the night someone knocked at Zadig's door; he was roused from sleep, and a note from the queen was given him; he doubted whether or not it were a dream, and opened the letter with a trembling hand. What was his surprise, and who could express the consternation and despair with which he was overwhelmed, when he read these words: "Fly, this very moment, or you will be seized and put to death! Fly, Zadig; I command you in the name of our love and of my yellow ribbons. I have done nothing wrong, but I foresee that I am going to die like a criminal."

Zadig, who had scarcely strength enough to speak, sent for Cador, and then, without a word, gave him the letter. Cador forced him to obey its injunction, and to set out immediately for Memphis.

"If you venture to go in search of the queen," said he, "you will only hasten her death; if you speak to the king, that step again will lead to her destruction. Her fate shall be my care; do you follow your own. I will spread the report that you have taken the road to India. I will soon come and find you out, when I will tell you all that shall have passed at Babylon."

Cador, without a moment's delay, had two of the swiftest dromedaries brought to a private postern of the palace, and made Zadig mount one of them; he had to be carried, for he was almost ready to expire. Only one servant accompanied him, and soon Cador, plunged in astonishment and grief, lost sight of his friend.

The illustrious fugitive, when he arrived at the brow of a hill which commanded a view of Babylon, turned his gaze towards the queen's palace, and fainted. He recovered his senses only to shed tears and to wish that he was dead. At last, after having occupied his thoughts awhile with the deplorable fate of the most amiable of women and the best of queens, he returned for a moment to himself, and exclaimed:

"What, then, is human life? O virtue! Of what use hast thou been to me? Two women have basely deceived me, and the third, who is innocent and is more beautiful than the others, is about to die! All the good that I have done has always brought upon me a curse, and I have been raised to the height of grandeur only to fall down the most horrible precipice of misfortune. If I had been wicked, like so many others, I should be happy like them."

Overwhelmed with these gloomy reflections, his eyes shrouded with a veil of sorrow, the paleness of death on his countenance, and his soul sunk in the depths of a dark despair, he continued his journey towards Egypt.

CHAPTER IX

THE BEATEN WOMAN

ZADIG directed his course by the stars. The constellation of Orion and the bright star of Sirius guided him towards the harbor of Canopus. He marveled at those vast globes of light, which appear only like feeble sparks to our eyes, while the earth, which is in reality nothing more than an imperceptible point in nature, appears to our covetous eyes something grand and noble. He then pictured to himself men as they really are, insects devouring one another on a little atom of clay. This true image seemed to annihilate his misfortunes, by making him realize the insignificance of his own existence and that of Babylon itself. His soul launched forth into the infinitude of space, detached from the operation of the senses, and contemplated the unchangeable order of the universe. But when, afterwards returning to himself and once more looking into his own heart, he thought how Astarte was perhaps already dead for his sake, the universe vanished from his eyes, and he saw nothing in all nature save Astarte dying and Zadig miserable. As he gave himself up to this alternate flow of sublime philosophy and overwhelming grief, he approached the confines of Egypt; and his faithful servant was already in the first village, looking out for a lodging. Zadig was, meanwhile, walking towards the gardens which skirted the village, and saw, not far from the highroad, a woman in great distress, who was calling out to heaven and earth for succor, and a man who was following her in a furious rage. He had already reached her before Zadig could do so, and the woman was clasping his knees, while the man overwhelmed her with blows and reproaches. He judged from the Egyptian's violence and from the repeated prayers for forgiveness which the lady uttered, that he was jealous and she unfaithful; but after he had closely regarded the woman, who was of enchanting beauty, and who, moreover, bore a little resemblance to the unhappy Astarte, he felt moved with compassion towards her, and with horror towards the Egyptian.

"Help me!" she cried to Zadig in a voice choked with sobs; "deliver me out of the hands of this most barbarous man, and save my life!"

Hearing these cries, Zadig ran and threw himself between her and the barbarian; and having some knowledge of the Egyptian tongue, he addressed him in that language, and said:

"If you have any humanity, I entreat you to respect beauty and weakness. How can you illtreat so cruelly such a masterpiece of nature as lies there at your feet, with no protection but her tears?"

"Ah, ha!" answered the man, more enraged than ever; "then you are another of her lovers! And on you too I must take revenge."

Saying these words, he left the lady, whom he had been holding by the hair with one hand, and, seizing his lance, made an attempt to run the stranger through with it. But he, being cool and composed, easily avoided the thrust of one who was beside himself with rage, and caught hold of the lance near the iron point with which it was armed. The one tried to draw it back, while the other tried to wrench it out of his hand, so that it was broken between the two. The Egyptian drew his sword, Zadig did the same, and they forthwith attacked each other; the former dealing a hundred blows in quick succession, the latter skilfully warding them off. The lady, seated on a piece of turf, readjusted her headdress, and looked calmly on. The Egyptian was stronger than his antagonist, Zadig was the more dexterous. The latter fought like a man whose arm was guided by his head, the former like a madman who in blind frenzy delivered random strokes. Zadig, attacking him in his turn, disarmed his adversary; and while the Egyptian, rendered still more furious, tried to throw himself upon him, the other seized him with a tight grip, and threw him on the ground; then, holding his sword to his breast, he offered to give him his life. The Egyptian, transported with rage, drew his dagger, and therewith wounded Zadig, at the very instant that the conqueror was granting him pardon. Provoked beyond endurance, Zadig plunged his sword into the other's heart. The Egyptian uttered a horrible yell, and died struggling violently. Then Zadig advanced towards the lady, and said in a respectful tone:

"He forced me to kill him; you I have avenged, and delivered out of the hands of the most outrageous man I ever saw. What will you have me do for you now, madam?"

"To die, scoundrel," she replied; "to die! You have killed my lover; I would that I were able to tear out your heart."

"Truly, madam, you had a strange sort of lover in him," returned Zadig; "he was beating you with all his might, and he wanted to have my life because you implored me to help you."

"I wish he was beating me still," answered the lady, giving vent to loud lamentation; "I well deserved it, and gave him good cause for jealousy. Would to heaven that he were beating me and that you were in his place!"

Zadig, more surprised and indignant than he had ever been before in his life, said to her:

"Madam, beautiful as you are, you deserve to have me beat you in my turn for your unreasonable behavior, but I shall not take the trouble."

So saying, he remounted his camel, and advanced towards the village. He had hardly proceeded a few steps when he turned back at the clatter of four messengers riding post haste from Babylon. One of them, seeing the woman, exclaimed:

"That is the very person! She resembles the description that was given us."

They did not encumber themselves with the dead body, but forthwith caught hold of the lady, who never ceased calling out to Zadig:

"Help me once more, generous stranger! I beg your pardon for having reproached you: help me, and I will be yours till death."

Zadig no longer felt any desire to fight on her behalf.

"Apply to someone else," he answered, "you will not entrap me again."

Moreover he was wounded and bleeding; he had need of help himself; and the sight of the four Babylonians, probably sent by King Moabdar, filled him with uneasiness. So he hastened towards the village, unable to imagine why four messengers from Babylon should come to take this Egyptian woman, but still more astonished at the conduct of the lady.

CHAPTER X

SLAVERY

AS he entered the Egyptian village, he found himself surrounded by the people. Everyone was crying out:

"This is the fellow who carried off the lovely Missouf, and who has just murdered Cletofis!"

"Gentlemen," said he, "may Heaven preserve me from carrying off your lovely Missouf! She is too capricious for me; and with regard to Cletofis, I have not murdered him, I only fought against him in self-defense. He wanted to kill me because I had asked him most humbly to pardon the lovely Missouf, whom he was beating unmercifully. I am a stranger come to seek a refuge in Egypt; and it is not likely that, in coming to claim your protection, I should begin by carrying off a woman and murdering a man."

The Egyptians were at that time just and humane. The people conducted Zadig to the court-house. They began by getting his wound dressed, and then they questioned him and his servant separately, in order to learn the truth. They came to the conclusion that Zadig was not a murderer; but he was found guilty of homicide, and the law condemned him to be a slave. His two camels were sold for the benefit of the village; all the gold that he carried was distributed among the inhabitants; his person was exposed for sale in the market-place, as well as that of his fellow-traveler. An Arab merchant, named Setoc, made the highest bid for him; but the serving-man, as more fit for hard work, was sold at a much higher price than the master. There was no comparison, it was thought, between the two men; so Zadig became a slave of inferior position to his own servant. They were fastened together with a chain, which was passed round their ankles, and in that state they followed the Arab merchant to his house. Zadig, on the way, tried to console his servant, and exhorted him to be patient; and, according to his custom, he made some general reflections on human life.

"I see," he said, "that my unhappy fate has spread its shadow over yours. Hitherto at every turn I have met with strange reverses. I have been condemned to pay a fine for having seen traces of a passing bitch; I thought I was going to be impaled on account of a griffin; I have been sent to execution because I made some complimentary verses on the king; I was on the point of being strangled because the queen had yellow ribbons; and here am I a slave along with you, because a brute of a man chose to beat his mistress. Come, let us not lose courage; all this perhaps will come to an end. It must needs be that Arab merchants should have slaves; and why should not I be one as well as another, since I also am a man? This merchant will not be unmerciful; he must treat his slaves well, if he wishes to make good use of them."

Thus he spoke, but in the depths of his heart he was thinking only of the fate of the queen of Babylon.

Setoc the merchant started, two days afterwards, for Arabia Deserta, with his slaves and his camels. His tribe dwelt near the desert of Horeb, the way to which was long and dangerous. Setoc, on the journey, took greater care of the servant than of the master, because the former could load the camels much better, and any little distinction that was made between them was in his favor.

A camel died two days before they expected to reach Horeb, and its load was distributed among the men, so that each back had its burden, Zadig's among the rest. Setoc laughed to see how all his slaves were bent almost double as they walked. Zadig took the liberty of explaining to him the reason, and gave him some instruction in the laws of equilibrium. The astonished merchant began to regard him with other eyes. Zadig, seeing that he had excited his master's curiosity, increased it by teaching him many things that had a direct bearing on his business, such as the specific gravity of metals and commodities in equal bulk, the properties of several useful animals, and the way in which those might be rendered useful which were not naturally so, until Setoc thought him a sage. He now gave Zadig the preference over his comrade, whom he had before esteemed so highly. He treated him well, and had no reason to repent of it.

Having reached his tribe, the first thing Setoc did was to demand repayment of five hundred ounces of silver from a Jew to whom he had lent them in the presence of two witnesses; but these two witnesses were dead, and the Jew, assured that there was no proof of the debt, appropriated the merchant's money and thanked God for having given him the opportunity of cheating an Arab. Setoc confided his trouble to Zadig, who was now his adviser in everything.

"In what place was it," asked Zadig, "that you lent these five hundred ounces to the infidel?"

"On a large stone near Mount Horeb," answered the merchant.

"What kind of man is your debtor?" said Zadig.

"A regular rogue," returned Setoc.

"But I mean, is he hasty or deliberate, cautious or imprudent?"

"Of all bad payers," said Setoc, "he is the hastiest man I ever knew."

"Well," pursued Zadig, "allow me to plead your cause before the judge."

In the end he summoned the Jew to take his trial, and thus addressed the judge:

"Pillar of the throne of equity, I come here to claim from this man, in my master's name, repayment of five hundred ounces of silver which he will not restore."

"Have you witnesses?" asked the judge.

"No, they are dead; but there still remains a large stone upon which the money was counted out; and, if it please your lordship to order someone to go and fetch the stone, I hope that it will bear witness to the truth. We will remain here, the Jew and I, until the stone arrives; I will send for it at my master Setoc's expense."

"I am quite willing that that should be done," answered the judge; and then he proceeded to dispatch other business.

At the end of the sitting he said to Zadig:

"Well, your stone is not arrived yet, is it?"

The Jew laughed, and answered:

"Your lordship would have to remain here till tomorrow before the stone could be brought; it is more than six miles away, and it would take fifteen men to move it."

"Now then," exclaimed Zadig, "did I not say well that the stone itself would bear witness? Since this man knows where it is, he acknowledges that upon it the money was counted." The Jew was abashed, and was soon obliged to confess the whole truth. The judge ordered him to be bound to the stone, without eating or drinking, until the five hundred ounces should be restored, and it was not long before they were paid.

After that, Zadig the slave was held in high esteem throughout Arabia, and so was the stone.

CHAPTER XI

THE FUNERAL PILE

SETOC was so enchanted with his slave that he made him his intimate friend. He could no more dispense with him than the king of Babylon had done; and Zadig was glad that Setoc had no wife. He found in his master an excellent disposition, with much integrity and good sense; but he was sorry to see that he worshiped the host of heaven (that is to say, the sun, moon, and stars), according to the ancient custom of Arabia. He spoke to him sometimes on the subject with judicious caution. At last he told him that they were material bodies like other things, which were no more worthy of his adoration than a tree or a rock.

"But," said Setoc, "they are immortal beings, from whom we derive all the benefits we enjoy; they animate nature, and regulate the seasons; besides, they are so far from us that one cannot help worshiping them."

"You receive more advantages," answered Zadig, "from the waters of the Red Sea, which bear your merchandise to India. Why may it not be as ancient as the stars? And if you adore what is far away from you, you ought to adore the land of the Gangarides, which lies at the very end of the world."

"No," said Setoc; "the stars are so bright that I cannot refrain from worshiping them."

When the evening was come, Zadig lighted a great number of candles in the tent where he was to sup with Setoc; and, as soon as his patron appeared, he threw himself on his knees before those wax lights, saying:

"Eternal and brilliant luminaries, be ever propitious to me!"

Having offered this prayer, he sat down to table without paying any attention to Setoc.

"What is that you are doing?" asked Setoc in astonishment.

"I am doing what you do," answered Zadig; "I adore these candles, and neglect their master and mine."

Setoc understood the profound meaning of this parable. The wisdom of his slave entered into his soul; he no longer lavished his incense upon created things, but worshiped the Eternal Being who had made them.

There prevailed at that time in Arabia a frightful custom, which came originally from Scythia, and which, having established itself in India through the influence of the Brahmins, threatened to invade all the East. When a married man died, and his favorite wife wished to obtain a reputation for scanctity, she used to burn herself in public on her husband's corpse. A solemn festival was held on such occasions, called "The Funeral Pile of Widowhood," and that tribe in which there had been the greatest number of women consumed in this way was held in the highest honor. An Arab of Setoc's tribe having died, his widow, named Almona, who was very devout, made known the day and hour when she would cast herself into the fire to the sound of drums and trumpets. Zadig showed Setoc how contrary to the interests of the human race this horrible custom was, for young widows were every day allowed to burn themselves who might have presented children to the State, or at least have brought up those they already had; and he made him agree that so barbarous an institution ought, if possible, to be abolished.

Setoc replied: "It is more than a thousand years since the women acquired the right of burning themselves. Which of us will dare to change a law which time has consecrated? Is there anything more venerable than an ancient abuse?"

"Reason is more ancient," rejoined Zadig. "Do you speak to the chiefs of the tribes, and I will go and find the young widow."

He obtained admission to her presence; and after having insinuated himself into her good graces by commending her beauty, and after having said what a pity it was to commit such charms to the flames, he praised her again on the score of her constancy and courage.

"You must have loved your husband wonderfully?" said he.

"I? Oh no, not at all," answered the Arab lady. "I could not bear him, he was so brutal and jealous; but I am firmly resolved to throw myself on his funeral pile."

"Apparently," said Zadig, "there must be some very delicious pleasure in being burned alive."

"Ah! It makes nature shudder to think of it," said the lady; "but I must put up with it. I am a pious person, and I should lose my reputation and be mocked by everybody if I did not burn myself."

Zadig, having brought her to admit that she was burning herself for the sake of other people and out of vanity, spoke to her for a long time in a manner calculated to make her a little in love with life, and even managed to inspire her with some kindly feeling towards himself.

"What would you do now," said he, "if you were not moved by vanity to burn yourself?"

"Alas!" said the lady, "I think that I should ask you to marry me."

Zadig was too much engrossed with thoughts of Astarte to take any notice of this declaration, but he instantly went to the chiefs of the different tribes, told them what had passed, and advised them to make a law by which no widow should be allowed to burn herself until after she had had a private interview with a young man for the space of a whole hour. Since that time no lady has burned herself in Arabia. To Zadig alone was the credit due for having abolished in one day so cruel a custom, and one that had lasted so many ages. Thus he became the benefactor of all Arabia.

CHAPTER XII

THE SUPPER

SETOC, who could not part from the man in whom wisdom dwelt, brought him to the great fair of Bassora, whither the wealthiest merchants of the habitable globe were wont to resort. It was no little consolation to Zadig to see so many men of different countries assembled in the same place. It seemed to him that the universe was one large family which gathered together at Bassora. The second day after their arrival Zadig found himself at table with an Egyptian, an Indian from the banks of the Ganges, an inhabitant of China, a Greek, a Celt, and several other foreigners, who, in their frequent voyages to the Persian Gulf, had learned enough Arabic to make themselves understood. The Egyptian appeared exceedingly angry. "What an abominable country Bassora is!" said he; "I cannot get a loan here of a thousand ounces of gold on the best security in the world."

"How is that?" said Setoc; "on what security was that sum refused you?"

"On the body of my aunt," answered the Egyptian; "she was the worthiest woman in Egypt. She always accompanied me on my journeys, and died on the way hither. I have turned her into one of the finest mummies to be had, and in my own country I could get whatever I wanted by giving her in pledge. It is very strange that no one here will lend me even a thousand ounces of gold on such sound security."

In spite of his indignation, he was just on the point of devouring a capital boiled fowl, when the Indian, taking him by the hand, exclaimed in a doleful voice, "Ah! what are you about to do?"

"To eat this fowl," said the man with the mummy.

"Beware of what you are doing," said the man from the Ganges; "it may be that the soul of the departed has passed into the body of that fowl, and you would not wish to run the risk of eating up your aunt. To cook fowls is plainly an outrage upon nature."

"What do you mean with your nonsense about nature and fowls?" returned the wrathful Egyptian. "We worship an ox, and yet eat beef for all that."

"You worship an ox! Is it possible?" said the man from the Ganges.

"There is nothing more certain," replied the other; "we have done so for a hundred and thirty-five thousand years, and no one among us has any fault to find with it."

"Ah! A hundred and thirty-five thousand years!" said

the Indian. "There must be a little exaggeration there; India has only been inhabited eighty thousand years, and we are undoubtedly more ancient than you are; and Brahma had forbidden us to eat oxen before you ever thought of putting them on your altars and on your spits."

"An odd kind of animal, this Brahma of yours, to be compared with Apis!" said the Egyptian. "What fine things now has your Brahma ever done?"

"It was he," the Brahmin answered, "who taught men to read and write, and to whom all the world owes the game of chess."

"You are wrong," said a Chaldean who was sitting near him; "it is to the fish Oannes that we owe such great benefits; and it is right to render our homage to him alone. Anybody will tell you that he was a divine being, that he had a golden tail and a handsome human head, and that he used to leave the water to come to preach on land for three hours every day. He had sundry children who were all kings, as every one knows. I have his likeness at home, to which I pay all due reverence. We may eat as much beef as we please, but there is no doubt that it is a very great sin to cook fish. Moreover, you are, both of you, of too mean and too modern an origin to argue with me about anything. The Egyptian nation counts only one hundred and thirty-five thousand years, and the Indians can boast of no more than eighty thousand, while we have almanacs that go back four thousand centuries. Believe me, renounce your follies, and I will give each of you a beautiful likeness of Oannes."

The Chinaman here put in his word, and said:

"I have a strong respect for the Egyptians, the Chaldeans, the Greeks, the Celts, Brahma, the ox Apis, and the fine fish Oannes, but it may be that Li or Tien,[7] by whichever name one may choose to call him, is well worth any number of oxen and fishes. I will say nothing about my country; it is as large as the lands of Egypt, Chaldea, and India all put together. I will enter into no dispute touching antiquity, because it is enough to be happy, and it is a very little matter to be ancient. But if there were any need to speak about almanacs, I could tell you that all Asia consults ours, and that we had very good ones before anything at all was known of arithmetic in Chaldea."

"You are a set of ignoramuses, all of you!" cried the Greek; "is it possible that you do not know that Chaos is the father of all things, and that form and matter have brought the world into the state in which it is?"

This Greek spoke for a long time, but he was at last interrupted by the Celt, who, having drunk deeply while the others were disputing, now thought himself wiser than any of them, and affirmed with an oath that there was nothing worth the trouble of talking about except Teutates and the mistletoe that grows on an oak; that, as for himself, he always had some mistletoe in his pocket; that the Scythians, his forefathers, were the only honest people that had ever been in the world; that they had indeed sometimes eaten men, but that no one ought to be prevented by that from having a profound respect for his nation; and finally, that if anyone spoke evil of Teutates, he would teach him how to behave.

Thereupon the quarrel waxed hot, and Setoc saw that in another moment there would be bloodshed at the table, when Zadig, who had kept silent during the whole dispute, at last rose. He addressed himself first to the Celt as the most violent of them all; he told him that he was in the right, and asked him for a piece of mistletoe. He commended the Greek for his eloquence, and soothed the general irritation. He said very little to the Chinaman, because he had been the most reasonable of them all. Then he said to the whole party:

"My friends, you were going to quarrel for nothing, for you are all of the same opinion."

When they heard him say that, they all loudly protested.

"Is it not true," he said to the Celt, "that you do not worship this mistletoe, but Him who made the mistletoe and the oak?"

"Assuredly," answered the Celt.

"And you, my Egyptian friend, revere, as it would seem, in a certain ox Him who has given you oxen, is it not so?"

"Yes," said the Egyptian.

"The fish Oannes," continued Zadig, "must give place to Him who made the sea and the fishes."

"Granted," said the Chaldean.

"The Indian," added Zadig, "and the Chinaman recognize, like you, a first principle; I did not understand very well the admirable remarks made by the Greek, but I am sure that he also admits the existence of a Supreme Being, upon whom form and matter depend."

The Greek who was so much admired said that Zadig had seized his meaning very well.

"You are all then of the same opinion," replied Zadig, "and there is nothing left to quarrel over;" at which all the company embraced him.

Setoc, after having sold his merchandise at a high price, brought his friend Zadig back with him to his tribe. On their arrival Zadig learned that he had been tried in his absence, and that he was going to be burned at a slow fire.

CHAPTER XIII

THE ASSIGNATION

DURING his journey to Bassora, the priests of the stars had determined to punish Zadig. The precious stones and ornaments of the young widows whom they sent to the funeral pile were their acknowledged perquisite; it was in truth the least they could do to burn Zadig for the ill turn he had done them. Accordingly they accused him of holding erroneous views about the host of heaven; they gave testimony against him on oath that they had heard him say that the stars did not set in the sea. This frightful blasphemy made the judges shudder; they were ready to rend their garments when they heard those impious words, and they would have done so, without a doubt, if Zadig had had the means wherewith to pay them compensation, but dreadfully shocked as they were, they contented themselves with condemning him to be burned at a slow fire.

Setoc, in despair, exerted his influence in vain to save his friend; he was soon obliged to hold his peace. The young widow Almona, who had acquired a strong appetite for life, thanks to Zadig, resolved to rescue him from the stake, the misuse of which he had taught her to recognize. She turned her scheme over and over in her head, without speaking of it to anyone. Zadig was to be executed the next day, and she had only that night to save him in. This is how she set about the business, like a charitable and discreet woman. She anointed herself with perfumes; she enhanced her charms by the richest and most seductive attire, and went to ask the chief priest of the stars for a private audience. When she was ushered into the presence of that venerable old man, she addressed him in these terms:

"Eldest son of the Great Bear, brother of the Bull, and cousin of the Great Dog" (such were the pontiff's titles), "I come to confide to you my scruples. I greatly fear that I have committed an enormous sin in not burning myself on my dear husband's funeral pyre. In truth, what had I worth preserving? A body liable to decay, and which is already quite withered." Saying these words, she drew up her long silk sleeves, and displayed her bare arms, of admirable form and dazzling whiteness. "You see," said she, "how little it is worth."

The pontiff thought in his heart that it was worth a great deal. His eyes said so, and his mouth confirmed it; he swore that he had never in his life seen such beautiful arms.

"Alas!" said the widow, "my arms may be a little less deformed than the rest; but you will admit that my neck was unworthy of any consideration," and she let him see the most charming bosom that nature had ever formed. A rosebud on an apple of ivory would have appeared beside it nothing better than madder upon box-wood, and lambs just come up from the washing would have seemed brown and sallow. This neck; her large black eyes, in which a tender fire glowed softly with languishing luster; her cheeks, enlivened with the loveliest crimson mingled with the whiteness of the purest milk; her nose, which was not at all like the tower of Mount Lebanon; her lips, which were like two settings of coral enclosing the most beautiful pearls in the Arabian sea; all these charms conspired to make the old man fancy himself a youth of twenty summers. With stammering tongue he made a tender declaration; and Almona, seeing how he was smitten, craved pardon for Zadig.

"Alas!" said he, "my lovely lady, though I might grant you his pardon, my indulgence would be of no use, as the order would have to be signed by three others of my colleagues."

"Sign it all the same," said Almona.

"Willingly," said the priest, "on condition that your favors shall be the price of my compliance."

"You do me too much honor," said Almona; "only be pleased to come to my chamber after sunset; when the bright star *Sheat* shall rise above the horizon; you will find me on a rose-colored sofa, and you shall deal with your servant as you may be able."

Then she went away, carrying with her the signature, and left the old man full of amorous passion and of diffidence as to his powers. He employed the rest of the day in bathing; he drank a liquid compounded of the cinnamon of Ceylon, and the precious spices of Tidor and Ternat, and waited with impatience for the star *Sheat* to appear.

Meanwhile the fair Almona went in search of the second pontiff, who assured her that the sun, the moon, and all the lights of heaven were nothing but faint marsh fires in comparison with her charms. She asked of him the same favor, and he offered to grant it on the same terms. She allowed her scruples to be overcome, and made an appointment with the second pontiff for the rising of the star *Algenib*. Thence she proceeded to the houses of the third and fourth priests, getting from each his signature, and making one star after another the signal for a secret assignation. Then she sent letters to the judges, requesting them to come and see her on a matter of importance. When they appeared, she showed them the four names, and told them at what price the priests had sold Zadig's pardon. Each of the latter arrived at his appointed hour, and was greatly astonished to find his colleagues there, and still more at seeing the judges, before whom they were exposed to open shame. Thus Zadig was saved, and Setoc was so delighted with Almona's cleverness, that he made her his wife.

CHAPTER XIV

THE DANCE

SETOC was engaged to go on matters of business to the island of Serendib,[8] but the first month of marriage, which is, as every one knows, the moon of honey, permitted him neither to quit his wife, nor even to imagine that he could ever quit her; so he requested his friend Zadig to make the voyage on his behalf.

"Alas!" said Zadig, "must I put a yet wider distance between the beautiful Astarte and myself? But I must oblige my benefactors." He spoke, he wept, and he set forth on his journey.

He was not long in the island of Serendib before he began to be regarded as an extraordinary man. He became umpire in all disputes between the merchants, the friend of the wise, and the trusted counselor of that small number of persons who are willing to take advice. The king wished to see and hear him. He soon recognized all Zadig's worth, placed reliance on his wisdom, and made him his friend. The king's intimacy and esteem made Zadig tremble. Night and day he was pierced with anguish at the misfortune which Moabdar's kindness had brought upon him.

"The king is pleased with me," said he; "how shall I escape ruin?"

He could not however decline his majesty's attentions; for it must be confessed that Nabussan, King of Serendib, the son of Nussanab, the son of Nabassan, the son of Sanbusna, was one of the best princes in Asia; when anyone spoke to him, it was difficult not to love him.

This good monarch was continually praised, deceived, and robbed; officials vied with each other in plundering his treasury. The receiver-general of the island of Serendib always set the example, and was faithfully followed by the others. The king knew it, and had time after time changed his treasurer; but he had not been able to change the time-honored fashion of dividing the royal revenue into two unequal parts, the smaller of which always fell to His Majesty, and the larger to the administrative staff.

King Nabussan confided his difficulty to the wise Zadig: "You who know so many fine things," said he, "can you think of no method of enabling me to find a treasurer who will not rob me?"

"Assuredly," answered Zadig; "I know an infallible way of giving you a man who has clean hands."

The king was charmed, and, embracing him, asked how he was to proceed.

"All you will have to do," said Zadig, "is to cause all who shall present themselves for the dignity of treasurer to dance, and he who dances most lightly will be infallibly the most honest man."

"You are joking," said the king; "truly a droll way of choosing a receiver of my revenues! What! Do you mean to say that the one who cuts the highest capers will prove the most honest and capable financier?"

"I will not answer for his capability," returned Zadig;

"but I assure you that he will undoubtedly be the most honest."

Zadig spoke with so much confidence that the king thought he had some supernatural secret for recognizing financiers.

"I am not fond of the supernatural," said Zadig; "people and books that deal in prodigies have always been distasteful to me; if Your Majesty will allow me to make the trial I propose, you will be well enough convinced that my secret is the easiest and most simple thing in the world."

Nabussan, King of Serendib, was far more astonished at hearing that this secret was a simple matter, than if it had been presented to him as a miracle.

"Well then," said the king, "do as you shall think proper."

"Give me a free hand," said Zadig, "and you will gain by this experiment more than you think."

The same day he issued a public notice that all who aspired to the post of receiver-in-chief of the revenues of His Gracious Majesty Nabussan, son of Nussanab, were to present themselves in garments of light silk, on the first day of the month of the Crocodile, in the king's antechamber. They duly put in an appearance to the number of sixty-four. Fiddlers were posted in an adjoining hall; all was ready for dancing; but the door of the hall was fastened, and it was necessary, in order to enter it, to pass along a little gallery which was pretty dark. An usher was sent to conduct each candidate, one after another, along this passage, in which he was left alone for a few minutes. The king, prompted by Zadig, had spread out all his treasures in this gallery. When all the competitors had reached the hall, his majesty gave orders that they should begin to dance. Never did men dance more heavily and with less grace; they all kept their heads down, their backs bent, and their hands glued to their sides.

"What rogues!" said Zadig, under his breath.

There was only one among them who stepped out freely, with head erect, a steady eye, and outstretched arms, body straight, and legs firm.

"Ah! The honest fellow! The worthy man!" said Zadig.

The king embraced this good dancer, and declared him treasurer; whereas all the others were punished with a fine, and that most justly, for each one of them, during the time that he was in the gallery, had filled his pockets so that he could hardly walk. The king was grieved for the honor of human nature that out of those sixty-four dancers there should have been sixty-three thieves. The dark gallery was henceforth called *The Corridor of Temptation*. In Persia those sixty-three gentlemen would have been impaled; in other countries a court of justice would have been held which would have consumed in legal expenses three times as much as had been stolen; while in yet another kingdom they would have procured a complete acquittal for themselves, and brought the nimble dancer to disgrace; at Serendib they were only condemned to increase the public funds, for Nabussan was very indulgent.

He was also very grateful; he gave to Zadig a sum of money greater than any treasurer had stolen from his master the king. Zadig availed himself of it to send expresses to Babylon, who were to bring him information of Astarte's fate. His voice trembled while giving this order, his blood flowed back towards his heart, a mist covered his eyes, and his soul was ready to take its flight.

The messenger departed: Zadig saw him embark. He returned to the king, seeing no one, fancying himself in his own chamber, and pronouncing the name of "love."

"Ah! love," said the king; "that is precisely what is the matter with me; you have rightly divined where my trouble lies. What a great man you are! I hope you will teach me how to recognize a faithful and devoted wife, as you have enabled me to find a disinterested treasurer."

Zadig, having recovered his wits, promised to serve him in love as well as in finance, although the undertaking seemed still more difficult.

CHAPTER XV

BLUE EYES

"MY body and my heart——" said the king to Zadig.

At these words the Babylonian could not refrain from interrupting His Majesty.

"How glad I am," said he, "that you did not say *my heart and soul!* For one hears nothing else but those words in every conversation at Babylon, and one sees nothing but books devoted to discussions on the heart and soul, written by people who have neither one nor the other. But please, sire, proceed."

Nabussan then continued:

"My body and my heart are predisposed by destiny to love; the former of these two powers has every reason to be satisfied. I have here a hundred women at my disposal, all beautiful, buxom, and obliging, even voluptuously inclined, or pretending to be so when with me.

My heart is not nearly so well off. I have found only too often that they lavish all their caresses on the King of Serendib, and care very little for Nabussan. It is not that I think my women unfaithful; but I would fain find a soul to be my own; I would resign for such a treasure the hundred beauties of whose charms I am master. See if, out of these hundred ladies of my harem, you can find me a single one by whom I may feel sure that I am loved?"

Zadig answered him as he had done on the subject of the financiers:—

"Sire, leave the matter to me; but allow me first to dispose of what you displayed in 'The Corridor of Temptation.' I will render you a good account of all, and you shall lose nothing by it."

The king gave him unfettered discretion. He chose in Serendib thirty-three little hunchbacks, the ugliest he could find, thirty-three of the most handsome pages, and thirty-three of the most eloquent and most robust bonzes. He left them all at liberty to enter the ladies' private chambers. Each little hunchback had four thousand gold pieces to give them, and the very first day all the hunchbacks were happy. The pages, who had nothing to give away but themselves, failed to achieve a triumph till the end of two or three days. The bonzes had a little more difficulty; but at last thirty-three fair devotees surrendered to them. The king, through the shutter-blinds which admitted a view into each chamber, witnessed all these experiments, and was not a little astonished. Of his hundred women, ninety-nine had succumbed before his eyes. There yet remained one who was quite young and freshly imported, whom His Majesty had never admitted to his arms. One, two, three hunchbacks were successively told off to make her offers which rose to the sum of twenty thousand pieces; she was incorruptible, and could not help laughing at the idea which had entered into these hunchbacks' heads that money could render them less deformed. The two handsomest of the pages were presented to her; she said that she thought the king still more handsome. The most eloquent and afterwards the most intrepid of the bonzes were let loose upon her; she found the first an idle babbler, and would not deign even to form an opinion on the merits of the second.

"The heart is everything," said she; "I will never yield either to the gold of a hunchback, or the personal attractions of a young man, or the cunning enticements of a bonze. I will love no one but Nabussan, son of Nussanab, and will wait till he condescends to love me."

The king was transported with joy, astonishment, and tenderness. He took back all the money that had won the hunchbacks their success, and made a present of it to the fair Falide (for such was the young lady's name). He gave her his heart, and she well deserved it. Never was the flower of youth so brilliant, never were the charms of beauty so enchanting. Historical veracity will not allow me to conceal the fact that she curtsied awkwardly, but she danced like a fairy, sang like a siren, and spoke like one of the graces; she was full of accomplishments and virtues.

Nabussan, loved as he was by her, adored her in his turn. But she had blue eyes, and this was the source of the greatest misfortunes. There was an ancient law which forbade the kings to love one of those women whom the Greeks in later days called βοῶπις The chief of the bonzes had established this law more than five thousand years before that time, with a view to appropriating the mistress of the first king of the island of Serendib, whom the chief bonze had induced to pass an anathema upon blue eyes as a fundamental article of the constitution. All orders of society came to remonstrate with Nabussan. They publicly declared that the last days of the kingdom had arrived, that iniquity had reached its height, and that all nature was threatened with some untoward accident; that, in a word, Nabussan, son of Nussanab, was in love with two big blue eyes. The hunchbacks, financiers, bonzes, and brunettes, filled the palace with complaints.

The wild tribes that inhabit the north of Serendib took advantage of the general discontent to make an incursion into the territory of the good Nabussan. He demanded subsidies from his subjects; the bonzes, who owned half the revenues of the state, contented themselves with raising their hands to heaven, and refused to put them into their coffers to help the king. They offered up grand prayers to fine music, and left the State a prey to the barbarians.

"O my dear Zadig! Will you rescue me again from this horrible embarrassment?" dolefully exclaimed Nabussan.

"Very willingly," answered Zadig. "You shall have as much money from the bonzes as you wish. Abandon to the enemy the lands on which their mansions are built, and only defend your own."

Nabussan did not fail to follow this advice. The bonzes thereupon came and threw themselves at the king's feet, imploring his assistance. The king answered them in beautiful strains of music, the words to which they were an accompaniment being prayers to Heaven for the preservation of their lands. The bonzes at last gave some money, and the king brought the war to a prosperous conclusion. Thus Zadig, by his wise and successful counsel, and by his important services, drew upon himself the irreconcilable hatred of the most powerful men in the State: the bonzes and the brunettes took an oath to ruin him; the financiers and the hunchbacks did not spare him, but did all they could to make him suspected by the excellent Nabussan. "Good offices remain in the antechamber when suspicions enter the closet," as Zoroaster has wisely observed. Every day there were fresh accusations; if the first was repelled, the second might graze the skin, the third wound, and the fourth be fatal.

Zadig, after having advantageously transacted the business of his friend Setoc and sent him his money, thought of nothing now in his alarm but of leaving the island, and resolved to go himself in search of tidings of Astarte.

"For," said he, "if I stay in Serendib, the bonzes will cause me to be impaled. . . . But where can I go? In Egypt I shall be a slave; burnt, in all likelihood, in Arabia; strangled at Babylon. Still I must know what has become of Astarte. . . . Let us be gone, and see for what my sad destiny reserves me."

CHAPTER XVI

THE BRIGAND

ON arriving at the frontier which separates Arabia Petræa from Syria, as he was passing near a strong castle, a party of armed Arabs sallied forth. He saw himself surrounded, and the men cried out: "All that you have belongs to us, and your body belongs to our master."

Zadig, by way of answer, drew his sword; his servant, who had plenty of courage, did the same. They routed and slew the Arabs who first laid hands on them; their assailants now numbered twice as many as before, but they were not daunted, and resolved to die fighting. Then were seen two men defending themselves against a multitude. Such a conflict could not last long. The master of the castle, whose name was Arbogad, having seen from a window the prodigies of valor performed by Zadig, conceived such an admiration for him that he hastily descended, and came in person to disperse his men and deliver the two travelers.

"All that passes over my lands is my property," said he, "as well as whatever I find on the lands of other people; but you seem to me such a brave man, that I except you from the general rule."

He made Zadig enter his castle, and bade his people treat him well. In the evening Arbogad desired Zadig to sup with him.

Now the lord of the castle was one of those Arabs who are known as *robbers*; but he sometimes did a good action among a multitude of bad ones. He robbed with fierce rapacity, and gave away freely; he was intrepid in battle, though gentle enough in society; intemperate at table, merry in his cups, and above all, full of frankness. Zadig pleased him greatly, and his animated conversation prolonged the repast. At length Arbogad said to him:

"I advise you to enroll yourself under me; you cannot do better; this calling of mine is not a bad one, and you may one day become what I now am."

"May I ask you," said Zadig, "how long you have practiced this noble profession?"

"From my tenderest youth," replied the lord of the castle. "I was the servant of an Arab who was a pretty sharp fellow; I felt my position intolerable; it drove me to despair to see that in all the earth, which belongs equally to all mankind, fortune had reserved no portion for me. I confided my trouble to an old Arab, who said to me: 'My son, do not despair; there was once upon a time a grain of sand which bewailed its fate in being a mere unheeded atom in the desert; but at the end of a few years it became a diamond, and it is now the most beautiful ornament in the King of India's crown.' This story made a great impression on me. I was the grain of sand, and I determined to become a diamond. I began by stealing two horses; I then formed a gang, and put myself in a position to rob small caravans. Thus by degrees I abolished the disproportion which existed at first between myself and other men; I had my share in the good things of this world, and was even recompensed with usury. I was held in high esteem, became a brigand chief, and obtained this castle by violence. The satrap of Syria wished to dispossess me, but I was already too rich to have anything to dread; I gave some money to the satrap, and by this means retained the castle and increased my domains. He even named me treasurer of the tribute which Arabia Petræa paid to the king of kings. I fulfilled my duty well, so far as receiving went, but utterly ignored that of payment. The Grand Desterham of Babylon sent hither in the name of King Moabdar a petty satrap, intending to have me strangled. This man arrived with his orders; I was informed of all, and caused to be strangled in his presence the four persons he had brought with him to apply the bowstring to my neck; after which I asked him what his commission to strangle me might be worth to him. He answered me that his fees might amount to three hundred pieces of gold. I made it clear to him that there was more to be gained with me. I gave him a subordinate post among my brigands, and now he is one of my smartest and wealthiest officers. Take my word for it, you will succeed as well as he. Never has there been a better season for pillage, since Moabdar is slain and all is in confusion at Babylon."

"Moabdar slain!" said Zadig; "and what has become of Queen Astarte?"

"I know nothing about her," replied Arbogad; "all I know is that Moabdar became mad and was killed, that Babylon is one vast slaughter-house, that all the empire is laid waste, that there are fine blows to be struck yet, and that I myself have done wonders in that way."

"But the queen?" said Zadig; "pray tell me, know you nothing of the fate of the queen?"

"I heard something about a prince of Hyrcania," replied he; "She is probably among his concubines, if she has not been killed in the insurrection. But I have more curiosity in the matter of plunder than of news. I have taken a good many women in my raids, but I keep none of them; I sell them at a high price if they are handsome, without inquiring who or what they are, for my customers pay nothing for rank; a queen who was ugly would find no purchaser. Maybe I have sold Queen Astarte, maybe she is dead; it matters very little to me, and I do not think you need be more concerned about her than I am."

As he spoke thus he went on drinking lustily, and mixed up all his ideas so confusedly that Zadig could extract no information out of him.

He remained confounded, overwhelmed, unable to stir. Arbogad continued to drink, told stories, constantly repeated that he was the happiest of all men, and exhorted Zadig to render himself as happy as he was. At last, becoming more and more drowsy with the fumes of wine, he gradually fell into a tranquil slumber. Zadig passed the night in a state of the most violent agitation.

"What!" said he, "The king become mad! The king killed! I cannot help lamenting him! The empire is dismembered, and this brigand is happy! Alas for fate and fortune! A robber is happy, and the most amiable object that nature ever created has perhaps perished in a frightful manner, or is living in a condition worse than death. O Astarte! what has become of you?"

At break of day he questioned all whom he met in the castle, but everybody was busy, and no one answered him: new conquests had been made during the night, and they were dividing the spoils. All that he could obtain in the confusion that prevailed was permission to depart, of which he availed himself without delay, plunged deeper than ever in painful thoughts.

Zadig walked on restless and agitated, his mind engrossed with the hapless Astarte, with the king of Babylon, with his faithful Cador, with the happy brigand Arbogad, and that capricious woman whom the Babylonians had carried off on the confines of Egypt, in short, with all the disappointments and misfortunes that he had experienced.

CHAPTER XVII

THE FISHERMAN

AT a distance of several leagues from Arbogad's castle, he found himself on the brink of a little river, still deploring his destiny, and regarding himself as the very personification of misery. There he saw a fisherman lying on the bank, hardly holding in his feeble hand the net which he seemed ready to drop, and lifting his eyes toward heaven.

"I am certainly the most wretched of all men," said the fisherman. "I was, as everybody allowed, the most famous seller of cream cheeses in Babylon, and I have been ruined. I had the prettiest wife that a man could possess, and she has betrayed me. A mean house was all that was left me, and I have seen it plundered and destroyed. Having taken refuge in a hut, I have no resource but fishing, and I cannot catch a single fish. O my net! I will cast you no more into the water, it is myself that I must cast therein."

Saying these words, he rose and advanced in the attitude of a man about to throw himself headlong and put an end to his life.

"What is this?" said Zadig to himself; "there are men then as miserable as I!"

Eagerness to save the fisherman's life rose as promptly as this reflection. He ran towards him, stopped, and questioned him with an air of concern and encouragement. It is said that we are less miserable when we are not alone in our misery. According to Zoroaster this is due, not to malice, but to necessity; we then feel ourselves drawn towards a victim of misfortune as a fellow-sufferer. The joy of a prosperous man would seem to us an insult, but two wretched men are like two weak trees, which, leaning together, mutually strengthen each other against the tempest.

"Why do you give way to your misfortunes?" said Zadig to the fisherman.

"Because," answered he, "I see no way out of them. I was held in the highest esteem in the village of Derlback, near Babylon, and I made, with my wife's help, the best cream cheeses in the empire. Queen Astarte and the famous minister Zadig were passionately fond of them. I had supplied their houses with six hundred cheeses, and went one day into town to be paid, when, on my arrival at Babylon, I learned that the queen and Zadig had disappeared. I hastened to the house of the lord Zadig, whom I had never seen; there I found the police officers of the Grand Desterham, who, furnished with a royal warrant, were sacking his house in a perfectly straightforward and orderly manner. I flew to the queen's kitchens: some of the lords of the dresser told me that she was dead; other said that she was in prison; while others again declared that she had taken flight; but all assured me that I should be paid nothing for my cheeses. I went with my wife to the house of the lord Orcan, who was one of my customers, and we asked him to protect us in our distress. He granted his protection to my wife, and refused it to me. She was whiter than those cream cheeses with which my troubles began, and the gleam of Tyrian purple was not more brilliant than the carnation which animated that whiteness. It was this which made the lord Orcan keep her and drive me away from his house. I wrote to my dear wife the letter of a desperate man. She said to the messenger who brought it:

" 'Oh! Ah, yes! I know something of the man who writes me this letter. I have heard people speak of him; they say he makes capital cream cheeses. Let him send me some, and see that he is paid for them.' "

"In my unhappy state I determined to have recourse to justice. I had six ounces of gold left; I had to give two ounces to the lawyer whom I consulted, two to the attorney who undertook my case, and two to the secretary of the first judge. When all this was done, my suit was not yet commenced, and I had already spent

more money than my cheeses and my wife were worth.
I returned to my village, with the intention of selling my
house in order to recover my wife.

"My house was well worth sixty ounces of gold, but
people saw that I was poor and forced to sell. The first
man to whom I applied offered me thirty ounces for it,
the second twenty, and the third ten. I was ready at last
to take anything, so blinded was I, when a prince of
Hyrcania came to Babylon, and ravaged all the country on his way. My house was first sacked and then
burned.

"Having thus lost my money, my wife, and my house,
I retired to this part of the country where you see me.
I tried to support myself by fishing, but the fishes mock
me as much as men do; I take nothing, I am dying of
hunger, and had it not been for you, my illustrious con-
soler, I should have perished in the river."

The fisherman did not tell his story all at once; for
every moment Zadig in his agitation would break in
with: "What! Do you know nothing of what has befallen the queen?" "No, my lord," the fisherman would
make reply; "but I know that the queen and Zadig have
not paid me for my cream cheeses, that my wife has been
taken from me, and that I am in despair."

"I feel confident," said Zadig, "that you will not lose
all your money. I have heard people speak of this Zadig; he is an honest man, and if he returns to Babylon,
as he hopes to do, he will give you more than he owes
you. But as to your wife, who is not so honest, I recommend you not to try to recover her. Take my advice, go
to Babylon; I shall be there before you, because I am on
horseback, and you are on foot. Apply to the most noble
Cador, tell him you have met his friend, and wait for

me at his house. Go; perhaps you will not always be unhappy."

"O mighty Ormuzd," continued he, "thou dost make use of me to console this man, of whom wilt thou make use to console me?"

So saying, he gave the fisherman half of all the money he had brought from Arabia, and the fisherman, astonished and delighted, kissed the feet of Cador's friend, and said: "You are an angel sent to save me."

Meanwhile Zadig continued to ask for news, shedding tears as he did so.

"What, my lord," cried the fisherman, "can you then be unhappy, you who bestow bounty?"

"A hundred times more unhappy than you," answered Zadig.

"But how can it be," said the simple fellow, "that he who gives is more to be pitied than he who receives?"

"Because," replied Zadig, "your greatest misfortune was a hungry belly, and because my misery has its seat in the heart."

"Has Orcan taken away your wife?" said the fisherman.

This question recalled all his adventures to Zadig's mind; he repeated the catalogue of his misfortunes, beginning with the queen's bitch, up to the time of his arrival at the castle of the brigand Arbogad.

"Ah!" said he to the fisherman, "Orcan deserves to be punished. But it is generally such people as he who are the favorites of fortune. Be that as it may, go to the house of the lord Cador, and wait for me."

They parted. The fisherman walked on thanking his stars, and Zadig pressed forward still accusing his own.

CHAPTER XVIII

THE COCKATRICE

HAVING arrived at a beautiful meadow, Zadig saw there several women searching for something with great diligence. He took the liberty of approaching one of them, and of asking her if he might have the honor of helping them in their search.

"Take good heed not to do that," answered the Syrian damsel; "what we are looking for can only be touched with impunity by women."

"That is very strange," said Zadig; "may I venture to ask you to tell me what it is that only women are allowed to touch?"

"A cockatrice," said she.

"A cockatrice, madam! And for what reason, if you please, are you looking for a cockatrice?"

"It is for our lord and master, Ogul, whose castle you see on the bank of that river, at the end of the meadow. We are his most humble slaves; the lord Ogul is ill, his physician has ordered him to eat a cockatrice stewed in rose-water, and, as it is a very rare animal, and never allows itself to be taken except by women, the lord Ogul has promised to choose for his well-beloved wife, whichever of us shall bring him a cockatrice. Let me pursue the search, if you please; for you see what it would cost me, if I were anticipated by my companions."

Zadig left this Syrian girl and the others to look for their cockatrice, and continued to walk through the meadow. When he reached the brink of a little stream, he found there another lady lying on the turf, but not in search of anything. Her figure appeared majestic, but

her countenance was covered with a veil. She was leaning over the stream; deep sighs escaped from her mouth.
She held in her hand a little rod, with which she was
tracing characters on the fine sand which lay between the
grass and the stream. Zadig had the curiosity to look
and see what this woman was writing. He drew near,
and saw the letter Z, then an A. He was astonished.
When there appeared a D, he started. Never was there
surprise to equal his, when he saw the two last letters of
his name. He remained some time without moving, then,
breaking the silence, he exclaimed in an agitated voice:

"O noble lady, pardon a stranger who is in distress if
he ventures to ask you by what astonishing chance I
find here the name of Zadig traced by your adorable
hand."

At that voice, at those words, the lady raised her veil
with a trembling hand, turned her eyes on Zadig, uttered a cry of tenderness, surprise, and joy, and, overcome by all the varied emotions which simultaneously
assailed her soul, she fell fainting into his arms. It was
Astarte herself, it was the queen of Babylon, it was she
whom Zadig adored, and whom he reproached himself
for adoring, it was she for whom he had wept so much,
and for whom he had so often dreaded the worst stroke
of fate. For a moment he was deprived of the use of his
senses, then, fixing his gaze on Astarte's eyes, which
languidly opened once more with an expression in which
confusion was mingled with tenderness, he cried:

"O immortal powers, who preside over the destinies of
feeble mortals! Do ye indeed restore Astarte to me? At
what a time, in what a place, and in what a condition do
I see her again!"

He threw himself on his knees before Astarte and applied his forehead to the dust of her feet. The queen of

Babylon lifted him up, and made him sit beside her on
the bank of the stream, while she repeatedly dried her
eyes from which tears would soon begin again to flow.
Twenty times at least did she take up the thread of the
discourse which her sighs interrupted; she questioned
him as to what strange chance brought them once more
together, and she anticipated his answers by suddenly
asking fresh questions. She began to relate her own misfortunes, and then wished to know those of Zadig. At
last, both of them having somewhat appeased the tumult
of their souls, Zadig told her in a few words how it came
to pass that he found himself in that meadow.

"But, O unhappy and honored queen, how is it that I
find you in this remote spot, clad as a slave, and accompanied by other women slaves who are searching for a
cockatrice to be stewed in rose-water by a physician's
order?"

"While they are looking for their cockatrice," said the
fair Astarte, "I will inform you of all that I have suffered, and of how much I have ceased to blame heaven
now that I see you again. You know that the king, my
husband, took it ill that you were the most amiable of all
men, and it was for this reason that he one night took
the resolution to have you strangled and me poisoned.
You know how heaven permitted my little mute to give
me warning of His Sublime Majesty's orders. Hardly
had the faithful Cador forced you to obey me and to go
away, when he ventured to enter my chamber in the
middle of the night by a secret passage. He carried me
off, and brought me to the temple of Ormuzd, where
his brother, the magian, shut me up in a gigantic statue,
the base of which touches the foundations of the temple
while its head reaches to the roof. I was as buried there,
but waited on by the magian and in want of none of the

necessaries of life. Meanwhile at daybreak His Majesty's apothecary entered my chamber with a draught compounded of henbane, opium, black hellebore, and aconite; and another official went to your apartment with a bowstring of blue silk. Both places were found empty. Cador, the better to deceive him, went to the king, and pretended to accuse us both. He said that you had taken the road to India, and that I had gone towards Memphis; so officers were sent after each of us.

"The messengers who went in search of me did not know me by sight, for I had hardly ever shown my face to any man but yourself, and that in my husband's presence and by his command. They hastened off in pursuit of me, guided by the description that had been given them of my person. A woman of much the same height as myself, and who had, it may be, superior charms, presented herself to their eyes on the borders of Egypt. She was evidently a fugitive and in distress; they had no doubt that this woman was the queen of Babylon, and they brought her to Moabdar. Their mistake at first threw the king into a violent rage; but ere long, taking a nearer look at the woman, he perceived that she was very beautiful, which gave him some consolation. She was called Missouf. I have been told since that the name signifies in the Egyptian tongue *the capricious beauty*. Such in truth she was, but she had as much artfulness as caprice. She pleased Moabdar and brought him into subjection to such a degree that she made him declare her his wife. Thereupon her character developed itself in all its extravagance; she fearlessly gave herself up to every foolish freak of her imagination. She wished to compel the chief of the magi, who was old and gouty, to dance before her; and when he refused she persecuted him most bitterly. She ordered her master of the horse to make her

a jam tart. In vain did the master of the horse represent
to her that he was not a pastry cook: he must make the
tart; and he was driven from office because it was too
much burned. She gave the post of master of horse to
her dwarf, and the place of chancellor to a page. It was
thus that she governed Babylon, while all regretted that
they had lost me. The king, who had been a tolerably
just and reasonable man until the moment when he had
determined to poison me and to have you strangled,
seemed now to have drowned his virtues in the exorbitant
love that he had for the capricious beauty. He came to
the temple on the great day of the sacred fire, and I saw
him implore the gods on behalf of Missouf, at the feet of
the image in which I was confined. I lifted up my voice,
and cried aloud to him:

" 'The gods reject the prayers of a king who is become
a tyrant, who has been minded to put to death a sensible
wife to marry a woman of the most extravagant whims.'

"Moabdar was so confounded at these words, that his
head become disordered. The oracle that I had delivered,
and Missouf's domineering temper, sufficed to deprive
him of his senses, and in a few days he became quite
mad.

"His madness, which seemed a punishment from heav-
en, was the signal for revolt. There was a general insurrection, and all men ran to take up arms. Babylon, so
long plunged in effeminate idleness, became the scene of
a frightful civil war. I was drawn forth from the cavity
of my statue, and placed at the head of one party. Cador
hastened to Memphis, to bring you back to Babylon.
The prince of Hyrcania, hearing of these fatal dissensions, came back with his army to form a third party in
Chaldea. He attacked the king, who fled before him with
his wayward Egyptian. Moabdar died pierced with

wounds, and Missouf fell into the hands of the conqueror. It was my misfortune to be myself taken prisoner by a party of Hyrcanians, and I was brought before
the prince at precisely the same time as they were bringing in Missouf. You will be pleased, no doubt, to hear
that the prince thought me more beautiful than the
Egyptian; but you will be sorry to learn that he destined
me for his harem. He told me very decidedly that as
soon as he should have finished a military expedition
which he was about to undertake, he would come and
keep me company. You may fancy my distress! The tie
that bound me to Moabdar was broken, and I might
have been Zadig's, if this barbarian had not cast his
chains round me. I answered him with all the pride that
my rank and my resentment gave me. I had always heard
it said that heaven has connected with persons of my
condition a greatness of character, which, with a word or
a look, can reduce the presumptuous to an humble sense
of that deep respect which they have dared to disregard. I
spoke like a queen, but found myself treated like a domestic. The Hyrcanian, without deigning to address to me even
a single word, told his black eunuch that I was a saucy
minx, but that he thought me pretty; so he bade him
take care of me, and subject me to the diet of his favorites, that I might recover my complexion, and be rendered more worthy of his favors by the time when he
might find it convenient to honor me with them. I told
him that I would sooner kill myself. He answered, laughing, that there was no fear of that, and that he was used
to such displays of affectation; whereupon he left me
like a man who has just put a parrot into his aviary.
What a state of things for the first queen in all the world,
—I will say more, for a heart which was devoted to
Zadig!"

At these words Zadig threw himself at her knees, and bathed them with tears. Astarte raised him tenderly, and continued thus:

"I saw myself in the power of a barbarian, and a rival of the crazy woman who was my fellow-prisoner. She told me what had befallen her in Egypt. I conjectured from the description she gave of your person, from the time of the occurrence, from the dromedary on which you were mounted, and from all the circumstances of the case, that it was Zadig who had fought in her behalf. I had no doubt that you were at Memphis, and resolved to betake myself thither.

" 'Beautiful Missouf,' said I, 'you are much more pleasing than I am, and will entertain the prince of Hyrcania far better than I can do. Help me to effect my escape; you will then reign alone, and render me happy in ridding yourself of a rival.'

"Missouf arranged with me the means of my flight, and I departed secretly with an Egyptian woman slave.

"I had nearly reached Arabia, when a notorious robber, named Arbogad, carried me off, and sold me to some merchants, who brought me to this castle where the lord Ogul resides. He bought me without knowing who I was. He is a man of pleasure whose only object in life is good cheer, and who is convinced that God has sent him into the world to sit at table. He is excessively fat, and is constantly on the point of suffocation. His physician, in whom he believes little enough when his digestion is all right, exerts a despotic sway over him whenever he has eaten too much. He has persuaded him that he can cure him with a cockatrice stewed in rose-water. The lord Ogul has promised his hand to whichever of his female slaves shall bring him a cockatrice. You see how I leave them to vie with one another in their eagerness to win this honor, for, since heaven has permitted me to see you again, I have less desire than ever to find his cockatrice."

Then Astarte and Zadig gave expression to all that tender feelings had long repressed,—all that their love and misfortunes could inspire in hearts most generous and ardent; and the genii who preside over love carried their vows to the orb of Venus.

The women returned to Ogul's castle without having found anything. Zadig, having obtained an introduction, addressed him to this effect:

"May immortal health descend from heaven to guard and keep you all your days! I am a physician, and am come to you in haste on hearing the report of your sickness, and I have brought you a cockatrice stewed in rosewater. I have no matrimonial intentions with regard to you; I only ask for the release of a young female slave from Babylon, who has been several days in your possession, and I consent to remain in bondage in her place if I have not the happiness of curing the magnificent lord Ogul."

The proposal was accepted. Astarte set out for Babylon with Zadig's servant, having promised to send him a messenger immediately to inform him of all that might have happened. Their parting was as tender as their unexpected recognition. The moment of separation and the moment of meeting again are the two most important epochs of life, as is written in the great book of Zendavesta. Zadig loved the queen as much as he swore he did, and the queen loved Zadig more than she professed to do.

Meanwhile Zadig spoke thus to Ogul:

"My lord, my cockatrice is not to be eaten, all its virtue must enter into you through the pores. I have put it into a little leathern case, well blown out, and covered with a fine skin; you must strike this case of leather as hard as you can, and I must send it back each time; a few days of this treatment will show you what my art can do."[9]

The first day Ogul was quite out of breath, and thought that he should die of fatigue. The second day he was less exhausted, and slept better. In a week's time he had gained all the strength, health, lightness, and good spirits of his most robust years.

"You have played at ball, and you have been temperate," said Zadig; "believe me, there is no such creature in nature as a cockatrice, but with temperance and exercise one is always well, and the art of combining intemperance and health is as chimerical as the philosopher's stone, judicial astrology, and the theology of the magi."

Ogul's former physician, perceiving how dangerous this man was to the cause of medicine, conspired with his private apothecary to dispatch Zadig to hunt for cockatrices in the other world. Thus, after having already been punished so often for having done good, he was again nearly perishing for having healed a gluttonous nobleman. He was invited to a grand dinner and was to have been poisoned during the second course, but while they were at the first he received a message from the fair Astarte, at which he left the table, and took his departure. "When one is loved by a beautiful woman," says the great Zoroaster, "one is always extricated from every scrape."

CHAPTER XIX

THE TOURNAMENT

THE queen had been received at Babylon with the enthusiasm which is always shown for a beautiful princess who has been unfortunate. Babylon at that time seemed more peaceful. The prince of Hyrcania had been killed in a battle, and the victorious Babylonians declared that Astarte should marry the man whom they might elect for monarch. They did not desire that the first position in the world, namely, that of being husband of Astarte and king of Babylon, should depend upon intrigues and cabals. They took an oath to acknowledge as their king the man whom they should find bravest and wisest. Spacious lists, surrounded by an amphitheater splendidly decorated, were formed at a distance of several leagues from the city. The combatants were to repair thither armed at all points. Each of them had separate quarters behind the amphitheater, where he was to be neither seen nor visited by anyone. It was necessary to enter the lists four times, and those who should be successful enough to defeat four cavaliers were thereupon to fight against each other, and the one who should finally remain master of the field should be proclaimed victor of the tournament. He was to return four days afterwards with the same arms, and try to solve the riddles which the magi would propound. If he could not solve the riddles, he was not to be king, and it would be necessary to begin the jousts over again until a knight should be found victorious in both sorts of contest; for they wished to have a king braver and wiser than any other man. The queen, during all this time, was to be strictly guarded; she was only allowed to be present at the games covered with a veil, and she was not permitted to speak to any of the competitors, in order to avoid either favoritism or injustice.

This was the intelligence that Astarte sent her lover, hoping that for her sake he would display greater valor and wisdom than anyone else. So he took his departure, entreating Venus to fortify his courage and enlighten his mind. He arrived on the banks of the Euphrates the evening before the great day, and caused his device to be inscribed among those of the combatants, concealing his countenance and his name, as the law required. Then he went to take repose in the lodging that was assigned him by lot. His friend Cador, who had returned to Babylon after having vainly searched for him in Egypt, dispatched to his quarters a complete suit of armor which was the queen's present. He also sent him, on her behalf, the finest steed in Persia. Zadig recognized the hand of Astarte in these gifts; his courage and his love gained thereby new energy and new hopes.

On the morrow, the queen having taken her place under a jeweled canopy and the amphitheater being filled with ladies and persons of every rank in Babylon, the combatants appeared in the arena. Each of them came and laid his device at the feet of the grand magian. The devices were drawn by lot, and Zadig's happened to be the last. The first who advanced was a very rich lord named Itobad, exceedingly vain, but with little courage, skill, or judgment. His servants had persuaded him that such a man as he ought to be king; and he had answered them: "Such a man as I ought to reign." So they had armed him from head to foot. He had golden armor enameled with green, a green plume, and a lance decked with green ribbons. It was evident at once, from the

manner in which Itobad managed his horse, that it was
not for *such a man as he* that heaven reserved the scepter
of Babylon. The first knight who tilted against him un-
horsed him; the second upset him so that he lay on his
horse's crupper with both his legs in the air and arms extended. Itobad recovered his seat, but in such an un-
gainly fashion that all the spectators began to laugh. The
third did not condescend to use his lance, but after
making a pass at him, took him by the right leg, turned
him half round, and let him drop on the sand. The
squires of the tourney ran up to him laughing, and re-
placed him on his saddle. The fourth combatant seized
him by the left leg, and made him fall on the other
side. He was accompanied with loud jeers to his quarters,
where he was to pass the night according to the law of
the games; and he said as he limped along with difficulty:
"What an experience for such a man as I!"

The other knights acquitted themselves better. There
were some who defeated two antagonists one after the
other, a few went as far as three, but the prince Otame
was the only one who conquered four. At last Zadig
tilted in his turn; he unseated four cavaliers in succession in the most graceful manner possible. It then remained to be seen whether Otame or Zadig would be the
victor. The arms of the former were blue and gold, with
a plume of the same color, while those of Zadig were
white. The sympathies of all were divided between the
knight in blue and the knight in white. The queen,
whose heart was throbbing violently, put up prayers to
heaven that the white might be the winning color.

The two champions made passes and wheeled round
with such agility, they delivered such dexterous thrusts,
and sat so firmly on their saddles, that all the spectators,
except the queen, wished that there might be two kings

in Babylon. At last, their chargers being exhausted, and their lances broken, Zadig had recourse to this stratagem: he steps behind the blue prince, leaps upon the crupper of his horse, seizes him by the waist, hurls him down, takes his place in the saddle, and prances round Otame, as he lies stretched upon the ground. All the amphitheater shouts: "Victory to the white cavalier!" Otame rises, indignant at his disgrace, and draws his sword; Zadig springs off the horse's back, saber in hand. Then, lo and behold! both of them on foot in the arena begin a new conflict, in which strength and agility by turns prevail. The plumes of their helmets, the rivets of their arm-pieces, the links of their armor, fly far afield under a thousand rapid blows. With point and edge they thrust and cut, to right and left, now on the head, and now on the chest; they retreat, they advance, they measure swords, they come to close quarters, they wrestle, they twine like serpents, they attack each other like lions; sparks are sent forth every moment from their clashing swords. At last Zadig, recovering his coolness for an instant, stops, makes a feint, and then rushes upon Otame, brings him to the ground, and disarms him, when the vanquished prince exclaims: "O white cavalier, you it is who should reign over Babylon."

The queen's joy was at its climax. The cavalier in blue and the cavalier in white were conducted each to his own lodging, as well as all the others, in due accordance with the law. Mutes came to attend them and to bring them food. It may be easily guessed that the queen's little mute was the one who waited on Zadig. Then they were left to sleep alone until the morning of the next day, when the conqueror was to bring his device to the grand magian to be compared with the roll, and to make himself known.

In spite of his love Zadig slept soundly enough, so tired was he. Itobad, who lay near him, did not sleep a wink. He rose in the night, entered Zadig's quarters, took away his white arms and his device, and left his own green armor in their place. As soon as it was daylight, he went up boldly to the grand magian, and announced that ·such a man as he was victor. This was unexpected, but his success was proclaimed while Zadig was still asleep. Astarte, surprised, and with despair at her heart, returned to Babylon. The whole amphitheater was already almost empty when Zadig awoke; he looked for his arms, and found only the green armor. He was obliged to put it on, having nothing else near him. Astonished and indignant, he armed himself in a rage, and stepped forth in that guise.

All the people who were left in the amphitheater and arena greeted him with jeers. They pressed round him and insulted him to his face. Never did man endure such bitter mortification. He lost patience, and with his drawn sword dispersed the mob which dared to molest him; but he knew not what course to adopt. He could not see the queen, nor could he lay claim to the white armor which she had sent him, without compromising her; so that, while she was plunged in grief, he was tortured with rage and perplexity. He walked along the banks of the Euphrates, convinced that his star had marked him out for inevitable misery, reviewing in his mind all the misfortunes he had suffered, since his experience of the woman who hated one-eyed men up to this present loss of his armor.

"See what comes," said he, "of awaking too late; if I had slept less, I should now be king of Babylon and husband of Astarte. Knowledge, good conduct and courage have never served to bring me anything but trouble."

At last, murmurs against Providence escaped him, and he was tempted to believe that the world was governed by a cruel destiny, which oppressed the good, and brought prosperity to cavaliers in green. One of his worst grievances was to be obliged to wear that green armor which drew such ridicule upon him; and he sold it to a passing merchant at a low price, taking in exchange from the merchant a gown and a nightcap. In this garb he paced beside the Euphrates, filled with despair, and secretly accusing Providence for always persecuting him.

CHAPTER XX

THE HERMIT [10]

WHILE walking thus, Zadig met a hermit, whose white and venerable beard descended to his girdle. He held in his hand a book which he was reading attentively. Zadig stopped, and made him a profound obeisance. The hermit returned his salutation with an air so noble and attractive, that Zadig had the curiosity to enter into conversation with him. He asked him what book he was reading.

"It is the book of destiny," said the hermit; "do you desire to read aught therein?"

He placed the book in Zadig's hands, but he, learned as he was in several languages, could not decipher a single character in the book. This increased his curiosity yet more.

"You seem to me much vexed," said the good father.

"Alas, and with only too much reason!" answered Zadig.

"If you will allow me to accompany you," rejoined the old man, "perhaps I may be of service to you; I have sometimes poured consolation into the souls of the unhappy."

The hermit's aspect, his beard, and his book, inspired Zadig with respect. He found in conversing with him the light of a superior mind. The hermit spoke of destiny, of justice, of morality, of the chief good, of human frailty, of virtue and of vice with an eloquence so lively and touching, that Zadig felt himself drawn towards him by an irresistible charm. He earnestly besought him not to leave him, until they should return to Babylon.

"I myself ask the same favor of you," said the old man; "swear to me by Ormuzd that you will not part from me for some days to come, whatever I may do."

Zadig swore not to do so, and they set out together.

The two travelers arrived that evening at a magnificent castle, where the hermit craved hospitality for himself and for the young man who accompanied him. The porter, who might have been taken for a distinguished nobleman, introduced them with a sort of disdainful politeness. They were presented to one of the principal domestics, who showed them the master's splendid apartments. They were admitted to the lower end of his table, without being honored even with a look from the lord of the castle; but they were served like the others, with elegance and profusion. A golden bowl studded with emeralds and rubies was afterwards brought them, wherein to wash their hands. For the night they were consigned to fine sleeping apartments, and in the morning a servant brought each of them a piece of gold, after which they were courteously dismissed.

"The master of the house," said Zadig, when they were again on their way, "seems to me to be a generous man, but a little too proud; he practices a noble hospitality."

As he said these words, he perceived that a very wide sort of pocket which the hermit was wearing appeared stretched and stuffed out, and he caught sight of the golden bowl adorned with precious stones, which the hermit had stolen. He did not at first venture to take any notice of it, but he experienced a strange surprise.

Towards midday, the hermit presented himself at the door of a very small house, inhabited by a very rich miser, of whom he begged hospitable entertainment for a few hours. An old servant, meanly clad, received them roughly, and conducted the hermit and Zadig to the stable, where some rotten olives, moldy bread, and sour beer were given them. The hermit ate and drank with as contented an air as on the evening before; then, turning to the old servant who was watching them both to see that they stole nothing, and who kept urging them to go, he gave him the two pieces of gold which he had received that morning, and thanked him for all his attentions.

"Pray," added he, "let me speak a word to your master."

The astonished servant introduced the two strangers.

"Magnificent lord," said the hermit, "I cannot refrain from offering you my most humble thanks for the noble manner in which you have treated us; deign to accept this golden bowl as a slight token of my gratitude."

The miser almost fell backward from his seat, but the hermit, not giving him time to recover from his sudden surprise, departed with his young companion as quickly as possible.

"Father," said Zadig, "what is all this that I see? You do not seem to me to resemble other men in anything that you do; you steal a bowl adorned with precious stones from a nobleman who entertained you sumptuously, and you give it to a miser who treats you with indignity."

"My son," replied the old man, "that pompous person, who entertains strangers only out of vanity, and to excite admiration of his riches, will learn a needful lesson, while the miser will be taught to practice hospitality; be astonished at nothing, and follow me."

Zadig was still uncertain whether he had to do with a man more foolish or more wise than all other men, but the hermit spoke with a tone of such superiority, that Zadig, bound besides by his oath, felt constrained to follow him.

In the evening they arrived at a house built in a pleasing but simple style, where nothing betokened either prodigality or avarice. The master was a philosopher who, retired from the world, pursued in peace the study of wisdom and virtue, and who, nevertheless, felt life no tedious burden. It had pleased him to build this retreat, into which he welcomed strangers with a generosity which was free from ostentation. He went himself to meet the travelers, and ushered them into a comfortable apartment, where he first left them to repose awhile. Some time afterwards he came in person to invite them to a clean and well-cooked meal, during which he spoke with great good sense about the latest revolutions in Babylon. He seemed sincerely attached to the queen, and expressed a wish that Zadig had appeared in the lists as a competitor for the crown.

"But mankind," added he, "do not deserve to have a king like Zadig."

The latter blushed, and felt his disappointment return with double force. In the course of conversation it was generally agreed that matters in this world do not always fall out as the wisest men would wish. The hermit maintained throughout that we are ignorant of the ways of Providence, and that men are wrong in judging of the whole by the very small part which alone they are able to perceive.

They spoke of the passions. "Ah, how fatal they are!" said Zadig.

"They are the winds that swell the sails of the vessel," replied the hermit; "they sometimes sink the vessel, but it could not make way without them. The bile makes men choleric and sick, but without the bile they could not live. Everything here below has its danger, and yet everything is necessary."

Then they spoke of pleasure, and the hermit proved that it is a gift of the Deity.

"For," said he, "man can give himself neither sensation nor idea, he receives them all; pain and pleasure come to him from without like his very existence."

Zadig marveled how a man who had acted so extravagantly could argue so well. At length, after a discourse as profitable as it was agreeable, their host conducted the two travelers back to their apartment, blessing heaven for having sent him two men so virtuous and so wise; and he offered them money in a frank and easy manner that could give no offense. The hermit, however, refused it, and told him that he must now take leave of him, as he purposed departing for Babylon before morning. Their parting was affectionate; Zadig especially felt full of esteem and love for so amiable a man.

When the hermit and he were alone in their chamber,

they passed a long time in praising their host. The old man at daybreak awoke his comrade.

"We must start," said he, "while all the household is asleep. I wish to leave this man a token of my regard and affection."

Saying these words, he seized a light, and set fire to the house. Zadig uttered a cry of horror, and would fain have prevented him from committing so dreadful a deed, but the hermit dragged him away by superior force, and the house was soon in flames. The hermit, who was now at a safe distance with his companion, calmly watched it burning.

"Thank God!" said he; "there goes the house of my dear host, destroyed from basement to roof! Happy man!"

At these words Zadig was tempted at once to burst out laughing, to overwhelm the reverend father with reproaches, to beat him, and to fly from him. But he did none of these things; still overawed by the hermit's dominating influence, he followed him in spite of himself to their last quarters for the night.

It was at the house of a charitable and virtuous widow, who had a nephew fourteen years of age, full of engaging qualities, and her only hope. She did the honors of her house as well as she could, and on the morrow she bade her nephew conduct the travelers as far as a bridge which, having broken down a short time before, was now dangerous to cross. The lad walked before them with alacrity. When they were on the bridge, the hermit said to the youth:

"Come, I must prove my gratitude to your aunt."

Then he seized him by the hair and threw him into the river. The boy sank, rose for a moment above the water, and was then swallowed up by the torrent.

"O monster! Most wicked of all mankind!" exclaimed Zadig.

"You promised to be more patient," said the hermit, interrupting him. "Know that under the ruins of that house to which Providence set fire, the master has found an immense treasure; and that this youth, whose neck Providence has twisted,[11] would have murdered his aunt within a year, and yourself within two."

"Savage, who told you so?" cried Zadig; "and though you may have read this event in your book of destiny, are you allowed to drown a child who has done you no harm?"

While the Babylonian was speaking, he perceived that the old man had no longer a beard, and that his countenance assumed the features of youth. The habit of a hermit disappeared; four beautiful wings covered a form majestic and glittering with light.

"O messenger from heaven! Divine angel!" cried Zadig, falling on his knees; "art thou then descended from the empyrean to teach a feeble mortal to submit to the eternal decrees?"

"Mankind," said the angel Jesrad, "judges of everything when knowing nothing; of all men you were the one who most deserved to be enlightened."

Zadig asked if he might have permission to speak.

"I distrust myself," said he, "but may I venture to ask thee to resolve my doubt? Would it not have been better to have corrected this youth, and to have rendered him virtuous, than to drown him?"

Jesrad answered: "If he had been virtuous, and had continued to live, it would have been his destiny to be murdered himself, together with the wife he was to marry, and the son whom she was to bear."

"What!" said Zadig, "is it inevitable then that there

should be crimes and misfortunes? The misfortunes too, fall upon the good!"

"The wicked," answered Jesrad, "are always unhappy; they serve to try a small number of righteous men scattered over the earth, and there is no evil from which some good does not spring."

"But," said Zadig, "what if there were only good, and no evil at all?"

"Then," answered Jesrad, "this earth would be another world; the chain of events would be ordered by wisdom of another kind; and this order, which would be perfect, can only exist in the eternal abode of the Supreme Being, which evil cannot approach. He has created millions of worlds, not one of which can resemble another. This boundless variety is an attribute of His boundless power. There are not two leaves of a tree upon this earth, nor two globes in the infinite fields of heaven, which are alike, and everything that you see on this little atom where you have been born must fill its own place, and exist in its own fixed time, according to the immutable decrees of Him who embraces all. Men think that this child who has just perished fell into the water by accident, that it was by accident likewise that that house was burned; but there is no such thing as accident; all that takes place is either a trial, or a punishment, or a reward, or a providential dispensation. Remember that fisherman who deemed himself the most miserable of men. Ormuzd sent you to change his destiny. Feeble mortal, cease to dispute against that which it is your duty to adore."

"But," said Zadig.

As the word was on his lips, the angel was already winging his way towards the tenth sphere. Zadig on his knees adored Providence, and was resigned. The angel cried to him from on high:

"Take your way towards Babylon."

CHAPTER XXI

THE RIDDLES

ZADIG, in a state of bewilderment, and like a man at whose side the lightning has fallen, walked on at random. He entered Babylon on the day when those who had contended in the lists were already assembled in the grand vestibule of the palace to solve the riddles, and to answer the questions of the grand magian. All the knights were there, except him of the green armor. As soon as Zadig appeared in the city, the people gathered round him; they could not satisfy their eyes with the sight of him, their mouths with blessing him, or their hearts with wishing him to be king. The Envious man saw him pass, trembled, and turned aside, while the people escorted him to the place of assembly. The queen, to whom his arrival was announced, became a prey to the agitation of fear and hope; she was devoured with uneasiness, and could not comprehend why Zadig was unarmed, and how it came to pass that Itobad wore the white armor. A confused murmur arose at the sight of Zadig. All were surprised and delighted to see him again; but only the knights who had taken part in the tournament were permitted to appear in the assembly.

"I have fought like the others," said he; "but another here wears my armor, and, while I must wait to have the honor of proving it, I ask leave to present myself in order to explain the riddles."

The question was put to the vote; his reputation for integrity was still so deeply impressed on the minds of all, that there was no hesitation about admitting him.

The grand magian first proposed this question:

"What, of all things in the world, is alike the longest and the shortest, the quickest and the slowest, the most minutely divided and the most widely extended, the most neglected and the most regretted, without which nothing can be done, which devours everything that is little, and confers life on everything that is great?"

Itobad was to speak first; he answered that such a man as he understood nothing about riddles, that it was enough for him to have conquered by the might of his arm. Some said that the answer to the riddle was fortune; according to others it was the earth, and according to others again light. Zadig said that it was time:

"Nothing is longer," added he, "since it is the measure of eternity; nothing is shorter, since it fails to accomplish our projects. There is nothing slower to one who waits, nothing quicker to one who enjoys. It extends to infinity in greatness, it is infinitely divisible in minuteness. All men neglect it, all regret its loss. Nothing is done without it. It buries in oblivion all that is unworthy of being handed down to posterity; and it confers immortality upon all things that are great."

The assembly agreed that Zadig's answer was the right one.

The next question was:

"What is it which we receive without acknowledgment, which we enjoy without knowing how, which we bestow on others when we know nothing about it, and which we lose without perceiving the loss?"

Everybody had his own explanation. Zadig alone guessed that it was life, and explained all the other riddles with the same readiness. Itobad said on each occasion that nothing was easier and that he would have come to the same conclusion with equal facility if he had cared to give himself the trouble. Questions were afterwards propounded on justice, the chief good, and the art of government. Zadig's replies were pronounced the soundest.

"What a pity," it was said, "that one whose judgment is so good should be so bad a knight!"

"Illustrious lords," said Zadig, "I have had the honor of conquering in the lists. It is to me that the white armor belongs. The lord Itobad possessed himself of it while I slept; he thought, apparently, that it would become him better than the green. I am ready to prove upon his person forthwith before you all, in this garb and armed only with my sword, against all this fine white armor which he has stolen from me, that it was I who had the honor of vanquishing brave Otame."

Itobad accepted the challenge with the greatest confidence. He felt no doubt that, armed as he was with helmet, breastplate, and brassarts, he would soon see the last of a champion arrayed in a nightcap and a dressing gown. Zadig drew his sword, and saluted the queen, who gazed on him with the deepest emotion of mingled joy and alarm. Itobad unsheathed his weapon without saluting anyone. He advanced upon Zadig like a man who had nothing to fear, and made ready to cleave his head open. Zadig adroitly parried the stroke, opposing the strongest part of his sword to the weakest part of that of his adversary in such a way that Itobad's blade was broken. Then Zadig, seizing his enemy round the waist, hurled him to the ground, and, holding the point of his sword where the breastplate ended, said:

"Submit to be disarmed, or I take your life."

Itobad, who was always surprised at any disgrace which befell such a man as he, suffered Zadig to do what he pleased, who peaceably relieved him of his splendid helmet, his superb breastplate, his fine brassarts, and his glittering thigh-pieces, put them on himself again, and ran in this array to throw himself at Astarte's knees.

Cador had no difficulty in proving that the armor belonged to Zadig. He was acknowledged king by unanimous consent, and most of all by Astarte, who tasted, after so many adversities, the delight of seeing her lover regarded by all the world as worthy of being her husband. Itobad went away to hear himself called his lordship in his own house. Zadig was made king, and he was happy. What the angel Jesrad had said to him was present to his mind, and he even remembered the grain of sand which became a diamond. The queen and he together adored Providence. Zadig left the beautiful and capricious Missouf to range the world at will. He sent in search of the brigand Arbogad, gave him an honorable post in his army, and promised to promote him to the highest rank if he behaved himself like a true warrior, but threatened to have him hanged, if he followed the trade of a robber.

Setoc was summoned from the heart of Arabia, together with the fair Almona, and set at the head of the commerce of Babylon. Cador was loved and honored, receiving an appointment such as his services deserved; he was the king's friend, and Zadig was then the only monarch upon earth who had one. The little mute was not forgotten. A fine house was given to the fisherman, while Orcan was condemned to pay him a large sum and to give him back his wife; but the fisherman, now grown wise, took the money only.

The fair Semira was inconsolable for having believed

that Zadig would be blind of an eye; and Azora never ceased lamenting that she had wished to cut off his nose. He soothed their sorrow with presents. The Envious man died of rage and shame. The empire enjoyed peace, glory, and abundance; that age was the best which the earth had known, for it was ruled by justice and by love. All men blessed Zadig, and Zadig blessed heaven.

[The manuscript containing Zadig's history ends here. We know that he experienced many other adventures which have been faithfully recorded. Interpreters of oriental tongues are requested, if they should meet with any such records, to make them public.]

LORD CHESTERFIELD'S EARS

LORD CHESTERFIELD'S EARS

A True Story

CHAPTER I

THERE can be no doubt that everything in the world is governed by fatality. My own life is a convincing proof of this doctrine. Lord Chesterfield, with whom I was a great favorite, had promised me that I should have the first living that fell to his gift. An old incumbent of eighty happened to die, and I immediately traveled post to London, to remind the Earl of his promise. I was honored with an immediate interview, and was received with the greatest kindness; I informed his Lordship of the death of the Rector, and of the hope I cherished relative to the disposal of the vacant living, and he replied that truly I looked very ill. I answered, that, thanks to God, my greatest affliction was poverty.

"I am sorry for you," said his Lordship, "and will do all that I can toward your being perfectly cured of your complaint." So doing, he politely dismissed me with a letter of introduction to Mr. Sidrac, who dwelt in the vicinity of Guildhall. I ran as fast as I could to this gentleman's house, not doubting but that he would immediately install me in the wished-for living. I delivered the Earl's letter, and Mr. Sidrac, who had the honor to be my Lord's surgeon, asked me to sit down, and, producing a case of surgical instruments, began to assure me, that if I was afflicted with the stone, he would perform an operation, which he trusted would very soon relieve me.

You must know that his Lordship had understood that I was suffering under this dreadful complaint, and that he generously intended to have me cured at his own expense. The Earl had the misfortune to be as deaf as a post, a fact, with which I, alas, had not been previously acquainted.

During the time which I lost in defending my bladder against the attacks of Mr. Sidrac, who insisted positively upon probing it, whether I would or no, one, out of the fifty candidates who were all on the lookout, came to town, flew to my Lord, begged the vacant living, and obtained it.

I was deeply in love with an interesting girl, a Miss Fidler, who had promised to marry me upon condition of my being made Rector; my fortunate rival not only got the living, but my mistress into the bargain!

Lord Chesterfield, upon being told of his mistake, promised to make me ample amends, but alas, he died two days after.

Mr. Sidrac demonstrated to me that, according to his organic structure, my good patron could not have lived one hour longer; he also clearly proved that the Earl's deafness proceeded entirely from the extreme dryness of the drums of his ears, and kindly offered to harden both my ears by an application of spirits of wine, to such a degree, that I should, in one month only, become as deaf as any peer of the realm.

I discovered Mr. Sidrac to be a man of profound knowledge; he inspired me with a taste for the study of nature, and I could not but be sensible of the valuable acquisition I had made, in acquiring the friendship of a man, who was capable of relieving me, should anything happen to my bladder or its vicinity.—Following his advice, I applied myself closely to the study of nature, to console myself for the loss of the rectory and of my enchanting Miss Fidler.

CHAPTER II

AFTER making many profound observations upon nature (having employed in the research my five senses, my spectacles, and a very large microscope), I said one day to Mr. Sidrac, "Unless I am much deceived, philosophy laughs at us, I cannot discover any trace of what the world calls nature, on the contrary, everything seems to me to be the result of art.—By art the planets are made to revolve round the sun, while the sun revolves on his own axis. I am convinced that some genius, as clear as any member of the royal academy, has arranged things in such a manner, that the square of the revolutions of the planets is always in proportion to the cubic root from their distance to their center, and one had need be a magician to find out how this is accomplished.

"The tides of the sea are the result of art no less profound, and no less difficult to explain.

"All animals, vegetables and minerals are arranged with due regard to weight and measure, number and motion. All is performed by springs, levers, pullies, hydraulic machines, and chemical combinations, from the insignificant flea to the being called man, from the grass of the field to the far spreading oak, from a grain of sand to a cloud in the firmament of heaven—assuredly, everything is governed by art, and the word NATURE is but a chimera."

"You are right," replied Sidrac, "but you have not discovered what is called the root of the matter. What astonishes me, and what I most admire in this wonderful system, is that by means of incomprehensible art, two machines can be so constituted as to be made to produce a third."

"Alas!" said I, "I understand but too well your drift, and am only sorry that it was fixed from all eternity, that, in producing a third being, Miss Fidler should employ another machine than myself."

"What you say," answered Mr. Sidrac, "has been said many years ago, and so much the better, for the probability is greater that your remark is true; it is indeed very droll that two beings should have the power of producing a third, but this assertion is not correct with regard to all things. Two flowers cannot by a loving embrace produce a third, neither can two metals or two pebbles, and yet metals and pebbles are things that man with all his boasted ingenuity and power of invention would never be able to form. The greatest wonder is, that a man and a woman should always form a child and never a monster, and that two nightingales should produce a third nightingale, and never a sparrow. We ought to pass the one half of our lives in imitating these prodigies, and the other half in blessing him who originally planned and executed these wondrous mysteries. There are a thousand curious secrets in generation. The great Newton says, nature is everywhere alike. This famous remark of his is totally false with regard to love, or rather concupiscence. Neither birds, beasts nor fishes perform the rites of Venus in the same manner that we do, the whole is one infinite variety. The creating of active and thinking beings delights one. The nature of vegetables is also well worth our attention; I am always astonished when I reflect that a grain of wheat cast into the earth will produce in a short time above a handful of the same wheat."

"Stop," said I foolishly, "you forget that wheat must die before it can spring up again, at least so they say at college."

My friend Sidrac, laughing heartily at this interruption, replied,

"That assertion went down very well a few years ago, when it was first published by a fellow called Paul; but in our more enlightened age, the meanest day laborer knows that the thing is altogether too ridiculous even for argument." "My dear friend," said I, "excuse the absurdity of my remark, I have hitherto been a Theologian, and one cannot divest one's self in a moment of every silly opinion."

CHAPTER III

SOME time after this conversation between the disconsolate person whom we shall call Goodman and that clever anatomist, Mr. Sidrac, the latter, one fine morning, observed his friend in St. James's Park standing in an attitude of deep thought, and apparently more embarrassed than a mathematician who has just discovered a mistake in one of his most complicated calculations.

"What's the matter?" said the surgeon, "is there anything amiss with your bladder or colon?"

"No," replied Goodman, "but I confess I am a little troubled with bile; I have just seen the proud and haughty bishop of N—— roll past in an elegant carriage, while I am obliged to walk on foot, and I acknowledge that the thoughts suggested to me by this are not of the most agreeable nature. I was just calculating that if I wished to obtain a bishopric, the chances are at least ten thousand to one against my success. I am left without a patron in the world since the death of Lord Chesterfield, who had the misfortune to be so deaf. Now supposing there to be only ten thousand clergymen in England, and granting these ten thousand have each two patrons, the odds against my obtaining a bishopric are twenty thousand to one; a reflection quite sufficient to give any man the blue devils. I remember, it was once proposed to me, to go out as cabin-boy to the East Indies; I was told that I should make my fortune. But I did not think I should make a good admiral, whenever I should arrive at the distinction; and so, after turning my attention to every profession under the sun, I am fixed for life as a poor clergyman, good for nothing."

"Then be a clergyman no longer!" cried Sidrac, "and turn philosopher; what is your income?"

"Only thirty guineas a year, to be sure. At the death of my mother, it will be increased to fifty."

"Well, my dear Goodman, that sum is quite sufficient to support you in comfort, thirty guineas are six hundred and thirty shillings, almost two shillings a day; with this fixed income, a man need do nothing to increase it, but is at perfect liberty to say all he thinks of the East India Company, the House of Commons, the king and all the royal family, of man generally and individually, and lastly, of God and his attributes; and the liberty we enjoy of expressing our thoughts upon these most interesting topics, is certainly very agreeable and amusing.

"Come and dine at my table every day, that will save you some little money. We will afterwards amuse ourselves with conversation, and your thinking faculty will have the pleasure of communicating with mine by means of speech, which is certainly a very wonderful thing, though its advantages are not duly appreciated by the greater part of mankind."

CHAPTER IV

DIALOGUE BETWEEN GOODMAN AND SIDRAC UPON THE SOUL AND SEVERAL OTHER EQUALLY TRIFLING TOPICS

GOODMAN. But my dear Sidrac, why do you always say *my thinking faculty* and not *my soul?* If you used the latter term I should understand much better what you meant.

SIDRAC. And for my part, I freely confess, I should not understand what I meant myself. I *feel,* I *know,* that God has endowed me with the faculties of thinking and speaking, but I can neither *feel* nor *know* that God has given me a thing called a soul.

GOODMAN. Truly, upon reflection, I perceive that I know as little about the matter as you do, though I own that I have, all my life, been bold enough to believe that I knew. I have often remarked that the Eastern nations apply to the soul, the same word they use to express life. After their example, the Latins understood the word *anima* to signify the life of the animal. The Greeks called the breath the soul. The Romans translated the word breath by *spiritus,* and thence it is that the word spirit or soul is found in every modern nation. As it happens that no one has ever seen this spirit or breath, our imagination has converted it into a being, which it is impossible to see or touch. The learned tell us that the soul inhabits the body without having any place in it, that it has the power of setting our different organs in motion without being able to reach and touch them, indeed, what is there, that has not been said upon the subject? The great Locke was perfectly sensible into what a chaos these absurdities had plunged the human understanding. He did not compose a single chapter on the soul, in writing the only reasonable book upon metaphysics that has yet appeared in the world; and, if by chance he now and then makes use of the word, he only introduces it to stand for intellect or mind.

In fact, every human being, in spite of Bishop Berkeley, is sensible that he has a mind; that this mind or intellect is capable of receiving ideas, of collecting and dispersing them; but no one can feel that there is another being within him which gives him motion, feeling and thought: it is, in the abstract, ridiculous to use words we do not understand and to admit the existence of beings of whom we cannot arrive at the slightest knowledge.

SIDRAC. We are then agreed upon a subject which for so many centuries has been matter of dispute.

GOODMAN. And I must observe that I am surprised that we should so soon be agreed upon it.

SIDRAC. Oh, that is not so astonishing. We really wish to know what is truth. If we were among the academies, we should argue like the characters in Rabelais. If we had lived in those ages of darkness, the clouds of which so long enveloped Great Britain, one of us would very likely have burned the other. We are so fortunate as to be born in an age comparatively reasonable; we easily discover what appears to us to be truth, and we are not afraid to proclaim it.

GOODMAN. You are right, but I fear, that, after all, the truth we have discovered is not worth much. In the mathematics indeed, we have done wonders, from the most simple causes we have produced effects that would have astonished Apollonius or Archimedes, and have made those great men become our scholars; but what have we proved in metaphysics? Absolutely nothing but our own ignorance.

SIDRAC. And do you call that nothing? You grant the Supreme Being has given you the faculties of feeling and thinking, in the same manner that he has given your feet the faculty of walking, your hands power to do a thousand different things, your stomach the capability of digesting food, and your heart the power of throwing blood by means of the arteries into all parts of your body. Everything we enjoy is derived from God, and yet we are totally ignorant of the means by which He governs and conducts the universe: For mine own part, as Shakespeare says, I thank Him for having taught me that of the principles of things, I know absolutely nothing. It has always been a question, in what manner the soul acted upon the body; before attempting to answer this question, I must be convinced that I have a soul. Either God has given us this wonderful spark of intellect, or He has gifted us with some principle that answers equally well. In whatever manner He may have acted, we are still the creatures of His divine will and goodness—and that is all I know about the matter.

GOODMAN. But, if you do not know, tell me at least what you are inclined to think upon the subject—you have opened skulls, and have dissected many human fœtuses—have you ever, in these dissections, discovered any appearance of a soul?

SIDRAC. Not the least, and I have never been able to understand how an immortal and spiritual essence could dwell for nine months together, wrapped up in a stinking membrane, between the urine and the excrements. It appears to me difficult to conceive that this pretended soul existed before the foundation of the body; for in what could she have been employed during the many ages previous to her mysterious union with flesh? Again, how can we imagine a spiritual principle waiting patiently in idleness during a whole eternity, in order to animate a mass of matter for a space of time which compared with eternity is less than a moment.

What would have become of this unknown being, if the fœtus, for whose animation it was intended, had happened to die in the womb! It appears still more ridiculous to imagine that God creates a soul every time a man has connection with a woman; it seems to me little less than blasphemous to suppose that God watches for the consummation of adultery or incest in order to reward these crimes by creating souls for the fruits of them.

It is worse still, when I am told that God forms immortal souls out of nothing, and then cruelly dooms them to an eternity of flames and torments.

What? Burn a spirit, in which there can be nothing capable of burning; how can He burn the sound of a voice, or the wind that blows? Though both the sound and wind were material during the short time of their existence; but a pure spirit—a thought—a doubt—I am lost in the labyrinth; on whichsoever side I turn, I find nothing but obscurity and absurdity, impossibility and contradiction. But I am quite at ease when I say to myself God is master of all. He who can cause the stars to hold each its particular course through the broad expanse of the firmament can very easily give us sentiments and ideas, without our requiring this little pitiful atom, called the soul. It is certain that God has endowed all animals, in a greater or lesser degree, with thought, memory and judgment; He has given them life; it is demonstrated that they have feeling, since they possess all the organs of feeling; if then they have all this without a soul, why is it improbable that we have no souls? And why do mankind flatter themselves that they alone are gifted with a spiritual and immortal principle?

GOODMAN. Perhaps this idea arises from their inordinate vanity. I am persuaded that if the peacock could speak, he would boast of his soul, and would affirm that it inhabited his magnificent tail. I am very much inclined to believe with you, that God has created us thinking creatures, with the faculties of eating, drinking, feeling etc., without telling us one word about the matter. We are as ignorant as the peacock I just mentioned, and he who has said that we live and die without knowing how, why, or wherefore, has spoken nothing but the truth.

SIDRAC. A celebrated author, whose name I forget, calls us nothing more than the puppets of Providence, and this seems to me to be a very good definition; an infinity of movements are necessary to our existence, but we did not ourselves invent and produce motion; there is a Being, who has created light, caused it to move from the sun to our eyes, and to arrive upon the earth in about seven minutes. It is only by means of motion that my five senses are put in action, and it is only by means of my senses that I have ideas, hence it follows that my ideas are derived from the great Author of motion, and when He informs me in what manner He communicates these ideas to me, I will most sincerely tell Him, I am very much obliged to Him.

GOODMAN. And so will I; as it is, I constantly thank

Him for having permitted me, as Epictetus says, to contemplate for a period of some years this beautiful and glorious world. It is true that He could have made me happier, by putting me in possession of Miss Fidler and a good Rectory; but still, such as I am, with my income of six hundred and thirty-six shillings a year, I consider myself as under a great obligation to God's parental kindness and care.

SIDRAC. You say that it is in the power of God to give you a good living, and to make you still happier than you at present are. There are many persons who would not scruple flatly to contradict this proposition of yours. Do you forget that you yourself sometimes complain of fatality? A man, and particularly a priest, ought never to contradict one day an assertion he has perhaps made the day before. Do you not see that if you had had the living and the wife you desired, that it would be you that would have helped Miss Fidler to make a child, and not your rival? This child of whom she would have been brought to bed might perhaps have taken a liking to the sea; from a cabin-boy, he might very naturally have become an admiral, and in that capacity have gained a victory at the mouth of the Ganges, which might have dethroned the Great Mogul.—This event would have affected the whole constitution of the Universe. Indeed, it would have been necessary to create quite a different world in order that your rival should not have your living nor your mistress, and that your income should not exceed six hundred and thirty shillings a year, at least, until the death of your mother. All is a succession of links, and God is wiser than to break the eternal chain of events, even for the sake of my dear friend Goodman.

GOODMAN. I certainly did not foresee this argument,

when I was speaking of fatality; but to come at once to the point, if it be so, God is as much a slave as myself!

SIDRAC. He is the slave of His will, of His wisdom, and of the laws which He has himself instituted; and it is impossible that He can infringe upon any of them because it is impossible that He can become either weak or inconsistent.

GOODMAN. But my friend, what you say would tend to make us irreligious, for if God cannot change any of the affairs of the world what is the use of teasing Him with prayers, or of singing hymns to His praise?

SIDRAC. Well, who bids you worship or pray to God? Truly, He cares a vast deal about either your prayers or praises. We praise a man because we think him vain; we entreat of him when we think him weak, and likely to change his purpose on account of our petitions.—Let us do our duty to God by being just and true to each other; in that consists our real prayers and our most heartfelt praises.

GOODMAN. My friend, we have gone over a great deal of ground in this short conversation; for without reckoning Miss Fidler, we have examined whether we have a soul, if there be a God, or any other state of being beyond the grave, and several other interesting questions which I should have perhaps never considered, if I had been a Rector. As I have at present nothing to occupy my time, I really must examine a little into these things, the knowledge of which is necessary and so sublime.

SIDRAC. Very well; tomorrow Doctor Grout is coming to dine with me. He is a very learned man, who has been all round the world in company with Banks and Solander; he ought, therefore, to know much more concerning God and the soul than we, who have always been ants of the same dunghill. Besides, Doctor Grout, when a young man, made the tour of Europe, and was the intimate friend of the Rev. Father Malagrida, whom he had the pleasure to see burned at Lisbon for repeating what the Holy Virgin had revealed to him, respecting the manner in which she amused herself while in the womb of her mother Saint Anne; you will allow that a man who has seen as much as Doctor Grout ought to be one of the greatest metaphysicians in the world. So adieu, my dear Goodman, until tomorrow at dinner time.

GOODMAN. And the next day at dinner time too, my friend, for I fear I shall not be able to get much instruction during one dinner alone.

CHAPTER V

THE next day, our three philosophers dined together and, when they had freely circulated the bottle, began, as men generally do after a good dinner, to amuse themselves by discoursing upon the follies that disgrace, and the pestilences that destroy so large a proportion of our unfortunate species. This diversity of abominations could not fail of affording them infinite entertainment; indeed, conversation of this kind is a pleasure that cannot be enjoyed by plebeians who have never traveled out of the sound of the church bell near which they were brought into being, and who believe that all the rest of the world is precisely constituted like, Change Alley, or Whitechapel.

"I observe," said Doctor Grout, "that notwithstanding

the immense variety spread over the Globe, all the men I ever saw, whether black or brown, red or white, have alike two legs, two eyes, and a head on their shoulders, though St. Augustine, in his 27th Sermon, assures us that he has seen men born with only one eye, and others with only one leg, besides Anthropophagi, in great abundance.

"I have been often asked whether all the inhabitants of that large country called New Zealand, who are to this day the most barbarous of the barbarous, were baptized in the Catholic Faith. I have answered, I knew nothing about it, but that the thing might nevertheless be; that the Jews who were still greater barbarians than the New Zealanders, had two baptisms instead of one. I allude to their baptism of justice, and their baptism of dwelling."

"I am acquainted with them both," said Goodman, "and have often disputed the point with those who believe that the Christians were the inventors of baptism. No, Gentlemen, we have invented nothing, we have only pillaged from the religious ceremonies of other sects. But tell me, I beseech you, out of the eighty or ninety different systems of religion which you must have seen followed in some part or other of the world, which do you consider the most agreeable, that of the New Zealanders or that of the Hottentots?"

Dr. Grout replied: "None of them are at all comparable with that of the Island of Otaheite. I have traveled over the whole surface of the habitable globe, but have never seen anything that could equal Otaheite and its very religious queen, whom God preserve. It is only in Otaheite that nature really dwells; everywhere else the human animal wears a mask.

"In matters of religion, particularly, a gang of rogues,

under the name of priests, deceive the honest and simple-minded. They promise us riches and pleasures in another world, in return for those with which we endow them in this. Not so in Otaheite. This island is much more civilized than New Zealand or the country of the Caffres, and in some respects is far preferable to either France or England. Nature has favored it with a more fertile soil; she has given it the bread-fruit tree, a present equally useful and beneficent, and which is unknown except to the islands in the South Sea; besides, Otaheite possesses plenty of fowls, greens and fruits, so that there is no occasion for man to eat man; there is no want of food, but there is a want more natural and more congenial, which the religion of Otaheite ordains to be gratified in public. Of all the religious ceremonies I ever beheld, this is doubtless the most imposing and the most interesting. I witnessed it in common with the rest of the gentlemen on board our ship, and can therefore certify the truth of this singular ceremony, which has been slightly mentioned by Dr. Hawkesworth in his celebrated work upon the discoveries made by our enterprising countrymen in the South Sea.

"In company with Captain Cook, Messieurs Banks, Solander, and many others, I saw what I am now going to relate to you:—

"The Princess of Oberia, Queen of the Island of Otaheite."

But just as the Doctor commenced his singular narrative, coffee was brought in, and when it had been handed round, the speaker resumed his discourse thus:—

CHAPTER VI

"THE Princess Obeira, I was saying, after having with a degree of politeness worthy of the Queen of England, loaded us with valuable presents, was curious one morning to assist in celebrating the ceremonies of our religion, after the English Fashion.

"We accordingly went through the church service with all due pomp and splendor, and after dinner the queen invited us in return to witness the manner in which her subjects worshiped the Deity of Otaheite. We found about a thousand persons of both sexes ranged in a respectable manner round their queen, and forming an extensive circle.

"A young girl, extremely handsome, in a voluptuous *déshabille,* lay upon a kind of scaffold which served instead of an altar; then the queen commanded a well-made fellow, about twenty years of age, to go up and sacrifice. He immediately pronounced a kind of prayer, and most devoutly ascended the steps of the altar. Both he and the girl were then disencumbered of their clothes, and the queen, with a majestic air, showed the young and tender victim, how to proceed in order to consummate the sacrifice. All the Otaheitans round were so serious and silent that none of our sailors dared disturb the ceremony by even a profane laugh. I have now told you what I saw, and what was also seen by almost the whole ship's company; it is for you to draw what inference you please from the performance of this singular and sacred rite."

"This holy festival does not in the least astonish me," said Goodman. "I am persuaded that it is the first fête men ever thought of celebrating, and I do not see why we should not adore God prior to forming an image, as the Bible says, after his likeness, as well as say grace before we eat our dinner.

"Surely, to labor in the formation of a reasoning and thinking creature, is the most noble and pious action that can possibly be performed by man. Thus thought the first Indians who worshiped the lingam, as a symbol of generation; the ancient Egyptians who carried the phallus in solemn procession; the Greeks who erected temples in honor of Priapus, and lastly the Jews, if I may be permitted to mention a people who always purloined their religious ceremonies from surrounding nations, who have it written in one of their books that they also worshiped Priapus, and that the queen-mother of the Jewish king Asa was his grand priestess.

"However that may be, it is very true that no nation has ever been able to establish a theological system by means of libertinism alone; excess will after a time naturally enter into such a religion, but the beginning of it, as in Otaheite, is always pure and innocent. Our first 'agapes,' or love-feasts, during which the youth of both sexes modestly kissed each other's lips, did not for many ages degenerate into rendezvous for intrigue and infamy. Would to God that I might be permitted to offer sacrifice with Miss Fidler, in all due honor and respect, before the good and pious queen Obeira: the day on which that event took place, would certainly be the happiest day of my life."

Sidrac, who had until now kept silence because our friends Grout and Goodman engrossed all the conversation to themselves, at length spoke, and said:—

"I cannot sufficiently admire what I have just heard. Queen Obeira certainly appears to me to have been the greatest and wisest lady in the world; but, amid so much glory and happiness, there is one circumstance, the very thought of which makes me shudder, and which has been slightly touched upon by your friend Goodman. Is it true, Dr. Grout, that Captain Wallis, who visited the favored island of Otaheite long before you, brought away with him that most horrible scourge under which the human race suffers, I mean the venereal disease?" "Alas! for mankind," replied Grout. "It is impossible to say. The French accuse us of being the first propagators in Europe of this infernal disease, and we accuse the French of the same thing. Monsieur Bougainville says the English infected Queen Oberia, and Captain Cook affirms that the lady in question was infected by Monsieur Bougainville himself. However the truth of this may be, the venereal disease may be said to resemble the fine arts in respect of its being unknown who was the original inventor; but by degrees it has overrun all the four quarters of the world."

"I have now been a surgeon for many years," said Sidrac, "and I freely confess that it is to this disease I owe the greater part of the money I have acquired in the profession; but I assure you, I do not the less abhor the cursed pestilence. Mrs. Sidrac unfortunately infected me on our wedding night, and as she is excessively delicate in her feelings of honor, she put an advertisement in all the public papers, saying upon affidavit, that it was true she was suffering under the venereal disease, but that she had imbibed it in her mother's womb, and that it had been long hereditary in the family. What could Dame Nature have been thinking of, when she infused this dreadful poison into the very sources of life? It has been said, and I now repeat it, that it is the most abominable and detestable of all possible contradictions. What? Man we are told is made in the image of God, and it is in the spermatic vessels of this image that are fixed infection, misery, and death. What becomes of Lord Rochester's fine saying, that 'love alone would cause God to be adored; amid even a nation of Atheists'."

"Then," said our simple friend, Goodman, "Alas! I ought perhaps to thank God for not permitting me to marry my dear and ever-to-be-lamented Miss Fidler, for who knows what might not have happened? One can never be certain of anything in this world. However, come what may, remember, my dear Sidrac, you have promised your assistance, in case anything should incommode me in the vicinity of my bladder."

"I am always very much at your service," replied Sidrac, "but it is time enough to think of these things when they happen to us."

In saying what he did upon the subject, Goodman seemed partly to foresee his destiny.

CHAPTER VII

THE next day our three philosophers were discussing the grand and important question, what is the chief ruling principle that influences the actions of men? Goodman, who had not yet forgotten the loss of his rectory and his amiable Miss Fidler, said that the principle of all, the *primum mobile*, was a compound of love and ambition. Grout, who had traveled through more countries, and had consequently a larger view of human nature, pronounced it to be money. And the great anatomist, Sidrac, with an air of the profoundest gravity, gave it as his opinion, that the principle of all

was the stool. His friends were thunderstruck at so curious an assertion, and Sidrac went on to prove his singular
proposition.

"I have observed," said he, "throughout life, that all
the affairs of this world depend on the opinion and will
of some principal personage, whether King, Queen, or
Minister. Now this opinion and this will are the immediate effects of the manner in which the animal spirits
pass through the brain and marrow. These animal spirits
depend on the formation of the chyle, the chyle is
formed in the network of the mesentery.—The mesentery (attend to what I say) is attached to the intestines,
by a number of very fine threads; the intestines (if
I may be allowed to say so) are filled with stercoraceous
matter. Now, notwithstanding the three coats with
which each intestine is covered, it is perforated like a
sieve, for everything is open to nature, and there is no
grain of sand, however diminutive it may seem, that
has not hundreds of pores in it. It is ascertained that a
number of needles might be passed through a cannon
ball, if the needles could be fabricated of a texture sufficiently delicate and fine. If a man then be costive,
what a dreadful state his inside must fall into!—The
finer and purer essences escape from the excrements
and mingle with the chyle, passing thence with the blood
through the whole body—through the heart of the dash-
ing exquisite, as well as through the brain (if she have
any brain) of the gay and wanton coquette. If this happen to man, naturally of a warm and passionate temperament, his anger becomes perfect ferocity, the whites of
his eyes turn almost black, his lips are parched and burned up, his very look seems to threaten you; beware how
you approach him. If he be a minister of state, do not
present your petition while he is in this unfortunate sit-

uation; he regards all kinds of papers as if he wished to make use of them in that abominable manner after which the work of authors are too frequently treated. Give his valet half a crown, and get him to inform you whether his master has had a stool this morning.

"What I mention is of much greater importance than at first sight it appears to be. Costiveness has too often been the original cause of the most sanguinary and dreadful scenes. My grandfather, who lived to the age of a hundred, had the honor of being apothecary to the renowned Oliver Cromwell. He has often told me that when that usurper signed the warrant for the execution of Charles the First, he had not sacrificed to the Goddess Cloacina for above a week.

"Everybody knows that the Duke de Guise was warned not to affront Henry the Third of France during a northeast wind; for while the wind blew from that quarter, this monarch could very rarely relieve himself from the unpleasant load occasioned by extreme costiveness, accordingly the fumes mounted to his brain, and for a time he was capable of every act of violence. The Duke de Guise put no faith in the advice that was given him, and what was the consequence? Both the Duke and his brother were basely assassinated. Take another case: Henry's predecessor, Charles the Ninth, was the most costive man in the kingdom; the passage of his colon and rectum were so closely blocked up that blood at last burst out at the pores of his body. It is but too well known that his costive and unhappy temperament was one of the principal causes of the massacre of St. Bartholomew. On the contrary, those persons who are favored by a regular and daily discharge of that matter so strongly recommended by the Jewish God to the most holy prophet Ezekiel as a cheap substitute for butter, those persons, I say, who can evacuate as easily as spit, are mild, affable, and compassionate; a *no* from their mouths comes with more grace, than a *yes* ' from the mouth of one who has not the same happy capacity for going to stool.

"The water-closet has so much ascendancy over us, that an excessive purge often renders a man cowardly while suffering under its effects; a fit of dysentery acts in the same way. Order a man, laboring under an attack of cholera morbus, to attack a battery with the point of the bayonet, he will be altogether incapable of anything like a deed of heroism; for this reason, I cannot believe history, when it tells us that our valiant army were suffering severely from dysentery when they fought and won the battle of Agincourt, and that our soldiers actually charged the French with their breeches hanging down about their heels. It may be true that some few individuals were indisposed from having eaten too many plums, and hence this ridiculous report has arisen; in the same way the French have handed down to posterity an absurd tradition that our great King Edward the First was once about to hang up six of the principal citizens of Calais for having bravely defended that city against his attacks, and that his Queen with much difficulty procured their pardon; these romance writers do not know that in those barbarous ages it was a custom upon the surrender of any fortified place, for some of the citizens to present themselves before the conqueror with ropes round their necks, a mere form, to show that their lives were entirely at his mercy. It seems to me ridiculous to suppose that the generous Edward had any idea of twisting the necks of these citizens, whom on the contrary he loaded with riches and honors.

"I am quite tired of reading all the follies that are

palmed upon us, under the name of history. I hardly know whether to believe in the truth of the battle of Pharsalia. Certainly I do not give credit to above one half of the wonderful victories upon record; some of them are as preposterous as the story of Gideon, gaining a battle with his three hundred pitchers, or the mighty Samson, defeating the Philistines, and killing them by hundreds, with the jawbone of an ass. I have almost given up reading altogether, and am much more interested in attempting to plan a regimen which will keep my bowels properly open and procure me easy digestion followed by a refreshing sleep. Think on what I have said, drink brandy in the winter, and nothing stronger than wine in the summer; eat of that which best pleases your appetite and best agrees with your stomach, digest your food, sleep, take your pleasure, and laugh at the devil and all his works."

CHAPTER VIII

JUST as Mr. Sidrac had concluded these wise observations, comes his servant post-haste, to say that the steward of the late Lord Chesterfield was at the door in his cabriolet, and wished to speak to Mr. Goodman. Our friend the parson runs to meet the great man, who, to his astonishment, says,

"You have doubtless heard, my good Sir, of what happened to Mr. Sidrac and his interesting wife, on their wedding night."

"Yes, Sir, my friend has just communicated to me the particulars of that unfortunate event."

"Well," said the steward, "the very same thing happened to Miss Fidler and her husband the rector: the next day they quarreled about it, and the day after they separated. The rector must of course give up the living; to come at once to the point, I have long loved the charming Fidler, I well know that she loves you, though for all that I am not disagreeable to her. I care nothing for her being poxed, a surgeon can soon put all that to rights! I am in love, and am naturally of an intrepid, as well as an amorous disposition.

"Give up your claim to Miss Fidler, and I will in exchange immediately put you in possession of the living which is worth at least a hundred and fifty guineas a year. I give you ten minutes to consider my proposal."

"Sir," replied Goodman, "I will not detain you an instant. Only allow me to say three words to my dear friends, Grout and Sidrac."

He runs to these gentlemen. "I am convinced," said he, "that digestion does not alone decide the affairs of this world, but that love, ambition, and money, have also a great deal to do with them."

He then states the case and asks his friends for their opinion; they decided that for one hundred fifty guineas he might have all the girls in the parish, and Miss Fidler into the bargain. Goodman was sensible of the truth of this, he embraced the proposal of the amorous steward, he enjoyed the living, and Miss Fidler too in private, and liked her all the better for not being his wife. He is become one of the most zealous priests in England, a perfect Boanerges, and is more convinced than ever that everything in this best of all possible worlds is governed by Fatalism.

THE WHITE BULL

THE WHITE BULL

A Satirical Romance

CHAPTER I

HOW THE PRINCESS AMASIDIA MEETS A BULL

THE princess Amasidia, daughter of Amasis, King of Tanis in Egypt, took a walk upon the highway of Peluaium with the ladies of her train. She was sunk in deep melancholy. Tears gushed from her beautiful eyes. The cause of her grief was known, as well as the fears she entertained lest that grief should displease the king, her father. The old man, Mambres, ancient magician and eunuch of the Pharoahs, was beside her, and seldom left her. He had been present at her birth. He had educated her, and taught her all that a fair princess was allowed to know of the sciences of Egypt. The mind of Amasidia equaled her beauty. Her sensibility and tenderness rivaled the charms of her body; and it was this sensibility which cost her so many tears.

The princess was twenty-four years old; the magician, Mambres, about thirteen hundred. It was he, as every one knows, who had that famous dispute with Moses, in which the victory was so long doubtful between these two profound philosophers. If Mambres yielded, it was owing to the visible protection of the celestial powers, who favored his rival. It required gods to overcome Mambres!

Amasis made him superintendent of his daughter's

159

household, and he fulfilled this office with his usual prudence. His compassion was excited by the sighs of the beautiful Amasidia.

"O, my lover!" said she to herself, "my young, my dear lover! O, greatest of conquerors, most accomplished, most beautiful of men! Almost seven years have passed since thou disappeared from the world. What God hath snatched thee from thy tender Amasidia? Thou art not dead. The wise Egyptian prophets confess this. But thou art dead to me. I am alone in the world. To me it is a desert. By what extraordinary prodigy hast thou abandoned thy throne and thy mistress? Thy throne, which was the first in the world—however, that is a matter of small consequence; but to abandon me, who adore thee! O, my dear Ne——"

She was going on.

"Tremble to pronounce that fatal name," said Mambres, the ancient eunuch and magician of the Pharoahs. "You would perhaps be heard by some of the ladies of your court. They are all very much devoted to you, and all fair ladies certainly make it a merit to serve the noble passions of fair princesses. But there may be one among them indiscreet, and even treacherous. You know that your father, although he loves you, has sworn to put you to death, should you pronounce the terrible name always ready to escape your lips. This law is severe; but you have not been educated in Egyptian wisdom to be ignorant of the government of the tongue. Remember that Hippocrates, one of our greatest gods, has always his finger upon his mouth."

The beautiful Amasidia wept, and was silent.

As she pensively advanced toward the banks of the Nile she perceived at a distance, under a thicket watered by the river, an old woman in a tattered gray garment, seated on a hillock. This old woman had beside her a she-ass, a dog, and a he-goat. Opposite to her was a serpent, which was not like the common serpents; for its eyes were mild, its physiognomy noble and engaging, while its skin shone with the liveliest and brightest colors. A huge fish, half immersed in the river, was not the least astonishing figure in the group; and on a neighboring tree were perched a raven and a pigeon. All these creatures seemed to carry on a very animated conversation.

"Alas," said the princess in a low tone, "these animals undoubtedly speak of their loves, and it is not even allowed me to so much as mention the name of mine."

The old woman held in her hand a slender steel chain a hundred fathoms long, to which was fastened a bull who fed in the meadow. This bull was white, perfectly well-made, plump, and at the same time agile, which is a thing seldom to be found. He was indeed the most beautiful specimen that was ever seen of his kind. Neither the bull of Pasiphæ, nor that in whose shape Jupiter appeared when he carried off Europa, could be compared to this noble animal. The charming young heifer into which Isis was changed, would have scarce been worthy of his company.

As soon as the bull saw the princess he ran toward her with the swiftness of a young Arabian horse who pricks up his ears and flies over the plains and rivers of the ancient Saana to approach the lovely consort whose image reigns in his heart. The old woman used her utmost efforts to restrain the bull. The serpent wanted to terrify him by its hissing. The dog followed him and bit his beautiful limbs. The she-ass crossed his path and kicked him to make him return. The great fish remounted the Nile and, darting out of the water, threatened to devour him. The he-goat remained immovable, apparently struck with fear. The raven fluttered round his head as if it wanted to tear out his eyes. The pigeon alone accompanied him from curiosity, and applauded him by a sweet murmur.

So extraordinary a sight threw Mambres into serious reflections. In the meanwhile, the white bull, dragging after him his chain and the old woman, had already reached the princess, who was struck with astonishment and fear. He threw himself at her feet. He kissed them. He shed tears. He looked upon her with eyes in which there was a strange mixture of grief and joy. He dared not low, lest he should terrify the beautiful Amasidia. He could not speak. A weak use of the voice, granted by Heaven to certain animals, was denied him; but all his actions were eloquent. The princess was delighted with him. She perceived that a trifling amusement could suspend for some moments even the most poignant grief.

"Here," said she, "is a most amiable animal. I should like very much to have him in my stable."

At these words the bull bent himself on his knees and kissed the ground.

"He understands me," cried the princess. "He shows me that he wants to be mine. Ah, heavenly magician! Ah, divine eunuch! Give me this consolation. Purchase this beautiful bovine. Settle the price with the old woman, to whom he no doubt belongs. This animal must be mine. Do not refuse me this innocent comfort."

All the ladies joined their requests to the entreaties of the princess. Mambres yielded to them, and immediately went to speak to the old woman.

CHAPTER II

HOW THE WISE MAMBRES, FORMERLY MAGICIAN OF PHAROAH, KNEW AGAIN THE OLD WOMAN, AND WAS KNOWN BY HER

"MADAM," said Mambres to her, "you know that ladies, and particularly princesses, have need of amusement. The daughter of the king is distractedly fond of your bull. I beg that you will sell him to us. You shall be paid in ready money."

"Sir," answered the old woman, "this precious animal does not belong to me. I am charged, together with all the beasts which you see, to keep him with care, to watch all his motions, and to give an exact account of them. God forbid that I should ever have any inclination to sell this invaluable animal."

Mambres, upon this discourse, began to have a confused remembrance of something which he could not yet properly distinguish. He eyed the old woman in the gray cloak with greater attention.

"Respectable lady," said he to her, "I either mistake, or I have seen you formerly."

"I make no mistake, sir," replied the old woman. "I have seen you seven hundred years ago, in a journey which I made from Syria into Egypt some months after the destruction of Troy, when Hiram the Second reigned at Tyre, and Nephel Keres in ancient Egypt."

"Ah, Madam," cried the old man, "you are the remarkable witch of Endor."

"And you, sir," said the sorceress, embracing him, "are the great Mambres of Egypt."

"O, unforeseen meeting! Memorable day! Eternal decrees!" said Mambres. "It certainly is not without permission of the universal providence that we meet again in this meadow upon the banks of the Nile near the noble city of Tanis. What, is it indeed you," continued Mambres, "who are so famous upon the banks of your little Jordan, the first person in the world for raising apparitions?"

"What, is it you, sir," replied Miss Endor, "who are so famous for changing rods into serpents, the day into darkness, and rivers into blood?"

"Yes, madam, but my great age has in part deprived me of my knowledge and power. I am ignorant from whence you have this beautiful bull, and who these animals are that, together with you, watch round him."

The old woman, recollecting herself, raised her eyes to heaven, and then replied:

"My dear Mambres. We are of the same profession, but it is expressly forbidden me to tell you who this bull is. I can satisfy you with regard to the other animals. You will easily know them by the marks which characterize them. The serpent is that which persuaded Eve to eat an apple, and to make her husband partake of it. The ass, that which spoke to your contemporary, Balaam, in a remarkable discourse. The fish, which always carries its head above water, is that which swallowed Jonah a few years ago. The dog is he who followed Raphael and the young Tobit in their journey to Ragusa in Media, in the time of the great Salamanzar. This goat is he who expiates all the sins of your nation. The raven and the pigeon, those which were in the ark of Noah. Great event! Universal catastrophe! Of which almost all the world is still ignorant! You are now informed. But of the bull you can know nothing."

Mambres, having listened with respect, said:

"The Eternal, O illustrious witch! reveals and conceals what he thinks proper. All these animals who, together with you, are entrusted with the custody of the white bull, are only known to your generous and agreeable nation, which is itself unknown to almost all the world. The miracles which you and yours, I and mine, have performed, shall one day be a great subject of doubt and scandal to inquisitive philosophers. But happily these miracles shall find belief with the devout sages, who shall prove submissive to the enlightened in one corner of the world; and this is all that is necessary."

As he spoke these words, the princess pulled him by the sleeves, and said to him:

"Mambres, will you not buy my bull?"

The magician, plunged into a deep reverie, made no reply, and Amasidia poured forth her tears.

She then addressed herself to the old woman.

"My good woman," said she, "I conjure you, by all you hold most dear in the world, by your father, by your mother, by your nurse, who are certainly still alive, to sell me not only your bull, but likewise your pigeon, which seems very much attached to him.

"As for the other animals, I do not want them; but I shall catch the vapors if you do not sell me this charming bull, who will be all the happiness of my life."

The old woman respectfully kissed the fringe of her gauze robe, and replied:

"Princess, my bull is not to be sold. Your illustrious magician is acquainted with this. All that I can do for your service is to permit him to feed every day near your palace. You may caress him, give him biscuits, and make him dance about at your pleasure; but he must always be under the eyes of all these animals who accompany me, and who are charged with the keeping of him.

If he does not endeavor to escape from them, they will prove peaceable; but if he attempt once more to break his chain, as he did upon seeing you, woe be unto him. I would not then answer for his life. This large fish, which you see, will certainly swallow him, and keep him longer than *three* days in his belly; or this serpent, who appears to you so mild, will give him a mortal sting."

The white bull, who understood perfectly the old woman's conversation, but was unable to speak, humbly accepted all the proposals. He laid himself down at her feet; he lowed softly; and, looking tenderly at Amasidia, seemed to say to her:

"Come and see me sometimes upon the lawn."

The serpent now took up the conversation:

"Princess," said he, "I advise you to act implicitly as mademoiselle of Endor has told you."

The she-ass likewise put in her word, and was of the opinion of the serpent.

Amasidia was afflicted that this serpent and this ass should speak so well, while a beautiful bull, who had such noble and tender sentiments, was unable to express them.

"Alas," said she, in a low voice, "nothing is more common at court. One sees there every day fine lords who cannot converse, and contemptible wretches who speak with assurance."

"This serpent," said Mambres, "is not a contemptible wretch. He is perhaps a personage of the greatest importance."

The day now declined, and the princess was obliged to return home, after having promised to come back next day at the same hour. Her ladies of the palace were astonished, and understood nothing of what they had seen or heard. Mambres made reflections. The princess, recollecting that the serpent had called the old woman Miss, concluded at random that she was still unmarried, and felt some affliction that such was also her own condition. Respectable affliction, which she concealed, however, with as much care as the name of her lover.

CHAPTER III

HOW THE BEAUTIFUL AMASIDIA HAD A SECRET CONVERSATION WITH A BEAUTIFUL SERPENT

THE beautiful princess recommended secrecy to her ladies with regard to what they had seen. They all promised it, and kept their promise for a whole day.

We may believe that Amasidia slept little that night. An inexplicable charm continually recalled to her the idea of the beautiful bull. As soon, therefore, as she was at freedom with her wise Mambres, she said to him:

"O, sage, this animal turns my head."

"He employs mine very much," said Mambres. "I see plainly that this bovine is very much superior to those of his species. I see that there is a great mystery, and I suspect a fatal event. Your father Amasis is suspicious and violent, and this affair requires that you conduct yourself with the greatest precaution."

"Ah!" said the princess, "I have too much curiosity to be prudent. It is the only sentiment which can unite in my heart with that which preys upon me on account of the lover I have lost. Can I not know who this white bull is that gives me such strange disquiet?"

Mambres replied:

"I have already confessed to you, frankly, that my knowledge declines in proportion as my age advances;

but I mistake much if the serpent is not informed of what you are so very desirous of knowing. He does not want sense. He expresses himself with propriety. He has been long accustomed to interfere in the affairs of the ladies."

"Ah, undoubtedly," said Amasidia, "this is the beautiful serpent of Egypt, who, by fixing his tail into his mouth, becomes the emblem of eternity; who enlightens the world when he opens his eyes, and darkens it when he shuts them?"

"No, Miss."

"It is then the serpent of Esculapius?"

"Still less."

"It is perhaps Jupiter under the figure of a serpent?"

"Not at all."

"Ah, now I see, I see. It is the rod which you formerly changed into a serpent?"

"No, indeed, it is not; but all these serpents are of the same family. This one has a very high character in his own country. He passes there for the most extraordinary serpent that was ever seen. Address yourself to him. However, I warn you it is a dangerous undertaking. Were I in your place, I would hardly trouble myself either with the bull, the she-ass, the he-goat, the serpent, the fish, the raven, or the pigeon. But passion carries you on; and all I can do is to pity you, and tremble."

The princess conjured him to procure her a *tête-a-tête* with the serpent. Mambres, who was obliging, consented, and making profound reflections, he went and communicated to the witch in so insinuating a manner the whim of the princess, that the old woman told him Amasidia might lay her commands upon her; that the serpent was perfectly well bred, and so polite to the ladies that he wished for nothing more than to oblige them, and would not fail to keep the princess's appointment.

The ancient magician returned to inform the princess of this good news, but he still dreaded some misfortune, and made reflections.

"You desire to speak with the serpent, Princess. This you may accomplish whenever Your Highness thinks proper. But remember you must flatter him; for every animal has a great deal of self-love, and the serpent in particular. It is said he was formerly driven out of heaven for excessive pride."

"I have never heard of it," replied the princess.

"I believe it," said the old man.

He then informed her of all the reports which had been spread about this famous serpent.

"But, my dear princess, whatever singular adventures may have happened to him, you never can extort these secrets from him but by flattery. Having formerly deceived women, it is equitable that a woman in her turn should deceive him."

"I will do my utmost," said the princess, and departed with her maids of honor. The old woman was feeding the bull at a considerable distance.

Mambres left Amasidia to herself, and went and discoursed with the witch. One lady of honor chatted with the she-ass, the others amused themselves with the goat, the dog, the raven, and the pigeon. As for the large fish that frightened everybody, he plunged himself into the Nile by order of the old woman.

The serpent then attended the beautiful Amasidia into the grove, where they had the following conversation.

SERPENT. You cannot imagine, Princess, how much

I am flattered by the honor which Your Highness deigns to confer upon me.

PRINCESS. Your great reputation, sir, the beauty of your countenance, and the brilliancy of your eyes, have emboldened me to seek for this conversation. I know by public report (if it be not false) that you were formerly a very great lord in the empyrean heaven.

SERPENT. It is true, Princess, I had a very distinguished place there. It is pretended I am a disgraced favorite. This is a report which once was current in India. The Brahmins were the first who gave a history of my adventures. And I doubt not but one day or other the poets of the north will make them the subject of an extravagant epic poem;* for in truth it is all that can be made of them. Yet I am not so much fallen, but that I have left in this globe a very extensive dominion. I might venture to assert that the whole earth belongs to me.

PRINCESS. I believe it; for they tell me that your powers of persuasion are irresistible, and to please is to reign.

SERPENT. I feel, Princess, while I behold and listen to you, that you have over me the same power which you ascribe to me over so many others.

PRINCESS. You are, I believe, an amiable conqueror. It is said that your conquests among the fair sex have been numerous, and that you began with our common mother, whose name I have unfortunately forgotten.

SERPENT. They do me injustice. She honored me with her confidence, and I gave her the best advice. I desired that she and her husband should eat heartily of the fruit of the tree of knowledge. I imagined in doing this that

* A prophetic reference by the serpent to Milton's *Paradise Lost.*—E.

I should please the ruler of all things. It seemed to me that a tree so necessary to the human race was not planted to be entirely useless. Would the Supreme Being have wished to be served by fools and idiots? Is not the mind formed for the acquisition of knowledge and for improvement? Is not the knowledge of good and evil necessary for doing the one and avoiding the other? I certainly merited their thanks.

PRINCESS. Yet, they tell me that you have suffered for it. Probably it is since this period that so many ministers have been punished for giving good advice, and so many real philosophers and men of genius persecuted for their writings that were useful to mankind.

SERPENT. It is my enemies who have told you these stories. They say that I am out of favor at court. But a proof that my influence there has not declined is their own confession that I entered into the council when it was in agitation to try the good man Job: and I was again called upon when the resolution was taken to deceive a certain petty king called Ahab. I alone was charged with this honorable commission.

PRINCESS. Ah, sir! I do not believe that you are formed to deceive. But since you are always in the ministry, may I beg a favor of you? I hope so amiable a lord will not deny me.

SERPENT. Your Highness, your requests are laws; name your commands.

PRINCESS. I entreat that you will tell me who this white bull is for whom I feel such extraordinary sentiments which both affect and alarm me. I am told that you would deign to inform me.

SERPENT. Curiosity is necessary to human nature, and especially to your amiable sex. Without it they would live in the most shameful ignorance. I have always satisfied, as far as lay in my power, the curiosity of the ladies. I am accused indeed of using this complaisance only to vex the ruler of the world. I swear to you that I could propose nothing more agreeable to myself than to obey you; but the old woman must have informed you that the revealing of this secret will be attended with some danger to you.

PRINCESS. Ah, it is that which makes me still more curious.

SERPENT. In this I discover the sex to whom I have formerly done service.

PRINCESS. If you possess any feeling, if rational beings should mutually assist each other, if you have compassion for an unfortunate creature, do not refuse my request.

SERPENT. You affect me. I must satisfy you; but do not interrupt me.

PRINCESS. I promise you I will not.

SERPENT. There was a young king, beautiful, charming, in love, beloved——

PRINCESS. A young king! Beautiful, charming, in love, beloved! And by whom? And who was this king? How old was he? What has become of him? Where is his kingdom? What is his name?

SERPENT. See, I have scarce begun, and you have already interrupted me. Take care. If you have not more command over yourself, you are undone.

PRINCESS. Ah, pardon me, sir. I will not repeat my indiscretion. Go on, I beseech you.

SERPENT. This great king, the most valiant of men, victorious wherever he carried his arms, often dreamed when asleep, and forgot his dreams when awake. He wanted his magicians to remember and inform him what he had dreamed, otherwise he declared he would hang them; for that nothing was more equitable. It is now near seven years since he dreamed a fine dream, which he entirely forgot when he awoke; and a young Jew, full of experience, having revealed it to him, this amiable king was immediately changed into an ox for——

PRINCESS. Ah! It is my dear Neb——

She could not finish; she fainted away. Mambres, who had been listening at a distance, saw her fall, and believed her dead.

CHAPTER IV

HOW THEY WANTED TO SACRIFICE THE BULL, AND EXORCISE THE PRINCESS

MAMBRES runs to her, weeping. The serpent is affected. He, alas, cannot weep; but he hisses in a mournful tone. He cries out, "She is dead." The ass repeats, "She is dead." The raven tells it over again. All the other animals appeared afflicted, except the fish of Jonah, which has always been merciless. The lady of honor, the ladies of the court, arrive and tear their hair. The white bull, who fed at a distance and heard their cries, ran to the grove, dragging the old woman after him, while the echo of his loud bellowings made the neighborhood resound. To no purpose did the ladies pour upon the expiring Amasidia their bottles of rose-water, of pink, of myrtle, of benzoin, of balm of Gilead, of amomum, of gilly-flower, of nutmeg, of ambergris. She had not as yet given the smallest signs of life. But as soon as she perceived that the beautiful white bull was beside her, she came to herself, more blooming, more beautiful and lively than ever. A thousand times did she kiss this charming animal, who languishingly leaned his head on her snowy bosom. She called him, "My master, my king, my dear, my life!" She throws her fair arms round his neck, which was whiter than snow. The light straw is not drawn more closely to the amber, the vine to the elm, nor the ivy to the oak, than she was drawn to him. The sweet murmur of her sighs was heard. Her eyes were seen, now sparkling with a tender flame, and now obscured by those precious tears which love makes us shed.

We may easily judge into what astonishment the lady of honor and ladies of her train were thrown. As soon as they entered the palace, they related to their lovers this extraordinary adventure, and every one with different circumstances, which increased its singularity, and which always contributes to the variety of all histories.

No sooner was Amasis, king of Tanis, informed of these events, than his royal breast was inflamed with just indignation. Such was the wrath of Minos, when he understood that his daughter Pasiphæ lavished her tender favors upon the father of the Minotaur. Thus raged Juno, when she beheld Jupiter caressing the beautiful cow Io, daughter of the river Inachus. Following the dictates of passion, the stern Amasis imprisoned his unhappy daughter, the beautiful Amasidia, in her chamber, and placed over her a guard of black eunuchs. He then assembled his privy council.

The grand magician presided there, but had no longer the same influence as formerly. All the ministers of state concluded that this white bull was a sorcerer. It was quite the contrary. He was bewitched. But in delicate affairs they are always mistaken at court.

It was carried by a great majority that the princess

should be exorcised, and the old woman and the bull sacrificed.

The wise Mambres did not contradict the opinion of the king and council. The right of exorcising belonged to him. He could delay it under some plausible pretense. The god Apis [1] had lately died at Memphis. A god ox dies just like another ox. And it was not allowed to exorcise any person in Egypt until a new ox was found to replace the deceased.

It was decreed in the council to wait until the nomination of a new god should be made at Memphis.

The good old man, Mambres, perceived to what danger his dear princess was exposed. He knew who her lover was. The syllables NEBU——, which had escaped her, laid open the whole mystery to the eyes of this sage.

The dynasty of Memphis belonged at that time to the Babylonians. They preserved this remainder of the conquests they had gained under the greatest king of the world, to whom Amasis was a mortal enemy. Mambres had need for all his wisdom to conduct himself properly in the midst of so many difficulties. If the king Amasis should discover the lover of his daughter, her death would be inevitable. He had sworn it. The great, the young, the beautiful king of whom she was enamored, had dethroned the king her father, and Amasis had only recovered his kingdom seven years before. From that time it was not known what had become of the adorable monarch—the conqueror and idol of the nations—the tender and generous lover of the charming Amasidia. Sacrificing the white bull would inevitably occasion the death of the beautiful princess.

What could Mambres do in such critical circumstances? He went, after the council had broken up, to find his dear foster daughter.

"My dear child," he said, "I will serve you; but I repeat it, they will behead you if ever you pronounce the name of your lover."

"Ah, of what significance is my neck," replied the beautiful Amasidia, "if I cannot embrace that of Nebu——? My father is a cruel man. He not only refuses to give me a charming prince whom I adore, but he declares war against him; and after he was conquered by my lover, he has found the secret of changing him into an ox. Did one ever see more frightful malice? If my father were not my father, I do not know what I should do to him."

"It was not your father who played him this cruel trick," said the wise Mambres. "It was a native of Palestine, one of our ancient enemies, an inhabitant of a little country comprehended in that crowd of kingdoms which your lover subdued in order to polish and refine them.

"Such metamorphoses must not surprise you. You know that formerly I performed more extraordinary outrages. Nothing was at that time more common than those changes which at present astonish philosophers. True history, which we have read together, informs us that Lycaon, king of Arcadia, was changed into a wolf; the beautiful Calista, his daughter, into a bear; Io, the daughter of Inachus, our venerable Isis, into a cow; Daphne into a laurel; Sirinx into a flute; the fair Edith, wife of Lot—the best and most affectionate husband and father ever known in the world—has she not become, in our neighborhood, a pillar of salt, very sharp tasted, which has preserved both her likeness and form, as the great men attest who have seen it? I was witness to this change in my youth. I saw seven powerful cities in the most dry and parched situation in the world, all at once transformed into a beautiful lake. In the early part of my life, the whole world was full of metamorphoses.

"In fine, madam, if examples can soothe your grief, remember that Venus changed Cerastes into an ox."

"I do not know," said the princess, "that examples comfort us. If my lover were dead, could I comfort myself by the idea that all men die?"

"Your pain may at least be alleviated," replied the sage; "and since your lover has become an ox, it is possible from an ox he may become a man. As for me, I should deserve to be changed into a tiger or a crocodile, if I did not employ the little power I have in the service of a princess worthy of the adoration of the world,—if I did not labor for the beautiful Amasidia, whom I have nursed upon my knees, and whom fatal destiny exposes to such rude trials."

CHAPTER V

HOW THE WISE MAMBRES CONDUCTED HIMSELF WISELY

THE sage Mambres having said everything he could to comfort the princess, but without succeeding in so doing, ran to the old woman.

"My companion," said he to her, "ours is a charming profession, but a very dangerous one. You run the risk of being hanged, and your ox of being burned, drowned or devoured. I don't know what they will do with your other animals, for, prophet as I am, I know very little; but do you carefully conceal the serpent, and the fish. Let not the one show his head above water, nor the other venture out of his hole. I will place the ox in one of my stables in the country. You shall be there with him, since you say that you are not allowed to abandon him. The good scapegoat may upon this occasion serve as an expiation. We will send him into the desert loaded with the sins of all the rest. He is accustomed to this ceremony, which does him no harm; and every one knows that sin is expiated by means of a he-goat, who walks about for his own amusement. I only beg of you to lend me immediately Tobit's dog, who is a very swift greyhound; Balaam's ass, who runs better than a dromedary; the raven and the pigeon of the ark, who fly with amazing swiftness. I want to send them on an embassy to Memphis. It is an affair of great consequence."

The old woman replied to the magician:

"You may dispose as you please of Tobit's dog,[2] of Balaam's ass, of the raven and the pigeon of the ark, and of the scapegoat; but my ox cannot enter into a stable. It is said, Daniel, vi 21, That he must be always made fast to an iron chain, be always wet with the dew of heaven, and eat the grass of the field, and his portion be with the wild beasts.

"He is intrusted to me, and I must obey. What would Daniel, Ezekiel, and Jeremiah think of me, if I trusted my ox to any other than to myself? I see you know the secret of this extraordinary animal, but I have not to reproach myself with having revealed it to you. I am going to conduct him far from this polluted land, toward the lake Sirbon, where he will be sheltered from the cruelties of the king of Tanis. My fish and my serpent will defend me. I fear nobody when I serve my master."

"My good woman," answered the wise Mambres, "let the will of God be done! Provided I can find your white bull again, the lake Sirbon, the lake Maris, or the lake of Sodom, are to me perfectly indifferent. I want to do nothing but good to him and to you. But why have you spoken to me of Daniel, Ezekiel, and Jeremiah?"

"Ah, sir," answered the old woman, "you know as well as I what concern they have in this important affair. But I have no time to lose. I don't desire to be hanged. I do not wish my bull to be burned, drowned, or devoured. I go to the lake Sirbon by Canopus, with my serpent and my fish. Adieu."

The bull followed her pensively, after having testified his gratitude to the beneficent Mambres.

The wise Mambres was greatly troubled. He saw that Amasis, king of Tanis, distracted by the strange passion of his daughter for this animal, and believing her bewitched, would pursue the unfortunate bull everywhere, who would eventually be burned as a sorcerer in the public place of Tanis, or given to the fish of Jonah, or be roasted and served up for food. Mambres wanted at all events to save the princess from this cruel disaster.

He wrote a letter in sacred characters to his friend the high priest of Memphis upon the paper of Egypt, which was not yet in use. Here are the identical words of this letter:

"Light of the world, lieutenant of Isis, Osiris, and Horus, chief of the circumcised, you whose altar is justly raised above all thrones! I am informed that your god, the ox Apis, is dead. I have one at your service. Come quickly with your priests to acknowledge, to worship him, and to conduct him into the stable of your temple. May Isis, Osiris, and Horus, keep you in their holy and worthy protection, and likewise the priests of Memphis in their holy care.

Your affectionate friend,
Mambres."

He made four copies of this letter for fear of accidents, and enclosed them in cases of the hardest ebony.

Then, calling to him his four couriers, whom he had destined for this employment (these were the ass, the dog, the raven, and the pigeon), he said to the ass:

"I know with what fidelity you served Balaam my brother. Serve me as faithfully. There is not a unicorn who equals you in swiftness. Go, my dear friend, and deliver this letter to the person himself to whom it is directed, and return."

The ass answered:

"Sir, as I served Balaam, I will serve you. I will go, and I will return."

The sage put the box of ebony into her mouth, and she swiftly departed. He then called Tobit's dog.

"Faithful dog," said Mambres, "more speedy in thy course than the nimble-footed Achilles, I know what you performed for Tobit, son of Tobit, when you and the angel Raphael accompanied him from Nineveh to Ragusa in Medea, and from Ragusa to Nineveh, and that he brought back to his father ten talents, which the slave Tobit, the father, had lent to the slave Gabellus; for the slaves at that time were very rich. Carry this letter as it is directed. It is much more valuable than ten talents of silver."

The dog then replied:

"Sir, if I formerly followed the messenger of Raphael, I can with equal ease execute your commission."

Mambres put the letter into his mouth.

He next spoke in the same manner to the pigeon, who replied:

"Sir, if I brought back a bough into the ark, I will likewise bring you back an answer."

She took the letter in her bill, and the three messengers were out of sight in a moment. Then Mambres addressed the raven:

"I know that you fed the great prophet Elijah, when he was concealed near the torrent of Cherith, so much celebrated in the world. You brought him each day good bread and fat pullets. I only ask of you to carry this letter to Memphis."

The raven answered in these words:

"It is true, sir, that I carried each day a dinner to the great prophet Elijah the Tishbite. I saw him mount in a chariot of fire drawn by fiery horses, although this is not the usual method of traveling. But I always took care to eat half the dinner myself. I am very well pleased to carry your letter, provided you assure me of two good meals every day, and that I am paid money in advance for my commission."

Mambres, angry, replied:

"Gluttonous and malicious creature, I am not astonished that Apollo has made you black as a mole, after being white as a swan, as you were formerly, before you betrayed in the plains of Thessaly the beautiful Coronis, the unfortunate mother of Esculapius. Tell me, did you eat ribs of beef and pullets every day when you were ten whole months in the ark?"

"Sir," said the raven, "we were of very good cheer, there. They served up roast meat twice a day to all the fowls of my species who live upon nothing but flesh, such as the vultures, kites, eagles, buzzards, sparrowhawks, owls, tarsels, falcons, great owls, and an innumerable crowd of birds of prey. They furnished, with the most plentiful profusion, the tables of the lions, leopards, tigers, panthers, hyenas, wolves, bears, foxes, polecats, and all sorts of carnivorous quadrupeds. There were in the ark eight persons of distinction (and the only ones who were then in the world), continually employed in the care of our table and our wardrobe: Noah and his wife, who were about six hundred years old, their three sons and their three wives. It was charming to see with what care, what dexterity, what cleanliness, our eight domestics served four thousand of the most ravenous guests, without reckoning the amazing trouble which about ten or twelve thousand other animals required, from the elephant and the giraffe, to the silkworm and fly. What astonishes me, is that our purveyor Noah is unknown to all the nations of whom he is the stem, but I don't mind it much. I had already been present at a similar entertainment with Xesustres, king of Thrace. Such things as these happen from time to time for the instructions of ravens. In a word, I want to be of good cheer, and to be paid in ready money."

The wise Mambres took care not to give his letter to such a discontented and babbling animal; and they separated very much dissatisfied with each other.

But it is necessary to know what became of the white bull, and not to lose sight of the old woman and the serpent. Mambres ordered his intelligent and faithful domestics to follow them; and as for himself, he advanced in a litter by the side of the Nile, always making reflections.

"How is it possible," said he to himself, "that a serpent should be master of almost all the world, as he boasts, and as so many learned men acknowledge, and that he nevertheless obeys an old woman? How is it, that he is sometimes called to the council of the Most High, while he creeps upon earth? In what manner can he enter by his power alone into the bodies of men, and that so many men pretend to dislodge him by means of words? In short, why does he pass with a small neighboring people for having ruined the human race? And how is it that the human race are entirely ignorant of this? I am old, I have studied all my life, but I see a crowd of inconsistencies which I cannot reconcile. I cannot account for what has happened to myself, neither for the great things which I long ago performed, nor for those of which I have been witness. Everything well considered, I begin to think that this world subsists by contradictions, *rerum concordia discors,* as my master Zoroaster formerly said."

While he was plunged in this obscure metaphysical reasoning—obscure like all metaphysics—a boatman singing a jovial song made fast a small boat by the side of the river, and three grave personages, barely clothed in dirty tattered garments, landed from it; but preserved, under the garb of poverty, the most majestic and august air. These strangers were Daniel, Ezekiel, and Jeremiah.

CHAPTER VI

HOW MAMBRES MET THREE PROPHETS, AND GAVE THEM A GOOD DINNER

THESE three great men who had the prophetic light in their countenance knew the wise Mambres to be one of their brethren by some marks of the same light which he had still remaining, and prostrated themselves before his litter. Mambres likewise knew them to be prophets, more by their uncouth dress than by those gleams of fire which proceeded from their august heads. He conjectured that they had come to learn news of the white bull; and, conducting himself with his usual propriety, he alighted from his carriage and advanced a few steps toward them in a dignified manner. He raised them up, caused tents to be erected, and prepared a dinner, of which he rightly judged that the prophets had very great need.

He invited the old woman who was only about five hundred paces from them to join them. She accepted the invitation, and arrived, leading her white bull.

Two soups were served up, one *de Bisque*, and the other *à la Reine*. The first course consisted of a carp's tongue pie, livers of eel-pouts, and pikes; fowl dressed with pistachios, pigeons with truffles and olives; two young turkeys with gravy of cray fish, mushrooms, and morels; and a chipotata. The second course was composed of pheasants, partridges, quails, and ortalons, with four salads; the *epergne* was in the highest taste; nothing could be more delicious than the side dishes; nothing more brilliant and more ingenious than the dessert. But the wise Mambres took great care to have no boiled beef, nor short ribs, nor tongue, nor palate of an ox, nor cows' udder, lest the unfortunate monarch near at hand should think that they insulted him.

This great and unfortunate prince was feeding near the tent; and never did he feel in a more cruel manner the fatal revolution which had deprived him of his throne for seven long years.

"Alas!" said he, to himself, "this Daniel who has changed me into a bull, and this sorceress, my keeper, are of the best cheer in the world, while I, the sovereign of Asia, am reduced to the necessity of eating grass, and drinking water."

When they had drunk heartily of the wine of Engaddi, of Tadmor, and of Schiras, the prophets and the witch conversed with more frankness than at the first course.

"I must acknowledge," said Daniel, "that I did not live so well in the lions' den."

"What, sir," said Mambres, "did they put you into a den of lions? How came you not to be devoured?"

"Sir," said Daniel, "you know very well that lions never eat prophets."

"As for me," said Jeremiah, "I have passed my whole life in starvation. This is the only day I have ever eaten a good meal; and were I to spend my life over again, and have it in my power to choose my condition, I must own I would much rather be comptroller-general or bishop of Babylon, than prophet at Jerusalem."

Ezekiel cried, "I was once ordered to sleep three hundred and ninety days upon my left side, and to eat all that time bread of wheat, and barley, and beans, and lentiles, cooked in the strangest manner. . . . Still I must own that the cookery of Seigneur Mambres is much more delicate. However, the prophetic trade has its advantages, and the proof is, that there are many who follow it."

After they had spoken thus freely, Mambres entered upon business. He asked the three pilgrims the reason of their journey into the dominions of the king of Tanis. Daniel replied, "That the kingdom of Babylon had been all in a flame since Nebuchadnezzar had disappeared; that according to the custom of the court, all the prophets had been persecuted; that they passed their lives in sometimes seeing kings humbled at their feet, and sometimes receiving a hundred lashes from them; that at length they had been obliged to take refuge in Egypt for fear of being starved."

Ezekiel and Jeremiah likewise spoke a long time in such fine terms that it was almost impossible to understand them. As for the witch, she always kept a strict eye over her charge. The fish of Jonah continued in the Nile, opposite to the tent, and the serpent sported upon the grass. After drinking coffee, they took a walk by the side of the Nile; and the white bull, perceiving the three prophets, his enemies, bellowed most dreadfully, ran furiously at them, and gored them with his horns. As prophets never have anything but skin upon their bones, he would certainly have run them through; but the ruler of the world, who sees all and remedies all, changed them immediately into magpies; and they continued to chatter as before. The same thing has happened since to the Pierides;[3] so much has fable always imitated sacred history.

This incident caused new reflections in the mind of Mambres.

"Here," said he, "are three great prophets changed into magpies. This ought to teach us never to speak too much, and always to observe a suitable discretion."

He concluded that wisdom was better than eloquence, and was thinking profoundly as usual, when a great and terrible spectacle presented itself to his eyes.

CHAPTER VII

HOW KING AMASIS WANTED TO GIVE THE WHITE BULL TO BE DEVOURED BY THE FISH OF JONAH, AND DID NOT DO IT

CLOUDS of dust floated from south to north. The noise of drums, fifes, psalteries, harps, and sackbuts was heard. Several squadrons and battalions advanced, and Amasis, king of Tanis, was at their head upon an Arabian horse caparisoned with scarlet trappings embroidered with gold. The heralds proclaimed that they should seize the white bull, bind him, and throw him into the Nile, to be devoured by the fish of Jonah; "for the king our lord, who is just, wants to revenge himself upon the white bull, who has bewitched his daughter."

The good old man Mambres made more reflections than ever. He saw very plainly that the malicious raven had told all to the king, and that the princess ran a great risk of being beheaded.

"My dear friend," said he to the serpent, "go quickly and comfort the fair Amasidia, my foster daughter. Bid her fear nothing, whatever may happen, and tell her stories to alleviate her inquietude; for stories always amuse the ladies, and it is only by interesting them that one can succeed in the world."

Mambres next prostrated himself before Amasis, king of Tanis, and thus addressed him:

"O king, live forever! The white bull should certainly be sacrificed, for Your Majesty is always in the right; but the ruler of the world has said that this bull must not be swallowed up by the fish of Jonah till Memphis shall have found a god to supply the place of him who is dead. Then thou shalt be revenged, and thy daughter exorcised, for she is possessed. Your piety is too great not to obey the commands of the ruler of the universe."

Amasis, king of Tanis, remained for some time silent and in deep thought.

"The god Apis," said he, at length, "is dead! God rest his soul! When do you think another ox will be found to reign over the fruitful Egypt?"

"Sire," replied Mambres, "I ask but eight days."

"I grant them to you," replied the king, who was very religious, "and I will remain here the eight days. At the expiration of that time I will sacrifice the enemy of my daughter."

Amasis immediately ordered that his tents, cooks, and musicians should be brought, and remained here eight days, as it is related in Manethon.

The old woman was in despair that the bull she had in charge had but eight days to live. She raised phantoms every night, in order to dissuade the king from his cruel resolution; but Amasis forgot in the morning the phantoms he had seen in the night, similar to Nebuchadnezzar, who had always forgotten his dreams.

CHAPTER VIII

HOW THE SERPENT TOLD STORIES TO THE PRINCESS TO COMFORT HER

MEANWHILE the serpent was telling stories to the fair Amasidia to soothe her. He related to her how he had formerly cured a whole nation of the bite of certain little serpents, only by showing himself at the end of a staff. (*Num. xx: 9.*) He informed her of the conquests of a hero who made a charming contrast with Amphion, architect of Thebes. Amphion assembled hewn stones by the sound of his violin. To build a city he had only to play a rigadoon and a minuet; but the other hero destroyed them by the sound of rams' horns. He executed thirty-one powerful kings in a country four leagues in length and four in breadth. He made stones rain down from heaven upon a battalion of routed Amorites; and having thus exterminated them, he stopped the sun and moon at noonday between Gibeon and Ajalon, in the road to Beth-horon, to exterminate them still more, after the example of Bacchus, who had stopped the sun and the moon in his journey to the Indies.

The prudence which every serpent ought to have, did not allow him to tell the fair Amasidia of the powerful Jephthah, who made a vow and beheaded his daughter, because he had gained a battle. This would have struck terror into the mind of the fair princess. But he related to her the adventures of the great Sampson, who killed a thousand Philistines with the jawbone of an ass, who tied together three hundred foxes by the tail, and who fell into the snares of a lady, less beautiful, less tender, and less faithful than the charming Amasidia.

He related to her the story of the unfortunate Sechem and Dinah, as well as the more celebrated adventures of Ruth and Boaz; those of Judah and Tamar; those even of Lot's two daughters; those of Abraham and Jacob's servant maids; those of Reuben and Bilhah; those of David and Bath-sheba; and those of the great king Solomon. In short, everything which could dissipate the grief of a fair princess.

CHAPTER IX

HOW THE SERPENT DID NOT COMFORT THE PRINCESS

" ALL these stories tire me," said Amasidia, for she had understanding and taste. "They are good for nothing but to be commented upon among the Irish by that madman Abbadie, or among the Welsh by that prattler d'Houteville. Stories which might have amused the great, great, great grandmother of my grandmother, appear insipid to me who have been educated by the wise Mambres, and who have read *Human Understanding* by the Egyptian philosopher named Locke, and the *Matron of Ephesus.* I choose that a story should be founded on probability, and not always resemble a dream. I desire to find in it nothing trivial or extravagant; and I desire above all, that under the appearance of fable there may appear some latent truth, obvious to the discerning eye, though it escape the observation of the vulgar.

"I am weary of a sun and of a moon which an old beldam disposes of at her pleasure, of mountains which dance, of rivers which return to their sources, and of dead men who rise again; but I am above measure disgusted when such insipid stories are written in a bombastic and unintelligible manner. A lady who expects to see her lover swallowed up by a great fish, and who is apprehensive of being beheaded by her own father, has need of amusement; but suit my amusement to my taste."

"You impose a difficult task upon me," replied the serpent. "I could have formerly made you pass a few hours agreeably enough, but for some time past I have lost both my imagination and memory. Alas! What has become of those faculties with which I formerly amused the ladies? Let me try, however, if I can recollect one amusing tale for your entertainment.

"Five and twenty thousand years ago King Gnaof and Queen Patra reigned in Thebes with its hundred gates. King Gnaof was very handsome, and Queen Patra still more beautiful. But their home was unblessed with children, and no heirs were born to continue the royal race.

"The members of the faculty of medicine and of the academy of surgery wrote excellent treatises upon this subject. The queen was sent to drink mineral waters; she fasted and prayed; she made magnificent presents to the temple of Jupiter Ammon, but all was to no purpose. At length a——"

"*Mon Dieu!*" said the princess, "but I see where this leads. This story is too common, and I must likewise tell you that it offends my modesty. Relate some very true and moral story, which I have never yet heard, to complete the improvement of my understanding and my heart, as the Egyptian professor Lenro says."

"Here then, madam," said the beautiful serpent, "is one most incontestably authentic.

"There were three prophets all equally ambitious and discontented with their condition. They had in common the folly to wish to be kings: for there is only one step from the rank of a prophet to that of a monarch, and man always aspires to the highest step in the ladder of fortune. In other respects, their inclinations and their pleasures were totally different. The first preached admirably to his assembled brethren, who applauded him by clapping their hands; the second was distractedly fond of music; and the third was a passionate lover of the fair sex.

"The angel Ithuriel presented himself to them one day when they were at table discoursing on the sweets of royalty.

" 'The ruler of the world,' said the angel to them, 'sends me to you to reward your virtue. Not only shall you be kings, but you shall constantly satisfy your ruling passions. You, first prophet, I make king of Egypt, and you shall continually preside in your council, which shall applaud your eloquence and your wisdom; and you, second prophet, I make king over Persia, and you shall continually hear most heavenly music; and you, third prophet, I make king of India, and I give you a charming mistress who shall never forsake you.'

"He to whose lot Egypt fell, began his reign by assembling his council for foreign affairs, which was composed only of two hundred sages. He made them a long and eloquent speech, which was very much applauded, and the monarch enjoyed the pleasing satisfaction of intoxicating himself with praises uncorrupted by flattery.

"After the council for foreign affairs he assembled his privy council. This was much more numerous; and a new speech received still greater praise. And it was the same in the other councils. There was not a moment of intermission in the pleasures and glory of the prophet king of Egypt. The fame of his eloquence filled the world.

"The prophet king of Persia began his reign by an Italian opera, whose choruses were sung by fifteen hundred eunuchs. Their voices penetrated his soul even to the very marrow of the bones, where it resides. This opera was succeeded by another, and the second by a third, without interruption.

The king of India shut himself up with his mistress, and enjoyed perfect pleasure in her society. He considered the necessity of always flattering her as the highest felicity, and pitied the wretched situation of his two brethren, of whom one was obliged always to convene his council, and the other to be continually at an opera.

"It happened at the end of a few days, that each of these kings became disgusted with his occupation, and beheld from his window certain wood-cutters who had come from an ale-house, and who were going to work in a neighboring forest. They walked arm in arm with their sweethearts, with whom they were happy. The kings begged of the angel Ithuriel, that he would intercede with the ruler of the world, and make them wood-cutters."

"I do not know whether the ruler of the world granted their request or not," interrupted the tender Amasidia, "and I do not care much about it; but I know very well that I should ask for nothing of anyone, were I with my lover, with my dear NEBUCHADNEZZAR!"

The vaults of the palace resounded this mighty name. At first Amasidia had only pronounced Ne—, afterwards Neb—, then Nebu—. At length passion hurried her on, and she pronounced entire the fatal name, notwithstanding the oath she had sworn to the king, her father. All the ladies of the court repeated Nebuchadnezzar, and the malicious raven did not fail to carry the tidings to the king. The countenance of Amasis, king of Tanis, sank, because his heart was troubled. And thus it was that the serpent, the wisest and most subtle of animals, once again beguiled a woman, thinking to do her service.

Amasis, in a fury, sent twelve alguazils for his daughter. These men are always ready to execute barbarous orders, because they are paid for it.

CHAPTER X

HOW THEY WANTED TO BEHEAD THE PRINCESS, AND DID NOT DO IT

NO sooner had the princess entered the camp of the king, than he said to her: "My daughter, you know that all princesses who disobey their fathers are put to death; without which it would be impossible for a kingdom to be well governed. I charged you never to mention the name of your lover, Nebuchadnezzar, my mortal enemy, who dethroned me about seven years ago, and disappeared. In his place, you have chosen a white bull, and you have cried Nebuchadnezzar. It is just that I behead you."

The princess replied: "My father, thy will be done: but grant me some time to bewail my sad fate."

"That is reasonable," said King Amasis; "and it is a rule established among the most judicious princes. I give you a whole day to bewail your destiny, since it is your desire. Tomorrow, which is the eighth day of my encampment, I will cause the white bull to be swallowed up by the fish, and I will behead you precisely at nine o'clock in the morning."

The beautiful Amasidia then went forth in sorrow to bewail her father's cruelty, and wandered by the side of the Nile, accompanied by the ladies of her train.

The wise Mambres pondered beside her, counting the hours and the seconds.

"Well, my dear Mambres," said she to him, "you have changed the waters of the Nile into blood, according to custom, and cannot you change the heart of Amasis, king of Tanis, my father? Will you suffer him to behead me tomorrow, at nine o'clock in the morning?"

"That depends," replied the reflecting Mambres, "upon the speed and diligence of my couriers."

The next day, as soon as the shadows of the obelisks and pyramids marked upon the ground the ninth hour of the day, the white bull was securely bound, to be thrown to the fish of Jonah; and they brought to the king his large saber.

"Alas, alas!" said Nebuchadnezzar to himself, "I, a king, have been a bull for almost seven years; and scarcely have I found the mistress I had lost when I am condemned to be devoured by a fish."

Never had the wise Mambres made such profound reflections; and he was quite absorbed in his melancholy thoughts when he saw at a distance all he expected. An innumerable crowd drew nigh. Three figures of Isis,

Osiris, and Horus, joined together, advanced, drawn in a carriage of gold and precious stones, by a hundred senators of Memphis, preceded by a hundred girls, playing upon the sacred sistrums. Four thousand priests, with their heads shaved, were each mounted upon a hippopotamus.

At a great distance, appeared with the same pomp the sheep of Thebes, the dog of Babastes, the cat of Phœbe, the crocodile of Arsinoe, the goat of Mendez, and all the inferior gods of Egypt, who came to pay homage to the great ox, to the mighty Apis, as powerful as Isis, Osiris, and Horus, united together.

In the midst of the demigods, forty priests carried an enormous basket, filled with sacred onions. These were, it is true, gods, but they resembled onions very much.

On both sides of this aisle of gods, followed by an innumerable crowd of people, marched forty thousand warriors, with helmets on their heads, scimitars upon their left thighs, quivers at their shoulders, and bows in their hands.

All the priests sang in chorus, with a harmony which ravished the soul, and which melted it,

> "Alas! alas! our ox is dead—
> We'll have a finer in its stead."

And at every pause was heard the sound of the sistrums, of cymbals, of tabors, of psalteries, of bagpipes, harps, and sackbuts.

Amasis, king of Tanis, astonished at this spectacle, forgot to behead his daughter. He sheathed his scimitar.

CHAPTER XI

APOTHEOSIS OF THE WHITE BULL. TRIUMPH OF
THE WISE MAMBRES. THE SEVEN YEARS PRO-
CLAIMED BY DANIEL ARE ACCOMPLISHED. NEB-
UCHADNEZZAR RESUMES THE HUMAN
FORM, MARRIES THE BEAUTIFUL AMA-
SIDIA, AND ASCENDS THE THRONE OF
BABYLON

"GREAT king," said Mambres to him, "the order
of things is now changed. Your Majesty must
set the example. O king, quickly unbind the white bull,
and be the first to adore him."

Amasis obeyed, and prostrated himself with all his
people. The high priest of Memphis presented to the
new god Apis the first handful of hay; the Princess Amasidia tied to his beautiful horns festoons of roses, anemones, ranunculuses, tulips, pinks, and hyacinths. She
took the liberty to kiss him, but with a profound respect. The priests strewed palms and flowers on the road
by which they were to conduct him to Memphis. And
the wise Mambres, still making reflections, whispered to
his friend, the serpent:

*"Daniel changed this monarch into a bull, and I have
changed this bull into a god!"*

They returned to Memphis in the same order, and the
king of Tanis, in some confusion, followed the procession. Mambres, with a serene and diplomatic air, walked by his side. The old woman came after, much amazed.
She was accompanied by the serpent, the dog, the she-
ass, the raven, the pigeon, and the scapegoat. The great
fish mounted up the Nile. Daniel, Ezekiel, and Jeremiah,
changed into magpies, brought up the rear.

When they had reached the frontiers of the kingdom, which are not far distant, King Amasis took leave of the bull Apis, and said to his daughter:

"My daughter, let us return into my dominions, that I may behead you, as it has been determined in my royal breast, because you have pronounced the name of Nebuchadnezzar, my enemy, who dethroned me seven years ago. When a father has sworn to behead his daughter, he must either fulfill his oath, or sink into hell forever; and I will not damn myself out of love for you."

The fair princess Amasidia replied to the King Amasis:

"My dear father, go and behead whomever it pleases you, but it shall not be me. I am now in the territories of Isis, Osiris, Horus, and Apis. I will never forsake my beautiful white bull, and I will continue to kiss him, till I have seen his apotheosis in his stable in the holy city of Memphis. It is a weakness pardonable in a young lady of high birth."

Scarce had she spoken these words, when the ox Apis cried out:

"My dear Amasidia, I will love you while I live!"

This was the first time that the god Apis had been heard to speak during the forty thousand years that he had been worshiped.

The serpent and the she-ass cried out, "The seven years are accomplished!" And the three magpies repeated, "The seven years are accomplished!"

All the priests of Egypt raised their hands to heaven.

The god on a sudden was seen to lose his two hind legs; his two fore legs were changed into two human legs; two white strong muscular arms grew from his shoulders; his taurine visage was changed to the face of a charming hero; and he once more became the most beautiful of mortals.

"I choose," cried he, "to be the lover of the beautiful Amasidia rather than a god. I am NEBUCHADNEZZAR, KING OF KINGS!"

This metamorphosis astonished all the world, except the wise Mambres. But what surprised nobody, was that Nebuchadnezzar immediately married the fair Amasidia in the presence of this assembly.

He left his father-in-law in quiet possession of the kingdom of Tanis, and made noble provision for the she-ass, the serpent, the dog, the pigeon, and even for the raven, the three magpies, and the large fish; showing to all the world that he knew how to forgive as well as to conquer.

The old woman had a considerable pension placed at her disposal.

The scapegoat was sent for a day into the wilderness, that all past sins might be expiated; and had afterwards twelve sprightly goats for his companions.

The wise Mambres returned to his palace, and made reflections.

Nebuchadnezzar, after having embraced the magician, his benefactor, governed in tranquillity the kingdoms of Memphis, Babylon, Damascus, Balbec, Tyre, Syria, Asia Minor, Scythia, the countries of Thiras, Mosok, Tubal, Madai, Gog, Magog, Javan, Sogdiana, Aroriana, the Indies, and the Isles; and the people of this vast empire cried out aloud every morning at the rising of the sun:

"Long live great Nebuchadnezzar, King of Kings, who is no longer an ox!"

Since which time it has been a custom in Babylon, when the sovereign, deceived by his satraps, his magicians, treasurers or wives, at length acknowledges his errors, and amends his conduct, for all the people to cry out at his gate:

"Long live our great king, who is no longer an ox."

JEANNOT AND COLIN

JEANNOT AND COLIN

MANY trustworthy persons have seen Jeannot and Colin when they went to school at Issoire in Auvergne, a town famous all over the world for its college and its kettles. Jeannot was the son of a dealer in mules, a man of considerable reputation; Colin owed his existence to a worthy husbandman who dwelt in the outskirts of the town and cultivated his farm with the help of four mules, and who, after paying tolls and tallage, scutage and salt duty, poundage, poll-tax, and tithes, did not find himself particularly well off at the end of the year.

Jeannot and Colin were very handsome lads for natives of Auvergne; they were much attached to each other, and had little secrets together and private understandings, such as old comrades always recall with pleasure when they afterwards meet in a wider world.

Their school days were drawing near their end, when a tailor one day brought Jeannot a velvet coat of three colors with a waistcoat of Lyons silk to match in excellent taste; this suit of clothes was accompanied by a letter addressed to Monsieur de La Jeannotière. Colin admired the coat, and was not at all jealous, but Jeannot assumed an air of superiority which distressed Colin. From that moment Jeannot paid no more heed to his lessons, but was always looking at his reflection in the glass, and despised everybody but himself. Some time afterwards a footman arrived post-haste, bringing a second letter, addressed this time to His Lordship the Marquis de La Jeannotière; it contained an order from his father for the young nobleman, his son, to be sent to Paris. As Jeannot mounted the chaise to drive off, he stretched out his hand to Colin with a patronizing smile befitting his rank. Colin felt his own insignificance, and wept. So Jeannot departed in all his glory.

Readers who like to know all about things may be informed that Monsieur Jeannot, the father, had rapidly gained immense wealth in business. You ask how those great fortunes are made? It all depends upon luck. Monsieur Jeannotière had a comely person, and so had his wife; moreover her complexion was fresh and blooming. They had gone to Paris to prosecute a lawsuit which was ruining them, when Fortune, who lifts up and casts down human beings at her pleasure, presented them with an introduction to the wife of an army hospital contractor, a man of great talent, who could boast of having killed more soldiers in one year than the cannon had destroyed in ten. Jeannot took the lady's fancy, and Jeannot's wife captivated the gentleman. Jeannot soon became a partner in the business, and entered into other speculations. When one is in the current of the stream it is only necessary to let one's self drift, and so an immense fortune may sometimes be made without any trouble. The beggars who watch you from the bank, as you glide along in full sail, open their eyes in astonishment; they wonder how you have managed to get on; they envy you at all events, and write pamphlets against you which you never read. That was what happened to Jeannot senior, who was soon styled Monsieur de La Jeannotière, and, after buying a marquisate at the end of six months, he took the young nobleman, his son, away from school, to launch him into the fashionable world of Paris.

Colin, always affectionately disposed, wrote a kind letter to his old schoolfellow in order to offer his congratulations. The little marquis sent him no answer, which grieved Colin sorely.

The first thing that his father and mother did for the young gentleman was to get him a tutor. This tutor, who was a man of distinguished manners and profound ignorance, could teach his pupil nothing. The marquis wished his son to learn Latin, but the marchioness would not hear of it. They consulted the opinion of a certain author who had obtained considerable celebrity at that time from some popular works which he had written. He was invited to dinner, and the master of the house began by saying:

"Sir, as you know Latin, and are conversant with the manners of the Court——"

"I, sir! Latin! I don't know a word of it," answered the man of wit; "and it is just as well for me that I don't, for one can speak one's own language better, when the attention is not divided between it and foreign tongues. Look at all our ladies; they are far more charming in conversation than men, their letters are written with a hundred times more grace of expression. They owe that superiority over us to nothing else but their ignorance of Latin."

"There now! Was I not right?" said the lady. "I want my son to be a man of wit, and to make his way in the world. You see that if he were to learn Latin, it would be his ruin. Tell me, if you please, are plays and operas performed in Latin? Are the proceedings in court conducted in Latin when one has a lawsuit on hand? Do people make love in Latin?"

The marquis, confounded by these arguments, passed

sentence, and it was decided that the young nobleman should not waste his time in studying Cicero, Horace, and Virgil.

"But what is he to learn then? For still, I suppose, he will have to know something. Might he not be taught a little geography?"

"What good will that do him?" answered the tutor. "When my lord marquis goes to visit his country seat, will not his postillions know the roads? There will be no fear of their going astray. One does not want a sextant in order to travel, and it is quite possible to make a journey from Paris to Auvergne without knowing anything about the latitude and longitude of either."

"Very true," replied the father. "But I have heard people speak of a noble science, which is, I think, called *astronomy.*"

"Bless my soul!" rejoined the tutor. "Do we regulate our behavior in this world by the stars? Why should my lord marquis wear himself out in calculating an eclipse, when he will find it predicted correctly to a second in the almanac, which will, moreover, inform him of all the movable feasts, the age of the moon, and that of all the princesses in Europe?"

The marchioness was quite of the tutor's opinion, the little marquis was in a state of the highest delight, and his father was very undecided.

"What then is my son to be taught?" said he.

"To make himself agreeable," answered the friend whom they had consulted. "For, if he knows the way to please, he will know everything worth knowing; it is an art which he will learn from her ladyship, his mother, without the least trouble to either of them."

The marchioness, at these words, smiled graciously upon the courtly ignoramus, and said:

"It is easy to see, sir, that you are a most accomplished gentleman; my son will owe all his education to you. I imagine, however, that it will not be a bad thing for him to know a little history."

"Nay, madam,—what good would that do him?" he answered. "Assuredly the only entertaining and useful history is that of the passing hour. All ancient histories, as one of our clever writers [1] has observed, are admitted to be nothing but fables, and for us moderns it is an inextricable chaos. What does it matter to the young gentleman, your son, if Charlemagne instituted the twelve Paladins of France, or if his successor [2] had an impediment in his speech?"

"Nothing was ever said more wisely!" exclaimed the tutor. "The minds of children are smothered under a mass of useless knowledge, but of all sciences that which seems to me the most absurd, and the one best adapted to extinguish every spark of genius, is geometry. That ridiculous science is concerned with surfaces, lines, and points which have no existence in nature. In imagination a hundred thousand curved lines may be made to pass between a circle and a straight line which touches it, although in reality you could not insert so much as a straw. Geometry, indeed, is nothing more than a bad joke."

The marquis and his lady did not understand much of the meaning of what the tutor was saying; but they were quite of his way of thinking.

"A nobleman like his lordship," he continued, "should not dry up his brain with such unprofitable studies. If, some day, he should require one of those sublime geometricians to draw plans of his estates, he can have them measured for his money. If he should wish to trace out the antiquity of his lineage, which goes back to the most remote ages, all he will have to do will be to send for some learned Benedictine. It is the same with all the other arts. A young lord born under a lucky star is neither a painter, nor a musician, nor an architect, nor a sculptor; but he may make all these arts flourish by encouraging them with his generous approval. Doubtless it is much better to patronize them than to practice them. It will be quite enough if my lord the young marquis has taste; it is the part of artists to work for him, and thus there is a great deal of truth in the remark that people of quality (that is if they are very rich) know everything without learning anything, because, in point of fact and in the long run, they are masters of all the knowledge which they can command and pay for."

The agreeable ignoramus then took part again in the conversation, and said:

"You have well remarked, madam, that the great end of man's existence is to succeed in society. Is it, forsooth, any aid to the attainment of this success to have devoted one's self to the sciences? Does anyone ever think in select company of talking about geometry? Is a well-bred gentleman ever asked what star rises today with the sun? Does anyone at the supper table ever want to know if Clodion the Long Haired crossed the Rhine?"

"No, indeed!" exclaimed the Marchioness de La Jeannotière, whose charms had been her passport into the world of fashion; "and my son must not stifle his genius by studying all that rubbish. But, after all, what is he to be taught? For it is a good thing that a young lord should be able to shine when occasion offers, as my noble husband has said. I remember once hearing an abbé remark that the most entertaining science was something the name of which I have forgotten—it begins with a *B*."

"With a *B*, madam? It was not botany, was it?"

"No, it certainly was not botany that he mentioned; it began, as I tell you, with a *B*, and ended in *onry*."

"Ah, madam, I understand!—It was blazonry or heraldry. That is indeed a most profound science; but it has ceased to be fashionable since the custom has died out of having one's coat of arms painted on the carriage door, although it was the most useful thing imaginable in a well-ordered State. Besides, that line of study would be endless, for at the present day there is not a barber who is without his armorial bearings, and you know that whatever becomes common loses its attraction."

Finally, after all the pros and cons of the different sciences had been examined and discussed, it was decided that the young marquis should learn dancing.

Dame Nature, who disposes everything at her own will and pleasure, had given him a talent which soon developed itself with prodigious success: it was that of singing street ballads in a charming style. The youthful grace accompanying his superlative gift caused him to be regarded as a young man of the highest promise. He was a favorite with the ladies, and, having his head crammed with songs, he had no lack of mistresses to whom to address his verses. He stole the line "Bacchus with the Loves at play" from one ballad, and made it rhyme with "night and day" taken out of another, while a third furnished him with "charms" and "alarms." But inasmuch as there were always some feet more or less than were wanted in his verses, he had them corrected at the rate of twenty sovereigns a song. And *The Literary Year* placed him in the same rank with such sonneteers as La Fare, Chaulieu, Hamilton, Sarrasin, and Voiture.

Her ladyship the marchioness then believed that she

was indeed the mother of a genius, and gave a supper to all the wits of Paris. The young man's head was soon turned upside down, he acquired the art of talking without knowing the meaning of what he said, and perfected himself in the habit of being fit for nothing. When his father saw him so eloquent, he keenly regretted that he had not had him taught Latin, or he would have purchased some high appointment for him in the Law. His mother, who was of more heroic sentiments, took upon herself to solicit a regiment for her son. In the meantime he made love,—and love is sometimes more expensive than a regiment. He squandered his money freely, while his parents drained their purses and credit to a lower and lower ebb by living in the grandest style.

A young widow of good position in their neighborhood, who had only a moderate income, was well enough disposed to make some effort to prevent the great wealth of the Marquis and Marchioness de La Jeannotière from going altogether, by marrying the young marquis and so appropriating what remained. She enticed him to her house, let him make love to her, allowed him to see that she was not quite indifferent to him, led him on by degrees, enchanted him, and made him her devoted slave without the least difficulty. She would give him at one time commendation and at another time counsel; she became his father's and mother's best friend. An old neighbor proposed marriage; the parents, dazzled with the splendor of the alliance, joyfully fell in with the scheme, and gave their only son to their most intimate lady friend. The young marquis was thus about to wed a woman whom he adored, and by whom he was beloved in return. The friends of the family congratulated him, the marriage settlement was on the point of being signed, the bridal dress and the epithalamium were both well under way.

One morning our young gentleman was on his knees before the charmer whom fond affection and esteem were so soon to make his own; they were tasting in animated and tender converse the first fruits of future happiness; they were settling how they should lead a life of perfect bliss, when one of his lady mother's footmen presented himself, scared out of his wits.

"Here's fine news which may surprise you!" said he. "The bailiffs are in the house of my lord and lady, removing the furniture. All has been seized by the creditors. They talk of personal arrests, and I am going to do what I can to get my wages paid."

"Let us see what has happened," said the marquis, "and discover the meaning of all this."

"Yes," said the widow, "go and punish those rascals —go, quick!"

He hurried homewards, he arrived at the house; his father was already in prison, all the servants had fled, each in a different direction, carrying off whatever they could lay their hands upon. His mother was alone, helpless, forlorn, and bathed in tears; she had nothing left her but the remembrance of her former prosperity, her beauty, her faults, and her foolish extravagance.

After the son had condoled with his mother for a long time, he said at last:

"Let us not despair; this young widow loves me to distraction; she is even more generous than she is wealthy, I can assure you, I will fly to her for succor, and bring her to you."

So he returns to his mistress, and finds her conversing in private with a fascinating young officer.

"What! Is that you, my lord de La Jeannotière? What business have you with me? How can you leave your mother by herself in this way? Go, and stay with the poor woman, and tell her that she shall always have my good wishes. I am in want of a waiting-woman now, and will gladly give her the preference."

"My lad," said the officer, "you seem pretty tall and straight; if you would like to enter my company, I will make it worth your while to enlist."

The marquis, stupefied with astonishment, and secretly enraged, went off in search of his former tutor, confided to him all his troubles, and asked his advice. He proposed that he should become, like himself, a tutor of the young.

"Alas! I know nothing; you have taught me nothing whatever, and you are the primary cause of all my unhappiness." And as he spoke he began to sob.

"Write novels," said a wit who was present, "it is an excellent resource to fall back upon at Paris."

The young man, in more desperate straits than ever, hastened to the house of his mother's father-confessor, who was a Theatine monk of the very highest reputation, directing the souls of none but ladies of the first rank in society. As soon as he saw him, the reverend gentleman rushed to meet him.

"Good gracious! My lord Marquis, where is your carriage? How is your honored mother, the Marchioness?"

The unfortunate young fellow related the disaster that had befallen his family. As he explained the matter further the Theatine [3] assumed a graver air, one of less concern and more self-importance.

"My son, herein you may see the hand of Providence; riches serve only to corrupt the heart. The Almighty has shown special favor then to your mother in reducing her to beggary. Yes, sir, so much the better!—She is now sure of her salvation."

"But, father, in the meantime are there no means of obtaining some succor in this world?"

"Farewell, my son! There is a lady of the Court waiting for me."

The marquis felt ready to faint. He was treated after much the same manner by all his friends, and learned to know the world better in half a day than in all the rest of his life.

As he was plunged in overwhelming despair, he saw an old-fashioned traveling chaise, more like a covered tumbril than anything else and furnished with leather curtains, followed by four enormous wagons all heavily laden. In the chaise was a young man in rustic attire; his round and rubicund face had an air of kindness and good temper. His little wife, whose sunburned countenance had a pleasing if not a refined expression, was jolted about as she sat beside him. The vehicle did not go quite so fast as a dandy's chariot, the traveler had plenty of time to look at the marquis, as he stood motionless, absorbed in his grief.

"Oh, good heavens!" he exclaimed; "I believe that is Jeannot there!"

Hearing that name the marquis raised his eyes; the chaise stopped.

"'Tis Jeannot himself! Yes, it is Jeannot!"

The plump little man with one leap sprang to the ground, and ran to embrace his old companion. Jeannot recognized Colin; signs of sorrow and shame covered his countenance.

"You have forsaken your old friend," said Colin, "but be you as grand a lord as you like, I shall never cease to love you."

Jeannot, confounded and cut to the heart, told him with sobs something of his history.

"Come into the inn where I am lodging, and tell me the rest," said Colin; "kiss my little wife, and let us go and dine together."

They went, all three of them, on foot, and the baggage followed.

"What in the world is all this paraphernalia? Does it belong to you?"

"Yes, it is all mine and my wife's, we are just come from the country. I am at the head of a large tin, iron, and copper factory, and have married the daughter of a rich tradesman and general provider of all useful commodities for great folks and small. We work hard, and God gives us his blessing. We are satisfied with our condition in life, and are quite happy. We will help our friend Jeannot! Give up being a marquis; all the grandeur in the world is not equal in value to a good friend. You will return with me into the country; I will teach you my trade, it is not a difficult one to learn; I will give you a share in the business, and we will live together with light hearts in that corner of the earth where we were born."

Jeannot, overcome by this kindness, felt himself divided between sorrow and joy, tenderness and shame, and he said to himself:

"All my fashionable friends have proved false to me, and Colin, whom I despised, is the only one who comes to my succor. What a lesson!"

Colin's generosity developed in Jeannot's heart the germ of that good disposition which the world had not yet choked. He felt that he could not desert his father and mother.

"We will take care of your mother," said Colin; "and

as for your good father, who is in prison,—I know something of business matters,—his creditors, when they see that he has nothing more, will agree to a moderate compensation. I will see to all that myself."

Colin was as good as his word, and succeeded in effecting the father's release from prison. Jeannot returned to his old home with his parents, who resumed their former occupation. He married Colin's sister, who, being like her brother in disposition, rendered her husband very happy. And so Jeannot the father, and Jeannotte the mother, and Jeannot the son came to see that vanity is no true source of happiness.

THE STORY OF A GOOD BRAHMAN

THE STORY OF A GOOD BRAHMAN

I ONCE met, when on my travels, an old Brahman who was exceedingly wise, full of native intelligence, and profoundly learned. Moreover, he was rich, and, in consequence, all the more correct in his conduct, for, being in want of nothing, he had no need to deceive anybody. His household was very well managed by three handsome wives who laid themselves out to please him; and, when he was not entertaining himself with them, he was engaged in studying philosophy.

Near his house, which was a fine one situated in the midst of charming gardens, dwelt an old Hindoo woman, bigoted, half-witted, and extremely poor.

One day the Brahman said to me:

"Would that I had never been born!"

I asked him what made him say that, and he replied as follows:

"I studied for forty years, and they are so many years wasted; I have been teaching for the rest of my life, and I am ignorant of everything. This state of things fills my soul with such humiliation and disgust, that life is to me intolerable. I have been born into the world, I live subject to the limitations of time, and I know not what time is: I find myself on a point between two eternities, as our sages say, and I have no conception of eternity. I am composed of matter, and I can think, yet I have never been able to satisfy myself as to what produces thought: I know not whether my understanding is a simple faculty within me, like the power of walking or of digesting food, and whether I think with my head in the same way as I grasp with my hands. Not only is the essential nature of my powers of thought unknown to me, but that of my muscular movements is equally obscure. I cannot tell why I exist, yet I am questioned every day on all these points, and I am obliged to make some answer. I have nothing to say worth hearing, but I am not sparing of my words, and, after all has been said, I remain confused and ashamed of myself.

"It is even worse when people ask me if Brahma was produced by Vishnu, or if they are both eternal. Heaven is my witness that I know nothing about the matter, as my answers only too plainly show. 'Ah, reverend father,' they say, 'teach us how it is that evil floods the whole earth!' I am as much at a loss as those who ask me that question; I tell them sometimes that all is well and could not be better, but those who have been ruined and maimed in the wars do not believe a word of it, any more than I do myself. I retire into my own house crushed by the weight of my own ignorance and unsatisfied curiosity. I read our ancient books, and they only make my darkness greater. I speak to my companions; some tell me in reply that we must enjoy life and laugh at mankind, others think that they know a secret that explains everything, and lose themselves in a maze of extravagant notions. All tends to increase the painful feeling of uncertainty that possesses me, and I am ready sometimes to fall into despair, when I consider that, after all my investigations, I know neither whence I come, nor what I am, nor whither I go, nor what will become of me."

I was really pained at the state of this good soul; no one could be more rational than he was, nor more sincerely in earnest. I conceived that the brighter the light of his understanding, and the keener the sensibility of his heart, the greater was his unhappiness.

The same day I saw the old woman who lived in his neighborhood, and I asked her if she had ever been distressed at not knowing how her soul was formed. She did not even comprehend my question; she had never reflected for a single moment of her life on any one of those points which tormented the Brahman; she believed in the incarnation of Vishnu with all her heart, and provided she might sometimes have a little water from the Ganges with which to wash herself, she deemed herself the most fortunate of women.

Struck with this poor creature's happiness, I returned to my philosopher, and said:

"Are you not ashamed of being unhappy, while at your very gate there is an old automatom who thinks about nothing and lives contented?"

"You are right," he answered; "I have told myself a hundred times that I should be happy if I were as silly as my neighbor, and yet somehow I have no wish to attain such happiness."

This reply of my Brahman impressed me more than anything else. I examined my own heart and discovered that, if I had the offer, I should not have wished, any more than he, to be happy at the expense of my intelligence.

I referred the problem to some philosophers, and their opinions were the same as mine.

"For all that," said I, "There is a wild contradiction in this manner of thinking; for, after all, what is the question?—How to be happy. What does it matter whether one is intelligent or silly? Moreover, those who are contented with their existence are quite sure that they are so, whereas those who exercise their reason are by no means so certain that they exercise it aright. It is clear then," said I, "that we should be constrained to choose the loss of reason, if reason contributes to our unhappiness in however small a degree."

Everybody agreed with me in this opinion, and yet I found no one willing to accept the bargain, when it was a question of purchasing contentment at the price of becoming a fool. Hence I concluded that if we set a high value on happiness, we value reason even more.

But, after having reflected on this matter, it appears to me that to prefer reason to happiness is to be very senseless. How can this contradiction be explained? Like all the others—whereon there is a great deal to be said.

MEMNON, THE PHILOSOPHER

MEMNON, THE PHILOSOPHER

Notice by the Author

In all we undertake we miss the way:
That is, alas! our destined fate, it seems.
My brain at morn with wisest projects teems,
While folly chases folly all the day.

THIS little verse pretty aptly describes a large number of those who pride themselves on the possession of reason, and it is odd enough to see a grave director of souls ending his career in the criminal dock beside a fraudulent bankrupt.[1] In connection with this case, we reprint here the following little tale, though it had its origin elsewhere, for it is well that it should be known far and wide.

Memnon one day conceived the irrational design of being perfectly wise and prudent. There are very few persons who have not at some time or other had foolish thoughts of this kind pass through their heads. Memnon said to himself: "In order to be very wise, and consequently very happy, one has only to be without passions, and nothing is easier than that, as everybody knows. In the first place, I will never fall in love with a woman, for I will say to myself, whenever I see a sample of perfect beauty: 'Those cheeks will one day be wrinkled, those fine eyes will be rimmed with red, that swelling bosom will be flat and flabby, that lovely head will become bald.' I have only to see her now with the same eyes as those with which I shall see her then, and assuredly my head will not be turned by the sight of hers.

"In the second place, I will be always sober and temperate; good cheer, delicious wines, and the seductive charms of social intercourse will tempt me in vain. I shall have nothing to do but to bring before my mind the results of excess in a heavy head, a disordered stomach, the loss of reason, of health, and of time, and then I shall eat only for necessity, my health will be always well balanced, my thoughts always bright and clear. All this is so easy that there is no merit in such attainments.

"In the next place," said Memnon, "I must give a little consideration to my property; my desires are moderate, my wealth is well bestowed with the receiver-general of the revenues of Nineveh, I have enough to support myself in independence, and that is the greatest of blessings. I shall never be under the cruel necessity of cringing and flattering; I shall envy nobody, and nobody will envy me. All that is still very easy. I have friends," continued he, "and I shall keep them, for they will have nothing to quarrel about with me. I will never be out of temper with them, nor they with me; that is a matter that presents no difficulty."

Having thus laid down his little scheme of wisdom and prudence in his chamber, Memnon put his head out of the window, and saw two women walking up and down under some plane trees near his house. One of them was old, and appeared to have nothing on her mind; the other was young and pretty, and seemed to be lost in thought. She sighed, she wept, and her sighs and tears only added to her charms. Our sage was touched, not, of course, by the lady's beauty (he was quite confident of being above such weakness as that), but by the distress in which he saw her. He went down and accosted the fair Ninevite, with the intention of ministering wise consolation. That charming young person related to him, with the most simple and affecting air, all the injury done her by an uncle, who did not exist; she told him by what tricks he had deprived her of a fortune, which she had never possessed, and all that she had to fear from his violence.

"You seem to me," said she, "a man of such excellent judgment and good sense, that if you would only condescend to come to my house and inquire into my affairs, I feel sure that you could extricate me from the cruel embarrassment in which I find myself."

Memnon had no hesitation in following her, in order to make a judicious examination of her affairs, and to give her good advice.

The afflicted lady led him into a sweetly-scented chamber, and politely made him sit down with her on a large ottoman, where they both remained awhile, with legs crossed, facing each other. When the lady spoke she lowered her eyes, from which tears sometimes escaped, and, when she raised them, they always met the gaze of the sage Memnon. Her language was full of a tenderness which grew more tender each time that they exchanged glances. Memnon took her affairs zealously to heart, and every moment felt an increasing desire to oblige a maiden so modest and so unfortunate. By imperceptible degrees, as their conversation grew warmer, they ceased to sit opposite each other, and their legs were no longer crossed. Memnon pressed her so closely with good advice, and bestowed such tender admonitions, that neither of them could any longer talk about business, nor did they well know what they were about.

While they were thus engaged, the uncle, as might have been expected, arrived upon the scene. He was armed from head to foot, and the first thing he said was that he was going to kill, as was only just and proper, both the sage Memnon and his niece. The last remark that escaped him was that he might possibly pardon them for a large sum of money. Memnon was obliged to give him all that he had about him. In those times, fortunately, it was possible to get off as cheaply as that. America had not yet been discovered, and distressed damsels were not nearly so dangerous as they are nowadays.

Memnon returned home disconsolate and ashamed, and found a note there inviting him to dine with some of his most intimate friends.

"If I stay at home alone," said he, "I shall have my thoughts taken up with my unfortunate adventure, I shall be unable to eat anything, and shall certainly fall ill; it will be much better to take a frugal meal with my intimate friends. In the pleasure of their company I shall forget the piece of folly that I have committed this morning."

He goes to meet his friends, who find him a little out of spirits, and persuade him to drink away his melancholy. A little wine taken in moderation is a medicine for mind and body. So thinks the sage Memnon, and proceeds to get tipsy. Play is proposed after dinner. A modest game with one's friends is a blameless pastime. He plays, loses all that he has in his purse, and four times as much on his promise to pay. A dispute arises over the game, and the quarrel grows hot; one of his intimate friends throws a dice box at his head, and puts out an eye. The sage Memnon is carried home drunk, without any money, and with one eye less than when he went.

After he had slept himself sober, and his brain was grown a little clearer, he sent his servant for some of the money which he had lodged with the receiver-general of the revenues of Nineveh, in order to pay what he owed to his intimate friends. He was told that his debtor had that very morning been declared a fraudulent bankrupt, an announcement which had thrown a hundred families into consternation. Memnon, in a state bordering on distraction, went to court with a plaster over his eye and a petition in his hand to solicit justice of the king against the bankrupt. In an antechamber he met a number of ladies, all wearing with apparent ease hoops twenty-four feet in circumference. One of these ladies, who knew him slightly, exclaimed with a sidelong glance: "Oh, what a horror!" Another, who was on more familiar terms with him, addressed him thus:

"Good evening, Mr. Memnon. It is indeed a pleasure to see you, Mr. Memnon. By the way, Mr. Memnon, how is it you have lost an eye?" And she passed on without pausing for an answer. Memnon hid himself in a corner, and awaited the moment when he might cast himself at the monarch's feet. That moment came; he kissed the ground thrice, and presented his petition. His Gracious Majesty received him very favorably, and gave the document to one of his satraps to report upon it. The satrap drew Memnon aside, and said:

"What a comical kind of one-eyed fool you are, to address yourself to the king rather than to me! And still more ridiculous to dare to demand justice against a respectable bankrupt, whom I honor with my protection, and who is the nephew of my mistress's waiting-maid. Let this matter drop, my friend, if you wish to keep the eye you still have left you."

Thus Memnon, after having in the morning renounced the blandishments of women, intemperance at table, gambling and quarreling, and more than all else the

court, had ere nightfall been cajoled and robbed by a
fair deceiver, had drunk to excess, played high, been concerned in a quarrel, had an eye put out, and been to
court, where he had been treated with contempt and de-
rision.

Petrified with astonishment, and crushed with vexation, he turned his steps homeward, sick at heart. Intending to enter his house, he found bailiffs in possession removing the furniture on behalf of his creditors.
Almost fainting, he seated himself under a plane tree,
and there encountered the fair lady who had victimized
him in the morning. She was walking with her dear uncle, and burst out laughing when she saw Memnon with
the patch over his eye. Night came on; and Memnon
laid himself down on some straw beside the walls of his
house. There he was seized with ague, and in one of the
fits he fell asleep, when a celestial spirit appeared to him
in a dream.

He was all glittering with light. He had six beautiful
wings, but no feet, nor head, nor tail, and was like nothing he had ever seen before.

"Who art thou?" said Memnon.

"Thy good genius," answered the other.

"Give me back my eye then, my health, my house,
my property, and my prudence," said Memnon. Thereupon he told him how he had lost them all in one day.

"Such adventures as those never befall us in the world
which we inhabit," said the spirit.

"And what world do you inhabit?" asked the afflicted mortal.

"My home," replied he, "is at a distance of five hundred millions of leagues from the sun, in a little star
near Sirius, which thou seest from hence."

"Charming country!" exclaimed Memnon. "What!

Have you no sly hussies among you who impose upon a poor fellow, no intimate friends who win his money and knock out one of his eyes, no bankrupts, no satraps who mock you while they deny you justice?"

"No," said the inhabitant of the star, "nothing of the kind. We are never deceived by women, because we have none; we are never guilty of excesses at table, since we neither eat nor drink; we have no bankrupts, for gold and silver are unknown among us; we cannot have our eyes put out, because we do not possess bodies such as yours; and satraps never treat us with injustice, since all are equal in our little star."

Then said Memnon: "My lord, without the fair sex and without any dinner, how do you manage to pass the time?"

"In watching over the other worlds which are intrusted to our care," said the genius; "and I am come now to minister consolation to thee."

"Alas!" replied Memnon, "why didst thou not come last night to prevent me committing such follies?"

"I was with Hassan, your elder brother," said the celestial being. "He is more to be pitied than thou art. His Gracious Majesty, the King of India, to whose court he has the honor to be attached, has caused both his eyes to be put out for a slight act of indiscretion, and he is confined at the present moment in a dungeon, with chains upon his hands and feet."

"It is indeed well worth while to have a good genius in a family!" said Memnon; "of two brothers one has an eye knocked out, and the other loses both, one lies on straw, the other in prison."

"Thy lot will change," answered the inhabitant of the star. "It is true that thou wilt never recover thine eye, but, for all that, thou wilt be tolerably happy, provided that thou does never entertain the foolish idea of being perfectly wise and prudent."

"Is it impossible then to attain such a condition?" cried Memnon with a sigh.

"As impossible," replied the other, "as to be perfectly clever, perfectly strong, perfectly powerful, or perfectly happy. Even we ourselves are very far from being so. There is indeed a sphere where all that is to be found, but in the hundred thousand millions of worlds which are scattered through space everything proceeds by degrees. There is less wisdom and enjoyment in the second than in the first, less in the third than in the second, and so on to the last, where everybody is an absolute fool."

"I very much fear," said Memnon, "that our little terraqueous globe is precisely that lunatic asylum of the universe of which thou dost me the honor to speak."

"Not quite," said the spirit; "but it is not far off; everything must occupy its own place."

"In that case," said Memnon, "certain poets and certain philosophers are much mistaken when they say that *everything is for the best*, is it not so?"

"They are quite right," said the philosopher from the world above, "when the arrangement of the whole universe is taken into consideration."

"Ah! I shall never believe that," answered poor Memnon, "till I see out of two eyes again."

THE WORLD IS LIKE THAT, OR
THE VISION OF BABOUC

THE WORLD IS LIKE THAT, OR
THE VISION OF BABOUC

CHAPTER I

AMONG the genii who preside over the empires of the world, Ithuriel holds one of the first places, and has the province of Upper Asia. He came down one morning, entered the dwelling of Babouc, a Scythian who lived on the banks of the Oxus, and addressed him thus:

"Babouc, the follies and disorders of the Persians have drawn down upon them our wrath. An assembly of the genii of Upper Asia was held yesterday to consider whether Persepolis should be punished or utterly destroyed. Go thither, and make full investigation; on thy return inform me faithfully of all, and I will decide according to thy report either to chastise the city or to root it out."

"But, my lord," said Babouc humbly, "I have never been in Persia, and know no one there."

"So much the better," said the angel, "thou wilt be the more impartial. Heaven has given thee discernment, and I add the gift of winning confidence. Go, look, listen, observe, and fear nothing; thou shalt be well received everywhere."

Babouc mounted his camel, and set out with his servants. After some days, on approaching the plains of Sennah, he fell in with the Persian army, which was going to fight with the army of India.[1] He first accosted a soldier whom he found at a distance from the camp, and asked him what was the cause of the war.

"By all the gods," said the soldier, "I know nothing about it; it is no business of mine, my trade is to kill and be killed to get a living. It makes no odds to me whom I serve. I have a great mind to pass over tomorrow into the Indian camp, for I fear that they are giving their men half a copper drachma a day more than we get in this cursed service of Persia. If you want to know why we are fighting, speak to my captain."

Babouc gave the soldier a small present, and entered the camp. He soon made the captain's acquaintance, and asked him the cause of the war.

"How should I know?" said he. "Such grand matters are no concern of mine. I live two hundred leagues away from Persepolis; I hear it said that war has been declared; I immediately forsake my family, and go, according to our custom, to make my fortune or to die, since I have nothing else to do."

"But surely," said Babouc, "your comrades are a little better informed than yourself?"

"No," replied the officer, "hardly anybody except our chief satraps has any very clear notion why we are cutting each other's throats."

Babouc, astonished at this, introduced himself to the generals, and they were soon on intimate terms. At last one of them said to him:

"The cause of this war, which has laid Asia waste for the last twenty years, originally sprang out of a quarrel between a eunuch belonging to one of the wives of the great King of Persia, and a customhouse clerk in the service of the great King of India. The matter in dispute was a duty amounting to very nearly the thirtieth part of a daric.[2] The Indian and Persian prime ministers worthily supported their masters' rights. The quarrel grew hot. They sent into the field on both sides an army of a million troops. This army has to be recruited every year with more than 400,000 men. Massacres, conflagrations, ruin, and devastation multiply, the whole world suffers, and their fury still continues. Our own as well as the Indian prime minister often protests that they are acting solely for the happiness of the human race, and at each protestation some towns are always destroyed and some province ravaged."

The next day, on a report being spread that peace was about to be concluded, the Persian and Indian generals hastened to give battle; and a bloody one it was. Babouc saw all its mistakes and all its abominations: he witnessed stratagems carried on by the chief satraps, who did all they could to cause their commander to be defeated; he saw officers slain by their own troops; he saw soldiers dispatching their dying comrades in order to strip them of a few blood-stained rags, torn and covered with mud. He entered the hospitals to which they were carrying the wounded, most of whom died through the inhuman negligence of those very men whom the King of Persia paid handsomely to relieve them.

"Are these creatures men," cried Babouc, "or wild beasts? Ah! I see plainly that Persepolis will be destroyed."

Occupied with this thought, he passed into the camp of the Indians, and found there as favorable a reception as in that of the Persians, just as he had been led to expect; but he beheld there all the same abuses that had already filled him with horror.

"Ah!" said he to himself, "if the angel Ithuriel resolves to exterminate the Persians, then the angel of India must destroy the Indians as well."

Being afterwards more particularly informed of all that went on in both camps, he was made acquainted with acts of generosity, magnanimity, and humanity that moved him with astonishment and delight.

"Unintelligible mortals!" he exclaimed, "how is it that ye can combine so much meanness with so much greatness, such virtues with such crimes?"

Meanwhile peace was declared. The commanders of both armies, neither of whom had gained the victory but who had caused the blood of so many of their fellow-men to flow, only to promote their own interests, began to solicit rewards at their respective courts. The peace was extolled in public proclamations, which announced nothing less than the return of virtue and happiness to earth.

"God be praised!" said Babouc, "Persepolis will be the abode of purified innocence. It will not be destroyed, as those rascally genii wished: let us hasten without delay to this capital of Asia."

CHAPTER II

ON his arrival he entered that immense city by the old approach, which was altogether barbarous and offended the eye with its hideous want of taste.[3] All that part of the city bore witness to the time at which it had been built, for, in spite of men's obstinate stupidity in praising ancient at the expense of modern times, it must be confessed that in every kind of art first attempts are always rude.

Babouc mingled in a crowd of people composed of all the dirtiest and ugliest of both sexes, who with a dull and sullen air were pouring into a vast and dreary building. From the constant hum of voices and the movements that he remarked, from the money that some were giving to others for the privilege of sitting down, he thought that he was in a market where straw-bottomed chairs were on sale. But soon, when he observed several women drop upon their knees, pretending to look fixedly before them, but giving sidelong glances at the men, he became aware that he was in a temple. Grating voices, harsh, disagreeable, and out of tune, made the roof echo with ill-articulated sounds, which produced much the same effect as the braying of wild asses on the plains of the Pictavians,[4] when they answer the summons of the cow-herd's horn. He shut his ears, but he was yet more anxious to shut his eyes and nose, when he saw workmen entering this temple with crowbars and spades, who removed a large stone, and threw up the earth to right and left, from which there issued a most offensive smell. Then people came and laid a dead body in the opening, and the stone was put back above it.

"What!" cried Babouc, "these folk bury their dead in the same places where they worship the Deity, and their temples are paved with corpses! I am no longer surprised at those pestilential diseases which often consume Persepolis. The air, tainted with the corruption of the dead and by so many of the living gathered and crammed together in the same place, is enough to poison the whole earth. Oh, what an abominable city is this Persepolis! It would seem that the angels intend to destroy it in order to raise up a fairer one on its site, and to fill it with cleaner inhabitants, and such as can sing better. Providence may be right after all; let us leave it to take its own course."

CHAPTER III

MEANWHILE the sun had almost reached the middle of its course. Babouc was to dine at the other end of the town with a lady for whom he had letters from her husband, an officer in the army. He first took several turns in and about Persepolis, where he saw other temples better built and more tastefully adorned, filled with a refined congregation, and resounding with harmonious music. He observed public fountains, which, badly placed though they were, struck the eye by their beauty; open spaces, where the best kings who had governed Persia seemed to breathe in bronze, and others where he heard the people exclaiming: "When shall we see our beloved master here?" He admired the magnificent bridges that spanned the river, the splendid and serviceable quays, the palaces built on either side, and especially an immense mansion where thousands of old soldiers, wounded in the hour of victory, daily returned thanks to the God of armies.[5] At last he entered the lady's house, where he had been invited to dine with a select company. The rooms were elegant and handsomely furnished, the dinner delicious, the lady young, beautiful, clever and charming, the company worthy of their hostess, and Babouc kept saying to himself every moment: "The angel Ithuriel must set the opinion of the whole world at defiance, if he thinks of destroying a city so delightful."

CHAPTER IV

AS time went on he perceived that the lady, who had begun by making tender inquiries after her husband, was, towards the end of the repast, speaking more tenderly still to a young magian. He saw a magistrate who, in his wife's presence, was bestowing the liveliest caresses upon a widow; and that indulgent widow kept one hand round the magistrate's neck, while she stretched out the other to a handsome young citizen whose modesty seemed equal to his good looks. The magistrate's wife was the first to leave the table, in order to entertain in an adjoining chamber her spiritual director, who had been expected to dine with them but arrived too late; and the director, a man of ready eloquence, addressed her in that chamber with such vigor and unction, that the lady, when she came back, had her eyes moist and her cheeks flushed, an unsteady step, and a stammering utterance.

Then Babouc began to fear that the genius Ithuriel was in the right. The gift that he possessed of winning confidence let him into the secrets of his fair hostess that very day; she owned to him her partiality for the young magian, and assured him that in all the houses at Persepolis he would find the same sort of behavior as he had witnessed in hers. Babouc came to the conclusion that such a society could not long hold together; that jealousy, discord, and revenge were bound to make havoc in every household; that tears and blood must be shed daily; that the husbands would assuredly kill or be killed by the lovers of their wives; and, finally, that Ithuriel would do well to destroy immediately a city given up to continual dissensions.

CHAPTER V

HE was brooding over these doleful thoughts, when there appeared at the door a man of grave countenance, clad in a black cloak, who humbly entreated a word with the young magistrate. The latter, without getting up or even looking at him, gave him some papers with a haughty and absent air, and then dismissed him. Babouc asked who the man was. The mistress of the house said to him in a low tone:

"That is one of the ablest counselors we have in this city, and he has been studying the laws for fifty years. The gentleman yonder, who is but twenty-five years of age, and who was made a satrap of the law two days ago, has employed him to draw up an abstract of a case on which he has to pronounce judgment tomorrow, and which he has not yet examined."

"This young spark acts wisely," said Babouc, "in asking an old man's advice, but why is not that old man himself the judge?"

"You must be joking," was the reply; "those who have grown old in toilsome and inferior employments never attain positions of great dignity. This young man enjoys a high office because his father is rich, and because the right of administering justice is bought and sold here like a farm."

"O unhappy city, to have such customs!" cried Babouc. "That is the coping-stone of confusion. Doubtless those who have purchased the right of dispensing justice sell their judgments. I see nothing here but unfathomable depths of iniquity."

As he thus testified his sorrow and surprise, a young

warrior, who had that very day returned from the campaign, addressed him in the following terms:

"Why should you object to judicial appointments being made a matter of purchase? I have myself paid a good price for the right of facing death at the head of two thousand men under my command; it has cost me forty thousand gold darics this year to lie on the bare ground in a red coat for thirty nights together and to be twice wounded pretty severely by an arrow, of which I still feel the smart. If I ruin myself to serve the Persian emperor whom I have never seen, this gentleman who represents the majesty of the law may well pay something to have the pleasure of listening to litigants."

Babouc in his indignation could not refrain from condemning in his heart a country where the highest offices of peace and war were put up to auction; he hastily concluded that there must be among such people a total ignorance of legal and military affairs, and that even if Ithuriel should spare them, they would be destroyed by their own detestable institutions.

His bad opinion was further confirmed by the arrival of a fat man, who, after giving a familiar nod to all the company, approached the young officer, and said to him:

"I can only lend you fifty thousand gold darics; for to tell you the truth, the imperial taxes have not brought me in more than three hundred thousand this year."

Babouc inquired who this man might be who complained of getting so little, and was informed that there were in Persepolis forty plebeian kings,[6] who held the Persian empire on lease, and paid the monarch something out of what they made.

CHAPTER VI

AFTER dinner he went into one of the grandest temples in the city, and seated himself in the midst of a crowd of men and women who had come there to pass away the time. A magian appeared in a structure raised above their heads, and spoke for a long time about virtue and vice. This magian divided under several heads what had no need of division, he proved methodically what was perfectly clear, and taught what everybody knew already. He coolly worked himself into a passion, and went away perspiring and out of breath. Then all the congregation awoke, and thought that they had been listening to an edifying discourse. Babouc said:

"There is a man who has done his best to weary two or three hundred of his fellow-citizens, but his intention was good, and there is no reason in that for destroying Persepolis."

On leaving this assembly, he was taken to witness a public entertainment, which was exhibited every day in the year. It was held in a sort of hall, at the further end of which appeared a palace. The fairest part of the female population of Persepolis and the most illustrious satraps, seated in orderly ranks, formed a spectacle so brilliant that Babouc imagined at first that there was nothing more to be seen. Two or three persons, who seemed to be kings and queens, soon showed themselves at the entrance of the palace; their language was very different from that of the people; it was measured, harmonious, and sublime. No one slept, but all listened in profound silence, which was only interrupted by expressions of feeling and admiration on the part of the audience. The

duty of kings, the love of virtue, and the dangerous nature of the passions were set forth in terms so lively and
touching that Babouc shed tears. He had no doubt that
those heroes and heroines, those kings and queens, whom
he had just heard, were the preachers of the empire. He
even proposed to himself to persuade Ithuriel to come
and hear them, quite convinced that such a spectacle
would reconcile him forever to the city.

As soon as the entertainment was over, he was anxious to see the principal queen, who had delivered such
pure and noble sentiments of morality in that beautiful
palace. He procured an introduction to her majesty, and
was led up a narrow staircase to the second story, and
ushered into a badly furnished apartment, where he
found a woman meanly clad, who said to him with a
noble and pathetic air:

"This calling of mine does not afford me enough to
live upon; one of the princes whom you saw has got me
into the family way, and I shall soon be brought to bed.
I am in want of money, and one cannot lie in without
that."

Babouc gave her a hundred gold darics, saying to himself:

"If there were nothing worse than this in the city, I
think Ithuriel would be wrong in being so angry."

After that he went, under the escort of an intelligent
man with whom he had become acquainted, to pass the
evening in the shops of those who dealt in objects of
useless ostentation. He bought whatever took his fancy,
and everything was sold him in the most polite manner
at far more than it was worth. His friend, on their return to his house, explained to him how he had been
cheated, and Babouc made a note of the tradesman's
name, in order to have him specially marked out by

Ithuriel on the day when the city should be visited with punishment. As he was writing, a knock was heard at the door; it was the shopkeeper himself come to restore his purse, which Babouc had left by mistake on his counter.

"How comes it to pass," cried Babouc, "that you can be so honest and generous, after having had the face to sell me a lot of trumpery for four times as much as it is worth?"

"There is no merchant of any note in this city," answered the shopkeeper, "who would not have brought you back your purse, but whoever told you that you paid four times its proper value for what you bought from me, has grossly deceived you. My profit was ten times as much, and so true is this that if you wish to sell the articles again in a month's time, you will not get even that tenth part. But nothing is fairer; it is men's passing fancy which settles the price of such gewgaws; it is that fancy which affords a livelihood to the hundred workmen whom I employ; it is that which provides me with a fine house, a comfortable carriage, and horses; it is that which stimulates industry, and promotes taste, traffic, and plenty. I sell the same trifles to neighboring nations at a much dearer rate than to you, and in that way I am useful to my country."

Babouc, after a moment's reflection, scratched the man's name out of his pocket book.

"For after all," said he, "the arts that minister to luxury multiply and flourish in a country only when all the necessary arts are also practiced, and the nation is numerous and wealthy. Ithuriel seems to me a little too severe."

CHAPTER VII

BABOUC, much puzzled as to what opinion he ought to have of Persepolis, determined to visit the magi and men of letters, for, inasmuch as the former devote themselves to religion and the latter to wisdom, he had great hopes that they would obtain pardon for the rest of the people. So next morning he repaired to a college of the magi. The archimandrite acknowledged that he had an income of a hundred thousand crowns for having taken a vow of poverty, and that he exercised a very extensive dominion in virtue of his profession of humility; after which he left Babouc in the hands of a brother of low degree, who did the honors of the place.

While this brother was showing him all the magnificence of that home of penitence, a rumor spread that he was come to reform all those religious houses. He immediately began to receive memorials from each of them, all of which were substantially to this effect: "Preserve us, and destroy all the others."

To judge by the arguments that were used in self-defense, these societies were all absolutely necessary; if their mutual accusations were to be believed, they all alike deserved extinction. He marveled how there was not one of them but wished to govern the whole world in order to enlighten it. Then a little fellow, who was a demi-magian, came forward and said to him:

"I see clearly that the work is going to be accomplished, for Zerdust has returned to earth; little girls prophesy, getting themselves pinched in front and whipped behind. It is evident that the world is coming to an end; could you not, before the final catastrophe, protect us from the grand lama?"

"What nonsense!" said Babouc. "From the grand lama? From the pontiff-king who resides in Thibet?"

"Yes," said the little demi-magian, with a decided air; "against him, and none else."

"Then you wage war on him, and have armies?" asked Babouc.

"No," said the other, "but we have written three or four thousand books against him, that nobody reads, and as many pamphlets, which are read by women at our direction.[7] He has hardly ever heard us spoken of, he has only pronounced sentence against us, as a master might order the trees in his garden to be cleared of caterpillars."

Babouc shuddered at the folly of those men who made a profession of wisdom; the intrigues of those who had renounced the world; the ambition, greed, and pride of those who taught humility and unselfishness; and he came to the conclusion that Ithuriel had very good reason for destroying the whole brood.

CHAPTER VIII

ON his return to his lodging, he sent for some new books in order to soothe his indignation, and he invited some literary men to dinner for the sake of cheerful society. Twice as many came as he had asked, like wasps attracted by honey. These parasites were as eager to speak as they were to eat, and two classes of persons were the objects of their praise: the dead and their own selves,—never their contemporaries, the master of the house excepted. If one of them happened to make a clever remark, the countenances of all the others fell, and they gnawed their lips for vexation that it was not they who had said it. They did not disguise their real feelings so much as the magi, because their ambition was not pitched so high. There was not one of them but was soliciting some petty post or another, and at the same time wishing to be thought a great man. They said to each other's face the most insulting things, which they took for flashes of wit. Having some knowledge of Babouc's mission, one of them begged him in a whisper to annihilate an author who had not praised him as much as he thought proper, five years ago; another entreated the ruin of a citizen for having never laughed at his comedies; and a third desired the abolition of the Academy, because he himself had never succeeded in gaining admission. When the meal was finished, each went out by himself, for in all the company there were not two men who could endure or even speak a civil word to each other, outside the houses of those rich patrons who invited them to their table. Babouc deemed that it would be no great loss if all that breed of vermin were to perish in the general destruction.

CHAPTER IX

AS soon as he was rid of them, he began to read some of the new books, and recognized in them the same temper as his guests had shown. He saw with special indignation those gazettes of slander, those records of bad taste which are dictated by envy, baseness, and abject poverty; those cowardly satires in which the vulture is treated with respect while the dove is torn to pieces; and those novels, destitute of imagination, in which are displayed so many portraits of women with whom the author is totally unacquainted.

He threw all those detestable writings into the fire, and went out to take an evening stroll. He was introduced to an old scholar who had not made one of his late company of parasites, for he always avoided the crowd. Knowing men well, he made good use of his knowledge, and was careful to whom he gave his confidence. Babouc spoke to him with indignation of what he had read and what he had seen.

"You have been reading poor contemptible stuff," said the learned sage; "but at all times, in all countries, and in every walk of life, the bad swarm and the good are rare. You have entertained the mere scum of pedantry, for in all professions alike those who least deserve to appear always obtrude themselves with most effrontery. The men of real wisdom live a quiet and retired life; there are still among us some men and books worthy of your attention."

While he was speaking thus another man of letters joined them, and their conversation was so agreeable and instructive, so superior to prejudice and conformable to virtue, that Babouc confessed he had never heard anything like it before.

"Here are men," he said to himself, "whom the angel Ithuriel will not dare to touch, or he will be ruthless indeed."

Reconciled as he now was to the men of letters, Babouc was still enraged at the rest of the nation.

"You are a stranger," said the judicious person who was talking to him; "abuses present themselves to your eyes in a mass, and the good which is concealed, and which sometimes springs out of these abuses, escapes your observation."

Then he learned that among the men of literature there were some who were free from envy, and that even among the magi virtuous men were to be found. He understood at last that these great societies, which seemed by their mutual collisions to be bringing about their common ruin, were in the main beneficial institutions; that each community of magi was a check upon its rivals; that if they differed in some matters of opinion, they all taught the same principles of morality, instructed the people, and lived in obedience to the laws, like tutors who watch over the son of the house, while the master watches over them. Becoming acquainted with several of these magi, he saw souls of heavenly disposition. He found that even among the simpletons who aspired to make war on the grand lama there had been some very great men. He began to suspect that the character of the people of Persepolis might be like their buildings, some of which had seemed to him deplorably bad, while others had ravished him with admiration.

CHAPTER X

SAID Babouc to his literary friend:
"I see clearly enough that these magi, whom I thought so dangerous, are in reality very useful, especially when a wise government prevents them from making themselves too indispensable. But you will at least acknowledge that your young magistrates, who buy a seat on the bench as soon as they have learned to mount a horse, must needs display in your courts of law the most ridiculous incompetence and the most perverse injustice; it would undoubtedly be better to give these ap-

pointments gratuitously to those old lawyers who have passed all their lives in weighing conflicting arguments."

The man of letters made reply:

"You saw our army before your arrival at Persepolis; you know that our young officers fight very well, although they have purchased their commissions; perhaps you will find that our young magistrates do not pronounce wrong judgments, in spite of having paid for the positions they occupy."

He took Babouc the next day to the High Court of Judicature, where an important decision was to be delivered. The case was one that excited universal interest. All the old advocates who spoke about it were uncertain in their opinions. They quoted a hundred laws, not one of which had any essential bearing upon the question; they regarded the matter from a hundred points of view, none of which presented it in its true light. The judges were quicker in giving their decision than the advocates in raising doubts; their judgment was almost unanimous, and their sentence was just, because they followed the light of reason, whereas the others went astray in their opinions, because they had only consulted their books.

Babouc came to the conclusion that abuses often entail very good results. He had an opportunity of seeing that very day how the riches of the farmers of the revenue, which had given him so much offense, might produce an excellent effect, for the emperor, being in want of money, obtained in an hour by their means a sum that he would not have been able to procure in six months through the ordinary channels. He saw that those big clouds, swollen with the dews of earth, restored to it in rain all that they received from it. Moreover, the children of those self-made men, often better educated than those of the most ancient families, were sometimes of much greater value to their country; for there is nothing to hinder a man from making a good judge, a brave soldier, or a clever statesman, in the circumstance of his having had a good accountant for his father.

CHAPTER XI

BY degrees Babouc forgave the greed of the farmers of the revenue, who are not in reality more greedy than other men, and who are necessary to the welfare of the state. He excused the folly of those who impoverished themselves in order to be a judge or a soldier, a folly which creates great magistrates and heroes. He pardoned the envy displayed by the men of letters, among whom were to be found men who enlightened the world; he became reconciled to the ambitious and intriguing magi, among whom eminent virtues outweighed petty vices. But there remained behind abundant matter of offense: above all, the love affairs of the ladies. And the ruin which he felt sure must follow, filled him with disquietude and alarm.

As he wished to gain an insight into human life under all conditions, he procured an introduction to a minister of state, but on his way he was trembling all the time lest some wife should be assassinated by her husband before his eyes. On arriving at the statesman's house, he had to wait two hours in the antechamber before he was announced, and two hours more after that had been done. He fully made up his mind during that interval to report to the angel Ithuriel both the minister and his insolent lackeys. The antechamber was filled with ladies of every degree, with magi of all shades of opinion, with judges, tradesmen, officers, and pedants; all found fault with the minister. The misers and usurers said: "That fellow plunders the provinces, there's no doubt about it." The capricious reproached him with being eccentric. The libertines said: "He thinks of nothing but his pleasures." The factious flattered themselves that they should soon see him ruined by a cabal. The women hoped that they might ere long have a younger minister.

Babouc heard their remarks, and could not help saying:

"What a fortunate man this is! He has all his enemies in his antechamber; he crushes under his heel those who envy him; he sees those who detest him groveling at his feet."

At last he was admitted, and saw a little old man stooping under the weight of years and business, but still brisk and full of energy.[8]

He was pleased with Babouc, who thought him a worthy man, and their conversation became interesting. The minister confessed that he was very unhappy; that he passed for rich, but was really poor; that he was believed to be all powerful, yet was being constantly thwarted, that almost all his favors had been conferred on the ungrateful; and that amid the continual labors of forty years he had scarcely had a moment's peace. Babouc was touched with compassion, and thought that if this man had committed faults and the angel Ithuriel wished to punish him, he had no need to destroy him: it would be enough to leave him where he was.

CHAPTER XII

WHILE the minister and he were talking together, the fair dame with whom Babouc had dined, hastily entered, and in her eyes and on her forehead were seen symptoms of vexation and anger. She burst out into reproaches against the statesman; she shed tears; she complained bitterly that her husband had been refused a post to which his birth allowed him to aspire, and to which his services and his wounds entitled him. She expressed herself so forcibly, she made her complaints with so much grace, she overcame objections with such skill and reinforced her arguments with such eloquence, that ere she left the room she had made her husband's fortune.

Babouc held out his hand, and said:

"Is it possible, madam, that you can have given yourself all this trouble for a man whom you do not love, and from whom you have everything to fear?"

"A man whom I do not love!" she cried. "My husband, let me tell you, is the best friend I have in the world; there is nothing that I would not sacrifice for him, except my lover, and he would do anything for me, except giving up his mistress. I should like you to know her; she is a charming woman, full of wit, and of an excellent disposition; we sup together this evening with my husband and my little magian; come and share our enjoyment."

The lady took Babouc home with her. The husband, who had arrived at last, overwhelmed with grief, saw his wife again with transports of delight and gratitude; he embraced by turns his wife, his mistress, the little magian, and Babouc. Unity, cheerfulness, wit, and elegance were the soul of the repast.

"Learn," said the fair dame at whose house he was supping, "that those who are sometimes called women of no virtue have almost always merits as genuine as those of the most honorable man; and to convince yourself of it come with me tomorrow and dine with the fair Theona. There are some old vestals who pick her to pieces, but she does more good than all of them together. She would not commit even a trifling act of injustice to promote her own interests, however important; the advice she gives her lover is always noble; his glory is her sole concern; he would blush to face her if he had neglected any occasion of doing good; for a man can have no greater encouragement to virtuous actions than to have for a witness and judge of his conduct a mistress whose good opinion he is anxious to deserve."

Babouc did not fail to keep the appointment. He saw a house where all the pleasures reigned, with Theona at their head, who knew how to speak in the language of each. Her natural good sense put others at their ease; she made herself agreeable without an effort, for she was as amiable as she was generous, and, what enhanced the value of all her good qualities, she was beautiful.

Babouc, Scythian though he was, and though a spirit had sent him on his mission, perceived that, if he stayed any longer at Persepolis, he should forget Ithuriel for Theona. He felt fond of a city whose inhabitants were polite, good-humored and kind, however frivolous they might be, greedy of scandal, and full of vanity. He feared that the doom of Persepolis was sealed; he dreaded, too, the report he would have to give.

This was the method he adopted for making that report. He gave instructions to the best founder in the city to cast a small image composed of all kinds of metals, earth, and stones, alike the most precious and the most worthless. He brought it to Ithuriel, and said:

"Wilt thou break this pretty little image because it is not all gold and diamonds?"

Ithuriel understood his meaning before the words were out of his mouth, and determined that he would not think of punishing Persepolis, but would let the world go on in its own way; "for," said he, "if everything is not as it should be, there is nothing intolerably bad." So Persepolis was allowed to remain unharmed, and Babouc was very far from uttering any complaint like Jonah, who was angry because Nineveh was not destroyed. But when a man has been three days in a whale's belly, he is not so good-tempered as after a visit to the opera or to the play, or after having supped in good company.

COSI-SANCTA, OR A LITTLE HARM FOR A GREAT GOOD

COSI-SANCTA, OR A LITTLE HARM
FOR A GREAT GOOD

An African Tale

IT is a maxim founded upon error that it is not allow-
able to commit a small fault in order that a greater
good may result. St. Augustine was decidedly of this
opinion, as it is easy to see from his mention of that
little occurrence which took place in his diocese, under
the proconsulship of Septimus Acindynus, and which
is related in his work entitled *The City of God*.[1]

There lived at Hippo an old parish priest, a great
founder of brotherhoods and father-confessor to all the
young damsels in the neighborhood, who had the reputation of being a man inspired by God, because he took
upon himself to utter predictions, a vocation in which
he acquitted himself tolerably well.

One day a young girl was brought to him named Cosi-
Sancta, the most beautiful in all the province. Her father and mother were Jansenists, and they had brought her
up in the strictest principles of virtue; and of all the ad-
mirers that she had had, not one had been able to cause
her so much as a moment's distraction in the midst of
her devotions. She had been for some time betrothed to
a little withered old man, whose name was Capito, a
councilor in the inferior court of justice at Hippo. He
was a cross and crabbed little man, not without some
sense of humor, but affected in his conversation, given
to sneers, and fond of ill-natured ridicule. Moreover, he

was as jealous as a Venetian, and would not for all the world have consented to be on friendly terms with his wife's lovers. The young creature did all she could to love him, because he was to be her husband, and set herself to make the attempt with all sincerity, although she scarcely succeeded.

She went then to consult her parish priest, to know if her marriage would be happy. The good man told her in the tone of a prophet:

"My daughter, your virtue will cause you much unhappiness, but you will be one day canonized for having been three times unfaithful to your husband."

This oracle sorely astonished and perplexed the innocent young maiden. She shed tears, she asked for an explanation, thinking that some mysterious meaning must be concealed behind those words, but all the explanation that was vouchsafed her was that the three times were not to be understood as three assignations with the same lover, but as three different adventures.

Then Cosi-Sancta uttered loud cries; she even made some rude remarks to the old priest, and swore that she would never be made a saint. She was made one, however, in spite of that, as you will soon see.

She was married not long afterwards, and the wedding was a very grand one. She bore pretty well all the sly speeches that she had to encounter, all the coarse jokes, and all the ill disguised ribaldry with which it is the custom to embarrass the modesty of young brides. She danced extremely gracefully with several well-made and handsome young fellows, on whom her husband scowled with the most ferocious expression imaginable.

She lay down in bed beside little Capito with a certain amount of repugnance. She passed a considerable portion of the night in sleep, and awoke in a pensive

frame of mind. Her husband, however, was less the subject of her meditation than a young man named Ribaldos, who had got into her head without her knowing
anything about it. This young man seemed as if fash-
ioned by the hands of Cupid; he had the same winning
airs, the same impudence and roguish tricks. He was a
little too forward perhaps, but only with those ladies
who liked it: he was the darling of all Hippo. He had
set all the women in the place at variance one against
another, and he was at loggerheads with all the mothers
and husbands. His flirtations were generally prompted
by mere giddiness, not unmixed with vanity, but he
loved Cosi-Sancta from genuine inclination, and loved
her all the more desperately the more difficult it was to
make a conquest of her.

He endeavored in the first instance, like a sensible
man, to please the husband. He made a thousand advances, complimented him on his good looks, and on his
genial and generous temper, he lost money to him at
play, and was always having some insignificant secret to
tell him in confidence. Cosi-Sancta found him as amiable
as could possibly be; she loved him already more than
she imagined; indeed, she had no suspicion of it, but her
husband had instead. Although he was as self-conceited
as any little man could be, he could not help doubting
whether the visits of Ribaldos were for his sake only. He
broke with him on some frivolous pretext, and forbade
him to enter his house again.

Cosi-Sancta was very sorry for this, but did not dare
to say so, and Ribaldos, becoming more amorous as his
difficulties increased, passed all his time in watching for
opportunities of seeing her. He disguised himself as a
monk, as a dealer in old wardrobes, and as the exhibitor
of a puppet-show. But, after all, he did not succeed well

enough to gain a triumph over his mistress, though too well to escape being recognized by the husband. If Cosi-Sancta had been of one mind with her lover, they might have taken such precautions that her husband would not have been able to suspect anything, but as she resisted her inclination, and did nothing for which she could reproach herself, she saved everything that concerned her honesty, except appearances, and her husband believed her guilty to the last degree.

The little fellow, who was very passionate, and who fancied that his honor depended on his wife's fidelity, abused her cruelly, and punished her because other people could see her charms. She found herself in the most horrible situation that a woman can be in,—unjustly accused and ill-treated by a husband to whom she was faithful, and tortured by a violent passion which she did all she could to overcome.

She believed that if her lover ceased from pursuing her, her husband might cease to be unjust, and that she might be happy enough to be cured of a love which there would be nothing any longer to keep alive. Under this impression she ventured to write the following letter to Ribaldos:

"If you have any goodness, cease to render me miserable; you love me, and your love exposes me to the suspicions and violence of a master to whom I am bound for the remainder of my life. Would that this were the only risk I had to run! For pity's sake cease from pursuing me; I entreat you by that very love which constitutes your unhappiness and my own, and which can never render you happy."

Poor Cosi-Sancta had never foreseen that a letter so virtuous, though so tender, would produce an effect quite contrary to what she hoped. It inflamed her lover's heart more than ever, and he determined to risk his life in order to obtain a sight of his mistress.

Capito, who was fool enough to want to be informed of everything, and had trusty spies, was warned that Ribaldos had disguised himself as a mendicant friar of the Carmelite order to ask for charity from his wife. He thought that it was all over with him now, for he was of opinion that a Carmelite's costume was far more dangerous than any other for the honor of a husband. He placed people in ambush to give friar Ribaldos a good drubbing, and his orders were only too well executed. The young man on entering the house was received by these gentry; it was in vain that he cried out that he was an honest Carmelite, and that poor friars should not be treated so; he was beaten unmercifully, and a fortnight afterwards died from a blow which he received on his head. All the women in the city shed tears over him, and Cosi-Sancta was inconsolable. Capito himself was sorry, but for another reason, for he found himself in a very unpleasant scrape.

Ribaldos was a kinsman of the proconsul Acindynus. The representative of Rome wished to avenge the assassination in an exemplary manner, and as he had previously had some disputes with the inferior court of Hippo, he was not sorry to have an excuse for hanging one of its councilors. And he was particularly pleased that the lot should fall on Capito, who was by far the vainest and most intolerable little pettifogger in the country.

Thus Cosi-Sancta had seen her lover assassinated, and was near seeing her husband hanged, and all for having been virtuous; for, as I have already observed, if she had granted her favors to Ribaldos, she would have found it much more easy to deceive her husband.

And so you see how the first part of the priest's prediction was fulfilled. Cosi-Sancta then called to mind the oracle, and greatly feared lest the rest of it might also be accomplished. But having reflected that one cannot conquer one's fate, she resigned herself to Providence, which led her to her destination by ways the most honest in the world.

The proconsul Acindynus was a man devoted to profligacy rather than to pleasure, finding very little entertainment in preliminary dalliance, frankly brutal, a regular garrison hero, and much dreaded in the province. All the women in Hippo had had intrigues with him, only in order to escape his displeasure.

He sent for Madam Cosi-Sancta, and she arrived in tears, but none the less charming for that.

"Your husband, madam," he said, "is going to be hanged, and it is only you who can save him."

"I would give my life for his," said the lady

"That is not what is asked of you," replied the proconsul.

"What then is to be done?" said she.

"I only want you to pass one of your nights with me," answered the proconsul.

"They are not mine to dispose of," said Cosi-Sancta; "they belong to my husband. I will shed my blood to save him, but I cannot sacrifice my honor."

"But if your husband gives his consent?" urged the proconsul.

"He is my lord and master," answered the lady; "every one may do what he pleases with his own property. But I know my husband too well to think that he will do anything of the sort; he is a little man quite capable of letting himself be hanged sooner than allow anyone to touch me with the tip of his finger."

"We shall see about that," said the magistrate in a rage. He immediately caused the criminal to be brought before him, and offered him his choice, either to be hanged or to be horned; there must be no hesitation. The little fellow, notwithstanding, required some pressing. At last he did what anybody else would have done in his place, and his wife, out of charity, saved his life. This was the first of the three times. The same day her son fell ill of a most extraordinary disease, unknown to all the physicians in Hippo. There was only one who had a secret remedy for this disease, and he lived at Aquila, some leagues away from Hippo. At that time a physician established at one town was forbidden to leave it in order to go and practice his profession in another, so Cosi-Sancta was obliged to go herself to his house at Aquila, with a brother of hers to whom she was tenderly attached. On her way she was stopped by brigands. The chief of these worthies was not insensible to her charms, and, just as her brother was about to be killed, he approached her, and said that, if she would only be a little obliging, her brother's life should be spared, and that it should cost him nothing. The crisis was urgent: she had just saved the life of a husband for whom she had no great affection, she was about to lose a brother whom she loved much; moreover her son's dangerous condition alarmed her, and there was not a moment to be lost. So she commended herself to the care of Heaven, and did all that was required of her. This, then, was the second of the three times.

She arrived the same day at Aquila, and alighted at the leech's house. He was one of those fashionable physicians whom women send for when they have the vapors, or when they have nothing at all the matter with them. He was the confidant of some and the lover of others, a man of agreeable and polite manners, not quite on the best terms however with the Faculty, at whose expense he had occasionally made some very good jokes.

Cosi-Sancta related the symptoms of her son's disease, and offered him a high fee, a sum in fact that would amount to more than a thousand crowns in French money.

"It is not in such coin as this, madam, that I desire to be paid," said the gay physician; "I would myself offer you all I possess, if you were disposed to take payment for the cures you can effect; heal me only of the malady from which you make me suffer, and I will restore your son to health."

The proposal seemed extravagant to the lady, but her fate had accustomed her to queer proceedings. The physician was obstinate, and would take no other price for his specific. Cosi-Sancta had not her husband with her to consult, but how could she let a son whom she idolized die for the want of the smallest possible help that she could give him! She was as good a mother as she was sister: she bought the remedy at the required price. This was the last of the three times.

She returned to Hippo with her brother, who never ceased thanking her during the journey for the courage with which she had saved his life.

Thus Cosi-Sancta, who by being too scrupulous had been the cause of her lover's destruction and her husband's condemnation to death, by her readiness to oblige preserved the lives of her husband, her brother, and her son. Such a woman was deemed a very desirable acquisition in a family, so she was canonized after her death for having done so much good to her relations by mortifying her own inclinations, and the following epitaph was engraved on her tomb:

"A LITTLE HARM FOR A GREAT GOOD."

BABABEC AND THE FAKIRS

BABABEC AND THE FAKIRS

WHEN I was in the city of Benares on the banks of the Ganges, the ancient home of the Brahmins, I endeavored to gain some information. I understood Hindustani tolerably well; I heard much, and noticed everything. I lodged with my correspondent Omri, the worthiest man I have ever known. He was of the religion of the Brahmins, and I have the honor to be a Mussulman, yet we have never had heated words on the subject of Mohammed and Brahma. We made our ablutions each on his own side, we drank of the same sherbet, and we ate of the same dish of rice, like a pair of brothers.

One day we went together to the pagoda of Vishnu. We saw there several groups of fakirs, some of whom were Janghis, that is to say, fakirs devoted to contemplation, while the others were disciples of the ancient gymnosophists, who led an active life. They have, as every one knows, a learned language, which is that of the most ancient Brahmins, and, written in this language, a book which is called the Vedas. It is undoubtedly the most ancient book in the whole of Asia, not excepting even the Zendavesta.

I passed in front of a fakir who was reading this book.

"Ah, wretched infidel!" cried he, "you have made me lose the number of vowels which I was counting, and in consequence of that my soul will have to pass into the body of a hare, instead of going into that of a parrot, as I had good grounds for flattering myself would be the case."

I gave him a rupee to console him. A few steps further on, having been so unfortunate as to sneeze, the noise that I made roused a fakir who was in a trance.

"Where am I?" said he. "What a horrible fall I have had! I can no longer see the tip of my nose; the celestial light has vanished." [1]

"If I am the cause," said I, "that you see at last beyond the tip of your nose, here is a rupee to repair the damage that I have committed; so recover your celestial light."

Having thus got myself discreetly out of the scrape, I passed on to the gymnosophists, some of whom brought me very nice little nails, to thrust into my arms and thighs in honor of Brahma. I bought their nails, and used them to fasten down my carpets. Some were dancing on their hands, others were tumbling on the slack rope, others again kept hopping continually on one leg. There were some loaded with chains, some who carried a pack-saddle, and some who had their heads under a bushel; yet they were all eminent for their virtues. My friend Omri brought me into the cell of one of the most famous of these philosophers, whose name was Bababec. He was as naked as an ape, and had a big chain round his neck, which must have weighed more than sixty pounds. He was seated on a wooden chair, neatly furnished with sharp little nails which ran into his posteriors, and yet one would have supposed that he was sitting on a velvet cushion. Many women came to consult him as an oracle on family affairs, and it may be truly said that he enjoyed the very highest reputation. I heard the important conversation that Omri had with him.

"Do you think, father," said the former, "that after my soul has undergone the probation of seven trans-migrations, I may be able to reach the abode of Brahma?"

"That depends," said the fakir. "What is your manner of life?"

"I endeavor," said Omri, "to be a good citizen, a good husband, a good father, and a good friend. I lend money without interest to the rich when they have occasion for it, I give it away to the poor, and I maintain peace among my neighbors."

"Do you ever drive nails into your bottom?" asked the Brahmin.

"Never, reverend father."

"I am sorry for it," replied the fakir; "you certainly will not enter the nineteenth heaven, and that is a pity."

"Very good," said Omri; "I am quite contented with my lot. What does it matter to me about the nineteenth or twentieth heaven, provided I do my duty during my pilgrimage, and am well received at the last stage? Is it not enough to be an honest man in this world, and then to be happy in the land of Brahma? Into which heaven do you expect to go, Mr. Bababec, with your nails and your chains?"

"Into the thirty-fifth," said Bababec.

"You are a droll fellow," replied Omri, "to expect a higher lodging than I; that expectation can only proceed from an inordinate ambition. You condemn those who seek for honors in this life, why do you aim at such great ones yourself in the next? Besides, on what do you found your expectation of having better treatment than I? Let me tell you that I give away in alms more in ten days than all the nails which you drive into your back-side cost you in the course of ten years. What does it matter to Brahma that you pass your days stark naked, with a chain round your neck? That is a fine way of serving your country! I reckon that man is worth a hundred times more who sows pot-herbs, or plants trees, than the whole tribe of you and your fellows who look at the tips of their noses, or carry a pack-saddle to show the extreme nobility of their souls."

Having spoken thus, Omri soothed, coaxed, persuaded, and at last induced Bababec to leave his nails and his chain there and then, to come with him to his house, and to lead a respectable life. They scoured him well, they rubbed him all over with perfumed essences, they clothed him decently, and he lived for a fortnight in a thoroughly rational manner, confessing that he was a hundred times happier than before. But he lost credit with the people, and the women came no more to consult him, so he left Omri and betook himself once more to his nails in order to recover his reputation.

CANDIDE, *or*
ALL FOR THE BEST

CANDIDE, or
ALL FOR THE BEST

PART I

CHAPTER I

HOW CANDIDE WAS BROUGHT UP IN A FINE CASTLE, AND HOW HE WAS EXPELLED FROM THENCE

THERE lived in Westphalia, in the castle of my Lord the Baron of Thunder-ten-tronckh, a young man, on whom nature had bestowed the most agreeable manners. His face was the index of his mind. He had an upright heart, with an easy frankness; which, I believe, was the reason he got the name of *Candide*. He was suspected, by the old servants of the family, to be the son of my Lord the Baron's sister, by a good honest gentleman of the neighborhood, whom that young lady declined to marry because he could only produce seventy-one armorial quarterings, the rest of his genealogical tree having been destroyed through the injuries of time.

The Baron was one of the most powerful lords in Westphalia; for his castle had both a gate and windows; and his great hall was even adorned with tapestry. The dogs of his outer yard composed his pack upon occasion; his grooms were his huntsmen; and the vicar of the parish was his great almoner. He was called by everybody, *My Lord*; and every one would laugh when he told his anecdote.

My Lady the Baroness, who weighed about three hundred and fifty pounds, attracted by that means very great regard, and did the honors of the house with a dignity that rendered her still more respectable. Her daughter Cunegonde, aged about seventeen years, was of a high complexion, fresh, plump, and the object of desire. The Baron's son appeared to be in every respect worthy of his father. The preceptor, Pangloss, was the oracle of the house, and little Candide listened to his lectures with all the simplicity that was suitable to his age and his character.

Pangloss taught metaphysico-theologo-cosmolonigology. He proved most admirably that there could not be an effect without a cause; that, in this best of possible worlds, my Lord the Baron's castle was the most magnificent of castles, and my Lady the best of baronesses that possibly could be.

"It is demonstrable," said he, "that things cannot be otherwise than they are; for all things having been made for some end, they must necessarily be intended for the best end. Observe well that the nose has been made for carrying spectacles, therefore we have spectacles. The legs are visibly designed for stockings, and therefore we have stockings. Stones have been formed to be hewn, and to make castles; therefore my Lord has a very fine castle; and the greatest baron of the province ought to be the best lodged. Swine were made to be eaten, therefore we eat pork all the year round; consequently those who have asserted that all is good have said a foolish thing: they should have said that all is for the best."

Candide listened attentively, and believed implicitly; for he thought Miss Cunegonde extremely handsome, though he never had the courage to tell her so. He concluded that next to the good fortune of being born Baron of Thunder-ten-tronckh, the second degree of happiness was that of being Miss Cunegonde, the third to see her every day, and the fourth to hear Master

Pangloss, the greatest philosopher of the province, and consequently of the whole world.

One day Cunegonde, having taken a walk hard by the castle in a little wood which they called the park, espied among the bushes Doctor Pangloss giving a lecture in experimental philosophy to her mother's chambermaid, a little brown wench, very handsome, and very tractable. As Miss Cunegonde had a strong inclination for the sciences, she observed, without making any noise, the experiments repeated before her eyes; she saw very clearly the sufficient reason of the Doctor, the effects and the causes; and she returned greatly flurried, quite pensive, and full of desire to be learned; imagining that she might be a sufficient reason for young Candide, as he also might be the same to her.

In her return to the castle she met Candide, and blushed. Candide also blushed: she wished him good morrow with a faltering voice, and Candide made answer without knowing what he said. The next day after dinner, as they rose from table, Cunegonde and Candide happened to get behind the screen. Cunegonde dropped her handkerchief, and Candide took it up; she, not thinking any harm, took hold of his hand; and the young man, not thinking any harm either, kissed the hand of the young lady with an eagerness, a sensibility and grace wholly singular; their mouths met, their eyes sparkled, their knees trembled, their hands strayed—— The Baron of Thunder-ten-tronckh happening to pass close by the screen, and observing this cause and effect, kicked Candide out of the castle with lusty blows on the backside. Cunegonde fell into a swoon; and as soon as she came to herself was heartily cuffed on the ear by my Lady the Baroness. Thus all was thrown into confusion in the finest and most agreeable castle possible.

CHAPTER II

WHAT BECAME OF CANDIDE AMONG THE BULGARIANS

CANDIDE being expelled from the terrestrial paradise, rambled a long time without knowing where, in tears, lifting up his eyes to heaven, and sometimes turning them towards the finest of castles, which contained the handsomest of baronesses. He laid himself down without his supper in the open fields, between two furrows, while the snow fell in great flakes. Candide, almost frozen to death, crawled next morning to the neighboring village, which is called *Waldberghoff-trarbk-dik-dorff*. Having no money, and dying with hunger and fatigue, he stopped in a dejected posture before the gate of an inn. Two men dressed in blue observed him in such a situation. "Brother," says one of them to the other, "there is a young fellow well-built and of a proper height." They accosted Candide, and invited him very civilly to dinner. "Gentlemen," replied Candide with an agreeable modesty, "you do me much honor, but I have no money to pay for my shot." "O Sir," said one of the blues, "persons of your appearance and merit never pay anything: are you not five feet five inches high?" "Yes, Gentlemen, that is my height," returned he, making a bow. "Come, Sir, sit down at table; we will not only treat you, but we will never let such a man as you want money: men are made to assist one another." "You are in the right," said Candide; "that is what Pangloss always told me, and I see plainly that everything is for the best." They entreat him to take a few crowns; which he accepts, and would have given them his note, but they refused it, and sat down to table. "Do not you love tenderly——?" "O yes," replied he, "I love tenderly Miss Cunegonde. "No," said one of the gentlemen; "we ask you if you do not love tenderly the King of the Bulgarians?" "Not at all," said he, "for I never saw him." "What! He is the most charming of kings, and you must drink his health." "O, with all my heart, Gentlemen," and he drinks. "That is enough," said they to him; "you are now the bulwark, the support, the defender, the hero of the Bulgarians; your fortune is made, and you are certain of glory." Instantly they clap him in irons, and carry him to the regiment. He is made to turn about to the right and to the left, to draw the rammer, to return the rammer, to present, to fire, to double; and they give him thirty blows with a cudgel. The next day he performs his exercise not quite so badly, and receives but twenty blows; the third day the blows are restricted to ten, and he is looked upon by his fellow soldiers as a kind of prodigy.

Candide, quite stupified, could not yet well conceive how he had become a hero. One fine day in the spring it came into his head to take a walk, going straight forward, imagining that the human as well as the animal species were entitled to make whatever use they pleased of their limbs. He had not traveled two leagues when four other heroes, six feet high, came up to him, bound him, and put him into a dungeon. He is asked by a court martial whether he chooses to be whipped six and thirty times through the whole regiment, or receive at once twelve bullets through the forehead? He in vain argued that the will is free, and that he chose neither the one nor the other; he was obliged to make a choice: he therefore resolved, in virtue of God's gift called *free will*, to run the gauntlet six and thirty times. He underwent this discipline twice. The regiment being composed of two thousand men, he received four thousand lashes, which laid open all his muscles and nerves from the nape of the neck to the posteriors. As they were proceeding to a third operation, Candide being quite spent, begged as a favor that they would be so kind as to shoot him; he obtained his request; they blindfolded him, and made him kneel. The King of the Bulgarians, passing by, inquired into the crime of the delinquent; and as this prince was a person of great penetration, he discovered from what he heard of Candide that he was a young metaphysician, entirely ignorant of the things of this world, and he granted him his pardon, with a clemency which will be extolled in all histories and throughout all ages. An experienced surgeon cured Candide in three weeks with emollients prescribed by no less a master than Dioscorides. He had now acquired some skin, and was able to walk, when the King of the Bulgarians gave battle to the King of the Abares.

CHAPTER III

HOW CANDIDE MADE HIS ESCAPE FROM THE BULGARIANS, AND WHAT AFTERWARDS BEFELL HIM

NOTHING could be so fine, so neat, so brilliant, so well disposed, as the two armies. The trumpets, fifes, hautboys, drums, and the cannon formed harmony superior to what hell could invent. The cannon swept off at first about six thousand men on each side; afterwards the musketry carried away from the best of worlds, about nine or ten thousand rascals that infected its surface. The bayonet was likewise the sufficient reason of the death of some thousands of men. The whole number might amount to about thirty thousand souls. Candide, who trembled like a philosopher, hid himself as well as he could during this heroic butchery.

In short, while each of the two kings were causing *Te Deum* to be sung in their respective camps, he resolved to go somewhere else, to reason upon the effects and causes. He walked over heaps of the dead and dying and came at first to a neighboring village belonging to the Abares, but found it in ashes; for it had been burned by the Bulgarians, according to the laws of nations. Here were to be seen old men full of wounds, casting their eyes on their murdered wives, who were holding their infants to their bloody breasts. You might see in another place virgins having their bellies ripped up, after they had satisfied the natural desires of some of those heroes, breathing out their last sighs. Others half burned prayed earnestly for instant death. The whole field was covered with brains, and with legs and arms lopped off.

Candide betook himself with full speed to another village. It belonged to the Bulgarians, and had met with the same treatment from the Abarian heroes. Candide, walking still forward over quivering limbs, or through rubbish of houses, got at last out of the theater of war, having some small quantity of provisions in his knapsack, and never forgetting Miss Cunegonde. His provisions failed him when he arrived in Holland; but having heard that every one was rich in that country, and that they were Christians, he did not doubt but he should be as well treated there as he had been in my Lord the Baron's castle, before he had been expelled thence on account of Miss Cunegonde's sparkling eyes.

He asked alms from several grave looking persons; who all replied that if he continued that trade, they

282 VOLTAIRE'S ROMANCES AND TALES

would confine him in a house of correction, where he should learn to get his bread.

He applied himself afterwards to a man who for a whole hour had been discoursing on the subject of charity, before a large assembly. This orator looking on him askance, said to him, "What are you doing here? Are you for the good cause?" "There is no effect without a cause," replied Candide modestly; "all is necessarily linked, and ordered for the best. A necessity banished me from Cunegonde; a necessity forced me to run the gauntlet; and another necessity makes me beg for my bread, till I can fall on a business to earn it. All this could not be otherwise." "My friend," said the orator to him, "do you believe that the Pope is Antichrist?" "I never have heard whether he is or not," replied Candide; "but whether he is, or is not, I want bread." "You do not deserve to eat any," said the other; "get you gone, you rogue, get you gone, you wretch; never in thy life come near me again." The orator's wife, having popped her head out of the window, and seeing a man who doubted whether the Pope was Antichrist, poured on his head a full—— O heavens! To what excess does religious zeal transport the fair sex!

A man who had not been baptized, a good Anabaptist named James, saw the barbarous and ignominious manner with which they treated one of his brethren, a being with two feet, unfeathered, and endowed with a rational soul. He took him home with him, cleaned him, gave him bread and beer, made him a present of two florins; and offered to teach him the method of working in his manufactories of Persian stuffs, which are fabricated in Holland. Candide prostrating himself almost at his knees, cried out, "Mr. Pangloss argued well when he said that everything is for the best in this world; for I am infinitely more affected with your very great generosity than by the hard-heartedness of that gentleman with the black cloak, and the lady his wife."

Next day, as he was taking a walk, he met a beggar all covered over with sores, his eyes dead, the tip of his nose eaten off, his mouth turned to one side of his face, his teeth black, speaking through his throat, tormented with a violent cough, and spitting a tooth at every attempt to draw his breath.

CHAPTER IV

HOW CANDIDE MET HIS OLD MASTER OF PHILOSOPHY, DR. PANGLOSS, AND WHAT HAPPENED TO THEM

CANDIDE, moved more with compassion than horror, gave this frightful mendicant the two florins which he had received of his honest Anabaptist James. The specter fixed his eyes attentively upon him, dropped some tears, and was going to fall upon his neck. Candide affrighted, drew back. "Alas!" said the one wretch to the other, "don't you any longer know your dear Pangloss?" "What do I hear! Is it you, my dear master! You in this dreadful condition! What misfortune has befallen you? Why are you no longer in the most magnificent of castles? What is become of Miss Cunegonde, the nonpareil of the fair sex, the masterpiece of nature?" "I have no more strength," said Pangloss. Candide immediately carried him to the Anabaptist's stable, where he gave him a little bread to eat. When Pangloss was refreshed a little, "Well," said Candide, "what is become of Cunegonde?" "She is dead," replied the other. Candide fainted away at this word: but his friend brought back his senses, with a little bad vinegar which he found by chance in the stable. Candide, opening his eyes, cried out, "Cunegonde is dead! Ah, best of worlds, where art thou? But of what distemper did she die? Was not this the cause, her seeing me driven out of the castle by my Lord, her father, with great kicks on the breech?" "No," said Pangloss, "she was killed by some Bulgarian soldiers, after having been barbarously ravished; they knocked my Lord the Baron on the head, for attempting to protect her; my Lady the Baroness was cut in pieces; my poor pupil was treated precisely like his sister; and as for the castle, there is not one stone left upon another, nor a barn, nor a sheep, nor a duck, nor a tree. But we have been sufficiently revenged; for the Abarians have done the very same thing to a neighboring barony which belonged to a Bulgarian lord."

At this discourse Candide fainted away a second time, but coming to himself, and having said all that he ought to say, he inquired into the cause and the effect, and into the sufficient reason that had reduced Pangloss to so deplorable a condition. "Alas!" said the other, "it was love; love, the comforter of the human race, the preserver of the universe, the soul of all sensible beings, tender love." "Alas!" said Candide, "I know this love, the sovereign of hearts, the soul of our soul; yet it never cost me more than a kiss, and twenty kicks on the breech. But how could this charming cause produce in you so abominable an effect?"

Pangloss made answer as follows, "O my dear Candide, you knew Paquetta, that pretty attendant on our noble Baroness: I tasted in her arms the delights of paradise, which produced those torments of hell with which you see me devoured. She was infected, and perhaps she is dead. Paquetta received this present from a learned cordelier, who had traced it to the source, for he had it from an old countess, who had received it from a captain of horse, who was indebted for it to a marchioness, who got it from a page, who had received it from a Jesuit, who in his novitiate had it in a direct line from one of the companions of Christopher Columbus. For my part, I will give it to nobody, for I am dying."

"O Pangloss!" cried Candide, "what a strange genealogy! Has not the devil given rise to it?" "Not at all," replied this great man; "it was a thing indispensable, a necessary ingredient in the best of worlds: for if Columbus had not caught, in an island of America, this distemper which poisons the source of generation, frequently hinders generation, and is evidently opposite to the great design of nature, we should have had neither chocolate nor cochineal. It may also be observed, that to this day, upon our continent, this malady, like a point of controversy, is peculiar to us. The Turks, the Indians, the Persians, the Chinese, the Siamese, and the Japanese know nothing of it yet. But there is a sufficient reason why they, in their turn, should become acquainted with it, a few centuries hence. In the meantime, it has made a marvelous progress among us, and especially in those great armies composed of honest hirelings well disciplined, who decide the fate of states; for one may be assured that when thirty thousand men in a pitched battle fight against troops equal to them in number, there are about twenty thousand of them poxed on each side."

"That is surprising," said Candide; "but you must be cured." "Ah! How can I?" said Pangloss; "I have not a penny, my friend; and, throughout the whole extent of this globe, one cannot be let blood, nor get a clyster without paying for it, or some other person doing that office for us."

This last speech determined Candide. He went to throw himself at the feet of his charitable Anabaptist James; and gave him so striking a description of the state his friend was reduced to, that the good man did not hesitate to entertain Dr. Pangloss; and he had him cured at his own expense. During the cure, Pangloss lost only an eye and an ear. As he wrote well, and understood arithmetic perfectly, the Anabaptist James made him his bookkeeper. At the end of two months, being obliged to go to Lisbon about the affairs of his trade, he took the two philosophers with him in his ship. Pangloss explained to him how everything was such that it could not be better. James was not of this sentiment. "Mankind," said he, "must have a little corrupted their nature; for they were not born wolves, and yet they are become wolves: God has given them neither cannon of twenty-four pounds, nor bayonets; and yet they have made cannon and bayonets to destroy one another. I might throw into the account bankrupts; and the law, which seizes on the effects of bankrupts only to bilk the creditors." "All this was indispensable," replied the one-eyed doctor, "and private misfortunes constitute the general good; so that the more private misfortunes there are, the better is the whole." While he was reasoning, the air grew dark, the winds blew from the four quarters of the world, and the ship was attacked by a most dreadful storm, within sight of the harbor of Lisbon.

CHAPTER V

TEMPEST, SHIPWRECK, EARTHQUAKE, AND WHAT BECAME OF DR. PANGLOSS, CANDIDE, AND JAMES THE ANABAPTIST

ONE half of the passengers, being weakened and ready to breathe their last, with the inconceivable anguish which the rolling of the ship conveyed through the nerves and all the humors of the body, which were quite disordered, were not capable of being alarmed at the danger they were in. The other half uttered cries and made prayers; the sails were rent, the masts broken, and the ship became leaky. Every one worked that was able; nobody regarded anything, and no order was kept. The Anabaptist contributed his assistance to work the ship. As he was upon deck, a furious sailor rudely struck him, and laid him sprawling on the planks; but with the blow he gave him, he himself was so violently jolted, that he tumbled overboard with his head foremost, and remained suspended by a piece of a broken mast. Honest James runs to his assistance, and helps him to get up again; but in the attempt is thrown into the sea, in the sight of the sailor, who suffered him to perish without deigning to look upon him. Candide draws near, and sees his benefactor one moment emerging, and the next swallowed up forever. He was just going to throw himself into the sea after him, when the philosopher Pangloss hindered him, by demonstrating to him that the road of Lisbon had been made on purpose for this Anabaptist to be drowned there. While he was proving this *à priori*, the vessel foundered, and all perished except Pangloss, Candide, and this brute of a sailor, who drowned the virtuous Anabaptist. The villain luckily swam ashore, whither Pangloss and Candide were carried on a plank.

When they had recovered themselves a little, they walked towards Lisbon. They had some money left, with which they hoped to save themselves from hunger after having escaped from the storm. Scarce had they set foot in the city, bewailing the death of their benefactor, when they perceived the earth to tremble under their feet, and saw the sea swell and foam in the harbor, and dash to pieces the ships that were at anchor. The whirling flames and ashes covered the streets and public places, the houses tottered, and their roofs fell under the foundations, and the foundations were scattered; thirty thousand inhabitants of all ages and sexes were crushed to death in the ruins. The sailor, whistling and swearing, said, "There is some booty to be got here." "What can be the sufficient reason of this phenomenon?" said Pangloss. "This is certainly the last day of the world," cried Candide. The sailor ran immediately into the midst of the ruins, encountered death to find money, found it, laid hold of it, got drunk, and having slept himself sober, purchased the favors of the first good-natured girl he met with, upon the ruins of the demolished houses, and in the midst of the dying and the dead. In the meantime, Pangloss pulled him by the sleeve: "My friend," said he, "this is not right; you trespass against universal reason, you improve your time badly." "Brains and blood!" answered the other; "I am a sailor, and was born at Batavia; four times I have trampled upon the crucifix in four voyages to Japan; thou mayst go seek for thy man with thy universal reason."

Some pieces of stone having wounded Candide, he lay stretched in the street, and covered with rubbish.

"Alas!" said he to Pangloss, "get me a little wine and oil, I am a-dying." "This trembling of the earth is no new thing," answered Pangloss. "The city of Lima, in America, experienced the same concussions last year; the same cause has the same effects; there is certainly a train of sulphur under the earth from Lima to Lisbon." "Nothing is more probable," said Candide; "but, for God's sake, a little oil and wine." "How probable?" replied the philosopher; "I maintain that the point is demonstrable." Candide lost all sense; and Pangloss brought him a little water from a neighboring fountain.

The day following, having found some provisions in rummaging through the rubbish, they recruited their strength a little. Afterwards they employed themselves, like others, in administering relief to the inhabitants that had escaped from death. Some citizens who had been relieved by them, gave them as good a dinner as could be expected amid such a disaster. It is true that the repast was mournful, and the guests watered their bread with their tears, but Pangloss consoled them by affirming that things could not be otherwise: "For," said he, "if an universe exist, that universe must necessarily be the best. Now, in the best of worlds, all is good, all is well, all is for the best: comfort yourselves, be merry, and let us take a glass." A little man clad in black, who belonged to the inquisition, and sat at his side, took him up very politely, and said, "In all appearance, the gentleman does not believe in original sin; for if all is for the best, then there has been neither fall nor punishment."

"I most humbly ask your Excellency's pardon," answered Pangloss still more politely; "for the fall of man and the curse necessarily entered into the best of worlds possible." "Then the gentleman does not believe there is liberty," said the inquisitor. "Your Excellency will excuse me," said Pangloss; "liberty can consist with absolute necessity; for it was necessary we should be free; because, in short, the determinate will——"

Pangloss was in the middle of his proposition when the inquisitor made a signal with the head to his footman who waited upon him, to bring him a glass of port wine.

CHAPTER VI

HOW A FINE AUTO-DA-FÉ WAS CELEBRATED TO PREVENT EARTHQUAKES; AND HOW CANDIDE WAS WHIPPED

AFTER the earthquake, which had destroyed three-fourths of Lisbon, the sages of the country could not find any means more effectual to prevent a total destruction, than to give the people a splendid auto-da-fé. It had been decided by the university of Coimbra, that the spectacle of some persons burned by a slow fire, with great ceremony, was an infallible nostrum to hinder the earth from quaking.

In consequence of this resolution, they had seized a Biscayner, convicted of having married his godmother, and two Portuguese, who, in eating a pullet, had stripped off the fat. After dinner they came and secured Dr. Pangloss and his disciple Candide, the one for having spoke too freely, and the other for having heard with an air of approbation. They were both conducted to separate apartments, extremely cool, and never incommoded with the sun. Eight days after, they were both clothed with a *sanbenito*, and had their heads adorned with paper miters. Candide's miter and sanbenito were painted with inverted flames, and with devils that had neither tails nor claws: but Pangloss' devils had claws and tails, and the flames were pointed upwards. Being thus dressed, they marched in procession, and heard a very pathetic sermon, followed with fine music on a squeaking organ. Candide was whipped in cadence, while they were singing; the Biscayner, and the two men who would not eat fat, were burned; and Pangloss, though it was contrary to custom, was hanged. The same day the earth shook anew with a most dreadful noise.

Candide, affrighted, interdicted, astonished, all bloody, all panting, said to himself, "If this is the best of possible worlds, what then are the rest? Supposing I had not been whipped, I have been among the Bulgarians; but, O my dear Pangloss, thou greatest of philosophers, that it should be my fate to see you hanged without knowing for what! O my dear Anabaptist, thou best of men, that it should be thy fate to be drowned in the harbor! O Miss Cunegonde, the jewel of ladies, that it should be thy fate to have thy belly ripped up!"

He returned, with difficulty supporting himself, after being lectured, whipped, absolved, and blessed, when an old woman accosted him, and said, "Child, take courage, and follow me."

CHAPTER VII

HOW AN OLD WOMAN TOOK CARE OF CANDIDE, AND HOW HE FOUND THE OBJECT HE LOVED

CANDIDE did not take courage, but followed the old woman into a ruined house. She gave him a pot of pomatum to anoint himself, left him something to eat and drink, and showed him a very neat little bed, near which was a complete suit of clothes. "Eat, drink, and sleep," said she to him, "and may our Lady of Mocha, our Lord St. Antony of Padua, and our Lord St. James of Compostella take care of you. I will be back tomorrow." Candide astonished at all he had seen, at all he had suffered, and still more at the charity of the old woman, offered to kiss her hand. "You must not kiss my hand," said the old woman; "I will be back tomorrow. Rub yourself with the pomatum, eat, and take rest."

Candide, notwithstanding so many misfortunes, ate, and went to sleep. Next morning the old woman brought him his breakfast, looked at his back, and rubbed it herself with another ointment. She afterwards brought him his dinner; and she returned at night, and brought him his supper. The day following she performed the same ceremonies. "Who are you?" would Candide always say to her: "Who has inspired you with so much goodness? What thanks can I render you?" The good woman made him no answer; she returned in the evening, but brought him no supper. "Come along with me," said she, "and say not a word." She took him by the arm, and walked with him into the country about a quarter of a mile; they arrived at a house that stood by itself, surrounded with gardens and canals. The old woman knocked at a little door; which being opened, she conducted Candide by a private staircase into a gilded closet, and leaving him on a brocade couch, shut the door, and went her way. Candide thought he was in a revery, and looked upon all his life as an unlucky dream, but on the present moment as an agreeable dream.

The old woman returned very soon, supporting with difficulty a woman trembling, of a majestic bearing, glittering with jewels, and covered with a veil. "Take off that veil," said the old woman to Candide. The young man approaches, and takes off the veil with a trembling hand.

What joy! What surprise! He thought he saw Miss Cunegonde; he saw her indeed, it was she herself. His strength fails him, he cannot utter a word, but falls down at her feet. Cunegonde falls upon the carpet. The old woman applies aromatic waters; they recover their senses, and speak to one another. At first their words were imperfect, their questions and answers were carried on confusedly, with sighs, tears, and cries. The old woman advised them to make less noise, and then left them to themselves. "What, it is you!" said Candide to her; "are you still alive? Do I find you again in Portugal? Were you not ravished then? Was not your belly ripped up, as the philosopher Pangloss assured me?" "Yes, the case was so," said the lovely Cunegonde; "but death does not always follow from these two accidents." "But your father and mother, were not they killed?" "It is but too true," answered Cunegonde, weeping. "And your brother?" "My brother was killed too." "And why are you in Portugal, and how did you know that I was here, and by what strange adventure did you contrive to bring me to this house?" "I will tell you all that," replied the lady, "but first you must inform me of all that has happened to you since the harmless kiss you gave me, and the rude kicking which you received." Candide obeyed her with the most profound respect; and though he was forbidden to speak, though his voice was weak and faltering, and though his back still pained him, yet he related to her, in the most genuine manner, everything that had befallen him since the moment of their separation. Cunegonde lifted up her eyes to heaven; she shed tears at the death of the good Anabaptist, and of Pangloss; after which she spoke in the following terms to Candide, who lost not a word, but dwelled upon her eyes as if he would devour them.

CHAPTER VIII

THE HISTORY OF CUNEGONDE

"I WAS in my bed and fast asleep, when it pleased Heaven to send the Bulgarians to our fine castle of Thunder-ten-tronckh: they murdered my father and my brother, and cut my mother in pieces. A huge Bulgarian, six feet high, perceiving the sight had deprived me of my senses, set himself to ravish me. This abuse made me come to myself; I recovered my senses, I cried, I struggled, I bit, I scratched, I wanted to tear out the huge Bulgarian's eyes, not considering that what had happened in my father's castle was a common thing in war. The brute gave me a cut with his sword in the left flank, the mark of which I still bear upon me." "Ah! I hope I shall see it," said the simple Candide. "You shall," answered Cunegonde; "but let us continue." "Do so," replied Candide.

She then resumed the thread of her story in this manner. "A Bulgarian captain came in, and saw me bleeding; but the soldier was not at all disconcerted. The captain flew into a passion at the little respect the brute showed him, and killed him upon my body. He then caused me to be dressed, and carried me as a prisoner of war to his own quarters. I washed the little linen he had, and dressed his victuals. He found me very pretty, I must say; and I cannot deny that he was well shaped, and that he had a white, soft skin; but otherwise he had little sense or philosophy; one could easily see that he was not bred under Dr. Pangloss. At the end of three months, having lost all his money, and being grown out of conceit with me, he sold me to a Jew, named Don Issachar, who traded to Holland and Portugal, and who had a most violent passion for women. This Jew laid close siege to my person, but could not triumph over me: I have resisted him better than I did the Bulgarian soldier. A woman of honor may be ravished once, but her virtue gathers strength from such rudeness. The Jew, in order to render me more tractable, brought me to this country house that you see. I always imagined hitherto, that no place on earth was so fine as the castle of Thunder-ten-tronckh; but I am now undeceived.

"The grand inquisitor observing me one day at mass, ogled me pretty much, and got notice sent me that he wanted to speak with me upon private business. Being conducted to his palace, I informed him of my birth; upon which he slyly remarked how much it was below my family to belong to an Israelite. A proposal was then made by him to Don Issachar, to yield me up to my Lord. But Don Issachar, who is the court banker, and a man of credit, would not agree to these measures. The inquisitor threatened him with an auto-da-fé. At last my Jew, being affrighted, concluded a bargain, by which the house and myself should belong to them both in common; that the Jew should have Monday, Friday, and Saturday, and the inquisitor the other days of the week. This agreement has now existed six months. It has not, however, been without quarrels; for it has been often disputed whether Saturday night or Sunday belonged to the old or to the new law. For my part, I have hitherto resisted them both; and I believe that this is the reason I am still beloved by them.

"At length, to avert the scourge of earthquakes, and to intimidate Don Issachar, it pleased his Lordship the Inquisitor to celebrate an auto-da-fé. He did me the

honor to invite me to it. I got a very fine seat; and the
ladies were served with refreshments between the mass
and the execution. I was really seized with horror at seeing them burn the two Jews, and the honest Biscayner
who married his godmother: but how great was my surprise, my consternation, my anguish, when I saw in a
sanbenito and miter a person that somewhat resembled
Pangloss! I rubbed my eyes, I looked upon him very attentively, and I saw him hanged: I fell into a swoon;
and scarce had I recovered my senses, when I saw you
stripped stark naked; this was the height of horror, consternation, grief, and despair. I will frankly own to you,
that your skin is still whiter, and of a better complexion
than that of my Bulgarian captain. This sight increased
all the sensations that oppressed and distracted my soul.
I cried out, I was going to say, 'Stop, barbarians;' but
my voice failed me, and my cries would have been to
no purpose. When you had been severely whipped, 'How
is it possible,' said I, 'that the charming Candide and the
sage Pangloss should both be at Lisbon, the one to receive a hundred lashes, and the other to be hanged by
order of my Lord the Inquisitor, by whom I am greatly
beloved? Pangloss certainly deceived me most cruelly,
when he said that everything is for the best in the
world.'

"Being agitated, astonished, sometimes beside myself,
and sometimes ready to die with weakness, I had my
head filled with the massacre of my father, my mother,
and my brother; the insolence of the vile Bulgarian soldier, the stab he gave me with his sword; my abject
servitude, and acting as cook to the Bulgarian captain;
the rascal Don Issachar, my abominable inquisitor, the
execution of Dr. Pangloss, the grand *Miserere* on the organ while you were whipped, and especially the kiss I

gave you behind the screen, the last day I saw you. I praised the Lord for having restored you to me after so many trials. I charged my old woman to take care of you, and to bring you hither as soon as she could. She has executed her commission very well; I have tasted the inexpressible pleasure of seeing you, hearing you, and speaking to you. You must have a ravenous appetite by this time; I am hungry myself too; let us therefore sit down to supper."

On this they both sat down to table; and after supper they seated themselves on the fine couch which was mentioned before. They were there when Signor Don Issachar, one of the masters of the house, came thither. It was his sabbath-day; and he came to enjoy his right, and to express his tender love.

CHAPTER IX

WHAT HAPPENED TO CUNEGONDE, CANDIDE, THE GRAND INQUISITOR, AND THE JEW

THIS Issachar was the most choleric Hebrew that had been seen in Israel since the captivity in Babylon. "What," says he, "you bitch of a Galilean, is it not enough to take in Master Inquisitor, but must this varlet also share with me?" When he had thus spoke, he drew out a long poignard, which he always carried about him, and not suspecting that his antagonist had any arms, fell upon Candide; but our honest Westphalian had received a fine sword from the old woman, along with his full suit. He drew his rapier, and though he had the most agreeable temper, he laid the Israelite dead upon the spot, at the feet of Cunegonde.

"Holy Virgin!" cried she; "what will become of us, with a man murdered in my apartment? If the peace-officer come, we are ruined." "If Pangloss had not been hanged," said Candide, "he would have given us excellent advice in this emergency; for he was a great philosopher. In this extremity let us consult the old woman." —She was a very prudent woman, and began to give her advice, when another little door opened. It was now about one o'clock in the morning, and consequently the beginning of Sunday. This day was allotted to my Lord the Inquisitor. Entering, he saw the whipped Candide with a sword in his hand, a dead body stretched out on the floor, Cunegonde in a mighty fright, and the old woman giving advice.

See now what passed in Candide's mind at this instant, and how he reasoned. "If this holy man calls in assistance, he will infallibly have me burned; he may treat Cunegonde in the same manner; he has caused me be whipped without mercy; he is my rival; I am in the way of killing, there is no time to hesitate." This reasoning was clear and precipitate; and, without giving time to the inquisitor to recover from his surprise, he ran him through the body, and laid him by the side of the Jew. "Behold, here is a second killed," said Cunegonde; "there is no pardon for us; we are excommunicated, our last hour is come. How could you, that was born so gentle, kill in two minutes' time a Jew and a prelate?" "My fair Lady," answered Candide, "when one is in love, jealous, and whipped by the inquisition, one does not know what one does." The old woman then put in her word, and said, "There are three Andalusian horses in the stable, with their saddles and bridles, which the gallant Candide may get ready; Madam has some moidores and jewels; let us get on horseback without delay, though I cannot sit but on one buttock; and let us go to Cadiz: it is the finest season in the world, and very pleasant it is to travel in the cool of the night."

Candide immediately saddled the three horses. Cunegonde, the old woman and he traveled thirty miles on a stretch. While they were making the best of their way, the holy Hermandad came to the house; they buried my Lord in a magnificent church, and threw Issachar upon a lay-stall.

Candide, Cunegonde, and the old woman, had now got to the little town of Avacena, in the middle of the mountains of Sierra Morena; and spoke as follows in an inn.

CHAPTER X

IN WHAT DISTRESS CANDIDE, CUNEGONDE, AND THE OLD WOMAN ARRIVED AT CADIZ, AND OF THEIR EMBARKATION

"WHO could have robbed me of my pistoles and jewels?" said Cunegonde with tears in her eyes. "What shall we live on? What shall we do? Where shall I find inquisitors and Jews to give me more?" "Alas," said the old woman, "I strongly suspect a Rev. Father Cordelier, who lay yesterday in the same inn with us at Badajos. God preserve me from judging rashly, but he came twice into our chamber, and went away a long time before us." "Ah!" said Candide, "the good Pangloss has often demonstrated to me that the goods of the earth are common to all men, and that every one has an equal right to them. According to these principles, the Cordelier ought to have left us enough to carry us to our journey's end. Have you nothing at all left then, my pretty Cunegonde?" "Not a farthing," said she. "What course shall we take?" said Candide. "Let us sell one of the horses," said the old woman; "I will mount behind Miss, though I can hold myself only on one buttock, and we shall reach Cadiz."

In the same inn was a Benedictine prior, who bought the horse very cheap. Candide, Cunegonde, and the old woman passed through Lucena, Chillas, and Lebrixa, and arrived at length at Cadiz. They were fitting out a fleet, and assembling troops, for bringing to reason the reverend fathers the Jesuits of Paraguay, who were accused of having excited one of their hordes, near the city of St. Sacrament, to revolt from their allegiance to the Kings of Spain and Portugal. Candide having served among the Bulgarians, performed the exercise of that nation before the commander of this little army with so much grace, celerity, address, dexterity, and agility, that he gave him the command of a company of infantry. Being now made a captain, he embarked with Miss Cunegonde, the old woman, two valets, and the two Andalusian horses, which had belonged to his Lordship the grand inquisitor of Portugal.

During the whole voyage, they argued a great deal on the philosophy of poor Pangloss. "We are going to another world," said Candide; "it is there without doubt that everything is best. For it must be confessed, that one has reason to be a little uneasy at what passeth in our world, with respect both to physics and ethics." "I love you with all my heart," said Cunegonde; "but my mind is still terrified at what I have seen and experienced." "All will be well," replied Candide; "the sea of the new world is already preferable to those of our Europe; it is more calm, and the winds are more constant. Certainly the new world is the best of all possible worlds." "God grant it," said Cunegonde; "but I have been so terribly unfortunate in mine, that my heart is almost shut against hope." "You complain indeed," said the old woman to them; "alas! you have not met with such misfortunes as I have."

Cunegonde was almost ready to fall a-laughing, and thought the old woman very comical for pretending to be more unfortunate than herself. "Alas! my good dame," said Cunegonde, "unless you have been ravished by two Bulgarians, have received two cuts with a sword in your belly, have had two castles demolished, have had two fathers and two mothers murdered, and have seen two lovers whipped at an auto-da-fé, I cannot see how you can have the advantage of me. Add to this, that I was born a baroness with seventy-two armorial quarterings, and that I have been a cook-maid." "My Lady," answered the old woman, "you know nothing of my extraction; and were I to show you my backside, you would not talk as you do, but would suspend your judgment." This discourse having raised an insatiable curiosity in the minds of Cunegonde and Candide, the old woman related her story in the following terms.

CHAPTER XI

THE HISTORY OF THE OLD WOMAN

"I HAD not always eyes bleared, and bordered with red; my nose has not always touched my chin; nor have I been always a servant. I am the daughter of Pope Urban X and of the Princess of Palestrina. I was brought up till I was fourteen in a palace to which all the castles of your German barons would not have served for stables, and one of my robes cost more than all the magnificence in Westphalia. I increased in beauty, in charms, and in fine accomplishments, in the very center of pleasures, of homages, and of high expectations. I now began to captivate every heart. My neck was so formed, and what a neck! White, firm, and shaped like that of the Venus of Medicis. And what eyes! What eyelids! What fine black eyebrows! What flames sparkled from my eyeballs, and, as the poets of our country told me, eclipsed the twinkling of the stars! The maids who dressed and undressed me, fell into an ecstasy when they viewed me before and behind, and all the men would have been glad to have been in their places.

"I was betrothed to a prince, the sovereign of Massa Carara. What a prince! As handsome as myself, made up of sweetness and charms, of a witty mind, and burning with love. I loved him, as one is used to do for the first time, with idolatry, with transport. Preparations were made for our nuptials. The pomp and magnificence were inconceivable; nothing but continual feasts, carousals, and operas; and all Italy made sonnets upon me, of which there was scarce one tolerable. I was just on the point of reaching the summit of happiness, when an old marchioness, who had been mistress to my prince, invited him to drink chocolate at her house. He died there in less than two hours' time in terrible convulsions. But this is only a mere trifle. My mother, in despair, and yet less afflicted than I, resolved to retreat for some time from so mournful a place. She had a very fine seat near Gaietta. We embarked on board a galley of the country, gilded like the altar of St. Peter's at Rome. We were scarce out at sea, when a corsair of Sallee fell upon us, and boarded us. Our soldiers defended themselves like those of the Pope; they all fell down upon their knees, after throwing away their arms, and asked absolution *in articulo mortis* of the corsair.

"They instantly stripped us as naked as monkeys; my mother, our maids of honor, and myself too, meeting with no better usage. It is a very surprising thing with what expedition these gentry undress people. But what surprised me most was that they should put their fingers into a place into which we women seldom suffer anything to enter but pipes. This ceremony appeared very strange to me; but so we judge of everything that is not produced in our own country. I soon learned, however, that it was to search whether we had not concealed some of our jewels there. It is a custom established time out of mind among civilized nations that scour the sea. I know that the gentlemen the religious knights of Malta never omit to practice it, when they take Turks of either sex. It is one of the laws of nations, from which they never deviate.

"I need not tell you how great a hardship it is for a young princess and her mother to be carried as slaves to Morocco. You may easily form a notion of all that we must suffer on board the vessel of the corsair. My mother was still very handsome; our maids of honor, nay our plain chambermaids, had more charms than are to be found throughout all Africa. As for myself, I was all attraction, I was all beauty, and all charms, nay more, I was a virgin. However, I was not one long: this flower, which had been reserved for the accomplished Prince of Massa Carara, was taken from me by the captain of the corsair. He was an ugly negro, but fancied he did me a great deal of honor. Indeed her Highness the Princess of Palestrina and myself must have been very strong to resist all the violence we met with till our arrival at Morocco. But let me pass over that; these are such common things that they are scarce worth the mentioning.

"Morocco was overflowed with blood when we arrived there. Fifty sons of the Emperor Muley Ismael had each their adherents: this produced in effect fifty civil wars, of blacks against blacks, of blacks against tawnies, of tawnies against tawnies, and of mulattoes against mulattoes. In a word, there was one continued carnage all over the empire.

"No sooner were we landed, than the blacks of a party inimical to that of my corsair made an attempt to rob him of his booty. Next to the jewels and the gold, we were the most valuable things he had. I was here witness to such a battle as you never saw in your European climates. The people of the north have not so much fire in their blood; nor have they that raging passion for women that is so common in Africa. One would think that you Europeans had nothing but milk in your veins; but it is vitriol and fire that runs in those of the inhabitants of Mount Atlas and the neighboring countries. They fought with the fury of lions, tigers, and serpents of the country, to know who should have us. A moor seized my mother by the right arm, while my captain's lieutenant held her by the left; a moorish soldier then took hold of her by one leg, and our pirates held her by the other. All our women found themselves almost in a moment seized thus by four soldiers. My captain kept me concealed at his back. He had a scimitar in his hand, and killed every one that opposed his fury. In short, I saw all our Italian women, and my mother, torn in pieces, hacked, and mangled by the brutes that fought for them. My fellow-prisoners, those who had taken them, soldiers, sailors, blacks, whites, mulattoes, and lastly my captain himself, were all killed; and I remained expiring upon a heap of dead bodies. These barbarous scenes extended, as every one knows, over more than three hundred leagues, without ever omitting the five prayers a day ordained by Mahomet.

"I disengaged myself with great difficulty from the weight of so many bloody carcasses heaped upon me, and made a shift to crawl to a large orange tree on the bank of a neighboring rivulet, where I fell down oppressed with fear, fatigue, horror, despair, and hunger. Soon after, my senses, being overpowered, were locked up in a sleep which resembled a fit rather than sleep. I was in this state of weakness and insensibility, between death and life, when I felt myself pressed by something that moved upon my body. I opened my eyes, and saw a white man, of a very good aspect, who sighed, and muttered these words between his teeth, O *che sciagura d'essere senza coglioni! i. e.* 'O this misfortune of being deprived of testicles!' "

CHAPTER XII

THE SEQUEL OF THE OLD WOMAN'S ADVENTURES

"ASTONISHED and transported to hear my own native language, and not less surprised at the words uttered by the man, I made answer that there might be far greater misfortunes than those he complained of. I then gave him a short hint of the horrid scenes I had undergone, and relapsed again into a swoon. He carried me to a neighboring house, caused me to be put to bed, gave me something to eat, waited upon me, comforted and flattered me, and said that he had never seen anyone so handsome as me, and that he never regretted so much the loss of what no one could restore to him. 'I was born at Naples,' said he, 'where they castrate two or three thousand children every year; some die of the operation, others acquire a finer voice than that of any woman, and others become sovereigns of states. This operation was performed on me with great success, and I became a singer in the chapel of her Highness the Princess of Palestrina.' 'Of my mother!' cried I. 'Of your mother!' cried he again, shedding tears. 'What! are you that young princess whom I had the care of bringing up till she was six years old, and who promised even then to be as handsome as you are now?' 'It is I myself: my mother lies about four hundred paces from hence, cut into four quarters, under a heap of dead bodies.'

"I related to him all that had befallen me: he likewise told me his adventures; and informed me that he was sent to the King of Morocco by a Christian power, to conclude a treaty with that monarch by which he was to furnish him with ammunition, artillery, and ships, to enable him entirely to destroy the commerce of other Christians. 'My commission is fulfilled,' said the honest eunuch to me; 'I am going to embark at Ceuta, and will carry you to Italy. But O my misfortune in wanting testicles!'

"I thanked him with tears of gratitude; but instead of conducting me to Italy, he carried me to Algiers, and sold me to the Dey of that province. Scarce was I sold, when the plague, which had made the tour of Africa, Asia, and Europe, broke out at Algiers with great fury. You have seen earthquakes; but pray, Miss, have you ever had the plague?" "Never," replied the Baroness.

"If you had had it," replied the old woman, "you would confess that it is far more terrible than an earthquake. It is very common in Africa; I was seized with it. Figure to yourself the situation of a Pope's daughter, about fifteen years of age, who, in the space of three months, had undergone poverty and slavery, had been ravished almost every day, had seen her mother cut into four quarters, had experienced both famine and war, and was dying of the plague at Algiers. I did not die for all that. But my eunuch, and the Dey, and almost all the seraglio at Algiers perished.

"When the first ravages of this dreadful pestilence were over, they sold the slaves belonging to the Dey. A merchant purchased me, and carried me to Tunis. There he sold me to another merchant, who sold me again at Tripoli; from Tripoli I was sold again to Alexandria; from Alexandria I was sold again to Smyrna; and from Smyrna to Constantinople. At last I became the property of an aga of the Janissaries who was soon after ordered to go to the defense of Asoph, then besieged by the Russians.

"The aga, who was a man of great gallantry, took all his seraglio along with him, and lodged us in a small fort on the Palus Mæotis, under the guard of two black eunuchs and twenty soldiers. We killed a great number of the Russians, who returned the compliment with interest. Asoph was put to fire and sword, and no regard was paid to age or sex. There remained only our little fort, which the enemy resolved to reduce by famine. The twenty Janissaries had sworn that they would never surrender. The extremities of famine to which they were reduced obliged them to eat our two eunuchs, for fear of violating their oath; and a few days after they resolved to devour the women.

"We had an Iman, a very religious and humane man. He preached an excellent sermon to them, in which he dissuaded them from killing us all at once. 'Cut off only one of the buttocks of these ladies,' said he, 'and you will fare extremely well: if you must come to it again, you will have the same entertainment a few days hence; Heaven will bless you for so charitable an action, and you will find relief.'

"As he had an eloquent tongue, he easily persuaded them. This horrible operation was performed upon us; and the Iman applied the same balsam to us that is applied to children after they are circumcised. We were all ready to die.

"The Janissaries had scarce finished the repast with which we had supplied them, when the Russians came in flat-bottomed boats, and not a single Janissary escaped. The Russians showed no concern about the condition we were in. As there are French surgeons in every country, one of them who was a person of very great skill, took us under his care and cured us; and I will remember all my life that when my wounds were pretty well healed, he made me amorous proposals. To be short, he bid us all comfort ourselves, and assured us that the like misfortune had happened in several sieges, and that it was the law of war.

"As soon as my companions were able to walk, they were obliged to go to Moscow. I fell to the lot of a Boyard, who made me his gardener, and gave me twenty lashes with his whip every day. But my Lord having been broke on the wheel within two years after, along with thirty more Boyards, on account of some bustle at court, I availed myself of this event and made my escape. After traversing all Russia, I was a long time servant to an innkeeper at Riga, afterwards at Rostock, Wismar, Leipsic, Cassel, Utrecht, Leyden, the Hague, and Rotterdam. I grew old in misery and disgrace, having only one half of my posteriors, but still remembering that I was a Pope's daughter. A hundred times have

I had thoughts of killing myself; but still I was fond of life. This ridiculous weakness is perhaps one of our most melancholy foibles. For can anything be more stupid than to be desirous of continually carrying a burden which one has a mind to throw down on the ground? To dread existence, and yet preserve it? In a word, to caress the serpent that devours us, till he has gnawed our very heart?

"In the countries through which it has been my fate to travel, and in the inns where I have been a servant, I have seen a prodigious number of people who looked upon their own existence as a curse, but I never knew of more than eight who voluntarily put an end to their misery, *viz:* three negroes, four Englishmen, and a German professor, named Robeck. My last service was with Don Issachar the Jew, who placed me near your person, my fair Lady. I am resolved to share your fate; and I have been more affected by your misfortunes than my own. I should never have spoke of my sufferings, if you had not vexed me a little, and if it had not been customary on board a ship to tell stories, by way of amusement. In short, Miss, I have a good deal of experience, and I have known the world. Divert yourself, and prevail upon each passenger to tell you his story; and if there is one found who has not frequently cursed his life, and has not as often said to himself, that he was the unhappiest of mortals, I will give you leave to throw me into the sea, with my head foremost."

CHAPTER XIII

HOW CANDIDE WAS OBLIGED TO PART FROM THE FAIR CUNEGONDE AND THE OLD WOMAN

THE beautiful Cunegonde having heard the old woman's story, paid her all the civilities that were due to a person of her rank and merit. She approved of her proposal; and engaged all the passengers, one after another, to relate their adventures, and then both Candide and she confessed that the old woman was in the right. "It is a great pity," said Candide, "that the sage Pangloss was hanged, contrary to custom, at the auto-da-fé, for he would tell us most surprising things concerning the physical and moral evil which cover both land and sea; and I should be bold enough, with due respect, to propose some objections."

While each passenger was relating his story, the ship advanced in her voyage. They landed at Buenos Aires. Cunegonde, Captain Candide, and the old woman waited on the governor, Don Fernandes d'Ibaraa, y Figueora, y Mascarenes, y Lampourdos, y Souza. This nobleman was possessed of pride suitable to a person dignified with so many titles. He spoke to other people with so noble a disdain, carried his nose so high, raised his voice so intolerably, assumed so imperious an air, and affected so lofty a gait, that all those who saluted him were tempted to beat him. He was an excessive lover of the fair sex. Cunegonde appeared to him the prettiest woman he had ever seen. The first thing he did, was to ask whether she was not the Captain's wife. The manner in which he proposed the question alarmed Candide. He dared not say that she was his wife, because in reality she was not;

he dared not tell him that she was his sister, because she was not that either, and though this officious lie might have been of service to him, yet his soul was too refined to betray the truth. "Miss Cunegonde," said he, "intends to do me the honor of marrying me, and we beseech your Excellency to grace our nuptials with your presence."

Don Fernandes d'Ibaraa, y Figueora, y Mascarenes, y Lampourdos, y Souza, turning up his mustaches, forced a grim smile, and ordered Captain Candide to go and review his company. Candide obeyed, and the Governor remained alone with Miss Cunegonde. He declared his passion, protested that he would marry her the next day in the face of the church, or otherwise, as it should be agreeable to a person of her charms. Cunegonde desired a quarter of an hour to consider the proposal, to consult with the old woman, and to take her resolution.

Says the old woman to Cunegonde: "Miss, you can reckon up seventy-two descents in your family, and not one farthing in your pocket. It is now in your power to be wife to the greatest lord in South America, who has very pretty whiskers; and what occasion have you to pique yourself upon inviolable fidelity? You have been ravished by the Bulgarians; a Jew and an inquisitor have been in your good graces. Misfortunes have no law on their side. I confess, were I in your place, I should have no scruple to marry the governor, and to make my Lord Captain Candide's fortune."

While the old woman was thus speaking, with all the prudence which age and experience dictated, they descried a small vessel entering the port, which had on board an alcaid and alguazils. The occasion of their voyage was this.

The old woman had shrewdly guessed that it was a

cordelier with a great sleeve that stole the money and jewels from Cunegonde in the city of Badajox, when she and Candide were making their escape. This friar offered to sell some of the diamonds to a jeweler, but he knew them to be the inquisitor's. The cordelier, before he was hanged, confessed he had stolen them. He described the persons he had stolen them from, and told the route they had taken. The flight of Cunegonde and Candide being by this means discovered, they were traced to Cadiz, where a vessel was immediately sent in pursuit of them, and now the vessel was in the port of Buenos Aires. A report was spread that an alcaid was going to land, and that he was in pursuit of the murderers of my Lord the grand inquisitor. The old woman saw in a moment what was to be done. "You cannot run away," said she to Cunegonde, "and you have nothing to fear; it was not you that killed my Lord; and besides, the governor, who is in love with you, will not suffer you to be illtreated; therefore stay here." She then ran to Candide. "Fly," said she, "or in an hour you will be burned alive." He had not a moment to lose; but how could he part from Cunegonde, and where could he fly for shelter?

CHAPTER XIV

HOW CANDIDE AND CACAMBO WERE RECEIVED BY
THE JESUITS OF PARAGUAY

CANDIDE had brought such a valet with him from Cadiz, as one often meets with in abundance on the coasts of Spain, and in the colonies. He was a fourth part a Spaniard, born of a mongrel in Tucuman; and had been a singing-boy, a sexton, a sailor, a monk, a factor, a soldier, and a lackey. His name was Cacambo, and he had an entire regard to his master, because his master was a very good sort of man. Having saddled the two Andalusian horses with all expedition, he said: "Let us go, Master, let us follow the old woman's advice, let us set off, and run without looking behind us." Candide dropped some tears: "O my dear Cunegonde," says he, "must I leave you just at a time when the governor is going to see us married! Cunegonde, when you are brought so far, what will become of you?" "She will do as well as she can," said Cacambo; "women are never at a loss; God will provide for her; let us run." "Whither art thou carrying me?" said Candide: "Where are we going? What shall we do without Cunegonde?" "By St. James of Compostella," said Cacambo, "you were going to fight against the Jesuits; now let us go and fight for them. I know the road perfectly well; I will conduct you to their kingdom; they will be charmed to have a captain that knows the Bulgarian exercise; you will make a prodigious fortune; though one cannot find his account in one world, he may in another. It is a great pleasure to see variety of objects, and to perform new exploits."

"Have you then been at Paraquay?" said Candide. "Yes, in truth, I have," said Cacambo; "I was usher to the College of Assumption, and am acquainted with the government of the good fathers as well as I am with the streets of Cadiz. It is an admirable sort of government. The kingdom is upwards of three hundred leagues in diameter, and divided into thirty provinces. The fathers there are masters of everything, and the people have nothing. It is the masterpiece of reason and justice. For my part, I see nothing so divine as the good fathers, who wage war here against the Kings of Spain and Portugal, and in Europe are their confessors; who in this country kill Spaniards, and at Madrid send them to heaven. This transports me: let us therefore push forward; you are going to be the happiest of mortals. What pleasure will it be to those fathers, when they know that a captain who understands the Bulgarian exercise comes to offer them his service!"

As soon as they reached the first pass, Cacambo told the advance guard that a captain desired to speak with my Lord the commandant. They went to inform the main guard of it. A Paraguayan officer ran on foot to the commandant, to impart the news to him. Candide and Cacambo were at first disarmed, and their two Andalusian horses seized. The two strangers were introduced between two files of musketeers: the commandant was at the further end, with a three-cornered cap on his head, his gown tucked up, a sword by his side, and a spontoon in his hand. He made a signal, and straightway four and twenty soldiers surrounded the new comers. A sergeant told them they must wait; that the commandant could not speak to them; that the Rev. Father Provincial does not permit any Spaniard to open his mouth but in his presence, or to stay above three hours in the province. "And where is the Rev. Father Provincial?" said Cacambo. "He is upon the parade, after saying mass," answered the sergeant; "and you cannot kiss his spurs in less than three hours." "But," said Cacambo, "my master, the Captain, who is ready to die for hunger, as well as myself, is not a Spaniard, but a German. Cannot we have something for breakfast, while we wait for his Reverence?"

The sergeant went that instant to give an account of this discourse to the commandant. "God be praised," said the Rev. Commandant; "since he is a German, I may speak with him; bring him into my arbor." Candide was immediately conducted into a green pavilion, decorated with a very handsome balustrade of green and gold marble, with intertextures of vines, containing parrots, humming-birds, fly-birds, guinea hens, and all other sorts of rare birds. An excellent breakfast was provided in vessels of gold, and while the Paraguayans were eating Indian corn out of wooden dishes, in the open fields, exposed to the sultry heat of the sun, the Rev. Father Commandant retired to his arbor. He was a very handsome young man, with a full face, tolerably fair, fresh colored, his eyebrows were arched, his eye full of fire, his ear red, his lips like vermilion; his air was somewhat fierce, but of a fierceness which differed both from that of a Spaniard and a Jesuit. They now returned to Candide and Cacambo their arms, which had been taken from them, together with the two Andalusian horses; which Cacambo took the liberty to feed near the arbor, keeping his eye upon them, for fear of a surprise.

Candide immediately kissed the hem of the commandant's garment; after which they both, by his order, sat down to table. "You are a German then?" said the Jesuit to him in that language. "Yes, my Reverend Father," said Candide. In pronouncing these words, they looked on each other with an extreme surprise, which they were not able to account for. "And what part of Germany do you belong to?" said the Jesuit. "To the lower part of Westphalia," said Candide: "I was born in the castle of Thunder-ten-tronckh." "Heavens, is it possible!" cried the commandant. "What a miracle is this!" cried Candide. "Is it you?" said the commandant. "'Tis impossible!" said Candide. On this they both fell backwards, but getting up again, embraced each other, and shed tears. "What, is it you, my Reverend Father? You, the brother of the fair Cunegonde? You that was slain by the Bulgarians? You, the Baron's son, are you a Jesuit at Paraguay? I must confess that this is a strange world indeed! Ah Pangloss! Pangloss! How glad would you have been, if you had not been hanged!"

The commandant ordered the negro slaves, and the Paraguayans who poured out their liquor into cups of rock crystal, to retire. He thanked God and St. Ignatius a thousand times; folded Candide in his arms, their faces being all the while bathed in tears. "You will be more astonished, more affected, more out of your wits," said Candide, "when I tell you that Miss Cunegonde, your sister, who you thought was ripped up, is as well as I am." "Where?" "In your neighborhood, at the house of the governor of Buenos Aires; and I was coming to fight against you." Every word they spoke in this long conversation heaped surprise upon surprise. Their souls dwelt upon their tongues, listened in their ears, and sparkled in their eyes. As they were Germans, they made a long meal (according to custom), waiting for the Reverend Father the Provincial, while the commandant thus addressed his dear Candide.

CHAPTER XV

HOW CANDIDE KILLED THE BROTHER OF HIS DEAR CUNEGONDE

"I SHALL ever have present in my memory that horrible day wherein I saw my father and mother killed, and my sister ravished. When the Bulgarians were gone, my sweet sister was nowhere to be found; and I, together with my father and mother, two maids, and three little lads that were murdered, were slung into a cart, in order to be buried in a chapel which belonged to the Jesuits, about two leagues distant from our family castle. A Jesuit sprinkled us with holy water, which being very salt, and some drops falling into my eyes, the Father could perceive my eyeballs move, on which he put his hand upon my side and felt my heart beat; I was taken care of, and in about three weeks' time, no one would have thought that anything had ailed me. You know very well, my dear Candide, I was very handsome, but I grew more so, on which account the Reverend Father Didrius, superior of the house, conceived a very great affection for me; gave me the habit of a novice; and some time after, sent me to Rome. The superior was then looking out for a recruit of young Jesuits from Germany. For the rulers of Paraguay take as few Spanish Jesuits as they can, but choose foreigners, because they think they can tyrannize over them as they please. I was therefore made choice of by the Reverend Father General, as a proper person to go to work in this vineyard. I set sail in company with a Polander and a Tirolesian. On my arrival I was honored with a subdeaconry and a lieutenancy. At present I am a colonel and a priest. We shall give the King of Spain's army a warm reception; I can assure you that they will be excommunicated and beaten. Providence has sent you hither to assist us. But is it true, that my dear sister Cunegonde is in our neighborhood, at the governor of Buenos Aires' house?" Candide swore that it was as true as the gospel. On this their tears gushed out afresh.

The Baron could not refrain from embracing Candide, whom he called his brother and his protector. "Ah, perhaps," said he, "we two may enter the city in triumph, and recover my sister Cunegonde." "There is nothing I could wish for more," said Candide; "for I expected to be married to her before tomorrow, and I have some hopes I shall yet." "The insolence of the fellow!" replied the Baron; "would you have the impudence to marry my sister, who can show seventy-two quarterings in her coat of arms?" Candide, being quite thunderstruck at this, made him the following reply: "My Reverend Father, all the quarterings in the world do not signify a farthing. I have delivered your sister from the hand of a Jew and an inquisitor; she lies under a great many obligations to me, and is willing to marry me. Master Pangloss always told me that all men are equal. I am sure I shall have her." "We will see whether you shall or no, you villain!" said the Jesuit Baron of Thunder-ten-tronckh; and at the same time gave him a blow on the face with the flat part of his sword. Candide drew his immediately, and plunged it up to the hilt in the Baron's body; but drawing it out again, and looking upon it as it reeked, he cried out, "O God! I have killed my old master, my friend, my brother-in-law. I am one of the best-natured men in the world, yet I have killed three men, and of the three, there were two of them priests." Cacambo, who stood sentry at the door of the arbor, and who heard the noise, ran in. "We have nothing now to do but to sell our lives as dear as we can," said his master to him; "and if they should force their way into the arbor, let us at least die with our arms in our hands."

Cacambo, who had been in circumstances of a similar nature, did not stand to rack his brains for an expedient, but took the Jesuit's dress, which the Baron wore, put it upon Candide, gave him the dead man's cap, and made him mount his horse. All this was done in the twinkling of an eye. "Let us gallop away, Master," says he; "everybody will take you for some Jesuit that is going express, and we shall get to the frontiers before they can overtake us." He fled like lightning, before these words were quite out of his mouth, crying out in Spanish, "Make way, make way for the Reverend Father, the Colonel."

CHAPTER XVI

WHAT PASSED BETWEEN OUR TWO TRAVELERS, AND TWO GIRLS, TWO MONKEYS, AND THE SAVAGES CALLED OREILLONS

CANDIDE and his valet had got beyond the pass before any person in the camp knew a syllable of the death of the German Jesuit. The provident Cacambo had taken care to fill his wallet with bread, chocolate, hams, and some bottles of wine. They pushed with their Andalusian horses into a strange country, where they could not discover any path or road. At last a pleasant meadow, which was divided by a river, presented itself to their eyes. Our two travelers turned their horses a-grazing. And Cacambo made a proposal to his master to eat a bit, and at the same time set him the example. "Do you think," said Candide, "that I can feast upon ham when I have killed the Baron's son, and find myself under a necessity never to see Cunegonde again, as long as I live? What signifies it to prolong my days in misery, since I must drag them out far from her, a prey to remorse and despair? And what will the Journal of Trevoux say of me?"

Having thus spoken, he refused to eat a morsel. The sun was now set, when our two wanderers, to their very great surprise, heard a faint cry, which seemed to come from some women. It was not easy to determine whether it was occasioned by distress or mirth; they rose immediately with all the anxiety and apprehension to which people are subject in a strange place. The noise was made by two girls that ran stark naked on the banks of the meadow, pursued by two large monkeys that bit their backsides. Candide was moved with pity; and as he had learned to shoot among the Bulgarians, and was so good a marksman that he would hit a nut in a bush without touching the leaves, he took up his Spanish fuzee, which was double-charged, and killed the two monkeys. "God be praised, my dear Cacambo," said he, "I have delivered the two poor girls from this great danger; however, if I have been guilty of a sin in killing the inquisitor, I have now made ample amends for it by saving the lives of the two girls. They may chance to prove a couple of ladies of rank; and who knows but this adventure may do us some service in this country?"

He was going on at this rate, thinking that he had done a great feat; but how great was his surprise, when, instead of rejoicing, he saw the two girls embracing the monkeys with all the marks of the most tender affection! They bathed their bodies with tears, and filled the air with shrieks that testified the deepest distress. "I could never have expected to have seen so much as this," said he to Cacambo, who replied, "You have done a fine piece of work indeed, Sir, you have killed the ladies' two sweethearts." "Their sweethearts! Is it possible? You are in jest, sure, Cacambo: who the deuce could believe you to be in earnest?" "My dear Sir," replied Cacambo, "you are always for making mountains of molehills; why should you think it incredible that there are some countries where monkeys enjoy the favors of the ladies? Why, they are got by human creatures, in the same manner as I was got by a Spaniard." "Ay," replied Candide, "now I recollect, Mr. Pangloss has told me that there may be many an instance of this kind, and that these mixtures gave birth to the Egipans, Fauns, and Satyrs; that a great many of the ancients had seen them with their own eyes; but I always looked upon it as a mere romance." "You ought, now, to see your mistake," said Cacambo, "and own that the Doctor was in the right. And you may see what influence the prejudice of education has upon the understanding. All I am afraid of is that these ladies will play us some unlucky trick."

These wise reflections induced Candide to quit the meadow and take to a wood, where he and Cacambo supped together, and, after heartily cursing the Portuguese inquisitor, the governor of Buenos Aires, and the Baron, they fell asleep.

On their waking, they found that they could not stir, for the Oreillons, the inhabitants of the country, whom the two lasses had informed of their adventure, had bound them in the night time with cords made of the bark of a tree. They were surrounded by a body of fifty Oreillons, stark naked, armed with arrows, clubs, and hatchets made of flint; some of them were making a great caldron boil, others preparing spits; and all of them crying out, "He's a Jesuit, he's a Jesuit; we will make him pay sauce for it, we will pick his bones for him; let us eat the Jesuit, let us eat the Jesuit."

"You may remember I told you, my dear master," cried Cacambo in a lamentable tone, "that those two lasses would play us some ugly trick."

Cacambo was never at a loss for an invention: "Never despair," said he to the disconsolate Candide. "I understand the jargon of these people a little, and am going to speak to them." "Don't fail," said Candide, "to represent to them the inhumanity of dressing men for meat, and set forth what an unchristian practice it is."

"Gentlemen," says Cacambo, "you fancy that you shall feast on a Jesuit today; a very good dish, I make no doubt, nor is there anything more just than to serve one's enemies so. In effect, the law of nature teaches us to kill our neighbor, and it is a principle which is put in practice all over the globe. If we do not make use of the right of eating him, it is because we have plenty of victuals without it; but as you have not that advantage, it must certainly be better for you to eat your enemies, than fling away the fruit of your victories as a feast to crows and ravens. But, gentlemen, I suppose you would not be for eating your friends. You fancy you are going to spit a Jesuit, but, believe me, I assure you it is your defender, it is the enemy of your enemies that you are going to roast. As for my part, I was born among you. The gentleman you see here is my master, and so far from being a Jesuit, he has just now killed a Jesuit, and he is only dressed in his spoils, which is the cause of your mistake. In order to confirm my assertion, let one of you take his gown off, carry it to the first pass of the government of the fathers, and inform himself whether my master has not killed a Jesuit officer. It is an affair that won't take up much time, and you may always have it in your power to eat us if you catch me in a lie. But if I have told you the truth, and nothing but the truth, you are too well acquainted with the principles of natural right, morality, and law, not to show us some favor."

The Oreillons were so fully convinced of the reasonableness of his proposal, that they deputed two of their chiefs to go and inform themselves of the truth of what he had told them. The two deputies acquitted themselves of their charge like men of sense, and returned soon with a favorable account. The Oreillons then unbound their prisoners, showed them a thousand civilities, offered them women, gave them something to refresh them, and conducted them back again to the confines of their state, crying all the while, like madmen, "He is no Jesuit, he is no Jesuit."

Candide could not help wondering at his deliverance. "What a people!" said he; "What men! What manners! If I had not had the good luck to stab Miss Cunegonde's brother through the lungs, I should inevitably have been eaten up. But, after all, the dictates of pure nature are always best, since this people, instead of eating me, showed me a thousand civilities as soon as they knew that I was not a Jesuit."

CHAPTER XVII

THE ARRIVAL OF CANDIDE AND HIS MAN AT THE COUNTRY OF ELDORADO, AND WHAT THEY SAW THERE

WHEN they had reached the frontiers of the Oreillons, "You see now," said Cacambo to Candide, "that this part of the world is not one pin better than the other. Take a fool's advice for once, and let us return to Europe as fast as ever we can." "How is that possible?" said Candide: "And pray what part of it would you have us go to? Shall I go into my own country? The Bulgarians and Abarians kill all they meet with there; if I return to Portugal, I am sure I shall be burned alive; if we stay in this country, we run the hazard of being roasted every moment. And again, how can I think of leaving that part of the globe where Miss Cunegonde lives?"

"Why then, let us take our course towards Cayenne," said Cacambo; "we shall meet with some Frenchmen there, for you know they are to be met with all over the globe; perhaps they will give us some relief, and God may have pity upon us."

It was no easy matter for them to go to Cayenne, as they did not know whereabouts it lay; besides, mountains, rivers, precipices, banditti, and savages were difficulties they were sure to encounter within their journey. Their horses died of fatigue, and their provisions were soon consumed. After having lived a whole month on wild fruits, they found themselves on the banks of a small river bordered by cocoa trees, which at once preserved their lives and kept up their hopes.

Cacambo, who was on all occasions as good a councilor as the old woman, said to Candide, "We can hold out no longer; we have walked enough already, and here's an empty canoe upon the shore. Let's fill it with cocoa, then get on board, and let it drift with the stream: a river always carries one to some inhabited place. If we don't meet with what we like, we are sure to meet with something new." "Why, what you say is very right, so let us go," said Candide, "and recommend ourselves to the care of Providence."

They rowed some leagues between the two banks, which were enameled with flowers in some places, in others barren, in some parts level, and in others very steep. The river grew broader as they proceeded, and at last lost iself in a spacious horizon that was bounded by some frightful rocks, which reached as high as the clouds. Our two travelers had the courage to trust themselves to the stream. The river, being very narrow in this place, drove them along with such a rapidity and noise as filled them with the utmost horror. In about four and twenty hours they got sight of daylight again, but their canoe was dashed in pieces against the breakers. They were obliged to crawl from one rock to another for a whole league; after which they got sight of a spacious plain, bounded with inaccessible mountains. The country was cultivated both for pleasure and profit; which latter was always mixed with the agreeable. The roads were covered, or, more properly speaking, were adorned with carriages, whose figure and materials were very brilliant; they were full of men and women of an extraordinary beauty, and drawn with great swiftness by large red sheep, which for fleetness surpassed the finest horses of Andalusia, Tetuan, or Mequinez.

"This certainly," said Candide, "is a better country than Westphalia." He and Cacambo got on shore near the first village they came to. The very children of the village were dressed in gold brocades, all tattered, playing at quoits at the entrance of the town. Our two travelers from the other world amused themselves with looking at them. The quoits were made of large round pieces, yellow, red, and green, and cast a surprising light. Our travelers' hands itched prodigiously to be fingering some of them, for they were almost certain that they were either gold, emeralds, or rubies, the least of which would have been no small ornament to the throne of the Great Mogul. "To be sure," said Cacambo, "these must be the children of the king of the country, diverting themselves at quoits." The master of the village coming at that instant to call them to school: "That's the preceptor to the royal family," cried Candide.

The little brats immediately quitted their play, leaving their quoits and other playthings behind them. Can-

dide picked them up, ran to the schoolmaster, and
presented them to him with a great deal of humility, ac-
quainting him, by signs, that their Royal Highnesses
had forgot their gold and jewels. The master of the village smiled, and flung them upon the ground; and having stared at Candide with some degree of surprise,
walked off.

Our travelers did not fail immediately to pick up the
gold, rubies, and emeralds. "Where are we got to now?"
cried Candide. "The princes of the blood must certainly
be well educated here, since they are taught to make so
light of gold and jewels." Cacambo was as much surprised as Candide. At length they drew near to the first
house in the village, which was built like one of our
European palaces. There was a vast crowd of people at
the door, and still a greater within. They heard very good
music, and their nostrils were saluted by a most refreshing smell from the kitchen.

Cacambo went up to the door, and heard they were
speaking the Peruvian language, which was his mother-
tongue, for every one knows that Cacambo was born
at Tucuman, in a village where they make use of no
other language. "I'll be your interpreter, Master," cries
Cacambo, in the greatest raptures, "this is an inn; in
with you, in with you."

Immediately two waiters and two maids that belonged
to the house, dressed in clothes of gold tissue, and having their hair tied back with ribands, invited them to
sit down to table with the landlord. They served up four
soups, each garnished with two parroquets, a large dish
of *bouillé*, that weighed about two hundred weight; two
apes roasted, of an excellent taste; three hundred humming-birds in one plate, and six hundred fly-birds in another; together with exquisite ragouts, and the most de-

licious tarts, all upon plates of a species of rock-crystal. After which the lads and maids served them with a great variety of liquors made from the sugar-canes.

The guests were mostly tradesmen and carriers, all extremely polite, who asked some questions of Cacambo with the greatest discretion and circumspection, and received as satisfactory answers.

When the repast was ended, Cacambo thought, as well as Candide, to discharge their reckoning by putting down two of the large pieces of gold which they had picked up. But the landlord and landlady burst out into a prodigious fit of laughing, and could not restrain it for some time. Recovering themselves at last: "Gentlemen," says the landlord, "we can see pretty well that you are strangers; we are not much used to such guests here. Pardon us if we fell a-laughing when you offered us the stones of our highways in discharge of your reckoning. It is plain you have got none of the money of this kingdom; but there is no occasion for it in order to dine here. All the inns, which are established for the conveniency of trade, are maintained by the government. You have had but sorry entertainment here, because this is only a poor village, but anywhere else you will be sure to be received in a manner suitable to your merit."

Cacambo explained the host's speech to Candide, who heard it with much astonishment and wonder as his friend Cacambo interpreted it. "What country can this be," said they to each other, "which is unknown to the rest of the earth, and of so different a nature from ours? It is probably that country where everything is right, for it is necessary that there should be one of that sort. And for all Doctor Pangloss has said, I could not help taking notice many a time that things were very bad in Westphalia."

CHAPTER XVIII

WHAT THEY SAW IN THE COUNTRY OF ELDORADO

CACAMBO could not conceal his curiosity from his landlord. "For my part," said the landlord to him, "I am very ignorant, though not the worse on that account; but we have an old man here, who has retired from court, and is reckoned both the wisest and the most communicative person in the kingdom." And saying this, without any more ado, he conducted Cacambo to the old man's house. Candide acted now only a second character in the play, and followed his servant. They entered into a very plain house, for the door was nothing but silver, and the ceilings nothing but gold, but finished with so much taste that the richest ceilings of Europe could not surpass them. The antechamber was indeed only covered with rubies and emeralds, but the order in which everything was arranged made amends for this great simplicity.

The old gentleman received the two strangers on a sofa stuffed with the feathers of humming-birds, and ordered them to be served with liquors in vessels of diamond; after which he satisfied their curiosity in the following manner:

"I am now in my hundredth and seventy-second year, and I have heard my deceased father, who was groom to His Majesty, mention the surprising revolutions of Peru, of which he was an eye witness. The kingdom we are in at present is the ancient country of the Incas, who left it very indiscreetly in order to conquer one part of the world; instead of which, they themselves were all destroyed by the Spaniards.

"The princes of their family who remained in their native country were more wise; they made a law, by the unanimous consent of the whole nation, that none of our inhabitants should ever go out of our little kingdom, and it is owing to this that we have preserved both our innocence and our happiness. The Spaniards have had some confused idea of this country, and have called it *El Dorado;* and an Englishman, named Sir Walter Raleigh, has likewise been on our coasts above a hundred years ago, but as we are surrounded by inaccessible rocks and precipices, we have always been hitherto sheltered from the rapacity of the European nations, who are inspired with an inconceivable rage for the stones and dirt of our land, and who, to possess themselves of them, would murder us all, to the very last man."

Their conference was pretty long, and turned upon the form of their government, their manners, their women, their public shows, and their arts. At last Candide, who had always a taste for metaphysics, bid Cacambo ask, if there was any religion in that country?

The old gentleman reddened a little, "How is it possible," said he, "that you should question it? Do you take us for ungrateful wretches?" Cacambo then humbly asked him, what the religion of Eldorado was. This made the old gentleman redden again. "Can there be more religions than one?" said he: "We profess, I believe, the religion of the whole world; we worship the Deity from evening to morning." "Do you worship but one God?" said Cacambo, who still acted as interpreter in representing Candide's doubts. "You may be sure we do," said the old man; "since it is evident there can be neither two, nor three, nor four. I must confess that the people of your world propose very odd questions." Candide was not yet wearied in interrogating the good old man: he wanted to know how they prayed to God in Eldorado. "We never pray at all," said the good respectable sage; "we have nothing to ask of Him; He has given us all we need, and we incessantly return Him thanks."

Candide had a curiosity to see their priests, and bid Cacambo ask where they were. This made the old gentleman smile. "My friends," said he, "we are all of us priests; the King, and the heads of every family, sing their solemn songs of thanksgiving every morning, accompanied by five or six thousand musicians." "What," said Cacambo, "have you no monks to preach, to dispute, to tyrannize, to set people together by the ears, and get those burned who are not of the same sentiments as themselves?" "We must be very fools indeed if we had," said the old gentleman; "we are all of us of the same opinion here, and we don't understand what you mean by your monks."

Candide was in an ecstasy during all this discourse, and said to himself, "This place is vastly different from Westphalia, and my Lord the Baron's castle. If our friend Pangloss had seen Eldorado, he would never have maintained that nothing upon earth could surpass the castle of Thunder-ten-tronckh. It is plain everybody should travel."

After this long conversation was finished, the good old man ordered a coach and six sheep to be got ready, and twelve of his domestics to conduct the travelers to the court. "Excuse me," says he to them, "if my age deprives me of the honor of attending you. The King will receive you in a manner that you will not be displeased with, and you will, I doubt not, make allowance for the customs of the country, if you should meet with anything that you disapprove of."

Candide and Cacambo got into the coach; the six sheep flew, and in less than four hours they reached the King's palace, which was situated at one end of the metropolis. The gate was two hundred and twenty feet high, and one hundred broad; it is impossible to describe the materials it was composed of. But one may easily guess, that it must have prodigiously surpassed those stones and the sand which we call gold and jewels.

Candide and Cacambo, on their alighting from the coach, were received by twenty maids of honor, of an exquisite beauty, who conducted them to the baths, and presented them with robes made of the down of the humming-birds; after which the great officers and their ladies introduced them into His Majesty's apartment, between two rows of musicians, consisting of a thousand in each, according to the custom of the country.

When they approached the foot of the throne, Cacambo asked one of the great officers in what manner they were to behave when they went to pay their respects to his Majesty, whether they were to fall down on their knees or their bellies; whether they were to put their hands upon their heads or upon their backsides; whether they were to lick up the dust of the room; and, in a word, what the ceremony was? "The custom is," said the great officer, "to embrace the King, and kiss him on 'both sides.'" Candide and Cacambo accordingly clasped His Majesty round the neck, who received them in the most polite manner imaginable, and very gently invited them to sup with him.

In the interim, they showed them the city, the public edifices, that reach almost as high as the clouds, the market places embellished with a thousand columns; fountains of pure water, besides others of rose water, and of the liquors that are extracted from the sugar-canes, which played incessantly in the squares, which were paved with a kind of precious stones that diffused a fragrance like that of cloves or cinnamon. Candide asking them to show them one of their courts of justice, and their parliament house; they told him they had none, and that they were strangers to lawsuits. He then inquired if they had any prisons, and was told they had not. What surprised him most, and gave him the greatest pleasure, was the palace of sciences, in which he saw a gallery of two thousand paces, full of instruments for making experiments in philosophy.

After having gone over about a thousandth part of the city in the afternoon, they were reconducted to the palace. Candide seated himself at table with His Majesty, his valet Cacambo, and a great many ladies. Never was there a better entertainment seen, and never was more wit shown at table than that His Majesty displayed. Cacambo interpreted the King's repartees to Candide, and though they were translated, they appeared repartees still; a thing which surprised Candide more than anything else.

They spent a whole month in this hospitable manner. Candide was continually saying to Cacambo, "I must say it again and again, my friend, that the castle where I was born was nothing in comparison to this country where we are now; but yet Miss Cunegonde is not here, and, without doubt, you have left a sweetheart behind you in Europe. If we stay where we are, we shall be looked upon only like other folks; whereas if we return to our own world only with twelve sheep loaded with the pebbles of Eldorado, we shall be richer than all the kings put together; we shall have no need to be afraid of the inquisitor; and we may easily recover Miss Cunegonde."

This proposal was extremely agreeable to Cacambo; so fond are we of running about, of making a figure among our countrymen, and of making orations on what we have seen in our travels that these two really happy men resolved to be no longer so, and accordingly asked his Majesty's leave to depart.

"You are guilty of a very great weakness," said his Majesty to them: "I am not ignorant that my country is a trifling place; but providing it be but passable, you had better stay in it. I must indeed confess, that I have no right to detain people of another nation; it is a degree of tyranny inconsistent with our customs and laws; all men are free; you may go when you please; but you ought first to be informed that you cannot leave us without some difficulty. It is impossible to go against the current up the rapid river which runs under the rocks; your passage hither was a kind of miracle. The mountains which surround my kingdom are a thousand feet high, and as steep as a wall; they are at least ten leagues over, and their descent is nothing but precipices. However, since you seem determined to leave us, I will give orders immediately to the constructors of my machines to contrive one to transport you with the greatest ease. When they have conveyed you to the other side of the mountains, no one must attend you; because my subjects have made a vow never to pass beyond them, and they are too wise to break it. There is nothing else you can ask of me which shall not be granted." "We ask your Majesty," said Cacambo, very eagerly, "only a few sheep loaded with provisions, together with some of the common stones and dirt of your country."

The King smiled heartily: "I cannot," said he, "conceive what pleasure you Europeans find in our yellow clay; but you are welcome to take as much of it as you please, and much good may it do you."

He gave immediate orders to his engineers to construct a machine to hoist up and transport these two extraordinary persons out of his kingdom. Three thousand able mechanics set to work; and in a fortnight's time the machine was completed, which cost no more than twenty millions sterling of their currency.

Candide and Cacambo were both placed in the machine, together with two large red sheep bridled and saddled for them to ride on when they were got clear of the mountains; twenty sheep of burden loaded with provisions; thirty with the greatest curiosities of the country, by way of present; and fifty with gold, precious stones, and diamonds. The King took his leave of our two vagabonds with the greatest marks of affection.

It was a very fine sight to see them depart, and the ingenious manner in which they and the sheep were slung over the mountains. The philosophers took their leave of them, after having got them safe over; and now Candide had no other desire, no other aim, than to go to present his sheep to Miss Cunegonde. "We have now got enough," said he, "to pay for the ransom of Miss Cunegonde, if the governor of Buenos Aires will but part with her. Let us march towards Cayenne, there take ship, and then we will look out for some snug kingdom to make a purchase of."

CHAPTER XIX

WHAT HAPPENED TO THEM AT SURINAM, AND HOW CANDIDE GOT ACQUAINTED WITH MARTIN

THE first day's journey of our two travelers was very agreeable, being elated with the idea of finding themselves masters of more treasure than Asia, Europe, or Africa could scrape together. Candide was so transported that he cut out the name of Cunegonde upon almost every tree that he came to. The second day two of their sheep sunk in a morass, and were lost with all that they carried; two others died of fatigue a few days after; seven or eight died at once for want in a desert; and some few days after, some others fell down a precipice. To be short, after a march of one hundred days, their whole stock amounted to no more than two sheep.

Says Candide, then, to Cacambo, "My friend, you see how perishable the riches of this world are; there is nothing durable, nothing to be depended on but virtue, and the happiness of once more seeing Miss Cunegonde." "I grant it," said Cacambo; "but we have still two sheep left, besides more treasure than ever the King of Spain was master of; and I see a town a good way off that I take to be Surinam, belonging to the Dutch. We are at the end of our troubles, and at the beginning of our happiness."

As they drew nigh to the city, they saw a negro stretched on the ground, with only one half of his clothes, that is to say, having only a pair of drawers of blue cloth; the poor fellow had lost his left leg and his right hand. "Good God!" said Candide to him in Dutch, "friend, what do you do here, in this terrible condition?"

"I am waiting for my master Mynheer Vanderdendur, the great merchant," replied the negro. "And was it Mynheer Vanderdendur that used you in this manner?" said Candide. "Yes, Sir," said the negro, "it is the custom of the country. They give us a pair of linen drawers for our whole clothing twice a year. If we should chance to have one of our fingers caught in the mill, as we are working in the sugarhouses, they cut off our hand; if we attempt to run away, they cut off one of our legs; and I have had the misfortune to be found guilty of both these charges. Such are the conditions on which you eat sugar in Europe! Yet, when my mother sold me for ten crowns of Patagon on the coast of Guinea, she said to me, 'My dear boy, bless our benefactors, be always very dutiful to them, they will make you live happily: you have the honor to be a slave to our lords the whites, and will by that means be in way of making the fortunes both of your father and mother.' Alas! I do not know whether I have made their fortunes, but I am sure they have not made mine. The dogs, monkeys, and parrots are a thousand times less wretched than we. The Dutch missionaries who converted me, told me every Sunday that we all are sons of Adam, both blacks and whites. I am not a genealogist myself; but if these preachers speak the truth, we are all cousin-germans; and then you must own that it is a shocking thing for them to use their relations in this barbarous manner.

"Ah! Pangloss," cried Candide, "you never dreamed of such an abominable piece of villainy; there is an end of the matter; I see I must at last renounce your optimism." "What do you mean by optimisim?" said Cacambo. "Why," said Candide, "it is the folly of maintaining that everything is right, when it is wrong." He then looked upon the negro, with tears in his eyes, and in that condition entered into Surinam.

The first thing they did here was to inquire whether there was any vessel in the harbor that might be hired for Buenos Aires. The person they applied themselves to was no other than a Spanish commander, who offered to make an honorable bargain with them. He appointed to meet them at an inn, whither Candide and the faithful Cacambo went to wait for him with their two sheep.

Candide, who had his mind in his tongue, told the Spaniard all his adventures, and confessed to him that he was determined to run away with Miss Cunegonde. "I shall take care how I carry you to Buenos Aires, if that is the case," said the captain; "for I would be hanged, and so would you. The fair Cunegonde is my Lord's favorite mistress."

This was a thunder-clap to Candide; he wept a long time, but at last, drawing Cacambo aside, "I will tell you, my dear friend," says he, "what I would have you do. We have each of us about five or six millions of diamonds in our pockets; and as you are a much cleverer fellow than I am, I would have you go and fetch Miss Cunegonde from Buenos Aires. If the Governor should make any difficulties, give him a million of them; if that do not succeed, give him two. As you did not murder the inquisitor, they will have no suspicion of you; in the meantime, I will fit out another vessel, and go and wait for you at Venice; that is a safe place, and I need not be afraid there of Bulgarians, Abares, Jews, or inquisitors." Cacambo cried up the wisdom of this proposal. He was indeed under great concern to leave so good a master, who used him like a familiar friend; but the pleasure of being serviceable to him soon got the better of the sorrow he felt in parting with him.

They took leave of each other with tears; Candide recommending to him at the same time not to forget their good old woman. The same day Cacambo set sail. This Cacambo was a very honest fellow.

Candide stayed some time at Surinam, waiting for another vessel to carry him and the two sheep which remained to Italy. He hired servants, and purchased everything necessary for a long voyage; at last, Mynheer Vanderdendur, the master of a large vessel, came and offered his service. "What will you have," said Candide to our Dutchman, "for carrying me, my family, goods, and these two sheep you see here, directly to Venice?" The master of the vessel asked ten thousand piastres, and Candide made no answer.

"O, O," said the crafty Vanderdendur to himself, after he had left him, "if this stranger can give ten thousand piastres without bargaining, he must be immensely rich." Returning a few minutes after, he let him know that he could not go for less than twenty thousand. "Well, you shall have them then," said Candide.

"Odso!" said the captain with a low voice, "This man makes no more of twenty thousand piastres than he did of ten!" He then returned a second time, and said that he could not carry him to Venice for less than thirty thousand piastres. "You shall have thirty thousand then," replied Candide.

"O, O," said the Dutch trader again to himself, "this man makes nothing of thirty thousand piastres, no doubt but the two sheep are loaded with immense treasures; let us stand out no longer; let us however finger the thirty thousand piastres first, and then we shall see."

Candide sold two small diamonds, the least of which was worth more than what the Captain had asked. He advanced him the money. The two sheep were put on board the vessel. Candide followed in a small wherry, intending to join the vessel when at sea. But the Captain seized his opportunity, unfurled his sails, unmoored, and met with a favorable gale. Candide, distracted and out of his wits, soon lost sight of him. "Ah!" cried he, "this is a trick worthy of the old world." He returned on shore overwhelmed with sorrow; for he had certainly lost more than would set up a score of kings.

He ran immediately to the Dutch judge, and as he was not quite master of himself, knocked very loud at the door; he went in, told his case, and raised his voice a little louder than became him. The judge began with making him pay ten thousand piastres for the noise he had made. After which he heard him very patiently, and promised to examine into the affair as soon as ever the trader should return, at the same time making him pay ten thousand piastres as the expense of the hearing.

This proceeding made Candide stark mad. He had indeed experienced misfortunes a thousand times more affecting; but the coolness of the judge, and the knavish trick of the master of the vessel who had robbed him, fired his spirits, and plunged him into a profound melancholy. The villainy of mankind presented itself to his mind in all its deformity, and he dwelled upon nothing but the most dismal ideas. At last, a French vessel being ready to sail for Bourdeaux, as he had no sheep loaded with diamonds to carry with him, he paid the common price as a cabin passenger, and ordered the crier to give notice all over the city that he would pay for the passage and diet of any honest man that would go the voyage with him, and he would give him two thousand piastres besides, on condition that he would make it appear that he was the most dissatisfied with his circumstances, and the most unfortunate person in that province.

A vast multitude of candidates presented themselves, enough to have manned a fleet. Candide, desirous to pick from among the best, marked out twenty, who seemed to him to have the best pretensions, and to be the most sociable. But as every one of them thought the preference due to himself, he invited them all to his inn, and gave them a supper, on condition that each of them should take an oath that he would relate his adventures faithfully, promising to choose that person who seemed to be the greatest object of pity, and had the greatest reason to be dissatisfied with his lot, and to give a small present to the rest, as a gratification for their trouble.

The assembly continued till four the next morning. As Candide was employed in hearing their adventures, he could not help recollecting what the old woman had told him in their voyage towards Buenos Aires, and the bargain she had made in case he met with a single person in the ship that did not esteem himself most miserable. He thought upon Pangloss at every incident that was related. "That Pangloss," said he, "would be hard put to it to defend this system. I wish he was but here. Indeed, if everything is ordered for the best, it must be at Eldorado, but nowhere else on earth." At last, he determined in favor of a poor scholar, who had written ten years for the booksellers at Amsterdam. For he thought there could not be a more disagreeable employment on the face of the earth.

This scholar, though in other respects a good sort of a man, had been robbed by his wife, beaten by his son, abandoned by his daughter, who got a Portuguese to run away with her; had been stripped of a small employment, which was all he had to subsist on; and was persecuted by the priests at Surinam because they took him for a Socinian.

It must indeed be confessed that some of the other candidates were at least as unhappy as he; but he met with a preference because Candide thought that a scholar would be the most proper person to divert him during the voyage. All his competitors thought that Candide did them a great piece of injustice; but he soon convinced them to the contrary, by giving them a hundred piastres apiece.

CHAPTER XX

WHAT HAPPENED AT SEA TO CANDIDE AND MARTIN

THE old scholar, who was named Martin, embarked for Bourdeaux along with Candide. They had both of them seen and suffered a great deal, and if the vessel had been to sail from Surinam to Japan, by the way of the Cape of Good Hope, they would have found enough to have entertained them on the subject of physical and moral evil during the whole voyage.

Candide, however, had one great advantage over Martin, which was that he still hoped to see Miss Cunegonde again; but as for Martin, he had nothing to hope for, to which we may add that Candide had both gold and diamonds; and though he had lost a hundred large red sheep loaded with the greatest treasure that the earth could produce, though the knavery of the Dutch captain was always uppermost in his thoughts; yet when he reflected upon what he had left in his pockets, and when he talked about Cunegonde, especially towards the latter end of a hearty meal, he inclined to Pangloss' hypothesis.

"But you, Mr. Martin," said he to the scholar, "what is your opinion? What is your notion of moral and physical evil?" "Sir," replied Martin, "the priests have accused me of being a Socinian; but the truth is, I am a Manichean." "You are in jest sure," said Candide; "there is not one Manichean in the world!" "I am one though," said Martin; "I cannot well account for it, but yet I am not able to think otherwise." "The devil must be in you then," said Candide. "He concerns himself so much in the affairs of this world," said Martin, "that he may possibly be in me, as well as anywhere else; but I must profess that when I cast my eyes upon this globe, or rather upon the globule, I cannot help thinking that the Deity has abandoned it to some malignant being. I always except Eldorado. I never met with a city that did not wish the destruction of its neighbor city, nor one family that did not desire to exterminate another family. All over the world the poor curse the rich, to whom they are obliged to cringe; and the rich treat them like so many sheep, whose wool and flesh is sold to the best bidder. A thousand assassins formed into regiments, running about from one extremity of Europe to another, practice murder and rapine according to discipline for their bread, because it is the most honorable profession in the world; and in those cities which seem to enjoy the sweets of peace, and where the arts are cultivated, mankind is devoured with greater envy, cares, and disquietudes, than a city meets with troubles when it is besieged. Private torments are still more insupportable than public calamities. In a word, I have seen and experienced so much, that I am become a Manichean."

"There's some good for all that," replied Candide.

"That may be," said Martin, "but I do not know where to find it."

In the middle of this dispute, they heard the report of cannon. The noise increasing every moment, each person took out his glass. By this means they espied two vessels engaging each other, about three miles distant. The wind brought the combatants so near the French vessel that they had the pleasure of seeing the fight very easily. At length, one of the vessels gave the other a broadside between wind and water, which sunk it to the bottom. Candide and Martin plainly perceived about a hundred men upon the deck of the ship which was sinking, lifting up their hands towards heaven, and making the most dismal lamentations; and in an instant they were all swallowed up by the sea. "Well," said Martin, "see how mankind treat one another." "It is true," said Candide, "there's something diabolical in it." As he was saying so, he perceived something red and glittering swimming near his ship. They immediately sent the longboat to see what it could be, and it proved to be one of his sheep. Candide felt more joy at the recovery of this sheep than he had trouble at the loss of a hundred loaded with the large diamonds of Eldorado. The French captain soon found that the captain of the conquering vessel was a Spaniard, and that the commander of the vessel which was sunk was a Dutch pirate, and the very same who had robbed Candide. The immense riches which the villain had amassed were buried in the sea along with him, and there was only a single sheep saved.

"You see," said Candide to Martin, "that wickedness sometimes meets with condign punishment: that rascal, the Dutch commander, has met with the fate merited." "Yes," said Martin; "but why should the passengers on board his ship also perish together with him? God indeed has punished the villain, but the devil has drowned the rest."

In the meantime, the Frenchman and the Spaniard continued their course, and Candide his debates with Martin. They disputed fifteen days without intermission; and at the end of the fifteen days, they were no farther advanced than when they began. But they chatted, they communicated their ideas to each other, and comforted each other reciprocally. Candide caressed his sheep. "Since I have found you," said he, "I have some hopes of recovering Cunegonde."

CHAPTER XXI

CANDIDE AND MARTIN DRAW NEAR TO THE COAST OF FRANCE, AND DISPUTE

AT length they descried the coast of France. "Have you ever been in France, Mr. Martin?" said Candide. "Yes," said Martin, "I have run over several of its provinces. In some, one half of the inhabitants are mere fools; in others they are too cunning; in others either very good-natured or very brutish; in others they affect to be wits; and in all of them, their ruling passion is love, the next lying, and the third to talk nonsense." "But, Mr. Martin, have you ever been at Paris?" "Yes, I have been at Paris: there are all these sorts there; it is a mere chaos; a crowd in which every one is in search after pleasure, but no one finds it, as far as I have been able to discover. I spent a few days there; and, at my arrival, was robbed of all I had by some sharpers at the fair of St. Germain. Nay, I myself was taken up for a robber and was eight days in prison; after which I turned corrector of the press, to get a small matter to carry me on foot to Holland. I know the whole tribe of scribblers, with malcontents and fanatics. They say the people are very polite in that city; I wish I could believe them." "For my part, I have no curiosity to see France," said Candide; "you may easily fancy that when a person has once spent a month at Eldorado, he is very indifferent whether he sees anything else upon earth, except Miss Cunegonde. I am going to wait for her at Venice; we will go through France on our way towards Italy. Won't you bear me company?" "With all my heart," said Martin; "they say that Venice is not fit for any but the noble Venetians; but, for all that, they receive strangers very well, provided they have a good deal of money. I have none; you have; therefore I'll follow you all the world over." "Now I think of it," said Candide, "do you imagine that the earth was originally nothing but water, as is asserted in the great book belonging to the Captain?" "I don't believe a word of it," said Martin, "no more than I do of all the reveries that have been published for some time." "But for what end was the world created then?" said Candide. "To make one mad," replied Martin. "Were not you vastly surprised," continued Candide, "at the passion which the two girls in the country of the Oreillons had for those two apes, whose story I related to you?" "Not at all," said Martin; "I see nothing strange in that passion, for I have seen so many strange things already, that I can look upon nothing as extraordinary." "Do you believe," said Candide, "that mankind always cut one another's throats; that they were always liars, knaves, treacherous, and ungrateful; always thieves, sharpers, highwaymen, lazy, envious, and gluttons; always drunkards, misers, ambitious, and bloodthirsty; always backbiters, debauchees, fanatics, hypocrites, and fools?" "Do you not believe," said Martin, "that hawks have always preyed upon pigeons, when they could light upon them?" "Certainly," said Candide. "Well then," said Martin, "if the hawks have always had the same nature, what reason can you give why mankind should have changed theirs?" "Aye," said Candide, "there is a great deal of difference, because free will. . . ." In the midst of this dispute, they arrived at Bourdeaux.

CHAPTER XXII

WHAT HAPPENED IN FRANCE TO CANDIDE AND MARTIN

CANDIDE stayed no longer at Bourdeaux than till he could dispose of some of the pebbles of Eldorado and furnish himself with a post chaise large enough to hold two persons, for he could not part with his philosopher Martin. He was indeed very sorry to part with his sheep, which he left at the academy of sciences at Bourdeaux, which proposed for the subject of this year's prize, the reason why this sheep's wool was red; and the prize was adjudged to a learned man in the North, who demonstrated, by A *plus* B *minus* C *divided by* Z, that the sheep must be red, and die of the rot.

In the meantime, all the travelers whom Candide met in the inns on the road, told him they were going to Paris, and this general eagerness to see the capital inspired him at length with the same desire, as it was not much out of the way in his journey towards Venice.

He entered Paris by the suburb of St. Marceau, and

fancied himself to be in the dirtiest village in West-phalia.

Candide was scarce got to his inn, when he was seized by a slight indisposition, caused by his fatigues. As he had a very large diamond on his finger, and the people had taken notice of a pretty heavy box among his baggage, in a moment's time he had no less than two physicians to attend him, who did not stay to be sent for; a few intimate friends, that never left him, sat up with him, together with a couple of female friends that took care to have his broths warmed. Said Martin, "I remember that when I was sick at Paris, in my first journey, I was very low in pocket, and could meet neither with friends, nurses, nor physicians; but I recovered."

In the meanwhile, what by medicines and bleedings, Candide's disorder beginning to grow a serious affair, the clerk of the parish came, with great modesty, to ask a bill for the other world, payable to the bearer. Candide refusing to accept it, the nurses assured him that it was a new fashion. Candide replied that he was resolved not to follow the fashion. Martin was going to throw the priest out of the window. The clerk swore that Candide should not be buried. Martin swore that he would bury the clerk, if he continued to be troublesome. The quarrel grew high, and Martin took the priest by the shoulders, and pushed him out of doors. This occasioning a great deal of scandal, an action was commenced against him.

Candide recovered; and all the while he was upon the mending hand, had the best of company to sup with him. They gamed high, and Candide was very much surprised that he never could throw an ace; but Martin was not surprised at all.

Among those who did him the honors of the town, was a little abbé of Perigord, one of those people that are always busy, always alert, always ready to do one service, forward, fawning, and accommodating themselves to every one's humor; who watch for strangers on their journey, tell them the scandalous history of the town, and offer them pleasures at all prices. This man carried Candide and Martin to the playhouse, where a new tragedy was to be acted. Candide found himself seated near some critics, but this did not keep him from crying at some scenes that were well acted. One of these critics, who stood at his elbow, said to him, between two of the acts, "You were in the wrong to shed tears; that's a shocking actress, the actor who plays with her is worse than she, and the piece is still worse than the actors. The author does not understand a single word of Arabic, and yet the scene lies in Arabia; but besides, he is a man who does not believe that our ideas are innate; I'll bring you twenty pamphlets against him by tomorrow morning." "Sir," said the abbé of Perigord, "did you take notice of that young man with the lively countenance and fine shape? He will not cost you more than ten thousand francs per month, and fifty thousand crowns in diamonds." "I have not above a day or two to spare," replied Candide, "because I have someone to meet at Venice, which hurries me."

In the evening, after supper was over, the insinuating Perigordin redoubled his compliments of service, and his officiousness. "You are then, Sir," said he, "under an engagement to go to Venice?" "Yes, Mr. Abbé," said Candide, "I am under a necessity to go to meet Miss Cunegonde." Being then invited to have the pleasure of speaking about the object he loved, he related, according to custom, a part of his adventures with that illustrious

Westphalian. "I fancy," said the Abbé, "that Miss Cunegonde is a lady of very great parts, and that she writes charming letters?" "I never received any from her," said Candide: "for you can imagine that being driven out of the castle on account of my passion for her, I could not write to her; that soon after I heard she was dead; that afterwards I found her, and lost her; and that I have now sent an express to her about two thousand five hundred leagues from hence, and wait for an answer."

The Abbé heard him with great attention, and appeared to be a little thoughtful. He soon took leave of the two strangers, after a most affectionate embrace. The next day, as soon as Candide awoke, he received a letter, couched in the following terms:

"Sir, my dearest love, I have been ill these eight days in this town, and have learned that you are here. I would fly to your arms, if I were able to stir. I knew of your passage to Bourdeaux, where I have left the faithful Cacambo and the old woman, who are to follow me very soon. The governor of Buenos Aires has taken all from me, but your heart is still left me. Come and see me; for your presence will either restore me to life, or kill me with pleasure."

This charming, this unexpected letter transported Candide with an inexpressible joy, and the indisposition of his dear Cunegonde overwhelmed him with sorrow. Distracted between these two passions, he took his gold and diamonds, and got somebody to conduct him and Martin to the house where Miss Cunegonde was lodged.

On his entrance he trembled in every limb, his heart beat quick, and his voice was choked up with sighs; he was going to open the curtains of the bed, and bid them bring him a light. "Take care, Sir," said the nurse, "she can't bear light for the world, it would overpower her;" and immediately she drew the curtains close again. "My dear Cunegonde," said Candide, dissolved in tears, "how do you find yourself? Though you can't see me, you may speak to me at least." "She can't speak," said the maid. The lady then put a plump hand out of the bed, which Candide for some time bathed with his tears, and afterwards filled with diamonds, leaving a bag full of gold upon the easy chair.

In the middle of his transports, a guardsman came in, followed by the Abbé Perigordin and a file of soldiers. "They," said he, "are the two suspected foreigners." He caused them be immediately seized, and ordered his men to drag them to prison. "It is not thus they treat travelers at Eldorado," said Candide. "I am more a Manichean than ever," said Martin. "But, pray, Sir, where are you going to carry us?" said Candide. "To a hole in the dungeon," said the guardsman.

Martin now finding his blood grow somewhat cool, fancied that the lass who pretended to be Cunegonde was a cheat; that the Abbé Perigourdin was a sharper, who had taken advantage of Candide's simplicity; and that the guardsman was another sharper, whom they might easily get clear of.

Rather than expose himself before a court of justice, Candide, swayed by his advice, and besides very impatient to see the real Cunegonde, offered the guardsman three small diamonds worth about three thousand pistoles each. "Ah, Sir," said the man with the ivory baton, "though you had committed all the crimes that can be imagined, this would make me think you are the honestest gentleman in the world! Three diamonds worth three thousand pistoles apiece! Sir, instead of putting you in a dungeon, I would lose my life for you; all strangers are arrested here, but let me alone for that. I have a brother at Dieppe in Normandy; I'll conduct you thither; and if you have any diamond to give him, he will take as much care of you as I myself."

"And why do they put all strangers under arrest?" said Candide. The Abbé Perigordin then put in his word: "Because," said he, " a beggar of Atrebatia listened to some foolish stories, which made him guilty of a parricide, not like that in May, 1610, but like that in December, 1594; and just like those that a great many other beggars have been guilty of, in other months and other years, after listening to foolish stories."

The guardsman then gave him a more particular account of their crimes. "O, the monsters!" cried Candide; "are there then such terrible crimes among people that can dance and sing? Can I not immediately get out of this country, where monkeys provoke tigers? I have seen bears in my own country, but I never met with men except at Eldorado. In the name of God, Mr. Officer, conduct me to Venice, where I am to wait for Miss Cunegonde." "I can conduct you nowhere except to Lower Normandy," said our mock officer. Immediately he ordered his irons to be struck off, said he was under a mistake, discharged his men, conducted Candide and Martin to Dieppe, and left them in the hands of his brother.

There was then a small Holland trader in the harbor. The Norman, by means of three more diamonds, become the most serviceable man in the world, put Candide and his attendants safe on board the vessel, which was ready to sail for Portsmouth in England. This was not indeed the way to Venice; but Candide thought he had escaped from hell, and resolved to resume his voyage towards Venice upon the first opportunity that offered.

CHAPTER XXIII

CANDIDE AND MARTIN GO TO THE ENGLISH COAST, AND WHAT THEY SAW THERE

" AH! Pangloss! Pangloss! Ah! Martin! Martin! Ah, my dear Cunegonde! What a world is this!" said Candide on board the Dutch ship. "A very foolish and abominable one indeed," replied Martin. "You are acquainted with England," said Candide to him; "are they as great fools as the French?" "They have a different kind of folly," said Martin; "you know that these two nations are at war about a few acres of snow towards Canada, and that they have spent a great deal more upon this fine war than all Canada is worth. To tell you with precision whether there are more people fit to send to a madhouse in one country than in the other, is more than my weak capacity is able to perform. I only know in general, that the people we are going to see are very melancholic."

As they were talking in this manner, they arrived at Portsmouth. The shore was covered with a multitude of people, who were looking very attentively at a pretty lusty man who was kneeling, with something tied before his eyes, on the deck of one of the men of war; four soldiers, that were placed opposite to him, lodged three balls apiece in his head, with the greatest coolness imaginable, and the whole assembly went away very well satisfied. "What is the meaning of this?" said Candide; "and what demon is it that exercises his dominion all over the globe?"

He inquired who the lusty gentleman was that was killed with so much ceremony. "He is an admiral *," replied some of them. "And why was this admiral killed?" "Because," said they, "he did not kill men enough himself. He engaged the French admiral, and was found guilty of not being near enough to him." "But then," said Candide, "was not the French admiral as far off from the English admiral, as he was from him?" "That surely cannot be doubted," replied they, "but in this country it is of very great service to execute an admiral now and then, in order to make the rest fight the better."

Candide was so astonished and shocked at what he had seen and heard, that he would not set foot on shore, but agreed with the master of the Dutch vessel (though he was sure to be robbed by him, as well as by his countryman at Surinam) to carry him directly to Venice.

The master was ready in two days. They coasted all along France. Passing within sight of Lisbon, Candide gave a very deep groan. They passed the Straits, made the Mediterranean, and at last arrived at Venice.

"The Lord be praised," said Candide, embracing Martin, "it is here that I shall see the fair Cunegonde again! I have as good an opinion of Cacambo, as of myself. Everything is right, everything goes well; everything is the best that it can possibly be."

*The author alludes to the case of Admiral Byng, who was shot on board the Monarque man of war at Portsmouth, March 14, 1757.

CHAPTER XXIV

CONCERNING PAQUETTA, AND FATHER GIROFFLÉE

AS soon as they arrived at Venice, he caused search for Cacambo in all the inns, in all the coffee houses, and among all the ladies of pleasure, but could not find him. He sent every day to all the ships and barks that arrived; but no news of Cacambo. "Well!" said he to Martin, "I have had time enough to go from Surinam to Bourdeaux, from Bourdeaux to Paris, from Paris to Dieppe, from Dieppe to Portsmouth; after that I have coasted along Portugal and Spain, and traversed the Mediterranean, and have now been some months at Venice, and yet, for all that, the lovely Cunegonde is not come. Instead of her, I have only met with a cheat and an abbé of Perigord. Cunegonde is certainly dead; and I have no more to do but to die too. Ah, it would have been far better for me to have stayed in that paradise, Eldorado, than to have returned again to this cursed Europe. You are certainly right, my dear Martin; all is illusion and misery here."

He fell into a deep melancholy, and never frequented the opera, or the other diversions of the carnival; nay, he was proof against all the charms of the fair sex. Martin said to him, "You are very simple indeed, to fancy that a mongrel valet, with five or six millions in his pocket, would go to the end of the world in quest of your mistress, and bring her to Venice. If he meets with her, he'll keep her for himself: if he cannot find her, he'll get somebody else. Let me advise you to forget both your valet Cacambo, and your mistress Cunegonde." Martin was a most wretched comforter. The melancholy of Candide increased; and Martin never ceased preaching that there was but very little virtue and as little happiness to be found on earth, excepting, perhaps, at Eldorado, where it was almost impossible for anyone to go.

As they were disputing on this important subject, and waiting for Cunegonde, Candide perceived a young Theatin * in the Place of St. Mark, with his arm around a girl. The Theatin friar looked fresh, plump, and full of vigor; his eyes were sparking, his air bold, his mien lofty, and his gait firm. This girl was tolerably handsome, and was singing a song; she ogled her Theatin friar with a great deal of passion, and now and then would give his fat cheeks a pinch.

"At least you will grant me," said Candide to Martin, "that these folks are happy. I have never found any but unhappy wretches till now all over this habitable globe, excepting at Eldorado; but as for the girl and the Theatin, I will lay any wager that they are as happy as happy can be." "I will lay they are not," said Martin. "Only let us invite them to dinner," said Candide, "and then you shall see if I am mistaken or not."

He immediately accosted them, made them a bow, and invited them to his inn to eat macaroni, partridges of Lombardy, and caviare, and to drink montepulciano, lachryma Christi, Cyprus, and Samos wine. The girl blushed; the Theatin accepted the invitation, and the girl followed him, looking at Candide with eyes of surprise and confusion, from which the tears trickled. Scarce was she entered into Candide's room, when she said to him, "What! Does not Mr. Candide know his old friend Paquetta again?" At these words, Candide, who had not yet looked at her with any degree of attention,

* An order of religious.

because Cunegonde engrossed all his thoughts, said to her, "Ah, my poor girl, is it you who reduced Dr. Pangloss to the fine plight in which I saw him?"

"Ay, Sir! 'tis I myself," said Paquetta; "I find you know the whole story; and I have been informed of all the terrible disasters which have happened to the family of my Lady the Baroness, and the fair Cunegonde. My fate, I assure you, has not been less melancholy. I was very innocent when you knew me. A cordelier, who was my confessor, easily seduced me. The effects of it were terrible: I was obliged to leave the castle some time after the Baron kicked you on your backside out of the door. If a celebrated quack had not taken pity on me, I should have perished. I was the quack's mistress for some time, by way of recompense. His wife, who was as jealous as the devil, beat me every day most unmercifully; she was a very fiend of hell. The Doctor was one of the ugliest fellows I ever saw in my life, and I one of the most wretched creatures that ever existed, to be beat every day for the sake of a man whom I hated. You know how dangerous it is for a scolding woman to be married to a doctor. Being quite exasperated with his wife's behavior, he gave her one day so efficacious a remedy to cure her of a slight cold she had that she died two hours after in the most horrid convulsions. My mistress's relations entered a criminal action against my master; he took to his heels, and I was carried to jail. My innocence would never have saved me, if I had not been rather handsome. The judge acquitted me, on condition of his succeeding the Doctor. I was soon afterwards supplanted by a rival, driven out of doors without any recompense, and obliged to continue this abominable occupation, which appears so pleasant to you men, while it is to us women the very abyss of misery. I am come to practice

my profession at Venice. Ah, Sir, if you could imagine
what it is to be obliged to caress indifferently an old
merchant, a councilor, a monk, a gondolier, or an abbé;
to be exposed to all sorts of insults and outrages; to be
often reduced to borrow a petticoat, to have it lifted up
by a disagreeable rascal; to be robbed by one gallant of
what one has got by another; to be ransomed by the
peace officer, and to have nothing else in prospect but a
frightful old age, a hospital, or a dunghill; you would
confess that I am one of the most unfortunate creatures
of the world."

Paquetta opened her mind in this manner to the good
Candide, in his closet, in the presence of Martin, who
said to Candide: "You see I have won one half of the
wager already."

Brother Girofflée waited in the dining room, and drank
a glass or two while he was waiting for dinner. "But,"
said Candide to Paquetta, "you had an air so gay, so
content, when I first met you, you sung, and caressed the
Theatin with so much warmth, that you seemed to me
as happy then as you pretend to be miserable now."
"Ah, Sir," replied Paquetta, "this is one of the miseries
of the trade. Yesterday I was robbed and beaten by an
officer, and today I am obliged to appear in good humor
to please a monk." Candide wanted no more to be satisfied, and owned that Martin was in the right. They sat
down to table with Paquetta and the Theatin; the repast was very entertaining, and, towards the end, they
began to speak to each other with some degree of confidence. "My father," said Candide to the monk, "you
seem to enjoy a state that all the world might look on
with envy. The flower of health blossoms on your countenance, and your physiognomy speaks nothing but happiness; you have a very pretty girl to divert you, and you

seem to be well satisfied with your station as a Theatin monk."

"'Faith, Sir," said Brother Girofflée, "I wish that all the Theatins were at the bottom of the sea. I have been tempted a hundred times to set fire to the monastery, and to go and turn Turk. My parents forced me, at the age of fifteen, to put on this cursed habit, to increase the fortune of an elder brother of mine, whom God confound. Jealousy, discord, and fury reside in the monastery. It is true indeed, I have preached a few paltry sermons, which brought me in a little money; one part of which the prior robs me of, the remainder serves me to spend upon the ladies; but every evening, when I enter the monastery, I am ready to dash out my brains against the wall of the dormitory; and all the brotherhood are in the same state."

Martin, turning towards Candide, with his usual coolness, "Well," said he to him, "have not I won the whole wager now?" Candide gave two thousand piastres to Paquetta, and one thousand to Brother Girofflée. "I'll answer for it," said he, "this will make them happy." "I don't believe a word of it," said Martin; "you may perhaps make them a great deal more miserable by your piastres." "Be that as it may," said Candide: "but one thing comforts me, I see that one often finds those persons whom one never expected to find any more; and as I have found my red sheep and Paquetta again, it may be I may find Cunegonde again too." "I wish," said Martin, "that she may one day make you happy; but it is what I very much question." "You are very incredulous," said Candide. "That is what I always was," said Martin. "But only look on those gondoliers," said Candide; "are they not perpetually singing?" "You don't see them at home, with their wives, and their monkeys of children," said Martin. "The doge has his inquietudes, and the gondoliers have theirs. Indeed, generally speaking, the condition of a gondolier is preferable to that of a doge; but I believe that the difference is so small, that it is not worth the trouble of examining into."

"People speak," said Candide, "of Seignor Pococurante, who lives in that fine palace upon the Brenta; and who entertains strangers in the most polite manner. They pretend that this man never felt any uneasiness." "I should be glad to see so extraordinary a phenomenon," said Martin. On which Candide instantly sent to Seignor Pococurante, to get permission to pay him a visit the next day.

CHAPTER XXV

THE VISIT TO SEIGNOR POCOCURANTE, THE NOBLE VENETIAN

CANDIDE and Martin went in a gondola on the Brenta, and arrived at the palace of the noble Pococurante. His gardens were very spacious, and ornamented with fine statues of marble, and the palace itself was a piece of excellent architecture. The master of the house, a very rich man, about threescore, received our two inquisitives very politely, but with very little heartiness; which, though it confused Candide, did not give the least uneasiness to Martin.

At first two young girls, handsome, and very neatly dressed, served them with chocolate, which was frothed extremely well. Candide could not help dropping them a compliment on their beauty, their politeness, and their address. "The creatures are well enough," said the Senator Pococurante; "I sometimes make them lie in my bed, for I am quite tired of the girls of the town, of their coquetry, their jealousies, quarrels, humors, monkey-tricks, pride, follies, and the sonnets one is obliged to make, or hire others to make for them; but, after all, these two girls begin to grow tiresome to me."

After breakfast, Candide, taking a walk in his long gallery, was charmed with the beauty of the pictures. He asked by what master were the two first. "They are by Raphael," said the Senator; "I bought them at a very high price, merely out of vanity, some years ago. They are said to be the finest paintings in Italy, but they do not please me at all; the colors are dead, the figures not finished, and do not appear with *relief* enough; the drapery is very bad. In short, let people say what they will, I do not find there a true imitation of nature. I do not like a piece unless it makes me think I see nature itself; but there are no such pieces to be met with. I have, indeed, a great many pictures, but I do not value them at all."

While they were waiting for dinner, Pococurante entertained them with a concert; Candide was quite charmed with the music. "This noise," said Pococurante, " might divert one for half an hour or so; but if it were to last any longer, it would grow tiresome to everybody, though no soul dares own it. Music is, nowadays, nothing else but the art of executing difficulties; and what has nothing but difficulty to recommend it, does not please in the long run.

"I might perhaps take more pleasure in the opera if they had not found out the secret of making such a monster of it as shocks me. Let those go that will see wretched tragedies set to music, where the scenes are composed for no other end than to lug in by the head and ears two or three ridculous songs, in order to set off the pipe of an actress. Let who will, or who can, die away with pleasure, at hearing a eunuch trilling out the part of Cæsar and Cato, and strutting upon the stage with a ridiculous and affected air. For my part, I have long ago bid adieu to those paltry entertainments, which constitute the glory of Italy and are purchased by crowned heads so extravagantly dear." Candide disputed the point a little, but with great discretion. Martin was entirely of the same sentiments as the Senator. They sat down to table, and, after an excellent dinner, went into the library. Candide, casting his eyes upon a Homer very handsomely bound, praised his High Mightiness for the goodness of his taste. "There," said he, "is a book that was the favorite of the great Pangloss, the best philosopher in Germany." "It is none of mine," said Pococurante, with great indifference; "I was made to believe formerly that I took a pleasure in reading him. But that continued repetition of battles that resemble each other; his gods, who are always very busy without bringing anything to a decision; his Helen, who is the subject of the war, and has scarce anything to do in the whole piece; that Troy, which is besieged, but never taken; I say, all these defects give me the greatest disgust. I have asked some learned men if they perused him with as little pleasure as I did. Those who were ingenuous professed to me that they could not keep the book in their hands; but that they were obliged to give it a place in their libraries, as a monument of antiquity, and as they do old rusty medals which are of no use in commerce."

"Your Excellence does not entertain the same opinion of Virgil?" said Candide. "I confess," replied Pococurante, "that the second, the fourth, and the sixth book of his Æneid are excellent; but as for his pious Æneas, his brave Cloanthus, his friend Achates, the little Ascanius, the infirm King Latinus, the burgess Amata, and the insipid Lavinia, I do not think anything can be more frigid, or more disagreeable. I prefer Tasso, and Ariosto's soporiferous tales far before him."

"Shall I presume to ask you, Sir," said Candide, "whether you do not enjoy a great deal of pleasure in perusing Horace?" "There are some maxims," said Pococurante, "which may be of some service to a man who knows the world, and being delivered in expressive numbers are imprinted more easily on the memory. But I place little value on his voyage to Brundusium, his description of his bad dinner, and the Billingsgate squabble between one Pupillus, whose speech he said was full of filthy stuff, and another whose words were as sharp as vinegar. I never could read without great disgust his indelicate lines against the old woman and witches; and I cannot see any merit in his telling his friend Mæcenas that if he should be ranked by him among the lyric poets, he would knock the stars with his lofty brow. Some fools admire everything in an author of reputation; for my part, I read only for myself; I approve nothing but what suits my own taste." Candide, having been taught to judge of nothing for himself, was very much surprised at what he heard; but Martin looked upon the sentiment of Pococurante as very rational.

"Oh, here's a Cicero," said Candide, "here is the great man whom I fancy you are never tired of reading." "I never read him at all," replied the Venetian. "What is it to me, whether he pleads for Rabirius or Cluentius? I have trials enough of my own. I might indeed have been a greater friend to his philosophical works, but when I found he doubted of everything, I concluded I knew as much as he, and that I had no need of a tutor to learn ignorance." "Well! Here are four and twenty volumes of the academy of sciences," cried Martin; "it is possible there may be something valuable in them." "There might," said Pococurante, "if but one of the authors of this hodge-podge had been only the inventor of the art of making pins; but there is nothing in all those volumes but chimerical systems, and scarce a single article of real use."

"What a prodigious number of theatrical pieces you have got here," said Candide, "in Italian, Spanish, and French!" "Yes," said the Senator, "there are about three thousand, and not three dozen good ones among them all. As for that collection of sermons, which all together are not worth one page of Seneca, and all those huge volumes of divinity, you must realize that they are never opened either by me or anybody else."

Martin, perceiving some of the shelves filled with English books, said, "I fancy, a republican, as you are, must generally be pleased with compositions that are written with so great a degree of freedom." "Yes," said Pococurante, "it is commendable to write what one thinks; it is the privilege of man. But all over our Italy they write nothing but what they don't think. Those who now inhabit the country of the Cæsars and Antonines dare not have a single idea, without taking out a license from a Jacobin. I should be very well satisfied with the freedom that breathes in the English writers, if passion and the spirit of party did not corrupt all that was valuable in it."

Candide, discovering a Milton, asked him if he did not look upon that author as a great genius? "What!" said Pococurante, "that blockhead, that has made a long commentary in ten books of rough verse, on the first chapter of Genesis; that gross imitator of the Greeks, who has disfigured the creation, and who, when Moses had represented the Eternal producing the world by a word, makes the Messiah take a large pair of compasses from the armory of God, to mark out his work. How can I have any esteem for one who has spoiled the hell and devils of Tasso; who turns Lucifer sometimes into a toad, and sometimes into a pigmy; makes him deliver the same speech a hundred times over; represents him disputing in divinity; and who, by a serious imitation of Ariosto's comic invention of firearms, represents the devils letting off their cannon in heaven? Neither I, nor anyone else in Italy, has it in his power to be pleased at these outrages against common sense: but the marriage of Sin and Death, and the snakes that proceed from her womb, are enough to make every person of the least delicacy of taste vomit. This obscure, fantastical, and disgusting poem was despised at its first publication, and I only treat the author now in the same manner as he was treated in his own country by his contemporaries. By the by, I speak what I think; and I give myself no uneasiness, whether or not other people think as I do."

Candide was vexed at this discourse; for he respected Homer, and was fond of Milton. "Ah!" said he, whispering to Martin, "I am very much afraid that this man here has a sovereign contempt for our German poets." "There would be no great harm in that," said Martin. "O what an extraordinary man!" said Candide, muttering to himself; "what a great genius is this Pococurante! Nothing can please him."

After having thus taken a view of all the books, they went down into the garden. Candide expatiated upon all its beauties. "I never knew anything laid out in so bad a taste," said the master; "we have nothing but trifles here, but, a day or two hence, I shall have one laid out upon a more noble plan."

When our two inquisitives had taken their leave of his Excellency, "Now, sure," said Candide to Martin, "you will confess that he is one of the happiest men upon earth, for he is above everything that he has." "Do not you see," said Martin, "that he is disgusted with everything that he has? Plato has said a long time ago, that the best stomachs are not those which cast up all sorts of victuals." "But," said Candide, "is not there a pleasure in criticizing upon everything? In perceiving defects where other people fancy they see beauties?" "That is as much as to say," replied Martin, "that there is a great pleasure in having no pleasure." "If that is the case," said Candide, "no person will be so happy as myself when I see Miss Cunegonde again." "We should always hope for the best," said Martin.

In the meantime days and weeks passed away, but no Cacambo was to be found. And Candide was so immersed in grief, that he did not recollect that Paquetta and Brother Girofllée never so much as once came to return him thanks.

CHAPTER XXVI

OF CANDIDE AND MARTIN'S SUPPING WITH SIX STRANGERS, AND WHO THEY WERE

ONE night as Candide, followed by Martin, was going to seat himself at table with some strangers who lodged in the same inn, a man of a complexion as black as soot, came behind him, and taking him by the arm, says to him, "Get yourself ready to go along with us; don't fail!" He turned his head, and saw Cacambo. Nothing but the sight of Cunegonde could have surprised or pleased him more. He was just ready to run mad for joy. Embracing his dear friend, "Cunegonde is here," said he, "without doubt; where is she? Carry me to her, that I may die with joy in her company!" "Cunegonde is not here," said Cacambo, "she is at Constantinople." "O heavens! at Constantinople? But, if she was at China, I would fly thither; let us be gone." "We will go after supper," replied Cacambo; "I can tell you no more; I am a slave; my master expects me, and I must go and wait at table; say not a word; go to supper, and hold yourself in readiness."

Candide, distracted between joy and grief, charmed at having seen his trusty agent, astonished at beholding him a slave, full of the idea of finding his mistress again, his heart palpitating, and his understanding confused, set himself down at the table with Martin, who saw all these scenes without the least emotion, together with six strangers that were come to spend the carnival at Venice.

Cacambo, who poured out wine for one of the six strangers, drew near to his master, towards the end of the repast, and whispered in his ear, "Sire, your Majesty may set out when you think proper, the ship is ready." On saying these words, he went out. The guests, surprised, looked at each other without speaking a word; when another servant approaching his master, said to him, "Sire, your Majesty's chaise is at Padua, and the yacht is ready." The master gave a nod, and the domestic retired. All the guests stared at one another again, and their common surprise was increased. A third servant approaching likewise the third stranger, said to him, "Sire, believe me, your Majesty must not stay here any longer; I am going to get everything ready." And immediately he disappeared.

Candide and Martin began by this time to make no

doubt but that this was a masquerade of the carnival. A fourth domestic said to the fourth master, "Your Majesty may depart whenever you please;" and went out as the others had done. The fifth servant expressed himself in terms to the same effect as the fourth; but the sixth servant spoke in a different manner to the sixth stranger, who sat near Candide: " 'Faith, Sir," said he, "no one will trust your Majesty any longer, nor myself neither; and we may both be sent to jail this very night, I shall however take care of myself. *Adieu.*"

All the domestics having disappeared, the six strangers, with Candide and Martin, remained in a profound silence. At last Candide broke it: "Gentlemen," said he, "this is something very droll; but why should you be all of you Kings, For my part, I own to you that neither I nor Martin are."

Cacambo's master then answered very gravely in Italian, saying, "I assure you I am not in jest; I am Achmet III. I was Grand Sultan for several years; I dethroned my brother; my nephew dethroned me; my viziers were beheaded: I am finishing my days in the old seraglio. My nephew, the Grand Sultan Mahmoud, permits me to take a voyage sometimes for the sake of my health, and I am come to pass the carnival at Venice."

A young man, who sat near Achmet, spoke next, and said, "My name is Ivan; I was Emperor of all the Russias, I was dethroned in my cradle, my father and mother were confined; I was brought up in prison. I have sometimes permission to travel, accompanied with two persons as guards; I am also come to pass the carnival at Venice."

The third said, "I am Charles Edward, King of England; my father has ceded his rights to the throne to me. I fought to support them; eight hundred of my adherents had their hearts taken out alive, and their heads struck off. I myself have been in prison: I am going to Rome to pay a visit to my father, who has been dethroned as well as myself and my grandfather; and am come to Venice to celebrate the carnival."

The fourth then said, "I am King of Poland; the fortune of war has deprived me of my hereditary dominions; my father experienced the same reverses; I resign myself to Providence, like the Sultan Achmet, the Emperor Ivan, and Charles Edward, whom God long preserve; and I am come to pass the carnival at Venice."

The fifth said, "I am likewise the King of Poland; I lost my kingdom twice; but Providence has given me another government, in which I have done more good than all the Kings of the Sarmatians put together have been able to do on the banks of the Vistula. I resign myself likewise to Providence, and am come to pass the carnival at Venice."

It now was the sixth monarch's turn to speak. "Gentlemen," said he, "I am not so great a prince as any of you, but for all that I have been a King as well as the best of you. I am Theodore; I was elected King of Corsica; I was once called 'Your Majesty,' but at present am scarce allowed the title of 'Sir.' I have caused money to be coined, but am not master at present of a farthing. I have had two secretaries of state, but now have scarce a single servant. I have seen myself on a throne, and have for some time lain upon straw in a common jail in London. I have been vastly afraid of meeting with the same treatment here, though I am come, like Your Majesties, to pass the carnival at Venice."

The five other kings heard this speech with a noble compassion. Each of them gave King Theodore twenty sequins to buy him some clothes and shirts, and Candide made him a present of a diamond worth two thousand sequins more. "Who," said the five kings, "can this private person be, who is both able to give, and really has given a hundred times as much as either of us?"

At the very instant they rose from table, there came into the same inn four Serene Highnesses, who had likewise lost their dominions by the fortune of war, and were come to pass the carnival at Venice, but Candide took no notice of those newcomers, his thoughts being taken up with nothing but going in search of his dear Cunegonde at Constantinople.

CHAPTER XXVII

CANDIDE'S VOYAGE TO CONSTANTINOPLE

THE faithful Cacambo had already prevailed on the Turkish captain who was going to carry Sultan Achmet back again to Constantinople, to receive Candide and Martin on board. They both of them embarked, after they had prostrated themselves before His Miserable Highness. As Candide was on his way, he said to Martin, "There were six dethroned kings that we supped with; and, what is still more, among these six kings there was one that I gave alms to. Perhaps there may be a great many other princes more unfortunate still. For my part, I have lost only one hundred sheep, and am going to fly into the arms of Cunegonde. My dear Martin, I must yet say, Pangloss was in the right; all things are for the best." "I wish they were," said Martin. "But," said Candide, "the adventure we met with at Venice is somewhat romantic. Such a thing was never heard of, that six dethroned kings should sup together at a common inn."

"This is not more extraordinary," replied Martin, "than the most of the things that have happened to us. It is a common thing for kings to be dethroned, and with respect to the honor that we had of supping with them, it is a trifle that does not merit our attention."

Scarce had Candide got on board when he leaped on the neck of his old servant and friend Cacambo. "Well," said he, "what news of Cunegonde? Is she still a miracle of beauty? Does she love me still? How does she do? No doubt but you have bought a palace for her at Constantinople?"

"My dear Master," replied Cacambo, "Cunegonde washes dishes on the banks of the Propontis, in the house of a prince who has very few to wash; she is a slave in the house of an ancient sovereign, named Ragotsky, to whom the Grand Turk allows three crowns a day to support him in his asylum; but, what is worse than all, she has lost her beauty, and is become shockingly ugly." "Well, handsome or ugly," replied Candide, "I am a man of honor, and it is my duty to love her still. But how came she to be reduced to so abject a condition, with the five or six millions that you carried her?" "And well," said Cacambo, "was not I to give two millions to Signor Don Fernandes d'Ibaraa, y Figueora, y Mascarenes, y Lampourdos, y Souza, the governor of Buenos Aires, for the permission of taking Miss Cunegonde back again? And did not a pirate bravely rob us of all the rest? Did not this pirate carry us to Cape Matapan, to Milo, to Nicaria, to Samos, to Dardanelles, to Marmora, to Scutari? Cunegonde and the old woman are servants to the prince I told you of, and I am a slave of the dethroned Sultan." "What a chain of shocking calamities!" said Candide. "But, after all, I have some diamonds, I shall easily purchase Cunegonde's liberty. It is pity that she is grown so ugly."

Then addressing himself to Martin, "Who do you think," says he, "is most to be pitied, the Sultan Achmet, the Emperor Ivan, King Charles Edward, or myself?" "I cannot tell," said Martin, "I must see into your hearts to be able to tell." "Ah!" said Candide, "if Pangloss were here, he would know and tell us." "I know not," replied Martin, "in what sort of scales your Pangloss would weigh the misfortunes of mankind, and appraise their sorrows. All that I can venture to say is that there are millions of men upon earth a hundred times more to be pitied than King Charles Edward, the Emperor Ivan, or Sultan Achmet." "That is possible," said Candide.

In a few days they reached the Black Sea. Candide began with ransoming Cacambo at an extravagant price; and, without loss of time, he got into a galley with his companions, to go to the banks of the Propontis, in search of Cunegonde, notwithstanding her loss of beauty.

Among the crew there were two slaves that rowed very ill, to whose bare shoulders the Levant trader would now and then apply a few strokes with a bull's pizzle. Candide, by a natural sympathy, looked at them more attentively than at the rest of the galley slaves, and went up to them with a heart full of pity. Some features of their faces, though very much disfigured, seemed to bear some resemblance to those of Pangloss, and the unfortunate Jesuit the Baron, the brother of Miss Cunegonde. This fancy affected him, and made him very gloomy. He looked at them again more attentively. "Really," said he to Cacambo, "if I had not seen Mr. Pangloss hanged, and had not had the misfortune to kill the Baron myself, I should think it was they that are rowing in this galley."

At the names of the Baron and Pangloss, the two galley slaves gave a loud shriek, held fast to the seat, and let their oars drop. The master of the Levanter ran up to them, and redoubled the lashes of the bull's pizzle upon them. "Hold! hold! Signor," cried Candide, "I will give you what money you please." "Lord, it is Candide!" said one of the galley slaves; "O, it is Candide!" said the other. "Do I dream?" said Candide; "am I awake? Am I in this galley? Is that Master Baron whom I killed? Is that Master Pangloss whom I saw hanged?"

"Yes, it is we, it is we!" replied they. "What, is that the great philosopher!" said Martin. "Harkee, Master Levant Captain," said Candide, "what will you take for the ransom of Master Thunder-ten-tronckh, one of the first Barons of the empire, together with Master Pangloss, the most profound metaphysician of Germany?" "You Christian dog," said the Levant captain, "since these two dogs of Christian slaves are barons and metaphysicians, which, without doubt, is a great degree of dignity in their own country, you shall give me fifty thousand sequins." "You shall have them, Sir; carry me back again, like lightning, to Constantinople, and you shall be paid directly. But stop, carry me to Miss Cunegonde first."

The Levant captain, on the first offer of Candide, had turned the head of the vessel towards the city, and made the slaves row faster than a bird cleaves the air.

Candide embraced the Baron and Pangloss a hundred times. "How happened it that I did not kill you, my dear Baron? And my dear Pangloss, how came you to life again, after being hanged? And how came you, both of you, to be galley slaves in Turkey?" "Is it true that my dear sister is in this country?" said the Baron. "Yes," replied Cacambo. "Then I see my dear Candide once more," said Pangloss.

Candide presented Martin and Cacambo to them: they embraced each other, and spoke all at the same time. The galley flew like lightning, and they were already in the port. A Jew was sent for, to whom Candide sold a diamond for fifty thousand sequins, which was worth a hundred thousand; who, notwithstanding, swore by Abraham that he could not give any more. He immediately paid the ransom of the Baron and Pangloss. The latter threw himself at the feet of his deliverer, and bathed them with his tears; as for the other, he thanked him with a nod, and promised to repay him the money the first opportunity. "But is it possible that my sister is in Turkey?" said he. "Nothing is more possible," replied Cacambo; "for she scours the dishes in the house of a prince of Transylvania!" Two more Jews were instantly fetched, to whom Candide sold some more diamonds; and they set out again all together in another galley, in order to deliver Cunegonde.

CHAPTER XXVIII

WHAT HAPPENED TO CANDIDE, CUNEGONDE, PANGLOSS, MARTIN, ETC.

"I ASK your pardon once more," said Candide to the Baron, "I ask pardon, my Reverend Father, for having given you a thrust with a sword through the body." "Don't let us say any more about it," said the Baron; "I was a little too hasty, I must confess. But since you desire to know by what fatality I came to be a galley slave, I will inform you. After I was cured of my wound by a brother, who was apothecary to the college, I was attacked and carried off by a party of Spaniards, who confined me in prison at Buenos Aires at the very time my sister was setting out from thence. I demanded leave of the Father General to return to Rome. I was nominated to go as almoner to Constantinople with the French ambassador. I had not been eight days engaged in this employment, when one evening I met with a young well-made icoglan. It was then very hot; the young man went to bathe himself, and I took this opportunity to bathe myself too. I did not know that it was a capital crime for a Christian to be found naked with a young Mussulman. A cadi ordered me to receive a hundred strokes of the bastinado on the soles of my feet, and condemned me to the galleys. I do not think there ever was a greater act of injustice. But I should be glad to know how it comes about that my sister is dishwasher in the kitchen of a Transylvanian prince, who is a refugee among the Turks."

"But you, my dear Pangloss, how came I ever to set eyes on you again?" It is true indeed," said Pangloss, "that you saw me hanged; I ought naturally to have been burned; but you may remember that it rained prodigiously when they were going to roast me; the storm was so violent that they despaired of lighting the fire. I was therefore hanged, because they could do no better. A surgeon bought my body, carried it home with him, and dissected me. He first made a crucial incision on me from the umbilicus to the clavicula. No one could have been more slovenly hanged than I was. The executioner of the holy inquisition, who was a subdeacon besides, burned people indeed to a miracle, but was not used to hanging. The cord being wet, did not slip properly, and the noose was badly tied: in short, I still drew my breath. The crucial incision made me give such a dreadful shriek that my surgeon fell down backwards, and, fancying he was dissecting the devil, he ran away, ready to die with the fright, and fell down a second time on the staircase, as he was making off. His wife ran out of an adjacent closet on hearing the noise, saw me extended on the table with my crucial incision, and being more frightened than her husband, fled also, and tumbled over him. When they were come to themselves a little, I heard the surgeon's wife say to him: 'My dear, how come you to be so weak as to venture to dissect a heretic? Don't you know that the devil always takes possession of the bodies of those people? I will go immediately and fetch a priest to exorcise him.' I shuddered at this proposal, and mustered up what little strength I had left to cry out, 'O, have pity upon me!' At length the Portuguese barber took courage, sewed up my skin, and his wife nursed me so well, that I was upon my feet again in about fifteen days. The barber got me a place to be footman to a knight of Malta, who was going to Venice, but my master not being able to pay me my wages, I engaged in the service of a Venetian merchant, and went along with him to Constantinople. One day the maggot took me to go into a mosque. There was nobody there but an old iman and a young devotee, very handsome, saying her prayers. Her breast was uncovered; she had in her bosom a beautiful nosegay of tulips, roses, anemones, ranunculuses, hyacinths, and auriculas; she let her nosegay fall; I took it up, and presented it to her with the most profound reverence. However, I was so long in giving it to her again that the iman fell in a passion, and seeing I was a Christian, called out for help. They carried me before the cadi, who ordered me to receive a hundred bastinadoes, and to be sent to the galleys. I was chained to the very same galley and the same bench with the Baron. There were on board this galley four young men from Marseilles, five Neapolitan priests, and two monks of Curfu, who told us that the like adventures happened every day. The Baron pretended that he had suffered more injustice than I; and I insisted that it was far more innocent to put a nosegay into a woman's bosom than to be found stark naked with an icoglan. We were perpetually disputing, and we received twenty lashes every day with a bull's pizzle, when the concatenation of events of this world brought you to our galley, and you ransomed us."

"Well, my dear Pangloss," said Candide to him, "when you were hanged, dissected, severely beaten, and tugging at the oar in the galley, did you always think that things in this world were for the best?" "I am still of my first opinion," answered Pangloss; "for as I am a philosopher, it would be inconsistent with my character to contradict myself, especially as Leibnitz could not be in the wrong; and his pre-established harmony is certainly the finest system in the world, as well as his plenum and subtile matter."

CHAPTER XXIX

HOW CANDIDE FOUND CUNEGONDE AND THE OLD WOMAN AGAIN

WHILE Candide, the Baron, Pangloss, Martin, and Cacambo were relating their adventures to each other, and disputing about the contingent and non-contingent events of this world, and while they were arguing upon effects and causes, moral and physical evil, on liberty and necessity, and the comforts a person may experience in the galleys in Turkey, they arrived on the banks of the Propontis, at the house of the Prince of Transylvania. The first objects which presented themselves were Cunegonde and the old woman, hanging out some table linen on the lines to dry.

The Baron grew pale at this sight. Even Candide, the affectionate lover, upon seeing his fair Cunegonde prodigiously tanned, with her eyelids reversed, her neck withered, her cheeks wrinkled, her arms red and full of scales, seized with horror, jumped near three yards backwards, but afterwards advanced to her out of good manners. She embraced Candide and her brother, who, each of them, embraced the old woman, and Candide ransomed them both.

There was a little farm in the neighborhood which the old woman advised Candide to hire, till they could meet with better accommodations for their whole company. As Cunegonde did not know that she was grown ugly, nobody having told her of it, she put Candide in mind of his promise in so peremptory a manner that the good man dared not refuse her. He then intimated to the Baron that he intended to marry his sister. "I will never suffer," said the Baron, "such meanness on her side, nor such insolence on yours. With this infamy I never will be reproached. The children of my sister can never be enrolled in the chapters of Germany. No; my sister shall never marry any but a Baron of the empire." Cunegonde threw herself at his feet, and bathed them with her tears, but he remained insensible. "You foolish puppy, you," said Candide to him, "I have delivered you from the galleys; I have paid your ransom; I have also paid that of your sister; she was a scullion here, and is very ugly; I have the goodness to make her my wife, and you pretend still to oppose it: I should kill you again, if I were to consult my passion." "You may indeed kill me again," said the Baron; "but you shall never marry my sister while I have breath."

CHAPTER XXX

THE CONCLUSION

CANDIDE had no great desire, at the bottom of his heart, to marry Cunegonde. But the extreme impertinence of the Baron determined him to conclude the match, and Cunegonde pressed it so earnestly, that he could not retract. He advised with Pangloss, Martin, and the trusty Cacambo. Pangloss drew up an excellent memoir, in which he proved, that the Baron had no right over his sister, and that she might, according to all the laws of the empire, espouse Candide with her left hand. Martin was for throwing the Baron into the sea; Cacambo was of opinion that it would be best to send him back again to the Levant captain, and make him work at the galleys; after which they might send him to Rome to the Father General by the first ship. This advice was thought good; the old woman approved it; and nothing was said to his sister about it. The scheme was put in execution for a little money; and so they had the pleasure of outwitting a Jesuit, and punishing the pride of a German Baron.

It is natural to imagine, that, after so many disasters, Candide married to his sweetheart, and living with the philosopher Pangloss, the philosopher Martin, the discreet Cacambo, and the old woman, and especially as he had brought so many diamonds from the country of the ancient Incas, must live the most agreeable life of any man upon earth. But he was duped so often by the Jews, that he had nothing left but the small farm; and his wife growing still more ugly, turned peevish and insupportable. The old woman was very infirm, and worse humored than Cunegonde herself. Cacambo, who worked in the garden, and went to Constantinople to sell its products, was worn out with labor, and cursed his fate. Pangloss was ready to despair, because he did not shine at the head of some university in Germany. As for Martin, as he was firmly persuaded that all was equally bad throughout, he therefore bore things with patience. Candide, Martin, and Pangloss disputed sometimes about metaphysics and ethics. They often saw passing under the windows of the farmhouse boats full of effendis, bashaws, and cadis, who were going into banishment to Lemnos, Mitylene, and Erzerum. They observed that other cadis, other bashaws, and other effendis succeeded in the posts of those who were exiled, and that they themselves were banished in their turns. They saw heads recently impaled, which were to be presented to the Sublime Porte. These spectacles increased the number of their disputations; and when they did not dispute, they were so prodigiously uneasy and unquiet in themselves, that the old woman took the liberty to say to them, "I want to know which is the worst, to be ravished a hundred times by negro pirates, to have a buttock cut off, to run the gauntlet among the Bulgarians, to be whipped and hanged at an auto-da-fé, to be dissected, to row in the galleys; in one word, to have suffered all the miseries we have undergone, or to stay here, without doing anything?" "That is a question not easily to be determined," said Candide.

This discourse gave rise to new reflections, and Martin concluded, upon the whole, that mankind are born to live either in the distractions of inquietude, or in the lethargy of disgust. Candide did not agree to that opinion, but remained in a state of suspense. Pangloss confessed that he had undergone terrible trials; but having once maintained that all things went wonderfully well, he still kept firm to his hypothesis, though quite opposite to his real sentiments. What contributed to confirm Martin in his shocking principles, to make Candide puzzle more than ever, and to embarrass Pangloss, was that one day they saw Paquetta and Brother Girofflée, who were in the greatest distress, at their farm. They soon squandered away their three thousand piastres, had parted, were reconciled, quarreled again, had been confined in prison, had made their escape, and Father Girofflée had at length turned Turk. Paquetta continued her trade, wherever she went, but made nothing by it. "I could easily foresee," said Martin to Candide, "that your presents would soon be squandered away, and would render them more miserable. You and Cacambo have swallowed millions of piastres and are not a bit happier than Brother Girofflée and Paquetta." "Ha! ha!" said Pangloss to Paquetta, "has Providence then brought you among us again, my poor child! Do you know that you have cost me the tip of my nose, one eye, and one of my ears, as you may see you have? What a world is this!" This new adventure set them a-philosophizing more than ever. There lived in the neighborhood a very famous dervish, who passed for the greatest philosopher in Turkey. They went to consult him. Pangloss was chosen speaker, and said to him, "Master, we are come to desire you to tell us why so strange an animal as man was created."

"What's that to you?" said the dervish; "is it any business of thine?" "But, my Reverend Father," said Candide, "there is a shocking sight of evil upon earth." "What signifies," said the dervish, "whether there be good or evil? When His Sublime Highness sends a vessel to Egypt, does it trouble him whether the mice on board are at their ease or not?" "What would you have one do then?" said Pangloss. "Hold your tongue," said the dervish. "I promised myself the pleasure," said Pangloss, "of reasoning with you upon effects and causes, the best of possible worlds, the origin of evil, the nature of the pre-established harmony." The dervish, at these words, shut the door against them.

During this conference, news was brought that two viziers and a mufti were strangled at Constantinople, and a great many of their friends impaled. This catastrophe made a great noise for some hours. Pangloss, Candide, and Martin, in their return to the little farm, met a good-looking old man, taking the air at his door, under an arbor of orange trees. Pangloss, who had as much curiosity as philosophy, asked him the name of the mufti, who was lately strangled. "I know nothing at all about it," said the good man; "and what's more, I never knew the name of a single mufti, or a single vizier, in my life. I am an entire stranger to the story you mention; and presume, that, generally speaking, they who trouble their heads with state affairs, sometimes die shocking deaths, not without deserving it: but I never trouble my head about what is doing at Constantinople; I content myself with sending my fruits thither, the produce of my garden, which I cultivate with my own hands!" Having said these words, he introduced the strangers into his house. His two daughters and two sons served them with several kinds of sherbet, which they made themselves, besides caymac, enriched with the peels of candied citrons, oranges, lemons, bananas, pistachio nuts, and Mocca coffee unadulterated with the bad coffee of Batavia and the isles. After which, the two daughters of this good mussulman perfumed the beards of Candide, Pangloss, and Martin.

"You must certainly," said Candide to the Turk, "have a very large and very opulent estate!" "I have only twenty acres," said the Turk; "which I, with my children, cultivate. Labor keeps us free from three of the greatest evils, tiresomeness, vice, and want." As Candide returned towards his farm, he made deep reflections on the discourse of the Turk. Said he to Pangloss and Martin, "The condition of this good old man seems to me preferable to that of the six Kings with whom we had the honor to sup." "The grandeurs of royalty," said Pangloss, "are very precarious, in the opinion of all philosophers. For, in short, Eglon, King of the Moabites, was assassinated by Ehud; Absalom was hung by the hair of his head, and pierced through with three darts; King Nadab, the son of Jeroboam, was killed by Baasha; King Elah by Zimri; Ahaziah by Jehu; Athaliah by Jehoiadah; the Kings Joachim, Jechonias, and Zedekias, were carried into captivity. You know the fates of Crœsus, Astyages, Darius, Dionysius of Syracuse, Pyrrhus, Perseus, Hannibal, Jugurtha, Ariovistus, Cæsar, Pompey, Nero, Otho, Vitellius, Domitian, Richard II., Edward II., Henry VI., Richard III., Mary Stuart, and Charles I., of England, the three Henrys of France, and the Emperor Henry IV. You know——" "I know very well," said Candide, "that we ought to look after our garden." "You are in the right," said Pangloss: "for when man was placed in the garden of Eden, he was placed there, *ut operaretur eum*, to cultivate it; which proves that mankind are not created to be idle." "Let us work," said Martin, without disputing; "it is the only way to render life supportable."

All their little society entered into this laudable design, according to their different abilities. Their little piece of ground produced a plentiful crop. Cunegonde indeed was very ugly, but she turned out an excellent pastry-cook. Paquetta worked at embroidery, and the old woman took care of the linen. There was no idle person in the company, not excepting even Brother Girofflée; he made a very good carpenter, and became too a very honest man.

Pangloss would sometimes say to Candide: "All events are linked together in this best of all possible worlds. For if you had not been driven with great blows on the backside out of a very fine castle, on account of your passion for Miss Cunegonde; if you had not been thrown into the inquisition; if you had not rambled through America on foot; if you had not given the Baron a hearty blow with your sword; if you had not lost all the sheep that you brought from that good country Eldorado; you would not have eaten here preserved citrons and pistachio nuts." "That is well said," said Candide; "but let us cultivate our garden."

The End of the First Part

NOTE

This second part of "Candide" was published first in 1761. Although attributed then to Voltaire, its authorship was neither admitted nor denied. The best opinion now seems to be that it was not written by Voltaire, but is the work of Thorel de Campigneulles, who died in 1809.

PART II

CHAPTER I

HOW CANDIDE PARTED FROM HIS COMPANY, AND WHAT RESULTED FROM IT

M AN soon grows weary of everything in life; riches are a burden to the possessor; ambition, when sated, leaves regrets; the sweets of love lose their delight; and Candide, born to experience all the vicissitudes of fortune, at last was tired of cultivating his garden. "Master Pangloss," said he, "if we are in the best of *possible worlds,* you must confess at least that I do not enjoy a suitable proportion of *possible happiness,* since I live unknown in a small corner of the Propontis, having no other support than that of my hands, which may soon lose their strength; no other pleasure than that which I have from Miss Cunegonde, who is very ugly, and, what is worst of all, she is my wife; no other company than yours, which often tires me; or that of Martin, which makes me gloomy; or that of Girofllée, who lately has turned good; or that of Paquette, which, you know, is very dangerous; or that of the old woman with one buttock, who tells me a parcel of long-spun stories."

Then Pangloss replied, "Philosophy teaches us that the *monads,* infinitely divisible, arrange themselves with a wonderful intelligence to form the different bodies that we remark in nature. The heavenly bodies are what they *ought* to be; they are placed where they *ought* to be placed; they describe the circles that they *ought* to describe; man follows the inclination that he *ought* to follow, he is what he *ought* to be, he does what he *ought* to do. You are cast down and complain, O Candide, because the *monad* of your soul is weary; but this weariness in a modification of the soul, and is no argument against everything being for the best with respect to yourself and others. When you saw me overrun with ulcers, I stood firm to my opinion: for if Miss Paquette had not given me a relish for the pleasures of love and its poison, I should not have met with you in Holland; I should not have given an occasion to James the Anabaptist to do a meritorious action; I should not have been hanged at Lisbon for the edification of our neighbor; I should not be here to comfort you with my advices, to live and die in the opinion of Leibnitz. Yes, my dear Candide, the whole is a concatenation, everything is necessary in the best of possible worlds. There is an absolute necessity for the burgess of Montauban to instruct kings, and the worm of Quimper-Corentin to criticize, criticize, criticize. The impeacher of philosophers is necessitated to be crucified in St. Denis's street; and the same necessity obliges the flogging pedant of the *Recollêts* and the archdean of St. Malo to distil gall and calumny from their *Christian Journals*. Philosophy lies under the necessity to be impeached at the tribunal of Melpomene. Philosophers are obliged to continue to enlighten mankind, notwithstanding the snarling envious brutes that grovel in the mud of literature. And were you to be kicked from the finest of castles, and under the necessity of learning again the Bulgarian exercise, run the gauntlet, suffer once more the effects of a Dutch vrow, and be sent back to Lisbon to be cruelly scourged by order of the holy inquisition, to undergo the same dangers among the Padres, the Oreillons, and the French; if you were, in short, to bear all *possible* calamities, and though you did not understand Leibnitz better than I do myself, you would always maintain that everything is *right,* and *for the best;* that the *plenum,* and the *materia subtilis,* the *pre-established harmony,* and the *monads,* are the prettiest things in the world; and that Leibnitz is a great man, even to those who do not understand him."

To this fine discourse, Candide, the mildest of all the beings of nature, though indeed he had killed three men, two of whom were priests, did not give an answer; but being weary of the Doctor and his company, he set out, the next morning by break of day, with a white stick in his hand, not knowing whither he was going, in search of a place devoid of weariness, and where men should not be men, as in the good country of Eldorado.

Candide, less unhappy since he no longer was in love with Miss Cunegonde, got his subsistence from the liberality of different people, who were not Christians, but were charitable. He arrived after a very tedious and painful march, at Tauris, a city on the frontiers of Persia, famous for the cruelties exercised there alternately by Turks and Persians.

Candide being quite spent with fatigue, having scarcely as many clothes as could cover the distinguishing mark of man, and what man calls his shame, was beginning to doubt whether he should believe Pangloss, when a Persian made up to him in a very polite manner, and entreated him to ennoble his house by his presence. "You joke, surely," said Candide; "I am a poor devil, who have left a wretched habitation that I had at the Propontis because I married Miss Cunegonde, who is become very ugly, and because I was weary. I am not indeed fit to ennoble anyone's house. I am not noble myself, thanks be to God; if I had the honor to be so, the Honorable

Baron of Thunder-ten-tronckh should have paid very dearly for the kicks on the breech he thought proper to give me, or I should have died for shame, which would have been too philosophical. Besides, I was scourged very ignominiously by the executioners of the holy inquisition, and by two thousand heroes, whose pay is three farthings a day. Give me whatever you please, but do not insult me in my distress by banters that would depreciate the merit of your favors." "My Lord," replied the Persian, "you may be a beggar, and it is pretty visible you are so; but my religion obliges me to be hospitable. You are a fellow-creature, and in want, therefore the apple of my eye shall be your path. Deign to ennoble my house by your radiant presence." "I shall do as you please," replied Candide. "Step in," said the Persian. They walked in; and Candide, full of admiration, was quite astonished at the respect that his landlord showed him. The slaves anticipated all his desires. The whole house seemed intent to procure him full satisfaction. "Provided this continues," said Candide, "matters are not so bad in this country." Three days elapsed, and the Persian generosity lasted as usual and Candide began to exclaim, "O Master Pangloss, I suspected always that you were in the right; for you are a great philosopher!"

CHAPTER II

WHAT HAPPENED TO CANDIDE IN THIS HOUSE, AND HOW HE LEFT IT

CANDIDE well-fed, well-clothed, and in high spirits, soon became again as ruddy, as fresh, and as pretty as when he was in Westphalia. This change gave no small pleasure to Ishmael Rahab, his landlord. This man, who was six feet high, had two small red sparkling eyes; and his pimpled nose, of a pretty large size, was a sufficient indication that he infringed the law of Mahomet. His whiskers were renowned in the province, and mothers were earnestly praying that their sons might have the like mustaches. Rahab had wives, because he was rich; but he was of an opinion that prevails but too commonly in the East, and in some colleges of Europe. "Your excellence is more beautiful than the stars," said the artful Persian one day to our unsuspecting hero, gently stroking him under the chin; "your charms must have captivated many hearts; you were born to give and to enjoy happiness." "Alas!" replied Candide, "I was but half happy behind the screen, for I was far from being at my ease. Cunegonde was then handsome—Cunegonde, poor innocent!" "Follow me, my Lord," said the Persian; and Candide followed him.

They came to a most enchanting inclosure at the bottom of a wood, where silence and voluptuousness seemed to reign. There Ishmael Rahab, tenderly embracing Candide, in few words declared a passion for him like that which the beautiful Alexis so feelingly describes in the Bucolics of Virgil. Candide was unable to recover from his astonishment. "No," cried he, "I will never submit to such infamy! What a strange cause, and what a shocking effect! I had rather suffer death." "Thou shalt die then," said the furious Ishmael. "How! Christian dog, because I very politely meant to give thee pleasure —resolve to satisfy me, or to endure the most cruel death." Candide did not long hesitate. The Persian's powerful arguments were sufficient to make him tremble; but he feared death like a philosopher.

Custom soon reconciles us to anything. Candide, well-

fed, well-instructed, though confined, was not absolutely dissatisfied with his situation. Good living, and
the various entertainments exhibited by the slaves of
Ishmael, gave some intermission to his griefs; he was unhappy only when he reflected; and so are the greatest
part of mankind.

About this time one of the chief supports of the
church militant of Persia, the most learned of all the
Mahometan doctors, who understood Arabic to his fingers' ends, and even the Greek which is at this day spoken
in the country of Demosthenes and Sophocles, the Rev.
Ed-Ivan-Baal-Denk, returned from Constantinople,
where he had been disputing with the Rev. Mamoud-Ab-
ram on a very delicate point of doctrine, namely, whether the prophet had plucked the quill with which he wrote
the Alcoran out of the wing of the angel Gabriel, or
whether Gabriel had presented it to him? They had disputed, during three days and three nights, with a zeal
worthy of the ages most renowned for controversy, when
the Doctor returned persuaded, like all the disciples of
Ali, that Mahomet had plucked the quill; and Mamoud-
Abram remained convinced, like the rest of the sect of
Omar, that the prophet was incapable of such a piece of
rudeness, and that the angel presented it to him with the
most becoming grace imaginable.

It was reported that there had been, at Constantinople, a kind of free thinker who had insinuated that
it was proper to inquire into the truth of the Alcoran's
having been actually written with a quill taken from the
angel Gabriel; but he was stoned.

Candide's arrival made a great noise in Tauris; several
persons who had heard of contingent effects, and effects
not contingent, began to doubt of his being a philosopher. They mentioned it to the Rev. Ed-Ivan-Baal-

Denk; he was curious to see him; and Rahab, who could not refuse a person of his consideration, ordered Candide into his presence. He seemed entirely satisfied with Candide's manner of reasoning on physical and moral evil, on things active and passive. "I understand you are a philosopher, and that is sufficient," said the venerable Cenobite: "it is very improper that so great a man as you are should be treated unworthily, which I am informed is the case. You are a stranger, Ishmael Rahab has no right over you. I will take you to court, where you will meet with a favorable reception: the Sophi is fond of the sciences. Ishmael, deliver this young philosopher into my hands, or you will incur the displeasure of your prince, and draw upon you the vengeance of Heaven, but more especially of its ministers." These last words terrified the intrepid Persian; he consented to everything; and Candide, blessing Heaven and the priesthood, set out from Tauris that very day with the Mahometan doctor. They took the road to Ispahan, where they arrived amid the blessings and acclamations of the people.

CHAPTER III

CANDIDE'S RECEPTION AT COURT, AND WHAT FOLLOWED

THE Rev. Ed-Ivan-Baal-Denk made no delay in presenting Candide to the King. His Majesty took a singular pleasure in listening to his discourse, and placed him among the learned men of his court; but these learned men treated him as an ignorant fool, and an idiot, which very much contributed to persuade His Majesty that he was a great man. "Because," said he to them, "you cannot comprehend Candide's arguments, you affront him; but, for my part, though I understand them no better than you, I assure you that he is a great philosopher; I swear it by my whiskers." These words imposed silence on the learned.

Candide was lodged in the palace, and allowed slaves for his service; he was clothed in a magnificent suit, and the Sophi commanded that, let him say what he would, no one should dare to prove him in the wrong. His Majesty did not stop here. The venerable priest ceased not to importune him in favor of Candide; and he resolved, at last, to rank him with his most intimate favorites.

"God be praised and our holy prophet," said the Iman, addressing Candide, "I have brought you a most agreeable piece of intelligence. How happy are you, my dear Candide! How will you be envied! You will swim in opulence; you may aspire to the most illustrious employments of the empire. Forget me not, however, my dear friend; remember that you are obliged to me for the favors with which you will soon be honored. The King will bestow upon you a kindness which is greatly esteemed, and you will shortly exhibit an entertainment which the court has not enjoyed this two years." "And pray, what are the honors designed for me by the prince?" said Candide. "This very day," replied the priest, quite delighted, "you will receive fifty strokes upon the soles of your feet, with a bull's pizzle, in the presence of his Majesty. The eunuchs, who are to perfume you, will be here immediately; prepare to support with becoming resolution this little trial, and make yourself worthy of the king of kings." "Let the king of kings keep his favors," cried Candide, "if, to deserve them, I must receive fifty strokes with a bull's pizzle." "It is his custom," replied the Doctor coldly, "with those on whom he would bestow his favors. I esteem you too much to report your reluctance, and I will make you happy in spite of yourself."

They had scarce done speaking when the eunuchs entered, preceded by the executor of his Majesty's small pleasures, who was one of the tallest and most robust lords of the court. Candide would rather have been excused, but, in spite of all he could say or do, they perfumed his legs and feet according to custom. Four eunuchs conducted him to the place appointed for the ceremony, in the midst of a double rank of soldiers, to the sound of musical instruments, cannon, and the ringing of bells. The Sophi was already there, attended by his principal officers, and the most intelligent of his courtiers. Candide was stretched in a moment on a gilded bench, and the executor of the small pleasures was preparing to enter upon his office. "O Pangloss, Pangloss, if you were here!" said Candide, crying and weeping with all his might; which would have been thought very indecent, if the priest had not asserted that his favorite behaved in this manner only to give his Majesty more entertainment. In truth, this great king laughed most immoderately; he was so pleased with the sight, that, when the fifty strokes were given, he ordered fifty more. But his prime minister having represented, with uncommon boldness, that this favor, conferred on a stranger, might alienate the hearts of his subjects, he revoked his order, and Candide was remanded back to his apartment.

They put him to bed, having bathed his feet with vinegar. The nobility came, one after another, to congratulate him; even the Sophi honored him with his presence; he not only suffered him to kiss his hand, but gave him a devilish drive in the chaps with his fist. The politicians thence conjectured that his fortune was made, and, what is more extraordinary, though politicians, they were not mistaken.

CHAPTER IV

CANDIDE RECEIVES NEW FAVORS. HIS ELEVATION

OUR hero was no sooner recovered than he was presented to the King, in order to express his gratitude for the favors with which he had been honored. The monarch received him graciously; moreover, he deigned to give him two or three slaps in the face during the conversation; and when he took his leave, condescended to kick his a—— as he went along, even as far as the guardroom: the courtiers were all ready to die with envy. Since the time His Majesty had first begun to bruise his special favorites, no one had ever had the honor to be so thoroughly bruised as Candide.

Three days after this audience, our philosopher, who was ready to go mad at the favors he had received, and began to think that things went very ill, was named governor of Chusistan, with despotic power. He was decorated with a fur cap, which in Persia is a mark of high distinction. Having taken leave of the Sophi, who honored him with the repetition of some favors, he set out for Sus, the capital of the province. From the moment Candide had appeared at court, the grandees of the empire conspired his destruction. The excessive favors which the Sophi had so lavishly bestowed on him served only to increase the storm which was ready to burst over his head. Nevertheless, he rejoiced in his good fortune, and especially in his remote situation: his ideas anticipated the pleasures of supremacy, and he said from the bottom of his heart,

Thrice happy they who from their sovereign dwell
Far distant!————

Scarce had he traveled twenty miles from Ispahan, when, on a sudden, a body of five hundred cavalry saluted him with a furious discharge of their carbines. Candide thought at first it was intended as a compliment; but a ball which shattered his leg to pieces soon convinced him of his mistake. His people threw down their arms, and Candide, almost dead, was carried to a desolate castle. His baggage, his camels, his slaves, his white eunuchs, his black eunuchs, and thirty-six wives which the Sophi had given him for his own use, all became the spoil of the conquerors. They cut off the leg of our hero to prevent a mortification, and endeavored to preserve his life to the intent that he might suffer a more cruel death.

"O Pangloss, Pangloss, what would become of your optimism, if you now beheld me, with only one leg, in the hands of my most cruel enemies? When I had just entered the path of felicity; just made governor, or rather king, of one of the most considerable provinces of the empire of ancient Media; when I became possessed of camels, slaves, white eunuchs and black eunuchs, and thirty-six wives for my own needs, and of which I had yet made no use." Thus Candide spoke when he was able to speak.

But while he thus bewailed his misery, fortune stood his friend. The prime minister being informed of the violence which had been committed, had dispatched a sufficient body of veterans in pursuit of the rebels; and the priest Ed-Ivan-Baal-Denk had published, by means of other priests, that Candide being favored by the priests, was consequently a favorite with God. Besides, those who were acquainted with the conspiracy were the more impatient to discover it, since the ministers of religion had declared in the name of Mahomet that if anyone had eaten swine's flesh, drank wine, passed several days without bathing, or visited a woman at an improper time, contrary to the express commands of the Alcoran, he should, upon declaring what he knew of the conspiracy, be *ipso facto* absolved. Candide's prison was soon discovered; it was instantly forced open, and, as religion was concerned, the vanquished were, according to rule, exterminated. Candide, marching over heaps of dead bodies, triumphed over the greatest danger he had ever yet experienced, and, together with his attendants, continued his route towards his government, where he was received as a peculiar favorite who had been honored with the bastinado in the presence of the king of kings.

CHAPTER V

HOW CANDIDE WAS A GREAT PRINCE, BUT NOT SATISFIED

PHILOSOPHY inspires men with the love of their fellow-creatures: Pascal is almost the only philosopher who seems endeavoring to make us hate them. Happily Candide had never read Pascal: he loved poor humanity with all his soul. Honest men perceived his disposition: they had hitherto been kept at a distance from the *Missi Dominici* of Persia; but it was not difficult for them to assemble in the presence of Candide, and to assist him with their counsel. He made many wise regulations for the encouragement of agriculture, population, commerce, and the arts. He rewarded those who had made useful experiments; and even those who had only written books met with encouragement. When all my subjects are contented (said Candide to himself with the most charming candor imaginable), then possibly I may be happy. He was but little acquainted with human nature. His reputation was attacked in seditious libels, and he was calumniated in a work called *l'Ami des hommes*. He found, that by endeavoring to make men happy, he did but excite their ingratitude. "O," cried Candide, "how difficult it is to govern these unfledged animals which vegetate on the face of the earth! Why did I not remain on my little farm, in the company of Master Pangloss, Cunegonde, the daughter of Pope Urban X who has but one buttock, Friar Girofflée, and the voluptuous Paquette!"

CHAPTER VI

CANDIDE'S PLEASURES

CANDIDE, in the extremity of his grief, wrote a most pathetic letter to the Right Reverend Ed-Ivan-Baal-Denk; who was so exceedingly moved with the sad picture of his misery that he persuaded the Sophi to dismiss Candide from his employment. His Majesty, in recompense for his services, granted him a very considerable pension. Thus eased of the weight of grandeur, our philosopher sought the optimisim of Pangloss in the pleasures of private life. Hitherto he seemed to have lived for others, and to have forgot that he had a seragl-

10. He now recollected this circumstance with that emotion which the very idea of a seraglio inspires. "Let all things be prepared," said he to his prime eunuch, "for my entrance among my wives." "My Lord," replied the squeaking gentleman, "it is now that your Excellence deserves the name of *wise*. Men, for whom you have done so much, were unworthy your attention; but women——" "It may be so," said Candide very modestly.

In the center of a garden, in which nature was assisted by art to develop her charms, stood a small fabric whose structure was simple, yet elegant, and therefore quite different from those which are seen in the suburbs of the most magnificent cities in Europe. Candide approached this temple, but not without a blush. The soft air spread a delicious fragrance round the peaceful mansion. The flowers, amorously entwined, seemed guided by the instinct of pleasure; nor were they only the flowers of a day: the rose never lost its vermilion. The remote view of a shaggy rock, whence fell a rapid torrent, seemed calculated to invite the soul to that sweet melancholy which precedes enjoyment. Candide, trembling, entered the saloon, where taste and magnificence were elegantly displayed; a secret charm thrilled through every sense. He beholds, breathing upon the canvas, the youthful Telemachus in the midst of the nymphs of Calypso's court. He then turns his eyes to a half-naked Diana flying into the arms of Endymion. But his agitation increased when he beheld a Venus faithfully copied from that of Medici. All at once he is struck with the sound of divine music; a number of young Circassian women appear covered with their veils; they form around him a dance agreeably imagined, and more veritable than those which are exhibited upon the stage after the death of your Cæsars and your Pompeys.

At a certain signal, their veils dropped; their expressive features add new life to the entertainment; they practice every bewitching attitude, but without any apparent design; one by her enticing eyes expressed a boundless passion; another in a soft languor seemed to expect pleasure without seeking it; a third bends forward, but raises herself immediately so as to afford a transient glance at those ravishing charms which at Paris the fair sex so profusely display; a fourth carelessly throws back the skirt of her robe, and discovers a leg which of itself was sufficient to inflame a man of delicacy. The dance ceases, and the beauties stand motionless.

The silence that reigns recalls Candide to himself; the fury of love rushes into his heart; his insatiable looks wander on all sides; he kisses the inflaming lips and moistened eyes; he put his hand on globes whiter than alabaster, their heaving and elastic motion makes the hand recoil, he admires the due proportions, he observes the ruddy tips, like the buds of the new-springing rose, that do not blow till recreated by the beneficent rays of the sun; he kisses them with ecstasy, and his mouth sticks close to them. Our philosopher contemplates with attention one of a more delicate shape and majestic deportment than the rest; but throws his handkerchief to a young nymph whose languishing eyes seemed peculiarly to court his affection, and whose beauty was improved by her blushes. The eunuch instantly opened the door of an apartment which was consecrated to the mysteries of love. The lovers entered, and the eunuch said to his master, "You are now going to be happy." "O," replied Candide, "I hope I am."

The ceiling and the walls of this delightful chamber were covered with mirrors, and in the middle stood a couch of black satin. Here he seated the fair Circassian, and began to undress her with inconceivable alertness. The good creature did not interrupt him, except to express her affection by her kisses. "O, my Lord," said she, like a true Mahometan, "how happy you have made your slave! How you honor her by your transports!" These few words charmed our philosopher. He was lost in ecstasy, and everything he beheld was entirely new to him. What difference between Cunegonde grown ugly, and violated by Bulgarian heroes, and a young Circassian of eighteen, who was never ravished! This was the first time that poor Candide had tasted pleasure. The objects which he devoured were repeated in the glass. Whichsoever way he turned his eyes, he saw the black satin contrasted with the whitest skin in the universe. He beheld——but I am obliged to comply with the false delicacy of our language. Let it suffice to say that our philosopher was completely happy.

"O Master, my dear Master Pangloss!" cried Candide quite enrapt, "all is full as well here as in Eldorado; nothing but a fine woman can satisfy the desires of man. I am as happy as it is possible to be. Leibnitz is in the right, and you are a great philosopher: for instance, I make no doubt but you, my lovely angel, are inclined towards optimism, as you have always been happy." "Alas!" replied the lovely angel, "I know not what you mean by optimism; but your slave was never happy before today. If my Lord will deign to hear me, I will convince him of this by a concise relation of my adventures." "With all my heart," said Candide, "I am in a proper state of tranquillity to listen to a story." And so the charming slave began her tale, as in the following chapter.

CHAPTER VII

THE HISTORY OF ZIRZA

"MY father was a Christian, and I also am a Christian, as he told me. He lived in a little hermitage in the neighborhood of Cotatis, where he attracted the veneration of the faithful by his servile devotion and an austerity of manners which was shocking to human nature. The women came in crowds to pay him homage, and took a singular pleasure in kissing his backside, which was every day gored with stripes of discipline. I certainly owe my being to one of the most devout of them. I was brought up in a subterraneous cave near my father's cell. I was twelve years old, without having once issued from this tomb, as I may call it, when the earth trembled with a terrible noise; the vault where I lay sank down, and I was with difficulty taken from under the rubbish. I was half dead, when, for the first time in my life, my eyes were struck with the light of day. My father took me into his hermitage as a predestined child: the whole affair appeared strange to the people. My father cried out a miracle, and the people joined in the cry.

"I was named Zirza, which, in the Persian language signifies *child of Providence*. It was not long before the beauty of your poor slave excited the curiosity of the public. The women began to visit the hermitage less frequently, and the men much oftener. One of them said he loved me. 'Wicked wretch,' cried my father, 'art thou qualified to love her? She is a treasure which God hath committed to my care: he appeared to me last night in the figure of a venerable hermit, and commanded me not to part with her for less than two thousand crowns. Be gone, vile beggar, lest thy impure breath should contaminate her charms.' 'I confess,' answered the youth, 'that I have only a heart to offer her; but, monster, art thou not ashamed to prostitute the name of the Deity to thy avarice? With what face, wretch as thou art, dost thou dare to assert that God spake to thee? It is degrading the Almighty to represent him conversing with men like thee.' 'O blasphemy!' cried my father in a violent passion, 'God himself commanded that blasphemers should be stoned.'

"Saying these words, he murdered my unhappy lover, and his blood spurted in my face. Now, though I was yet unacquainted with love, I found myself so far interested in the fate of my lover that the sight of my father became insupportable to me. I resolved to leave him: he perceived my design. 'Ungrateful girl,' said he, 'it is to me thou art indebted for thy being; thou art my daughter, and yet thou hatest me! But thou shalt no longer hate me without cause.' He kept his word but too religiously. During five sad years which I passed in tears and groans, neither my youth nor faded beauty had power to relax his severity. Sometimes he would thrust a thousand pins into every part of my body; then with his discipline he would cover my backside with blood." "That gave you less pain than the pins," said Candide. "True, my Lord," replied Zirza. "At last, however, I found means to escape; and not daring to confide in any man, I hid myself in the woods. Three days I spent without food, and should certainly have died of hunger, but for a tiger to whom I had the good fortune to be agreeable, and who was kind enough to divide his prey with me. But I was often dreadfully frightened by this terrible animal; the brute had once like to have ravished from me the flower, the plucking of which has given your Lordship so much pain and pleasure. My food gave me the scurvy, but I was no sooner cured than I followed a slave-merchant who was traveling to Tiflis, where the plague then raged, and I soon became infected. These misfortunes, however, had so little affected my charms, that the purveyor of the court thought fit to purchase me for your use. It is now three months that I have languished among the rest of your wives; we all began to imagine ourselves despised. O, Sir, if you did but know how disagreeable and improper these eunuchs are to console neglected girls. In short, I have not yet lived eighteen years, twelve of which I passed in a dungeon; I have felt an earthquake; I was sprinkled with the blood of the first amiable man I had seen; during five whole years I endured the most cruel torture; I have had the scurvy and the plague. Pining in the midst of a company of black and white monsters, still preserving that which I had saved from the fury of a tiger, and cursing my destiny, I spent three long months in this seraglio; and should most certainly have died of the green sickness, if your Excellence had not honored me with your embraces."

"O heavens!" said Candide, "is it possible at your age to have experienced such sad misfortunes? What would Pangloss say if he could hear your story? But your misfortunes are at an end as well as mine. Things are not now so bad; do you think they are?" Saying these words he renewed his caresses, and became more and more confirmed in the opinions of Pangloss.

CHAPTER VIII

CANDIDE'S DISGUST. A MEETING WHICH HE DID
NOT EXPECT

OUR philosopher, in the midst of his seraglio, distributed his favors with tolerable impartiality;
he enjoyed the pleasure of variety, and returned with
fresh ardor to the *child of Providence*. But this did not
continue long. He now began to feel violent pains in his
loins, and was also frequently afflicted with the colic. In
being happy he became emaciated. Zirza's neck appeared
neither so white nor so admirably turned; her shape lost
half its delicacy; her eyes, in the eyes of Candide, seemed
less sparkling; her complexion appeared less beautiful,
and the ravishing vermilion of her lips seemed quite
faded. He perceived that she did not walk well, and was
not entirely satisfied with her breath. He also discovered
a mole where he had conceived no blemish. The impetu-
osity of her passion became troublesome. In his other
wives he coolly observed many defects which, during
his first transports, had escaped his notice: their lewd-
ness grew offensive. He was ashamed to have followed
the example of the wisest of all men, *et invenit amarior-
em morte mulierem.*

Candide, still firm in his Christian sentiments, saun-
tered for want of employment in the streets of Sus,
where, to his great surprise, a gentleman richly dressed
caught him in his arms, calling him by his name. "Is it
possible," said Candide, "bless my spirit; it cannot be——
Yet there is so striking a resemblance—— Abbé Perigordin——" "It is even so," replied Perigordin. Candide stepped back three paces, and ingenuously said,

"But are you happy, my dear Sir?" "A fine question truly," answered Perigordin, "the little trick which I put upon you at Paris served only to establish my credit. The police employed me a while; but disagreeing with them at last, I threw off the ecclesiastical habit, which was of use to me no longer, and went over to England, where those of my profession are better paid. I revealed all that I knew, and all that I did not know, of the strength and weakness of the country I had quitted. I swore that the French were a rascally people, and that London was the only store of good sense; in short, I made a considerable fortune, and am come hither to negotiate a treaty at the court of Persia, in which the Sophi is bound to exterminate every European who shall enter his dominions in search of cotton or silk, to the prejudice of the English." "The object of your embassy," said our philosopher, "is doubtless very commendable; but, Sir, you are a great rascal: I do not like villainy, and I have come into influence at court: tremble, therefore, for your prosperity is at an end; you will soon feel the punishment due to your crimes." "O Most Noble Lord Candide," said Perigordin, falling on his knees, "have mercy on me: I am driven to wickedness by an irresistible impulse, in the same manner as you are impelled to virtue. I perceived this fatal inclination the moment I was acquainted with Mr. Walsp, and became a writer in the Feuilles——*" "Feuilles!" cries Candide, "what are those?" "They are," replied Perigordin, "certain pamphlets of seventy pages, in which the public are periodically

* This is one of the thirty or forty periodical papers printed at Paris. It is only known in France, where it meets with success among all ranks. But these loose sheets of seventy-two pages must not be confounded with others, comprised under the same number of pages, wherein the author is indulgent to himself, and these papers, however, are much valued by philosophers.

entertained with scandal, satire, and Billingsgate. It is an honest man who, having learned to read and write, and not being able to continue Jesuit so long as he could have wished, set about this pretty little performance, in order to buy lace for his wife, and bring up his children in the fear of God. There are also a set of *honest gentlemen* who for a few pence, and now and then a gill of bad wine, assist the other *honest* man in carrying on his work. This Monsieur Walsp is a member of an extraordinary club, whose chief amusement is to make a few drunken people deny their God; or to assist some poor fool in spending his fortune, break his furniture, and then send him a challenge: these are no more than little gentilities, which these gentlemen call *mystifications,* and which nevertheless merit the notice of the police. In short, this very honest Monsieur Walsp, who denies his ever having been sent to the galleys, is blessed with a lethargy which renders him insensible to the severest truth; and it is impossible to rouse him but by certain violent means, which he endures with a magnanimity and resignation beyond all belief. I labored some time under this celebrated author; I became famous in my turn, and had just left Monsieur Walsp, with an intention to begin for myself, when I had the honor to pay my respects to you at Paris——" "You are a vile rogue," said Candide; "but your sincerity moves me. Go directly to court, and present yourself to the Right Reverend Ed-Ivan-Baal-Denk. I will write to him in your favor, on condition that you promise to become an honest man, and that you do not insist on having thousands of people murdered, for the sake of a little silk and cotton." Perigordin promised all that Candide desired of him, and they parted friends.

CHAPTER IX

CANDIDE'S DISGRACE, TRAVELS, AND ADVENTURES

PERIGORDIN was no sooner arrived at court than he used all his art to gain the minister and ruin his benefactor. He reported that Candide was a traitor, and that he had spoken disrespectfully of the sacred whiskers of the king of kings. It was the general opinion of the courtiers that he ought to be roasted at a slow fire; but the Sophi, with more humanity, was graciously pleased to condemn him only to perpetual banishment, after having kissed the soles of his accuser's feet, according to the custom of Persia. Perigordin set out in order to put this sentence in execution; he found our philosopher in tolerable health, and almost disposed to renew his happiness. "My dear friend," said the English ambassador, "with the utmost regret I come to acquaint you that you must quit this kingdom with all possible expedition, and also that you must kiss the soles of my feet with sincere contrition, for the enormous crimes of which you have been guilty." "Kiss the soles of your feet!" cried Candide; "upon my word, Mr. Abbé, you carry your jokes too far: I do not comprehend you." He had scarce spoken, before the mutes which attended Perigordin entered the room, and immediately took off his shoes. He was then told, that he must either submit to this humiliation, or be impaled. Candide, in virtue of his free agency, kissed the Abbé's feet. They clothed him in a robe of coarse canvas, and the hangman drove him out of the city, crying aloud, "He is a traitor! He has spoken disrespectfully of the Sophi's whiskers, even of the whiskers of the great king!"

But what was the officious Cenobite doing, while his favorite was thus disgraced? I really cannot tell. Possibly he was grown weary of patronizing Candide. Who can depend on priests or princes!

In the meantime, our hero trudged sorrowfully along. "I never in my life," said he to himself, "spoke of the king of Persia's whiskers. I am fallen at once from the pinnacle of fortune into the abyss of misery, because I am accused by a wretch who has violated all laws, of a crime which I never committed; and this fellow, this persecutor of virtue—is happy."

Candide, after several days' march, found himself on the borders of Turkey. He directed his steps toward Propontis, being determined to fix there once more, and to spend the remainder of his life in cultivating his garden. In passing through a small town, he observed a multitude of people gathered together. He inquired the cause of this effect. " 'Tis a very odd affair," answered an old man: "you must know, that some time ago the rich Mehemet obtained in marriage the daughter of the Janissary Zamoud: he found her not a virgin, and very naturally, according to law, cut off her nose, and sent her back to her father. Zamoud, enraged at the affront, as was quite natural, in the first transport of his fury cut off the head of his disfigured daughter, at one stroke of his scimitar. His eldest son, who had a great affection for his sister, which you know is natural enough, in the violence of his passion very naturally plunged a dagger into his father's breast; then like a lion, whose rage increases at the sight of his own blood, the young Zamoud flew to the house of Mehemet, and having killed half a dozen slaves who opposed his entrance, he murdered Mehemet, his wives, and two children in the cradle; after which he put an end to his own life with the dagger, yet reeking with the blood of his father, and of his enemies, which, you know, was also quite natural——" "O horrible!" cried Candide. "O Master Pangloss! if these barbarities are natural, would you not confess that nature is corrupted, and that all things are not——" "No," replied the old man; "the pre-established harmony——" "O heavens!" cried Candide, "Am I deceived? Are you not Pangloss himself?" " 'Tis even so," said the old man; "I knew you at first, but I had a mind to penetrate into your sentiments before I disclosed myself. Come, let us reason a little upon contingent effects: let me see what progress you have made in the school of wisdom." "Truly, Master Pangloss," said Candide, "you time it very ill: inform me rather what is become of Cunegonde, and where is Friar Girofflée, Paquette, and the daughter of Pope Urban." "I know nothing of the matter," replied Pangloss; " 'tis now two years since I left our habitation in search of you. I have traveled over all Turkey, and was now going to the court of Persia, where, as I was informed, you had made your fortune. I remained in this town among these good people, only to recover a little strength in order to pursue my journey." "What do I see!" said Candide in astonishment, "You have lost an arm, my dear Pangloss." "That's nothing at all," replied Pangloss; "there is nothing more common than to see people with but one eye and one arm in this best of worlds. The accident happened in my journey from Mecca. Our caravan was attacked by a troop of Arabs; and as our escort made resistance, the Arabs, being stronger, according to the laws of war massacred us all.

"There perished in this affair about five hundred people, among whom were about a dozen women with child. For my part, I escaped with only a cloven skull, and with the loss of an arm. You see I am still living, and have always found that everything was for the best. But you yourself, my dear Candide, how happens it that you have a wooden leg?"

Candide then related his adventures. Our philosophers returned to Propontis, amusing themselves as they went along with reasoning on physical and moral evil, on free will and predestination, on *monads* and pre-established harmony.

CHAPTER X

THE ARRIVAL OF CANDIDE AND PANGLOSS IN PRO-PONTIS, WHAT THEY SAW THERE, AND WHAT BECAME OF THEM

"OMY dear Candide," said Pangloss, "why did you grow weary of cultivating your garden? Why could not we be content with our preserved citron, and pistachio nuts? Why were you tired of being happy? Why because all things are necessary in the best of worlds, was it therefore requisite that you should undergo the bastinado in the presence of the king of Persia; that you should have your leg cut off to make the Susians happy, to try the ingratitude of mankind, and to draw down punishment upon the heads of some villains who deserved to suffer."

Thus conversing, they arrived at their old habitation. The first objects which struck their eyes were Martin and Paquette, in the habit of slaves. "Whence comes this strange metamorphose?" said Candide, tenderly embracing them. "Alas!" they replied, sighing, "you have no longer a place of abode; another is intrusted with the cultivation of your garden; he eats your preserved citron and pistachio nuts, and uses us like negroes." "Who is this other?" said Candide. " 'Tis," said they, "the general of the marine, the least humane of all human beings. The Sultan, wishing to reward his services without being at any expense, confiscated all your possessions, under pretense that you were gone over to his enemy, and condemned us to slavery." "Believe me, Candide," added Martin, "and proceed on your journey. I have always told you that everything is for the worst; the sum of evil greatly exceeds the sum of good; depart, and I do not despair of your becoming a Manichean, if you are not one already." Pangloss was going to argue in form; but Candide interrupted him by inquiring after Cunegonde, the old woman, Friar Giroflée, and of Cacambo. "Cacambo is here," replied Martin; "he is now busy in cleaning the common sewer. The old woman is dead of a kick in the breast which was given her by an eunuch. Friar Giroflée is entered among the Janissaries. Madam Cunegonde is grown fat again, and has recovered her former beauty; she is in our master's seraglio." "What a string of unhappy wretches!" said Candide. "Was it necessary that Cunegonde should recover her beauty to make me a cuckold?" "It is of little importance," said Pangloss, "whether Madam Cunegonde be handsome or ugly; whether she is in your arms, or in those of another; it makes no difference in the general system: for my part, I wish her a numerous posterity. Philosophers never concern themselves by whom women have children, provided they have them at all. Population——" "Alas," said Martin, "philosophers had much better employ themselves in contributing to the happiness of a few individuals, than undertake to multiply the suffering species." While they were speaking, they heard a great noise. 'Twas the general who had ordered a dozen slaves to be flogged for his amusement. Pangloss and Candide, terrified, left their friends with tears in their eyes, and hastily took the road to Constantinople. Here they found everybody in an uproar; the fire began in the suburbs of Pera: it had already consumed five or six hundred houses, and two or three thousand people had perished in the flames. "What a shocking disaster!" cried Candide. "All for the best," said Pangloss: "these little accidents happen every year. It is very natural that fire should catch wooden houses, and that those houses should burn. Besides, it delivers many honest people from a miserable existence." "What do I hear?" said one of the officers of the Sublime Porte. "How, wretch, darest thou say it is all for the best, when half Constantinople is on fire? Go, dog, cursed prophet, go receive the punishment due to thy presumption."

In saying these words, he took Pangloss by the middle, and threw him headlong into the flames. Candide, half dead with fear, crept, as well as he could, into a neighboring quarter, where things were more quiet; and what became of him, we shall see in the next chapter.

CHAPTER XI

CANDIDE CONTINUES HIS JOURNEY; AND IN WHAT CAPACITY

"I HAVE now no other course to take," said our philosopher, "than to sell myself for a slave, or turn Turk. Happiness has abandoned me forever. A turban would corrupt all my pleasures. I feel myself incapable of enjoying peace of mind in a religion full of imposture, and which I should never embrace but from the base motive of interest. No, I shall never be content if I cease to be an honest man: I will therefore become a slave." No sooner had Candide taken this resolution than he determined to put it in practice. He fixed upon an Armenian merchant for his master; his character was very good, and he was reputed to have as much virtue as an Armenian could possibly have. This Armenian was ready to sail for Norway; he took Candide with him, hoping that a philosopher might be serviceable to him in his trade. They embarked, and the wind was so favorable to them that they made their passage in half the time which is generally required. They had no occasion to purchase a wind of the Lapland magicians, and therefore thought it sufficient to give them some trifle, that they might not interrupt their good fortune by their witchcraft, which sometimes happens, if one may believe Moreri's dictionary. As soon as they were landed, the Armenian made his purchase of whale blubber, and ordered our philosopher to traverse the country in search of dried fish. He acquitted himself of his commission as well as he could, and was returning with a number of reindeer loaded with this commodity, reflecting deeply on the amazing difference which he discovered between the Laplanders and other men, when he was accosted by an extremely small Laplandese. Her head was rather larger than the rest of her body, her eyes red and fiery, her nose flat, and her mouth reached from ear to ear; she bade him good morrow with the most engaging air imaginable. "My dear little lord," said this animal, who herself was but one foot ten inches high, "you are exceedingly charming; be so kind as to love me a little."

So saying, she threw her arms about his neck. Candide pushed her from him with inexpressible horror. She cried out; her husband advanced, accompanied by a number of his countrymen. "What is the meaning of this noise?" said they. "'Tis," said the little animal, "only this stranger——alas! I cannot speak for grief; he despises me." "I understand you," said the husband. "Impolite, uncivil, brutal, infamous, cowardly rascal, thou hast brought shame upon my house; thou hast done me the greatest injury; thou hast refused to lie with my wife." "Is the man mad?" said our hero. "What would you have said, had I lain with her?" "I should have wished you all manner of prosperity," said the enraged Laplander; "but thou deservest my utmost indignation." So saying, he exercised his stick upon the shoulders of Candide without mercy. The reindeer were seized by the relations of the affronted husband, and Candide, fearing worse treatment, was obliged to betake himself to his heels, and evermore to renounce his good master; for he dared not appear before him without money, without fish, and without reindeer.

CHAPTER XII

CANDIDE CONTINUES HIS JOURNEY. NEW ADVENTURES

CANDIDE strolled a long time without even knowing whither he would go; he determined, at last, to make the best of his way to Denmark, where, he had heard, things went well. He found himself possessed of some little money which the Armenian had given him; and, with this weak support, he hoped to accomplish his journey. This hope kept up his spirits, and he still enjoyed some happy moments. He chanced, one day, to meet in an inn with three travelers, who were talking with earnestness of a *plenum* and *materia subtilis*. Right, said Candide to himself, these are philosophers. "Gentle-men," said he, "as to the *plenum,* it is incontestable, there is no *vacuum* in nature, and the *materia subtilis* is well imagined." "Then you are a Cartesian," said the travel-ers. "Yes," said Candide; "and, what is still more, I am a Leibnitzian." "So much the worse for yourself," replied the philosophers. "Descartes and Leibnitz had not com-mon sense. As for us, we are Newtonians, and we glory in the distinction: if we dispute, it is only to strengthen our own sentiments, for we are all of the same mind.

"We seek the truth upon Newtonian principles, be-cause we are convinced that Newton is a great man." "And so is Descartes, so is Leibnitz, so is Pangloss," said Candide: "these are great men worth all the others." "You are very impertinent, friend," replied the philoso-phers. "Are you acquainted with the laws of refrangi-bility, of attraction, and of motion? Have you read Doc-tor Clark's refutation of your Leibnitz? Do you know what is meant by the centrifugal and centripetal force? Do you know that colors are formed by density? Have you any notion of the theory of light, and of gravita-tion? Are you ignorant of the period of 25,920 years, which unfortunately does not agree with chronology? No; I warrant your ideas of all these things are false and imperfect: learn to keep silence therefore, for the pitiful *monad* you are; and be careful how you affront gentle-men, by comparing them with pigmies." "Gentlemen," said Candide, "if Pangloss was here, he would teach you surprising things, for he is a great philosopher: he has an absolute contempt for your Newton, and, as I am his disciple, Newton is no great favorite of mine."

The philosophers, quite enraged, fell upon Candide, and our poor hero was drubbed most philosophically.

Their wrath appeasing, they begged the hero's pardon

for their rashness; then one of them began to speak, and made a very beautiful discourse on *mildness* and *moderation*.

During this conversation there happened to pass by a very pompous funeral, whence our philosophers took occasion to comment on the ridiculous vanity of mankind. "Would it not," says one of them, "be much more rational for the relations and friends of the deceased to carry, without pomp, the corpse upon their own shoulders? Would not the mournful employment more effectually excite the idea of death, and produce the most salutary and philosophical effect? Would not this reflection naturally arise? *This body which I carry is that of my friend, my relation; he is no more, and, like him, I must cease to exist?* Might not such a custom, in some measure, diminish the crimes committed in this unhappy world, and reclaim beings which believe in the soul's immortality? Mankind are but too willing to keep the thought of death at a distance, that we should be afraid of reminding them of their mortality too often. Why are not the weeping mother or husband present at this solemnity? The plaintive accents of nature, the piercing cries of despair, would do more honor to the ashes of the dead than all those sable mutes, and that string of clergy, jovially singing psalms which they do not understand." "It is well said," replied Candide. "If you did but always talk in this manner, without beating people, you would be a great philosopher."

Our travelers separated with marks of mutual confidence and friendship. Candide, steering his course towards Denmark, soon found himself in the middle of a wood; in ruminating on the misfortunes which had befallen him in this best of worlds, he had lost his way. The day had considerably declined when he perceived his mistake. His courage failed, and sorrowfully lifting his eyes to heaven, our hero, leaning against a tree, expressed himself in the following words: "I have traversed half this globe; I have seen fraud and calumny triumphant: my sole intention has been to be serviceable to mankind, yet I have been constantly persecuted. A great king honors me with his favor, and the bastinado. I am sent to a delightful province, but with a wooden leg: there I tasted pleasure after my misfortunes. An abbé arrives, and I protect him; by my means he insinuates himself at court, and I am obliged to kiss the soles of his feet. I meet my poor Pangloss again, only to see him burned. I stumble upon a company of philosophers, a species of animals the mildest and most sociable of any that are spread upon the face of the earth, and they beat me most unmercifully. Yet all must be right, because Pangloss said so; nevertheless I am the most miserable of all possible beings."

His meditations were suddenly interrupted by piercing cries, which seemed not far off. His curiosity led him on. He beheld a young woman tearing her hair in the most violent agitation of despair. "Whosover you are," said she, "if you have a heart, follow me." He followed her, and the first object he beheld was a man and a woman extended on the grass; their aspect bespoke the elevation of their minds and their distinguished origin; their features, though disfigured by grief, expressed something so interesting that Candide sympathized with their sorrows, and could not help eagerly inquiring the cause of their misfortunes. "These," said the young woman, "are my parents; yes, they are the authors of my unhappy being," continued she, throwing herself into their arms. "They were forced to fly to avoid the rigor of an unjust sentence: I attended them in their flight, and was contented to share their misfortunes, in hopes that I might be of some service in procuring nourishment for them in the desert we were going to enter. We stopped here to repose a while, and unhappily discovering that tree, I was deceived in its fruit. O Sir! I am a most horrid criminal! Arm yourself in defense of virtue, and punish me as I deserve. Strike!——That fruit——I gave it to my parents; they ate of it with pleasure: I rejoiced that I had relieved them from the torment of thirst. Unhappily, I presented them with death: the fruit is poison."

Candide shook with horror; his hair stood upright; a cold sweat covered his whole body. He immediately did all in his power to assist this wretched family; but the poison had already made so much progress that the best antidote would now have been ineffectual. "Dear, dear child, our only hope and comfort!" said the expiring parents, "Forgive thyself; we sincerely forgive thee; it was thy excessive tenderness which deprives us of life——O generous stranger! Be careful of our daughter: her heart is noble and formed for virtue: it is a treasure which we commit to thy care, infinitely more precious than our past fortune.——Dearest Zenoide, receive our last embraces; mix thy tears with ours. O heaven, what delightful moments are these! Thou hast opened to us the door of the comfortless dungeon, in which we have lived forty tedious years. We bless thee with our last breath, praying that thou mayst never forget the lessons which our prudence dictated; and that they may preserve thee from the danger to which thou wilt necessarily be exposed!"

Pronouncing these words, they expired. Candide had great difficulty in bringing Zenoide to herself. The solitude of the place, and the pale light of the moon, rendered the melancholy scene still more affecting. The day began to dawn before Zenoide recovered the use of her senses. She no sooner opened her eyes, than she desired Candide to dig a hole to inter the bodies; even she herself assisted with astonishing resolution. This duty being discharged, she gave vent to her tears. Our philosopher persuaded her to quit this fatal spot, and they walked along for some time, without knowing whither they went. At length they perceived a little cottage, which was inhabited by an old man and his wife, who, in the midst of this desert, were always ready to render all the service in their power to their distressed brethren. This couple were, in fact, what Philemon and Baucis are said to have been. They had enjoyed the sweets of Hymen forty years, without one bitter draught. Constant health, the produce of temperance and tranquillity; a pleasing simplicity of manners; an inexhaustible fund of candor in their disposition; all the virtues for which man is indebted to himself alone, composed the happy lot which heaven had been pleased to grant them. They were held in great veneration in the neighboring hamlets, whose inhabitants, happy in their rusticity, might have passed for very honest people, if they had been Catholics. They considered it as their duty to support Agaton and Suname (such were the names of this old couple), and they now extended their charity to the two strangers. "Alas!" said Candide, "what pity it was that you, my poor Pangloss, were burned: I know you were quite right; but it was not in those parts of Europe and Asia which we traversed together that all is for the best: it is in Eldorado, which it is impossible to reach; and in a little cottage, situated in the coldest, the most barren, and the most dismal country in the whole world. What pleasure should I have had to hear you, in this cabin,

talk of pre-established harmony and *monads!* I should
like to spend the rest of my days among these honest
Lutherans, but it would oblige me to renounce going
to mass, and expose me to the lash of the *Journal Chré-
tien.*"

Candide was very anxious to know the adventures of
Zenoide. Modesty hindered him from inquiring. She observed this, and satisfied his impatience by the following
narrative.

CHAPTER XIII

THE STORY OF ZENOIDE—HOW CANDIDE BECAME
ENAMORED OF HER, AND THE CONSEQUENCES

"I AM descended from one of the most ancient houses
of Denmark; one of my ancestors perished in that
place where the wicked Christiern caused such a number of
senators to be put to death. The accumulated riches and
honors of my family served only to render their misfortunes more illustrious. My father had the boldness to dis-
oblige a man in power by speaking the truth; he sub-
orned false accusers, who charged him with several im-
aginary crimes. The judges were deceived. Alas, what
judge can always avoid the snares which calumny spreads
for innocence? My father was condemned to lose his
head on a scaffold. Flight only could preserve him, and
he took refuge with a friend, one whom he thought
worthy of this amiable appellation. We continued some
time concealed in a castle on the seashore, which belonged
to him, and here we might have been still secure, if the
cruel wretch, taking advantage of our deplorable situation, had not exacted a price for his friendship which
made us regard him with detestation. The infamous

creature had conceived a violent passion for my mother and me: he made an attempt on our virtue by methods unworthy of a gentleman, and, to avoid the effects of his brutality, we were obliged to expose ourselves to the most frightful dangers: we betook ourselves to flight a second time, and you know the rest."

Here Zenoide finished her narration, and she began to weep afresh. Candide dried up her tears, and said, in order to comfort her: "It is all for the best, my dear Miss, for if your father had not been poisoned, he would, most infallibly, have been discovered, and they would have cut off his head; your mother would have died of grief, perhaps, and we should not now be in this poor cottage, where all things are much better than in the most charming castle imaginable." "Alas! Sir," replied Zenoide, "my father never told me that all was for the best. We all belong to one God, who loves us; but he will not exempt us from the devouring cares, the cruel distempers, the innumerable evils to which human nature is liable. In America, poison and the bark grow close to each other. The happiest of mortals has shed tears. A mixture of pleasures and pain constitutes what we call life; that is to say, a determined space of time (always too long in the opinion of wisdom), which ought to be employed in being useful to the society of which we are members, to rejoice in the works of the Almighty, without foolishly inquiring into their causes; to regulate our conduct upon the testimony of our conscience; and, above all, to respect our religion. Happy if we could always observe its precepts!

"In this manner have I heard my honored father frequently speak. What presumptuous wretches, would he say, are those rash scribblers who seek to penetrate into the secrets of the Almighty? On the principle that God expects to be honored by the numberless atoms to whom he has given existence, mankind have united ridiculous chimeras with the most respectable truths. The Dervish among the Turks, the Brahman in Persia, the Bonze in China, the Talapoin in India, all worship the Deity in a different manner; nevertheless they enjoy peace of mind, though bewildered in obscurity; those who would endeavor to dispel the mist, would do them no service; he cannot be said to love mankind, who would remove their prejudices."

"You speak like a philosopher," said Candide: "may I presume to ask you, my dearest young lady, of what religion you are." "I was brought up a Lutheran," replied Zenoide; "it is the religion of my country." "Everything you say," continued Candide, "is a ray of light which penetrates my soul: you fill me with esteem and admiration. How is it possible that so much sense should inhabit so fair a body? Indeed, my dear Miss, I love and admire you to such a degree——" Candide stammered out something more; but Zenoide, perceiving his confusion, retired; from that moment, she avoided all occasions of being alone with him, and Candide sought every opportunity of being either alone with her, or entirely by himself. He was seized with a melancholy, which, however, was not unpleasing; he was violently in love with Zenoide, yet endeavored to dissemble his passion; but his looks betrayed the secret of his heart. "Alas!" said he, "if Pangloss was here, he would give me good advice, for he was a great philosopher."

CHAPTER XIV

CONTINUATION OF CANDIDE'S AMOUR

CANDIDE was forced to be content with the poor consolation of conversing with the beautiful Zenoide in the presence of the old man and his wife. "And was it possible," said he one day to the mistress of his heart, "that the king, whom you were allowed to approach, could permit such a flagrant act of injustice to your family? You have great reason to hate him." "Alas!" replied Zenoide, "who can hate his king?

"Who can avoid loving him who is intrusted with the glittering blade of the law? Kings are the visible images of the Deity; we ought never to condemn their conduct; obedience and respect are the duties of good subjects." "I admire you more and more," answered Candide: "pray, Miss, are you acquainted with the great Leibnitz, and the great Pangloss, who was burned, after having escaped hanging? Do you know the *monads*, the *materia subtilis*, and the *vortices*?" "No, Sir," said Zenoide; "my father never mentioned any of these things; he gave me only a slight notion of experimental philosophy, and taught me to despise every kind of philosophy which did not directly tend to promote the happiness of mankind; which inspires one with false notions of his duty to himself and to his neighbor; which does not teach him how to regulate his manners; which serves only to fill his mind with unintelligible words, and rash conjectures; which cannot give a clearer idea of the author of our being than that which we form from his works, and the miracles which are daily performed before our eyes." "Upon my word, Miss," said Candide, "I admire you beyond expression; I am enchanted; I am ravished; you are certainly an angel sent from heaven to confute the sophisms of Master Pangloss. Ignorant animal that I was! After having endured a prodigious number of kicks on the backside, of stripes across my shoulders, of strokes with a bull's pizzle on the soles of my feet; after having felt an earthquake; after having been present at the hanging of Doctor Pangloss, and lately seeing him burned alive; after having been ignominiously used by a vile Persian; after having been plundered by order of the divan, and drubbed by a company of philosophers; notwithstanding all this, I believed that all was for the best; but I am now entirely undeceived. Nevertheless, nature never appeared to me so beautiful as since I have beheld you. The rural concerts of birds strike my ears with a harmony to which, till now, I was quite insensible. All nature blooms, and the beauty of your sentiments seems to animate every object. I feel none of that voluptuous languor which I experienced in my garden at Sus; the passion you inspire is quite different." "Forbear," said Zenoide, "lest you offend that delicacy which you ought to respect." "I will be silent then," said Candide, "but that will only augment my passion."

He looked earnestly at Zenoide, as he pronounced these words; he perceived that she blushed, and thence, like a man of experience, he conceived the most flattering hopes. The young Dane continued for some time to shun her lover. One day as he was walking hastily in the garden, he cried out in a transport of love, "O that I had but my Eldorado sheep! Why am I not able to buy a little kingdom!——" "What would you make me?" said a voice that shot through the heart of our philosopher. "Is it you, charming Zenoide?" said he, falling upon his knees at her feet, "I thought myself alone. The few words you spoke seemed to flatter my hopes. I shall never be a king, and possibly never shall be rich; but if I were beloved by you—— O do not turn away those charming eyes, but let me read in them a confession which alone can make me happy. Beautiful Zenoide, I adore you: for Heaven's sake be merciful.—Ah! what do I see? You weep. Gods, I am too happy." "Yes," said Zenoide, "you are happy; nothing obliges me to conceal my sensibility from a person who deserves it. Hitherto you have been attached to my destiny by the ties of humanity only: it is now time to strengthen our union with more holy bonds. I have deliberately consulted my own heart; do you also maturely reflect, and above all things remember that by marrying me you engage to become my protector; to soften and participate in the miseries which fate may still have reserved for me." "Marry you?" said Candide; "these words have at once opened my eyes, and shown me the imprudence of my conduct. Alas! Sweet lady, I am unworthy of your goodness: Cunegonde is yet living." "Cunegonde, who is she?" "My wife," replied Candide, with his usual ingenuity.

Our lovers stood silent for some moments; they would have spoken, but the words expired upon their lips; their eyes swam in tears. Candide held both her hands in his; he pressed them to his heart; he devoured them with kisses. He had the courage to touch her heaving breast, and found that she breathed with difficulty. His soul rose up to his lips, which by pressing those of Zenoide, brought her to herself. Candide thought he saw his pardon written in her eyes. "Dear Candide," said she, "my displeasure would but ill repay those transports which my heart in spite of me approves. Yet hold; you will ruin me in the opinion of mankind, and you will cease to love me when I am become the object of their contempt. Stop then, and respect my weakness." "What!" said Candide, "because the stupid vulgar say that a girl is dishonored in making her lover happy in following the generous dictates of nature, which in the early ages of the world——"

We shall not relate all this interesting conversation; we shall content ourselves with saying that Candide's eloquence, embellished by the expressions of love, had all the effect that he could expect, on a young and tender-hearted female philosopher.

Our lovers, who had hitherto passed their time in disquietude and affliction, were now continually intoxicated with pleasure. The silence of the forest, the mountains covered with brambles and surrounded with precipices; the frozen waters, and barren fields with which they were environed, served but to persuade them of the necessity of love, they resolved never to quit this frightful solitude; but destiny was not yet weary in her persecutions, as we shall see in the next chapter.

CHAPTER XV

THE ARRIVAL OF VOLHALL. JOURNEY TO COPENHAGEN

CANDIDE and his mistress amused themselves with reasoning on the works of the Creator, on the worship due to him from mankind, on the duties of society, more especially on charity, which, of all other virtues, is the most useful to our fellow-creatures. They were not content with vain declamations: Candide taught youth to respect the sacred restrictions of the law, and

Zenoide instructed young maidens in their duty to their parents; they united their endeavors to sow the prolific seeds of religion in juvenile minds. One day as they were busied in this pious employment, Suname acquainted Zenoide that an old gentleman, with several attendants, was just come, and inquired for a person who, she was convinced by his description, could be no other than the beautiful Zenoide. The gentleman, who followed her close, entered almost at the same instant. Zenoide fainted away as soon as she saw him, but Volhall, unmoved at this affecting sight, took her by the hand and dragged her with so much violence that she came to herself; but it was only to shed a torrent of tears. "It is very well, niece," said he, with a severe smile, "I have caught you in fine company; no wonder you prefer it to the capital, to my house, and to your own family." "Yes, Sir," replied Zenoide, "I prefer the habitation of truth and candor to that of treachery and imposture. I shall never behold without horror the place where my misfortunes began, where I have had such convincing proofs of your baseness, and where you are the only relation I have." "No matter, Miss," replied Volhall, "you shall follow me, if you please, though you were to have another fit." So saying, he dragged her along, and put her into a chaise. She had but just time to bid Candide follow her, and to bless her kind host and hostess, promising to reward them for their generous hospitality.

One of Volhall's servants, being moved by Candide's affliction, and believing he had no other interest in the young lady than what virtue in distress might inspire, advised him to take a journey to Copenhagen. He told him he could probably get him admitted into Volhall's family if he had no other resource. Candide accepted his offer, and being arrived, his future comrade

428 VOLTAIRE'S ROMANCES AND TALES

presented him as a relation for whose fidelity he would answer. "Maraut," said Volhall, "I consent: you shall have the honor of waiting on a man of my rank and distinction, but be careful always to pay an implicit obedience to my will: anticipate my commands if you are endowed with sufficient penetration; remember that a man of my distinction degrades himself by conversing with such a wretch as you." Our philosopher replied with great submission to this impertinent harangue, and that very day he was dressed in his master's livery.

One may easily imagine Zenoide's astonishment and joy when she recognized her lover among her uncle's servants. She gave him all the opportunities she could, which Candide judiciously improved to their mutual satisfaction. They vowed an eternal constancy; nevertheless Zenoide was far from being quite easy: she sometimes condemned her passion for Candide, and would now and then afflict him for amusement, but Candide adored her; he knew that perfection did not fall to the lot of man, much less of woman. Zenoide recovered her good humor in his arms; the constraint they were obliged to observe increased their enjoyment, and they were yet happy.

CHAPTER XVI

HOW CANDIDE FOUND HIS WIFE AGAIN. HOW HE LOST HIS MISTRESS

OUR hero had no hardship to bear but the haughtiness of his master, and this was not purchasing at too dear a rate the favors of his mistress. Happy lovers cannot conceal their passion so easily as is generally imagined; they soon betrayed their own secret; their connection was no longer a mystery to anyone in the house, except to Volhall himself. Candide was honored with felicitations that made him tremble; he expected the storm which was about to burst over his head, and was in no doubt that the person who had been so dear to him was upon the point of accelerating his misfortunes.

For some days past Candide had observed a woman whose face bore a strong resemblance to that of Cunegonde; he now saw her again in the courtyard, but her garb was mean; besides, there was not the least probability that the favorite mistress of a rich Mahometan should appear in the courtyard of an inn at Copenhagen. Nevertheless, this disagreeable object fixed her eyes on Candide with great attention. She now precipitately approached, and saluted him with the most violent box on the ear he ever received in his life. "I was not deceived," cried our philosopher; "O heavens, who could have thought it! What business have you here, after suffering yourself to be ravished by a Mahometan? Go, perfidious spouse, I know nothing of you." "Thou shalt know me by my fury," said Cunegonde. "I know all thy wicked courses, thy intrigue with thy master's niece, thy contempt of me. Alas! It is three months since I was turned out of the seraglio, because I was no longer useful. A merchant bought me to mend his linen, and having occasion to make a voyage to these parts, brought me along with him. Martin, Cacambo, and Paquette, whom he also purchased, are of the party. Doctor Pangloss also, by the greatest chance imaginable, was a passenger in the same ship; we were cast away a few miles from hence. I escaped with honest Cacambo, whose flesh, I assure thee, is as firm as thine; and I have found thee again to my sorrow, for thy infidelity is manifest.

Tremble therefore, and dread the vengeance of an injured woman."

Candide was so stupified with this moving scene, that he suffered Cunegonde to depart without considering how necessary it is to keep on good terms with those who are in our secrets, when all at once Cacambo presented himself to his view. They tenderly embraced. Candide inquired into the truth of what he had heard, and was extremely afflicted at the loss of the great Pangloss, who, after having been hanged and burned, was most miserably drowned. He spoke of him with that effusion of heart which true friendship inspires. A *billet* which Zenoide threw out of the window put an end to their conversation. Candide opened it, and read as follows: "Fly, my dear lover, everything is discovered. An innocent and natural inclination, which does no injury to society, is a crime in the estimation of credulous and cruel men. Volhall has this moment left my chamber, after treating me with the utmost inhumanity; he is gone to obtain an order to have you immured in a dungeon. Fly, therefore, my dear, dear lover, and save a life which I am no longer suffered to enjoy. Those happy days are past, when our mutual tenderness—Ah, wretched Zenoide, what hast thou done to deserve the wrath of heaven! But I wander: O do not forget thy dear Zenoide. Dear Candide, thy image will never be effaced from my heart—— No, thou never knew how much I loved thee —O that thou couldst receive from my burning lips my last farewell, and my last sigh! I feel that I am ready to follow my unhappy father: I hold the world in abhorrence; it is all treachery and guilt."

Cacambo, always retaining his wisdom and prudence, drew along with him Candide, who had lost all the power of his sensitive faculties. They went by the shortest way out of the city. Candide did not open his mouth, and they had got at a pretty considerable distance from Copenhagen before he was roused from his lethargy, but at last staring at his faithful Cacambo, he spoke as follows.

CHAPTER XVII

HOW CANDIDE INTENDED TO KILL HIMSELF, AND
DID NOT EFFECTUATE IT. WHAT HAPPENED TO
HIM IN AN INN

"DEAR Cacambo, formerly my servant, now my equal and always my friend, thou hast partaken of some of my misfortunes, thou hast given me salutary advices, thou hast seen my love for Miss Cunegonde." "Alas! My dear old Master," said Cacambo, "it is she who played you this most base trick. Being informed by your companions that you were as deep in love with Zenoide as she was with you, she revealed the whole scene to the barbarous Volhall." "Since this is the case," said Candide, "death is my only refuge." Our philosopher then taking a penknife out of his pocket, began to whet it with a composure worthy of an ancient Roman, or of an Englishman. "What do you mean?" said Cacambo. "To cut my throat," said Candide. "An excellent thought," replied Cacambo; "but wisdom should never decide, till after mature deliberation: the means of death will be always in your own power, if you continue in the same mind. Be advised, my dear master, and put it off till tomorrow; the longer you defer it, the more courageous will be the action." "I like thy reasoning," said Candide; "besides, if I should cut my throat now, the gazetteer of Trevoux

would insult my memory; it is then determined, I will
not cut my throat for this two or three days at least."

Thus conversing they arrived at Elsinore, a rather considerable town, at a little distance from Copenhagen:
here they rested that night, and Cacambo applauded
himself for the good effect which sleep had produced in
the mind of Candide. They took their leave of this town
at break of day, and Candide, always a philosopher, for
the prejudices of youth are not easily effaced, entertained his friend Cacambo with a dissertation on moral
and physical good, with the discourses of the wise Zenoide, and the true lights he had received from her
learned conversation. "If Pangloss was not dead," said he,
"I would confute his system beyond contradiction. God
preserve me from becoming a Manichean. My dear mistress has taught me to respect the impenetrable veil by
which the Deity chooses to conceal his designs from mankind. Perhaps man himself is the cause of the misfortunes
under which he groans: fruit-eaters are become carnivorous animals. The savages we have seen devour only
the Jesuits, yet they live in perfect harmony among
themselves; and those which, by chance, are scattered
through the desert, and feed only upon roots and herbs,
are certainly happy. Society has given birth to the most
heinous crimes. There are people, who, from their situation, seem as it were obliged to desire the death of their
fellow-creatures. The shipwreck of a vessel, the burning
of a house, or the loss of a battle, is the occasion of
grief to some, and of joy to others. Things go very ill,
my dear Cacambo, and a wise man has nothing to do
but to cut his throat as gently as possible." "You are in the
right," said Cacambo, "but I perceive an inn, you must
be thirsty; come, my old master, let us take a glass, and
then we will proceed in our philosophical disquisitions."

They entered the inn, where a crowd of peasants were dancing in the middle of the court, to the sound of very bad instruments. A cheerful smile sat on every face; it was a picture worthy the pencil of Watteau. As soon as they perceived Candide, a young girl took him by the hand, intreating him to dance. "My sweet lass," replied Candide, "when a man has lost his mistress, found his wife, and but just heard of the death of the great Pangloss, he can have no inclination to cut capers. Besides, I intend to kill myself tomorrow, and you know, when a person has but a few hours to live, he should not waste his time in dancing." Cacambo then advanced, and expressed himself in the following manner: "Great philosophers have always had a passion for glory. Cato of Utica killed himself after having slept soundly; Socrates swallowed hemlock after familiarly conversing with his friends; several Englishmen have blown out their brains after coming from an entertainment: but I have never heard of any great man who cut his throat after dancing. No, my dear master, this glory is reserved for you. Let us dance our bellies full today, and we will kill ourselves tomorrow." "Dost thou not observe," replied Candide, "that pretty lively wench?" "There is something vastly striking in her countenance," said Cacambo. "She squeezed my hand," replied our philosopher. "Did you take notice," said Cacambo, "of her little round breasts, when her handkerchief flew back as she was dancing?" "Yes, I observed them well," said Candide: "if my heart was not full of the charms of Miss Zenoide——" But the little black girl interrupted Cacambo, and again besought him to dance. Our hero was at last persuaded, and danced with the genteelest air imaginable. He then embraced the pretty peasant, and retired to his seat without asking the queen of the ball to dance. Immediately there was a confused murmur; both the actors and spectators were shocked at such a manifest neglect. Candide was ignorant of his fault, and therefore could make no apology. At length a great clown came forward, and gave him a slap in the face, which was returned by Cacambo with a kick in the belly. The instruments were scattered about in an instant, the women lost their caps. Candide and Cacambo behaved like heroes; but they were forced to betake themselves to their heels, though quite crippled with the blows they had received.

"I am very unlucky," said Candide, leaning on his friend Cacambo; "I have experienced great misfortunes, but I never expected to have had my bones broke for dancing with a peasant at her own request."

CHAPTER XVIII

CANDIDE AND CACAMBO RETIRE TO A HOSPITAL. ADVENTURE THERE

CACAMBO and his quondam master were unable to proceed; they began to give way to that malady of the soul which destroys all its faculties: dejection and despair, when looking up, they espied a hospital built for travelers. Cacambo entered, and Candide followed him; they were treated in the manner in which people are generally treated for the love of God. Their wounds were speedily healed; but they both got the itch, which was not to be cured in a few days. This idea drew tears from the eyes of our philosopher, and, scratching himself, he said, "O my dear Cacambo, why didst thou hinder me from cutting my throat? Thy pernicious counsel hath plunged me again into disgrace and misfortune: if I

CANDIDE 435

should now cut my throat, they would say, in the *Journal of Trevoux,* 'He was a coward; he killed himself because he had the itch.' See to what thou hast exposed me by thy injudicious friendship." "Our misfortunes are not without a remedy," said Cacambo; "if you will follow my advice, we will become brothers of the hospital; I understand a little of surgery, and I will engage to render our woeful condition supportable." "Ah!" cried Candide, "a pox take all the asses in the world, and especially those chirurgical asses, so fatal to human nature! No, I will not suffer thee to pass for what thou art not; it were a piece of treachery, the consequences of which might be terrible. Besides, if thou didst but know, after having been viceroy of a rich province, after having been able to purchase kingdoms, after having been the happy lover of Miss Zenoide, how hard it is to resolve to serve as mate in a hospital. All this I know full well; but I also know that it is very hard to die of hunger. Besides, the plan which I propose is perhaps the only one to elude the cruelty of Volhall."

While he thus spake, one of the brothers of the hospital happening to pass, asked him a few questions, to which he replied properly. This brother assured them that the fraternity lived well, and enjoyed decent liberty. Candide made up his mind: they were admitted without scruple, and these two miserable beings began to administer comfort to beings yet more miserable.

One day as Candide was distributing some bad broth among the patients, an old man particularly caught his attention. He seemed in the agony of death. "Poor man," said Candide, "how I pity you! You must suffer terribly." "Indeed I do," he replied, with a hollow sepulchral voice: "they tell me that I have a complication of distempers, and that I am poxed to the very bone; if so, I must needs be extremely ill. Nevertheless, it is all for the best, and that is my consolation." "No man in the world," said Candide, "but Doctor Pangloss, could maintain optimism in such a deplorable situation, when every other mortal would preach pess———." "Do not pronounce that detestable word," said the poor old man; "I am that very Pangloss. Wretch, let me die in peace; all things are good, everything is best." The effort he made in pronouncing these words cost him his last tooth, and a few moments after he expired.

Candide bewailed his death, for he had a good heart; his obstinacy, however, afforded matter of reflection to our philosopher. He would frequently ruminate on his adventures. Cunegonde had remained at Copenhagen, where, he was informed, she mended shirts and stockings with great reputation. He had now lost all his passion for traveling. The faithful Cacambo assisted him with his advice and friendship. He never murmured at the dispensations of providence: "I know," he would sometimes say, "that happiness is not the lot of humanity; it is nowhere to be found except in the good country of Eldorado; but to go thither is impossible."

CHAPTER XIX

NEW ADVENTURES

CANDIDE was not quite unhappy, for he had a true friend. He had found, in an American mongrel valet, what in Europe we seek in vain. Perhaps nature, who has planted simples in America proper for the maladies of European bodies, may there also have sown remedies for the disorders of our hearts and minds.

Perhaps there are a species of men in this new world who are formed differently from us, who are not slaves to self-interest, who are capable of sincere friendship. 'Twere happy, if instead of bales of indigo and cochineal, stained with blood, they would bring us some of these men: this kind of commerce would be very advantageous to mankind. Cacambo was of more value to Candide than a dozen of red sheep loaded with the pebbles of Eldorado. Our philosopher now began to be reconciled to life. He consoled himself that he was employed in the preservation of the human species, and in not being a useless member of society. Heaven rewarded the purity of his intentions by restoring to him, as well as to his friend Cacambo, the blessing of health. They had no longer the itch, and they performed the duties of their function with great alacrity; but alas, fate soon broke in upon their peaceful security. Cunegonde, who had set her heart upon tormenting her husband, sallied forth from Copenhagen in pursuit of him; chance directed her to the hospital; she was accompanied by a man whom Candide soon discovered to be the Baron of Thunder-ten-tronckh: his surprise may be easily supposed. The Baron, perceiving it, spoke to him in these words. "I did not long continue to row in the Turkish galleys; the Jesuits, hearing of my misfortune, redeemed me for the honor of the society. I made a tour to Germany, where I received some civilities from my father's heirs. I left nothing unattempted to get intelligence of my sister, and hearing at Constantinople that she had embarked on board a vessel which was cast away on the coast of Denmark, I disguised myself and departed, being provided with proper letters of recommendation to Danish merchants in connection with the society: in short, I have found my sister again, who loves you notwithstanding your unworthiness of that honor; and since you have had the insolence to lie with her, I consent to the ratification, or rather a new celebration of your nuptials; that is to say, provided she gives you only her left hand, which is but reasonable, as she has no less than seventy-one quarters, and you have none at all." "Alas," says Candide, "all the quarters in the world without beauty——Miss Cunegonde was very ugly when I imprudently married her; she became handsome, and another has enjoyed her charms; she is again grown ugly, and you would have me give my hand to her a second time: no, no, Reverend father; send her back to her seraglio at Constantinople; she has done me but too much injury in this country." "Ungrateful man," said Cunegonde, making horrible contortions, "how can you be so hard-hearted? Do not oblige the Baron, now a priest, to wash the blot out of his escutcheon with your blood. Dost thou believe me capable of consenting to the act of infidelity? What wouldst thou have had me done when I was in the power of a Turk who thought me handsome? Neither tears, nor my cries, had any effect on his savage brutality, so that, finding it in vain to resist, I contrived to be as commodiously ravished as possible, as any other woman would have done in my situation: this is all my crime. But my greatest offense is having robbed thee of thy mistress, which, on the contrary, thou shouldst consider as a proof of my affection. Come, come, my dear little soul; if ever I should grow handsome again, if my breasts, which now are somewhat pendent, should recover their rotund elasticity, if—— they shall be all for thee alone, my dear Candide; we are no longer in Turkey, and I swear that I will never suffer myself to be ravished again."

This discourse made no very deep impression upon

Candide. He desired a little time for consideration. The Baron granted him two hours, which he spent in consulting with his friend Cacambo. After having weighed every argument *pro* and *con,* they determined to accompany the Baron and his sister to Germany. Accordingly everything being settled, they set out all together, not on foot, but mounted on good cavalry, which the Jesuit Baron had brought along with him. They were now arrived at the frontiers of the kingdom, when a tall ill-favored fellow fixed his eyes attentively on our hero. "It is the very man," said he; "pray, Sir, if I may be so bold, is not your name Candide?" "Yes, Sir," replied Candide, "so I have always been called." "I am extremely glad of it," said the man. "Yes indeed, you have black eyebrows, ears of moderate size, a round face, and ruddy complexion, and you appear to be about five feet five." "Yes, Sir," said Candide, "that is exactly my height; but what are my ears and my height to you?" "Sir," replied the man, "we cannot be too circumspect in our employment: permit me to ask you another question; were you not in the service of Squire Volhall?" "In truth, Sir," said Candide, a little disconcerted, "I do not understand——" "But I understand perfectly well that you are the person whose description I have in my hand. Please to walk into the guard room. Soldiers, conduct the gentleman in; prepare the black hole, and tell the smith to make a slight chain of about thirty or forty pound weight. Mr. Candide, you have got a good horse there; I want one of that color; we shall agree about him by and by."

The Baron did not dare to claim his beast. Cunegonde wept for a quarter of an hour. The Jesuit beheld the scene without emotion, "I should have been obliged," said he to his sister, "either to kill him or force him to remarry you; and, all things considered, it is the best that could happen for the honor of our family." Cunegonde and her brother set out for Germany; but the faithful Cacambo resolved not to abandon his friend in distress.

CHAPTER XX

THE CONTINUATION OF CANDIDE'S MISFORTUNES; HOW HE FOUND HIS MISTRESS AGAIN, AND WHAT WAS THE CONSEQUENCE

"O PANGLOSS!" said Candide, "it is a thousand pities that you have perished so miserably; you have been witness only to the smallest part of my misfortunes, and I was in hopes to make you reject that groundless opinion you so obstinately maintained, even unto death. There is not a man in the world who has experienced greater adversity than I have, and yet there is not a single soul who has not cursed his own existence, as the daughter of Pope Urban very pathetically told us. What will become of me, my dear Cacambo?" "I cannot tell," replied Cacambo; "all I know is, that I will never forsake you." "But Cunegonde has forsaken me," said Candide. "Alas! A wife is not worth an American friend."

This was the conversation of Candide and Cacambo in a dungeon, from whence they were dragged in order to be conveyed to Copenhagen, where our philosopher was to learn his fate. He feared it would be a dreadful one, as the reader may also apprehend; but Candide was mistaken, and so is the reader. He was destined to be happy at Copenhagen, where he was no sooner arrived than he was apprised of the death of Volhall; this brute died unlamented, and everybody concerned themselves about Candide. His chains were immediately knocked off, and liberty was the more agreeable to him, as it furnished him with the means of finding Zenoide. He hastened to her house; he was a long time before he could utter a syllable, but their silence was sufficiently expressive. They embraced; they endeavored to speak, but they could only weep. Cacambo enjoyed this delightful scene like a being of sensibility; he sympathized in his friend's joy, and was almost in the same situation. "My dear Cacambo, my beloved Zenoide," cried Candide, "I am now recompensed for all my sufferings. Love and friendship shall sweeten the remainder of my life. What numberless difficulties have paved the way to this unexpected happiness? But all is now forgotten, dearest Zenoide, I see you, you love me; all things go well with me now, everything is for the best."

The death of Volhall left Zenoide her own mistress, and the court allowed her a pension out of her father's fortune, which had been confiscated. She readily shared with Candide and Cacambo, whom she permitted to live in the same house, and industriously reported that, having received such signal services from these two strangers, she thought herself obliged to reward them with all the pleasures of life. Some shrewd people penetrated into the motives of her kindness, which was not very difficult, as her intrigue with Candide had unluckily transpired. Most people condemned her, and her conduct was approved only by a few people who knew the world. Zenoide, who paid some regard to the esteem of fools, was not quite happy in her situation. The death of Cunegonde, which the correspondents of trading Jesuits reported at Copenhagen, furnished Zenoide with an opportunity to reconcile the scrupulous; she ordered a pedigree to be made for Candide; and the author, who was a man of parts, proved him to be descended from one of the most ancient families in Europe; he even pretended that his real name was Canut, the name of an ancient Danish king, than which nothing could be more probable, for to change *did* into *ut* was no very extraordinary metamorphosis. In consequence of this trifling alteration, Candide became a nobleman of distinction. He was married publicly to Zenoide; they lived together as happily as it is possible to live. Cacambo was their common friend, and Candide used frequently to say, "All things are not so well with us here as in Eldorado, but yet they are pretty well."

REFERENCES

MICROMEGAS

[1] *i.e.*, the little great one.

[2] It is thought that Voltaire here alludes to his quarrel with Boyer, bishop of Mirepoix, who had assailed him for maintaining, in his *Lettres Philosophiques,* that human beings resemble animals in the gradual development of the soul in correspondence with that of the body. See note, p.

[3] Dr. Derham, F.R.S., Rector of Upminster in Essex from 1689 to 1735, was author, among other works, of *Astro-Theology,* to which allusion is here made.

[4] Huyghens, the discoverer of Saturn's ring, whose *Systema Saturnium* was published in 1659.

[5] The first edition of Louis Moreri's *Grand Dictionnaire Historique et Critique* appeared at Paris in 1673, and the last in 1759.

[6] "They" (*i.e.*, the astronomers of Laputa) "have likewise discovered two lesser stars, or satellites, which revolve about Mars." (*Gulliver's Travels,* part iii.) Strangely enough, this conjecture, which, it will be seen, Voltaire borrowed from Swift, has been verified by the progress of science, for in 1877 Professor Asaph Hall, of Washington, discovered that Mars is actually attended by two moons, which have received the appropriate names of "Phobos" and "Deimos" ("Fear" and "Terror").

[7] Buffon in his *Histoire Naturelle,* the first three volumes of which were published at Paris in 1749, had fully discussed these observations of Leuwenhoek and others.

[8] This expression was one which Fontenelle (*ob.* 1757) had employed in relating certain physiological observations of his own.

[9] The first part of *Gulliver's Travels,* containing the Voyage of Lilliput, was published in 1726. At Voltaire's suggestion the Abbé Desfontaines translated the whole work into French.

[10] The Crimea, which was annexed to Russia in 1783, after two wars with Turkey, to the earlier one of which (1736-1739) reference is here made.

[11] The derivation of Czar (or Tzar) from Cæsar is admitted by Skeat.

[12] Such as was worn by a Doctor of the Sorbonne.

ZADIG, OR DESTINY

[1] Our author has here a note to the effect that there was at that time a Babylonian [Parisian] named Arnoult, who, according to his announcement in the newspapers, cured and prevented all sorts of fits by means of a bag hung round the neck.

[2] This is an anagram of Boyer, a bishop by whom Voltaire had been subjected to repeated persecution, or what he considered such.

[3] The Abbé Desfontaines.

[4] Allusion is here made to the philosophical system of Leibnitz (d. 1716), in which "monads" figure largely as the ultimate atoms of nature, and the intimate connection between the mind and body is explained by a "pre-established harmony" which admits of perfect independence. The optimism of Leibnitz is ridiculed by Voltaire in *Candide*.

[5] A summary of various parts of the Zendavesta.

[6] That venomous serpents sting with their tongues is of course a popular error.

[7] Chinese words signifying respectively *reason* and *heaven*.

[8] The island of Ceylon is called by this name in the *Arabian Nights*.

[9] Compare the story of the Grecian king and the sage Durban in the *Arabian Nights' Entertainment*.

[10] This version of a moral tale, familiar to the English reader from Parnell's *Hermit* has a source at least as ancient as the mediæval *Gesta Romanorum*.

[11] The phrase would have been more appropriate if Voltaire had followed Parnell's version of this incident.

> "Before the pilgrims part, the younger crept
> Near the closed cradle where an infant slept,
> And writhed his neck," etc.
>
> (*The Hermit*, ll. 150-153.)

THE WHITE BULL

[1] According to Eschenburg, Apis is the name of the ox in which Osiris was supposed to reside, rather than a distinct deity. The ox thus honored was known by certain marks; his body was all black, excepting a square spot of white on his forehead, and a white crescent or sort of half-moon on his right side; on his back was the figure of an eagle; under his tongue a sort of knot resembling a beetle *(cantharus)*; and two sorts of hair upon his tail. This ox was permitted to live twenty-five years. His

body was then embalmed, placed in a chest, and buried with many solemnities. A season of mourning then followed, until a new Apis, or ox properly marked, was discovered.

[2] "Histories," says Pope, in his *Poetical Works,* vol. 4, p. 245, "are more full of examples of the fidelity of dogs than of friends, but I will only say for the honor of dogs, that the two most ancient and estimable books, sacred and profane, extant, viz. the Scripture and Homer, have shown a particular regard to these animals. That of Tobit is the most remarkable, because there seemed no manner of reason to take notice of the dog, besides the great humanity of the author. ['And the dog went after them,' *Tobit,* xi: 4.] Homer's account of Ulysses's dog, Argus, is the most pathetic imaginable, all the circumstances considered, and an excellent proof of the old bard's good nature. . . . Plutarch, relating how the Athenians were obliged to abandon Athens in the time of Themistocles, steps back again out of the way of his history, purely to describe the lamentable cries and howlings of the poor dogs they left behind. He makes mention of one that followed his master across the sea to Salamis, where he died, and was honored with a tomb by the Athenians, who gave the name of the Dog's Grave to that part of the island where he was buried. This respect to a dog, in the most polite people of the world, is very observable. A modern instance of gratitude to a dog is, that the chief order of Denmark, (now injuriously called the order of the elephant), was instituted in memory of the fidelity of a dog, named Wildbrat, to one of their kings who had been deserted by his subjects. He gave his order this motto, or to this effect, (which still remains), 'Wildbrat was faithful.' Sir William Trumbull has told me a story, which he heard from one that was present. King Charles I. being with some of his Court during his troubles, a discourse arose on what sort of dogs deserved pre-eminence, and it being on all hands agreed to belong either to the spaniel or greyhound, the King gave his opinion on the part of the greyhound, because (said he) it has all the good nature of the other without the fawning."

This satire upon fawning would no doubt have been as applicable to the court of King Amasis as to that of Charles I., for fawning has ever been the besetting sin of dogs and courtiers.

It is indeed a grand testimonial to the value of the greyhound, that his fleetness and fidelity were appreciated by Mambres, the great Egyptian magician, five thousand years before they were endorsed by the unfortunate English king. Miss Endor, Homer, Ulysses, Mambres, Tobit, Plutarch, the polite Athenians, Charles I., and Alexander Pope are certainly as respectable a list of references as the most aristocratic greyhound could desire.

[3] The nine daughters of Pierus, king of Emathia, were called Pierides. They entered into a contest with the Muses, and being conquered, were metamorphosed into birds.

REFERENCES

JEANNOT AND COLIN

tenelle, who died in the year 1757.

ègue, *i.e.*, the Stammerer, was third in succession from

[3] The ....tines are a religious brotherhood founded in 1524. Their first superior, one of the four founders of the order, was Caraffa, bishop of Theate (Chiete), hence their name.

MEMNON, THE PHILOSOPHER

[1] Billard and the Abbé Grizel.

THE WORLD IS LIKE THAT, OR THE VISION OF BABOUC

[1] Allusion is here made to the wars between England and France.

[2] A coin worth about five dollars.

[3] Allusion is here made to a quarter of Paris which formerly bore the name of the suburb of Saint Marceau.

[4] The Pictavi were the ancient inhabitants of the modern province of Poitou.

[5] The Hôtel des Invalides at Paris.

[6] The earlier editions have "seventy-two." The number of farmers-general of the taxes in France differed at different times.

[7] Satire is here aimed at the standing quarrel of the Jansenists with the Pope, their controversial works, and the nuns of Port Royal. The fanatical extravagance and claim to prophetic powers of their later disciples, the "convulsionnaires" of 1730, etc., are also turned into ridicule.

[8] This portrait is thought to be intended for Cardinal Fleury.

COSI-SANCTA, OR A LITTLE HARM
FOR A GREAT GOOD

[1] The reference should have been to St. Augustine's *Treatise upon the Sermon on the Mount* (lib. i. chap. xvi.).

BABABEC AND THE FAKIRS

[1] Voltaire has a note here: "When the fakirs wish to behold the celestial light, an aspiration which is very general among them, they turn their eyes towards the tip of the nose." Mr. Braid adopted a very similar process for inducing hypnotism. (See Dr. W. B. Carpenter's *Mental Physiology*, § 493, and Albert Moll's *Hypnotism*, p. 28.)